SHERLOCK
HOLMES

and the ICE PALACE MURDERS

Other Minnesota Mysteries by Larry Millett
Published by the University of Minnesota Press

Sherlock Holmes and the Red Demon
Sherlock Holmes and the Rune Stone Mystery
Sherlock Holmes and the Secret Alliance
The Disappearance of Sherlock Holmes
The Magic Bullet

SHERLOCK HOLMES

and the ICE PALACE MURDERS

Larry Millett

A Minnesota Mystery
Featuring Shadwell Rafferty

University of Minnesota Press
Minneapolis
London

The Fesler–Lampert Minnesota Heritage Book Series

This series is published with the generous assistance
of the John K. and Elsie Lampert Fesler Fund and David R. and
Elizabeth P. Fesler. Its mission is to republish significant out-of-print books
that contribute to our understanding and appreciation of
Minnesota and the Upper Midwest.

Originally published in 1998 by Viking Penguin

First University of Minnesota Press edition, 2011

Map on page vii drawn by Mark Melnick, based on a map prepared for
Lost Twin Cities, published by the Minnesota Historical Society, 1992.

Published by the University of Minnesota Press
111 Third Avenue South, Suite 290
Minneapolis, MN 55401-2520
http://www.upress.umn.edu

Library of Congress Cataloging-in-Publication Data

Millett, Larry.
Sherlock Holmes and the Ice Palace murders / Larry Millett. — 1st University of
Minnesota Press ed.
p. cm. — (The Fesler–Lampert Minnesota Heritage Book Series)
Originally published: New York : Viking, 1998.
"A Minnesota Mystery."
ISBN 978-0-8166-7482-4 (pb : alk. paper)
1. Holmes, Sherlock (Fictitious character) — Fiction. 2. Watson, John H.
(Fictitious character) — Fiction. 3. British — Minnesota — Fiction. 4. Private
investigators — Minnesota — Fiction. 5. St. Paul (Minn.) — Fiction. I. Title.
PS3563.I42193S46 2011
813'.54 — dc22
2011000795

Printed in the United States of America on acid-free paper

The University of Minnesota is an equal-opportunity educator and employer.

18 17 16 15 14 13 12 11   10 9 8 7 6 5 4 3 2 1

To John Mallander, friend for life

St. Paul in 1896

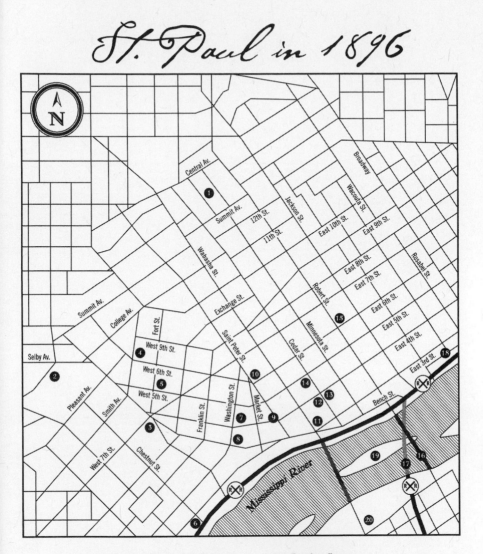

1. Central Park–Ice Palace
2. James J. Hill Mansion
3. Seven Corners
4. Hotel Barteau
5. Muskrat Club
6. City Dump–Upper Levee
7. Rice Park
8. Central Police Station
9. Costanza Apartments
10. St. Paul Cathedral
11. Bridge Square
12. Globe Building
13. Minnesota Club
14. Ramsey County Jail
15. Ryan Hotel (Rafferty's Saloon)
16. Robert Street Bridge
17. Railroad Bridge
18. Union Depot
19. Raspberry Island
20. West Side Flats

INTRODUCTION

Readers of *Sherlock Holmes and the Red Demon* may recall that near the end of that remarkable story, Dr. John Watson provided a tantalizing reference to another case in Minnesota in which he and the famous detective had been involved. This case, centering on a bizarre discovery in the Winter Carnival Ice Palace in St. Paul, occurred in January 1896, less than a year and a half after Holmes and Watson had solved the mystery of the Red Demon. But did Watson provide an account of this new adventure, and if so, where might it be found? Thus began a search that was to conclude with a quite unexpected discovery.[1]

I knew at the outset that Watson's own papers, kept at the British Museum in London, would prove of little help, since they have been so thoroughly scrutinized over the years by so many scholars that they are, for all practical purposes, mined out. Therefore, I concentrated my search in St. Paul. Since the manuscript of *Sherlock Holmes and the Red Demon* had been found in the mansion of James J. Hill, the railroad titan, I naturally began there. After all, Hill had hired Holmes once, to pursue the Red Demon, and there was good reason to believe that he might have done so again. But a new and extremely thorough search of Hill's Summit Avenue mansion in 1995 proved fruitless. There were no more secrets to be discovered within its walls.

Satisfied that I had closed this avenue of inquiry, I next examined Hill's voluminous papers, which are kept at the reference library he established in St. Paul. This was a Herculean task, since Hill left behind one of the largest paper trails in American history—a mass of documents rivaled in extent by few other private collections. Again, however, my labors went unrewarded, for I found no trace of any "ice palace" manuscript among Hill's papers. Nor did any of his descendants profess knowledge of such a manuscript.

I then tried another approach. Knowing that all of St. Paul's ice palaces were built in conjunction with the city's annual Winter Carnival, I spent a month inspecting Winter Carnival Association records, some dating back to the 1880s, in the archives of the Minnesota Historical Society. But here, too, I drew a blank, for there was simply no manuscript by Watson to be found. Hard as it was for me to accept the fact, I was finally forced to conclude that Watson, as with so many other of Holmes's adventures mentioned in passing, never bothered to "write up" the ice palace case.

Such was the state of affairs when, in late October 1996, I received a telephone call from a woman in Hudson, New York. The woman, who identified herself as Inez White, told me that she had read *Sherlock Holmes and the Red Demon* (which I edited for publication) and was intrigued by Watson's reference to the ice palace case. She knew all about it, she said, because she had found an account of the case in a handwritten manuscript that had only recently come into her possession. Mrs. White then went on to ask whether I would be interested in looking at the manuscript! My heart skipped a beat at that moment, and I accepted her offer at once.

The manuscript, entitled "Sherlock Holmes and the Ice Palace Murders," turned out to be everything I could have hoped for. One look at the document told me that it had come straight from the hand of Watson himself. Even so, I conducted a number of tests, similar to those used to authenticate *Sherlock Holmes and the Red Demon*, to satisfy myself that I had indeed come upon the genuine article.[2]

The story of the ice palace murders presents one of the most harrowing investigations of Holmes's long career, pitting him against villains of exceptional cunning and ruthlessness. Much of the tale takes place in and around the 1896 St. Paul Winter Carnival Ice Palace, which was among the largest structures of its kind ever built in North America, and this unusual setting adds a fantastic note to Watson's narrative. The case is also highly unusual in that Holmes finds himself competing with another detective, in the person of Shadwell Rafferty. A saloonkeeper and part-time private investigator in St. Paul, Rafferty emerges from the pages of Watson's manuscript as a most engaging character. Yet Holmes soon discovers that Rafferty is far more formidable than his rather genial facade might suggest, and the battle of wits between these two seemingly disparate men is fascinating to watch.

Rafferty is also a key figure in the manuscript's provenance, since he appears to have been the original owner of the only known copy of "Sherlock Holmes and the Ice Palace Murders." The history of the manuscript can be briefly summarized as follows:

When Rafferty died in St. Paul in 1928, at age eighty-five, his possessions were turned over to his only surviving relative, a younger sister who lived in Boston. This woman, Mrs. Mary Corcoran, was never close to her brother and apparently paid no attention to the various boxes of items—including the Watson manuscript—that came with Rafferty's estate. Instead, it was all consigned to storage and promptly forgotten.

Mrs. Corcoran herself died in the early 1930s, after which the manuscript came into the possession of her youngest daughter, Mrs. Julia Thompson, who was then married and living in Hudson. Being a busy woman with six children of her own, Mrs. Thompson had little time to sort through boxes of material left by her mother, and so the precious manuscript sat undisturbed in the attic of her home for many decades.

Mrs. Thompson was 101 years old when she died on September 14, 1996. After her death, the house in Hudson was put up for sale, and the task of cleaning it out fell to one of her daughters, the aforementioned Mrs. White, who finally came upon the forgotten manuscript. Mrs. White at first thought it was simply a piece of fiction penned by "mad old great-grandpa," as Rafferty was known in the family. But she concluded otherwise after having read, quite by chance, *Sherlock Holmes and the Red Demon*.

One obvious question is why Rafferty himself never sought to sell or publish the manuscript. Indeed, he seems to have kept it under close wraps, since there is no mention of it in various newspaper obituaries or any of his correspondence (which Mrs. White also found). There is, I believe, a ready explanation for Rafferty's reluctance to make the manuscript public. As readers of *Sherlock Holmes and the Ice Palace Murders* will discover, Rafferty's actions at the end of the case were so legally indefensible that he had good reason not to wish them publicized in his lifetime.[3]

Now, however, the true story can at last be told of the strange and terrible events that made the 1896 Winter Carnival the most memorable in St. Paul's history. And so, without further ado, I am pleased to offer you this long-forgotten account of *Sherlock Holmes and the Ice Palace Murders*.

Sherlock Holmes

and the

Ice Palace

Murders

1

WHERE IS THE GROOM?

In the years since I first began chronicling the adventures of my good friend Sherlock Holmes, I have often been asked which case inspired his greatest feat of detection. There is, I fear, no ready answer to this, and Holmes himself dismisses all such comparisons as pointless. As he once put it to me: "Every case is different, Watson, and I look upon them as a good father does his children; that is to say, though I may like some more than others, I must love them all." Be that as it may, I am inclined to believe that among our many adventures together, few presented Holmes with greater challenges, or put him in more frequent and deadly peril, than the singular case of the ice palace murders.

The case still lingers in my mind with a kind of faint miraculous glow, for it was exceptional in every respect. Its setting—in a vast, gleaming structure of ice—was utterly fantastic. Its crimes were gruesome and unprecedented, the product of both infinite calculation and the rash imperatives of the heart. Its cast of characters—most notably the giant Irishman whose deductive skills even Holmes could not help but admire—was extraordinary. Yet what I find most amazing about our wintry adventure in St. Paul is that Holmes survived it.

To this day I can scarcely believe how fortunate he was to escape the frigid death which, on one memorable night, seemed certain to claim him. It was as a direct result of this remarkable episode that he came to write his superb monograph on the muskrat, which has been so enthusiastically received in scientific circles.[1]

I am well aware, of course, that many words have already been written about the ice palace affair, which for a time cast its lurid glare across the front pages of every newspaper in America. Yet none of these accounts, including Mr. Steffens's recent and much celebrated article in *McClure's Magazine*, have penetrated to the dark heart of the matter, which was shocking almost beyond belief. Holmes, who usually reserves his criminal superlatives for the late Professor Moriarty, acknowledged to me not long ago that the ice palace case "presented villainy of such an extreme and vicious kind that we may not see its like again in our lifetimes."[2]

And now, as I take up my pencil to narrate this strange and horrible story to the world, I can only pray that Holmes was right.

On the second day of January in 1896, Sherlock Holmes received an invitation at our Baker Street residence which proved impossible to resist. It came in the form of a telegram from Potter Palmer, the famous Chicago real estate and hotel magnate, who requested assistance with a "most urgent and delicate matter" involving a member of his family. Palmer's message could not have come at a more propitious time, for Holmes's recent exertions in a case vital to the national interest had left him in a dark and restless mood, hungering for some new excitement.[3]

"Well, my dear Watson," he announced after reading the telegram, "I believe our ship has come in. Pack up your things immediately. We are once again off to America."

"I seem to recall," I said, "that after our last adventure on that continent you were not especially anxious to return. What has happened to change your mind?"

"Chicago," Holmes said simply, letting the word roll off his tongue as though it were pure ambrosia. "It is a city like no other, Watson, full of the wild energy of the New World and a veritable nursery of crime in all its manifestations. I am a student of crime, Watson, and a student must always go where he can best be educated. Chicago shall be my next university!"[4]

I knew that Holmes had always maintained a curious attachment to Chicago, but until this rather remarkable speech I had not realized the extent of his fascination with that city. In any event, I could tell by the excited glitter in Holmes's eyes that the opportunity to visit Chicago was precisely the sort of adventure he longed for, and I began at once to make arrangements for our trip.

By a stroke of good fortune, the Cunard Line's *Campania* was scheduled to sail from Southampton the very next day, and so within twenty-four hours we were once again on our way to America. Our crossing proved smooth and uneventful, which suited Holmes, who whiled away the hours in his cabin working almost continuously on his newest pastime—the building of a miniature ship in a bottle. The ship Holmes had chosen for this demanding task was, appropriately enough, the famous schooner yacht *America*, whose clean lines and speed before the wind he had always admired. When I asked why he had selected the *America*, he informed me that it was among the finest two-masters ever built and was therefore worthy of his time. For my part, I could only wonder why Holmes wished to embark upon an enterprise which promised little except a steady diet of tedium.[5]

Holmes, however, thought it fine fare indeed, and so immersed himself in his work that I hardly saw him during our passage across the North Atlantic. When I asked him to explain why he would devote himself to such a seemingly pointless project, his reply was instructive: "It is a thing which looks impossible, Watson, and that is why I am interested in it. You will note that I intend to insert my ship, when it is done, in a small whisky bottle"—here he showed me the chosen receptacle, from one of Scotland's lesser-known distilleries—"with a neck only one inch in diameter. It will be, I believe, the largest ship ever placed in so small a bottle. The trick, of course, is in the hinging of the masts, and I have devised a new technique which I am confident will one day be adopted by model makers around the world. I may even write up a little paper on the topic someday."

"I shall look forward to reading it," I lied, and thereafter left Holmes to his tiresome task.

Holmes had barely started work on the masts of his miniature masterpiece by the time we reached New York City on January 10, and it had to be carefully packed as we prepared for the next leg of our journey. That afternoon, we boarded the Pennsylvania Limited, whose swaying movements fortunately deterred Holmes from further work on his project. Twenty-four hours later, we reached Chicago, then in the grip of a bitter cold spell.

"It appears that in America we are destined for either fire or ice," remarked Holmes as we emerged from Chicago's cavernous Union Station into the frosty air. This was a reference, of course, to our decidedly warmer adventures in the Minnesota pineries on our first visit to the New World, in the late summer of 1894. Yet Chicago's piercing cold, as it turned out, was but a prelude to a much deeper chill that lay ahead.

We immediately settled in at Palmer's palatial estate near the shores of Lake Michigan. Despite its nostalgic castle-like appearance, the house was filled with blurry French paintings of the most modern kind, which Holmes found quite intriguing. Indeed, he seemed to spend more time admiring Palmer's art collection than investigating "the delicate matter" which had brought us to Chicago in the first place. This matter, Holmes quickly concluded, was "a mere trifle," and within the span of two days he had resolved it to everyone's satisfaction. I shall make no additional mention of the case here, other than to note that its solution depended on several brilliant deductions from the evidence of a single eyelash—a topic on which Holmes promises to produce a detailed study one day. So pleased were Palmer and his wife with Holmes's efficient work that they invited us to stay at their home for as long as we wished. Holmes readily accepted this generous and unexpected offer, since it gave him his chance to study the Chicago underworld.[6]

"The American criminal is a distinctive species," he remarked to me, "and well worth careful scrutiny. And nowhere has the American criminal mind developed more completely, or with more interesting variations, than in Chicago."

I did not share his enthusiasm in this regard, especially when it became apparent that Holmes's research would regularly take us to the so-called Levee, a sinkhole of unspeakable depravity located just south of Chicago's business district, commonly called the Loop. For the next week, we spent many of our days and most of our nights in this vile precinct devoted to gratification of every known vice and perversion. Our tour guide was none other than the celebrated police detective Clifton Wooldridge, who introduced us to such distinctive examples of American criminal enterprise as the "goosing slum," the "panel house," and the "blind pig."[7]

We also visited brothels, gambling dens, groggeries, and the notorious Lone Star Saloon, whose proprietor—a tough little Irishman named Mickey Finn—was well known for his mastery of the "knockout drop."[8] Our tour of this hideous netherworld brought us into contact with a variety of desperate characters, including several members of the Star Cleaners, a gang reputed to be the most bold and vicious in all of Chicago. We did not know it then, but we were soon to encounter one especially murderous member of the Star Cleaners under entirely different, and infinitely more dangerous, circumstances.

The highlight, if it can be called that, of our week-long expedition to Chicago's underbelly was a tour of the house of horrors at Wallace and Sixty-third Streets where the monster Henry H. Holmes had gone about his gruesome business only a few years earlier. "Mr. Holmes seems to have been a very bad man with a very good cognomen," remarked his namesake after we had finished our grisly tour, "though there can be no doubt that he will soon have a well-deserved date with the hangman."[9]

Holmes's dark fascination with the Levee district was quite beyond me, but I do not doubt that he would have haunted its streets for several more weeks had not a special delivery letter arrived one day from our old friend James J. Hill. The letter came as a complete surprise to me, since I had no idea that the St. Paul railroad baron knew we were in Chicago at Palmer's residence. Holmes, however, saw nothing to wonder at.

"Mr. Hill is a most resourceful man, Watson, and one should never forget that the heart of his business is keeping track of things. Therefore, you should not be in the least surprised that he has seen fit to keep track of us."

The letter—written in Hill's taut, distinctive hand—was much like Palmer's earlier telegram in that it contained an offer which Holmes found difficult to refuse. After the usual introductory pleasantries, Hill explained his purpose for writing:

A most unusual and, I dare say, unprecedented situation has developed here in St. Paul. It involves the disappearance

of a young man on the eve of his wedding amid circumstances that I think you will agree are most peculiar. If you
and Dr. Watson would care to come to St. Paul, you will not
want for hospitality at my house and you will doubtlessly
find ample opportunity to exercise your unique skills. I have
enclosed a newspaper article that will acquaint you with the
basic facts of the situation. Let me know at once if you propose to come.

Regards, J. J. Hill

P.S. The temperature here is five below zero and dropping. Do not fail to bring warm clothes.

The story enclosed with Hill's letter came from the January 22,
1896, edition of the St. Paul *Pioneer Press*, and since it proved to be a
crucial piece of evidence in the fantastic events which were to follow,
I have reprinted it here in its entirety:

ALL OF ST. PAUL WANTS TO KNOW: WHERE IS THE GROOM? —
YOUNG JONATHAN UPTON MISSING — TO BE WED SATURDAY IN
ICE PALACE — LAST SEEN SUNDAY NIGHT ON PALACE GROUNDS —
FAMILY CALLS IN AUTHORITIES — FIANCÉE PROSTRATE WITH GRIEF —
"WHERE HAS MY JOHNNY GONE?" SHE WAILS — UPTON APPEARED
"PERFECTLY NORMAL" TO FRIENDS — CHIEF O'CONNOR INVESTIGAT-
ING BUT REPORTS NO LEADS

St. Paul is today the scene of a prenuptial mystery unlike any other
in the city's history. Jonathan Upton, the young man who is to be
wed this Saturday in lavish ceremonies at the Winter Carnival Ice
Palace, has disappeared without a trace, and there are fears for his
well-being.

Upton, whose father is one of the merchant princes of this city,
was last seen in the early hours of Monday morning at the ice
palace grounds in Central Park. He had gone there to look for a
missing hat, which he apparently found, and was last seen walking
toward Cedar Street at about one in the morning. When he did not
appear by the following noon at the offices of his father, George
Upton, inquiries were immediately made as to his whereabouts.
These, however, proved fruitless, and after half a day had passed

with no communication from the young man, the family felt compelled to call in the authorities.

Young Upton's fiancée, Miss Laura Forbes of this city, is among those most anxiously awaiting word of his whereabouts and is reported to be inconsolable at the thought that some unhappy fate may have befallen him. "Oh, where has my Johnny gone?" she asks repeatedly, but thus far there is no answer to her plaintive query. The bride-to-be's father, Cadwallader Forbes, a businessman whose name is well known throughout the Northwest, is said to be equally distraught. Frederick Forbes, the bride-in-waiting's brother and a close friend of the missing man, told the *Pioneer Press* last night that he knew of no financial reversals or other circumstances which might have caused Jonathan Upton to flee the city. "His disappearance is a complete mystery," he said.

As there has never been any hint of impropriety connected with young Upton's name, nor any indication that he looked upon his impending marriage with anything other than the utmost joy, the authorities cannot help but fear that he has met with foul play. The family, however, continues to nourish the flame of hope, although as the hours pass, the light must inevitably dim. Mr. George Upton, in a rare interview last night at his Summit Avenue mansion, said his sole concern was "to have my boy back" and that he would "pay any price" to achieve that end. It is believed, in fact, that Mr. Upton has already hired private investigators to assist with the search, although he would not confirm this to be the case.

Young Upton, who is 25 years of age, has worked at his father's wholesale house in Lowertown for several years, and is highly regarded by all who know him for his business acumen, charming manner, and temperate habits. He has resided for the past year or so in bachelor quarters at the Costanza Apartments on St. Peter Street. The police have already made a thorough search of his apartment, hoping to find any irregularities which might explain his disappearance. But young Upton's clothes and other belongings were discovered to be in perfect order, and there was no sign of a struggle or any other untoward event.

No Unusual Behavior
The proprietor of the Costanza, Thomas Greene, reported that he last saw young Upton about five o'clock on Sunday afternoon as he was going out and that he exhibited no unusual behavior at that

time. As part of their investigation, the authorities have also interviewed many of the junior Upton's acquaintances, including members of the Muskrat Club, of which he is an active member, all to
no avail. It is known that Upton spent the late hours of Sunday at
the clubrooms on Washington Street. "He appeared perfectly normal and was the life of the party," said a club member. "He did not
seem to have a care in the world as he went out into the night.
None of us can imagine what happened to him, but we fear the
worst."

The Guard's Account

Naturally, the police have interviewed at length the night guard
at the palace grounds, a reliable and well-regarded Swede named
Lars Melander, who appears to have been the last person to see
young Upton. The guard gave this account to our reporter of the
events of early Monday:

"Young Mr. Upton came to the main gate a bit after midnight
with a lantern in his hand and asked to be let into the grounds. Of
course, I know the young man well, for he and his father have
been much involved in the building of the palace. In any event, Mr.
Upton said he believed he had left his fur hat in the rotunda some
days before. It seemed odd to me that he would come back at so
late an hour, but I supposed it was a valuable hat and that he did
not want to lose it. And as I had already had a busy time of it that
night, I guess I was not all that surprised to see him.

"I told him I would go help him look for the hat if he wished, but
he told me I must not leave my post and that, in any case, he knew
exactly where to look, so I did not think much of it. I let him in and
said he should call me if he needed help. He said he would do so
and walked off toward the rotunda without another word. I saw
him go through the big doorway into the rotunda.

"As there had been other people about that night, including the
construction superintendent, Mr. Riley, I did not see any reason to
pay particular attention to Mr. Upton. Besides, I had other things
to occupy my mind, because a few minutes later there developed
an awful row in the street. A couple of topers coming up from one
of the Front Street dives got into an argument, and then one of
them pulled a knife and began making dire threats, so I whistled
for the coppers. I forgot about young Mr. Upton in all of the commotion and it was about half an hour, I guess, before I saw him

coming back toward the gate. He had on a fur hat, and I told him I was pleased to see he had found what he was looking for. But he seemed to be in quite a hurry and just waved as he walked by. He went out in the direction of Cedar Street, and that was the last I saw of him."

O'Connor on the Case

Chief of Detectives O'Connor has taken personal charge of the investigation. O'Connor assured the *Pioneer Press* yesterday that all of the resources of the police department are being brought to bear on the matter. "If the lad is to be found, we will find him," he said, even as he acknowledged that few clues have presented themselves to this point. Nonetheless, he did note that the precinct of the ice palace is known to be frequented by strong-arm artists of the worst type, one of whom in recent weeks has relieved several passersby of their wallets. "We will be raising quite a ruckus among the ruffians of this city," O'Connor promised, "and if any of them are involved in this sorry affair, we will know about it soon enough."

In the meantime, all of St. Paul anxiously awaits word of young Upton's whereabouts and prays that he will be found, safe and sound, at the earliest possible moment.

"Well, what do you make of it?" I asked Holmes once he had finished reading the article with his usual rapidity. We were sitting in the study of Palmer's mansion, enjoying tea and a view across the windswept expanse of Lake Michigan. "Perhaps that young fellow Upton has simply decided that he's not quite ready for connubial bliss."

Holmes shrugged, set the clipping on his lap, and took a long draft of tea. "You may be right, Watson, in thinking that there is no more to this matter than what the Americans, I believe, call a case of 'cold feet.' The problem is that all we know at present comes from a single newspaper account, which may or may not be reliable. As I have always said, there are only three kinds of stories: those that are true, those that are false, and those that appear in the newspapers."

In fact, I had never heard Holmes say any such thing before, and I asked him to explain his puzzling remark.

"It means," he said, "that newspaper stories, which are invariably written quickly and with an incomplete set of facts at hand, are always difficult to interpret, for they tend to consist of both honest lies and deceptive truths. And that, my dear Watson, is why they must always be read between the lines if any sense is to be made of them. This story of the missing groom is a perfect case in point. It raises all manner of questions, and it is quite as interesting for what it does not say as for what it does."

I could tell by Holmes's tone of voice that the case interested him and that he had already made a decision. "I presume we shall be going to St. Paul, then," I said matter-of-factly. "Do you wish to catch a train tonight?"

Holmes smiled, stood up, and patted me on the shoulder. "Watson, you are becoming quite the soothsayer. Yes, I think we shall have to go to St. Paul, for I fear that young Mr. Upton may have colder feet than anyone imagines."

After wiring Hill that we would indeed come north for a visit, we bade farewell to Palmer and his vivacious wife late in the evening of January 23 (only hours after we had received Hill's letter). We then boarded one of the Chicago, Burlington & Quincy's fast trains to St. Paul, which we reached at nine o'clock the next morning. I felt an eerie sense of discomfort upon arriving at that city's Union Depot, for my mind was immediately flooded with memories of those strange and awful events which had culminated our first visit to Minnesota. But two familiar faces quickly put me in a better frame of mind.

The first was that of our old friend William Best, the stalwart engineer who had braved the terrible forest fire in Hinckley with us. Quite by accident, Holmes saw him tending the engine of a train which had apparently arrived a few minutes before ours, on the adjoining track. After warm handshakes and salutations all around, we learned that Best was now engineer of the Great Northern's finest continental train and had just come from the West Coast. Moments later, another voice joined our conversation:

"Welcome back to St. Paul," said Joseph Pyle, smiling broadly as he strode toward us along the platform. "It is a great pleasure to see you again."

Pyle was Hill's most trusted agent and the man whom the Empire Builder had dispatched to London in 1894 to invite us to Minnesota.

He was also the editor in chief of one of St. Paul's leading daily newspapers, the *Globe*, which Hill owned.

"Ah, Mr. Pyle," said Holmes, "the pleasure is all ours. Are we to be placed in your capable hands once again?"

"You are indeed. A sleigh is waiting out front. I must inform you, however, that neither Mr. Hill nor his family will be at home to see you. Mr. Hill has been called away to New York on urgent business—it is a matter involving certain bonds vital to the well-being of the Great Northern—and he has asked me to convey his sincere apologies. As for Mrs. Hill and the children, they have done the sensible thing and gone south for a few weeks to escape this beastly cold. But I have been instructed to help you in any way I can and to inform you that all of Mr. Hill's resources remain at your disposal."

After saying good-bye to Best, who pronounced himself much in need of refreshment following his long run in from the Pacific, we joined Pyle for the sleigh ride to Hill's mansion on Summit Avenue. Our patron had not lied about the weather—it was brutally cold, colder in fact than I had ever experienced—but heavy buffalo robes and foot and hand warmers kept us reasonably comfortable.

The scenery as we drove through St. Paul proved to be quite remarkable, for a storm some days earlier had cast a silvery spell over the entire city, which gleamed and shimmered in a carapace of ice. Ice clung to trees and power lines, coated windows and doors, spread into thin shining sheets on streets and sidewalks, and glinted from rooftops and steeples. Meanwhile, every building wore a spectacular necklace of icicles, as though dressed for the great winter celebration to come.

This extraordinary display of Nature's handiwork appeared to be of little interest to Holmes, however, and he barely looked up from beneath his robes as we made our way through the heart of the city's commercial district, which had been gaily decorated for the Winter Carnival. These adornments included banners, wreaths, festoons, lights, and innumerable ice carvings. Indeed, it appeared as though an army of sculptors had descended on the city, and their work could be seen in front of almost every building.

The size, variety, and brilliance of these crystalline sculptures amazed me. There were Indians in war bonnets, Eskimos with sled dogs, draped figures from classical antiquity, animals of every kind, whimsical gargoyles and fearsome monsters, miniature castles and cathedrals, obelisks and even a small representation of the Great Pyramid of Cheops.

One sculpture, however, easily eclipsed all the others, and we came to a stop to inspect it. Standing alone in a small downtown square and bathed in pale sunlight, it depicted a beautiful young woman in a long flowing gown, with a perfectly realized rose clasped in her hands. But it was the statue's face that held my gaze, for there was something forlorn and disquieting about the look in her translucent eyes. Was it fear, melancholy, disappointment, or even shame? I could not say, but the depth of her pain was undeniable. Even Holmes, normally insensible to feminine charms, was sufficiently struck by the statue to remark on its "distinctive qualities" to Pyle.

Once we resumed our course toward Hill's mansion, Pyle provided us with additional information regarding Jonathan Upton. A groom vanishing on the eve of his wedding was not uncommon, Pyle noted, for as he put it: "What normal man has not trembled before the prospect of eternal matrimony?" But Jonathan Upton was not just any young man, nor was he about to be the groom at just any wedding. He was, in fact, the only son of George Upton and therefore heir to one of St. Paul's great commercial fortunes. The jobbing firm of Upton & Son, founded in 1860, when St. Paul was yet an infant city, distributed hardware to dealers throughout the Northwest and garnered enormous profits doing so. According to Pyle, no wholesaler in the city could boast of a bigger trade, and the old man was reputed to be worth five million dollars easily, and perhaps a good deal more.

We learned that Upton's bride-in-waiting, Laura Forbes, came from equally privileged circumstances. Her father, Cadwallader Forbes, known as the "Commodore" because of his early career as a packet boat captain on the Red River of the North, was one of those rough and ready men who came to St. Paul early in the game; he was rewarded for his foresight with a fortune. He made his millions in timber, real estate, and railroading, among other enterprises, although it was widely believed that not all of his income derived from what Pyle called "conventional sources."

"In other words, I take it there are people who believe Mr. Forbes to be dishonest," said Holmes. "Tell me, is your employer among them?"

"I think that is a question best put to Mr. Hill himself," said Pyle, who then went on with his account of the Upton and Forbes families.

He pointed out that joining the two families would undoubtedly create the greatest fortune in St. Paul save that of Hill himself. As for Laura Forbes, Pyle informed us that she was widely regarded as the city's most beautiful woman, possessing long dark hair, flashing violet eyes, and a luxuriant figure. "She's caught the eye, and broken the heart, of many an eligible bachelor," said Pyle, with a touch of rue which led me to wonder whether he was among her rejected swains.

Not surprisingly, the Upton-Forbes union necessitated a wedding far beyond the ordinary, and it had therefore been decided that the couple should take their vows in the Winter Carnival Ice Palace, which both fathers had promoted tirelessly and had helped to finance.

"I must say that being married inside a big pile of ice hardly seems very romantic," I remarked as we turned onto Summit Avenue, where Hill's mansion, a vast pile of red stone rising above the white glare of snow all around it, immediately came into view.

"Oh, but it is," Pyle said, "and I think you'll understand why once you see the palace. It is quite remarkable. In fact, the very first ice palace in the world, built by the Empress Anna of Russia in 1740, was the site of a wedding. And there have been many marriages in the ice palaces here over the years."[10]

"How intriguing," Holmes said. "The warmest of human connections being celebrated in the coldest place imaginable! In any event, as I understand it, the Upton-Forbes nuptials were to have taken place tomorrow in the palace."

"Yes. It was supposed to be the social event of the season in St. Paul. Tomorrow is also the day that the Winter Carnival officially begins. But I imagine it will put quite a damper on the festivities if young Upton isn't found."

"No doubt," said Holmes, "though the same might be said if he is."

"What do you mean?" Pyle asked.

"That will become clear soon enough," Holmes replied, "for I have an idea or two as to where young Mr. Upton might be."

CHAPTER

2

THESE GENTLEMEN ARE WITH ME

Once we had arrived at Hill's mansion and warmed ourselves with hot cocoa, Holmes turned his attention to the
matter at hand. "I should like to see the newspapers," he
told Pyle, who had joined us in one of the sitting rooms, which offered a panoramic view of the wide, deep, and frozen Mississippi
Valley as it cut through the heart of St. Paul.

Pyle had anticipated the request, and the most recent editions
of four St. Paul newspapers—the *Pioneer Press*, the *Daily News*, the
Dispatch, and, of course, Pyle's own *Globe*—were brought in for
Holmes's inspection. Young Upton's disappearance, as might be expected, continued to occupy a prominent place on the front pages,
although I was pleased to see that there were also reports on Jameson's effort to overthrow the Boers—a story I had been following
closely.[1] The raid held no interest for Holmes, however, for when he
was on a case, events elsewhere mattered nothing to him. His brow
furrowed in concentration, Holmes perused every article relating
to Jonathan Upton's disappearance, in hopes of discovering useful
information.

His hopes were quickly dashed, for the stories offered little beyond a rehash of earlier events, well seasoned with wild speculation and dramatic accounts of the grieving bride-to-be. One story theorized that Upton had been spirited away by Indians upset over the desecration of an old burial ground beneath the ice palace. Another suggested that he may have been abducted or even killed by a group of labor "anarchists" said to be sworn enemies of the "capitalist class." Since Minnesota was reputed to be a hotbed of such radicalism, this theory struck me as promising, but Holmes gave it short shrift.

"It appears the journalists of St. Paul, finding themselves in possession of few new facts, have taken to spinning elaborate fictions," he said. "There is little here but a farrago of fantasy and idle gossip. However, I do note one item from today's edition of the *Globe* which is quite suggestive."

"And what is that?" Pyle asked.

Holmes then read aloud the following paragraph, which appeared near the end of the story: " 'It was learned Thursday that Miss Forbes has returned the bridal gown in which she was to have been wed Saturday in the ice palace. "I will have no use for it," she told Mrs. Swanson, the seamstress who had made the gown.' "

"Why do you find this piece of news so suggestive?" I asked Holmes. "The young bride obviously is distraught over her fiancé's disappearance."

"Perhaps, Watson, yet I find it odd that she would return the dress yesterday, two full days before the planned wedding. A young woman in her situation, I should think, would cling to the hope that her beloved would in fact be found and that the wedding would go forward. Instead, her actions suggest that she has either given up all hope or—" Holmes stopped, as though not quite certain of his own thoughts.

"Or what?" Pyle and I inquired in unison.

"Or there is another explanation," said Holmes with a cryptic smile. He abruptly stood up and went to one of the big windows overlooking the river. Snow had begun to fall, forming a white shroud which obscured our vista of the valley.

Staring out into the blankness, Holmes announced: "I must have time to think. There are certain features to this case which are most unusual, and I have not yet grasped all of their implications."

I knew that Holmes always preferred to think alone, and so Pyle and I went off to find some lunch, both of us still wondering what the other "explanation" for Laura Forbes's behavior might be.

Before sitting down to lunch, we encountered Laura Olson, the young woman whom I had helped rescue from a life of prostitution in Hinckley as one of the notorious "jack pine twins." She was overjoyed to see me, and I learned from her that she was now working as an upstairs maid in Hill's mansion. After we talked amiably for several minutes, I cautioned her not to identify Holmes or me by name, as we were working under cover. She readily agreed and promised that "our little secret," as she put it, would be safe with her.

Pyle and I then enjoyed a hearty lunch of turtle soup, cold cuts, and bread. As we ate, Pyle provided a brief history of the Winter Carnival and the extraordinary ice palaces which were so often a part of it.

The first St. Paul Winter Carnival, he said, had been staged in 1886 after a newspaper correspondent from New York likened the city to "another Siberia, unfit for human habitation in winter." St. Paulites responded to this insult by organizing their first carnival, which included a large ice palace modeled on similar structures built earlier in Montreal. So successful was this initial event, Pyle told me, that two other carnivals — each featuring a gigantic ice palace — followed. But unusually mild winters in 1889 and 1890 defeated St. Paul's palace builders, and then came the terrible depression of the early 1890s. "The city was in no mood for celebration after that," Pyle noted, "and it looked as though the ice palace of 1888 would be the city's last."[2]

Yet even though the economy was still less than robust, the city's business leaders — George Upton and Cadwallader Forbes among them — had determined to build the largest ice palace ever in 1896, as testimony of St. Paul's continuing vitality. "The businessmen believe a magnificent palace will renew the city's spirits and also symbolize its rising position in the world," said Pyle.

To my surprise, Pyle went on to say that the palace had taken little more than six weeks to build. Planning, however, had begun much earlier, in the spring of 1895. The senior Upton and Cadwallader Forbes first formed a group of business leaders known as the Ice Palace Committee. This body contributed twenty-five thousand dollars to the project, and a like amount was quickly raised by sell-ing stock to the citizens of St. Paul. The committee next engaged a prominent St. Paul architect named Cass Gilbert to design the palace, after which bids were let for the construction work.³

"Then it was just a matter of waiting for winter, which seldom disappoints in this part of the world," Pyle said.

By early December, the builders were ready to begin. First, crews cut large blocks of ice (weighing five hundred pounds apiece) from nearby lakes and rivers. Teamsters then hauled the blocks to the palace site on sleds, after which an expert team of masons, stone carvers, and laborers went to work. Abetted by a month of what Pyle called "perfect" weather ("cold enough to freeze the spit in your mouth," or so he claimed), the palace builders made rapid progress.

As for the actual construction of the palace, Pyle said: "That was the easy part. A block of good ice is no different than a block of good stone, Dr. Watson, except that it's not quite as strong and a bit more slippery. Once you've got the ice, all you need to build a palace are masons with heavy axes to 'trim' the ice blocks to their proper size and shape, a few derricks equipped with sharp iron tongs to lift the blocks into place, and then some men on scaffolds to 'mortar' the blocks together with slush. The slush soon freezes, and then you've got a solid bond. Why, Mr. Gilbert has told me the palace is so solid it could last until June."⁴

"And the palace is now complete?" I asked.

"Nearly," Pyle said. "There are the usual last-minute details to attend to, but as far as I know, it will open tomorrow as scheduled, despite Jonathan Upton's disappearance."

"It must be a wonderful sight," I said, "and I hope—"

"You hope, my dear Watson, that we shall have a chance to see it," said Holmes, who was standing behind us at the door to the dining room, "and we shall. In fact, I have so enjoyed Mr. Pyle's disquisition on the fine art of ice palace construction that I am of a mind to visit this marvel at once, before the snow renders travel too difficult. Would you care to join us, Mr. Pyle?"

Pyle glanced at his pocket watch. "I would very much like to, Mr. Holmes, but as it is already after one o'clock, I really must return to the office. I have a newspaper to put out. However, one of Mr. Hill's sleighs and a driver are at your disposal. It is but a few minutes' ride to the ice palace site."

"Then we shall be off," Holmes said, shaking Pyle's hand before turning toward me. "Come along, Watson, and dress warmly, for I anticipate that we will be spending a good deal of time outdoors."

"Oh, there is one more thing, Mr. Holmes," said Pyle as he prepared to leave. "What names will you be going by during your stay in St. Paul, and how shall I report your occupation if inquiries are made of me?"

I confess that I had not considered this issue. But Holmes obviously had, for he told Pyle: "I think the names which we used on our last visit to Minnesota will be perfectly adequate."

And so I once again took the name of Peter Smith, while Holmes became John Baker.

"Well, then, gentlemen, good luck to you," said Pyle. "And naturally, should you make any great discovery, an exclusive for the *Globe* would be most appreciated."

"Have no fear, Mr. Pyle," said Holmes with a smile, as servants brought our heavy coats. "If we come upon any news, you shall be the first to know about it."

The snow had begun to fall heavily by the time we left Hill's mansion in a large brougham sleigh pulled by two handsome black geldings. I had heeded Holmes's advice and was bundled up in a thick wool coat, wool mittens, and a stocking cap. Holmes, however, had dressed for the cold with more flair. He wore a long coat of fox fur, mukluks (a gift from Hill), and a beaver hat with long earflaps.

"You appear prepared for a trek across the Siberian wastes," I told him.

"Siberia, my dear Watson, would undoubtedly be no colder than this place," he said, his breath visible with every word, "for I am beginning to think that the Eastern newspaper correspondent who so enraged the good citizens of St. Paul was entirely correct in his assessment of the climate."

Our driver took us east along Summit Avenue, through a neighborhood of solid brick houses and apartment buildings. There was nothing exceptional about this scene until we rounded a corner and suddenly caught our first glimpse of the ice palace, which loomed up before us like some vast and improbable chimera. It was, as Pyle had promised, "quite remarkable," its fantastic dome rising amid a crystalline wilderness of ramparts, towers, turrets, and pinnacles, its translucent walls gleaming like diamonds. I could think of nothing that compared to it, except perhaps for Paxton's famous glass palace in London.[5] Even Holmes seemed astounded.

"St. Paul has outdone itself," he said. "The energies of the New World are most extraordinary, Watson."

Although the palace was indeed magnificent, its setting proved to be less so. The enormous structure occupied a small, sloping plot of land known as Central Park, located at the northern fringe of St. Paul's commercial district. Barely two city blocks in size, the park did not appear to be very central to anything, and its immediate neighborhood, while decent enough, hardly qualified as the most fashionable in the city. A few large houses of recent vintage, along with several apartment buildings and a scattering of insubstantial wooden dwellings, bordered the park, but these structures seemed absurdly prosaic compared to the towering palace in their midst.[6]

The palace's most remarkable feature was undoubtedly the huge dome, which Pyle had told us about. Built, as I later learned, by the technique of corbeling blocks inward as they rose in successive circular courses, the dome was essentially an igloo, but on a scale unknown to the primitive Eskimo. It appeared to be about eighty feet in diameter, with massive buttresses and thick lower walls to bear the weight of the circling ice above. A single archway, adorned with elaborate carvings, opened into the rotunda beneath the dome, the very same rotunda where Jonathan Upton was to have been married and where he had gone in search of his hat, only to vanish without explanation.

We observed these features as we approached the south side of the palace grounds, which were defined by a low perimeter wall of ice surmounted at regular intervals by small decorative evergreens. Two gates, one at the north end of the park and one at the south, admitted visitors to the grounds, which also contained a number of smaller ice structures, including a skating rink, a small maze, and what appeared to be an unfinished toboggan slide.

Holmes instructed our driver to let us off by the south gate and await our return. We took a moment to observe the activity within the grounds, where scores of men were working at a furious pace to ready the palace for its grand opening. They scurried and clambered all about the structure, seemingly oblivious to the dangers posed by the slick, treacherous ice. I twice saw gigantic blocks slip free from their tongs and go crashing to the ground amid loud cries of "Look out below!"

We walked up to the south gate, where a burly policeman stood guard beside a large hand-lettered sign which read: WORKMEN ONLY. NO VISITORS WITHOUT A PASS.

"Good afternoon," said Holmes to the policeman, who despite his heavy woolen attire looked quite miserable in the cold. "I am John Baker, a visitor from England, and this is my associate, Mr. Smith. We have come to write a magazine article for European readers on the wonders of St. Paul's Winter Carnival. Would it be possible for us to make a closer inspection of the palace?"

The policeman—a square-jawed giant with a wide, grim face that promised trouble to the unwary—gave Holmes a sour look and said: "You got a pass?"

"No, but as our magazine has many thousands of readers, I am sure an exception can be made in our case. If you would care to see our credentials—"

Jabbing his nightstick into Holmes's chest, the policeman said: "Yeah, and I'm Nelly Bly.[7] Now, why don't you two scammers beat it."

I was about to chastise the brute (Holmes, I had no doubt, planned an even more forceful response), when I heard a deep, rolling voice with a distinctive Irish lilt say: "These gentlemen are with me, Tommy, and I would be much obliged if you would refrain from man-handlin' them in my presence."

The speaker, who had come up behind us, was a rollicking bear of a man, perhaps in his mid-fifties, with a smile so broad and inviting that it seemed to warm the very air around him. His attire was equally jovial, for he was dressed from head to toe in heavy red woolens, which made him look for all the world like jolly old St. Nick himself. This curious resemblance was also evident in his round crinkled face, which, if I may borrow a handy phrase, was a study in scarlet: ruddy cheeks, full lips, a wide splotchy nose, and a long reddish beard, well flecked with gray. Yet there was nothing buffoonish about him, and his flinty blue eyes suggested great depths of character. He had one other feature of note—a short, wide scar which angled upward from one corner of his left eyebrow and lent a barbarous touch to his otherwise affable appearance.

The policeman grinned at the sight of this strange figure and said: "Well, now, I'll be d--ned. What are you doin' up here, Shad? Lookin' for some ice to water down your drinks?"

"No, Tommy, me boy," came the smiling response. "I'm lookin' for an honest copper, but as there does not appear to be one in the vicinity, I guess I will have to settle for you."

Both men laughed heartily, and I could only suppose that the exchange of insults was a regular occurrence with them. Nodding in our direction as if we were old friends, the man then put his arm around the policeman's shoulders and said: "I've come to show these English gents the ice palace, for they are most interested in St. Paul's monument to winter. Why, there's nothin' like it across the Atlantic, and that's a fact! Do you suppose we might take a little peek inside, Tommy?"

"Sorry, Shad," replied the policeman. "I got my orders right from the Bull himself. No one's to get in without a pass. Them's the rules."

"Of course they are," the man said amiably, "and rules is rules is what I say. Too bad, though."

"Meanin' what?" asked the policeman suspiciously.

The big man removed an envelope from his coat pocket. "Meanin', Tommy, that I happen to have two front-row tickets for tomorrow night's show at the Metropolitan. Miss Lillie Langtry herself will be there, as I'm sure you know.[8] Now, I'd like to see her, indeed I would, for they say the Jersey Lily's a mighty beautiful woman who don't like to discomfort herself with an excess of clothing. But the problem is, I'm always losin' things. Why, I might even drop this envelope right into your hand and completely forget about it, especially if my friends and I were to be preoccupied lookin' at this wondrous ice palace. But, of course, rules is rules—"

The policeman interrupted: "Well, why didn't you gentlemen just tell me in the first place that you had passes? If you'll let me just check them"—he took the envelope and opened it—"I'm sure everything . . . Oh yes, everything's in order. Well, then, go on in now and enjoy your visit."

"Thank you kindly," said the big man, "and give Miss Langtry my regards."

Once we were inside the grounds and well out of the policeman's hearing, Holmes finally uttered his first words to our mysterious benefactor: "We are grateful, sir, for your assistance, and I trust you will take no offense if I remark that you seem to possess a well-honed talent for bribery."

"No offense taken, though I do not care much for the word. 'Bribery' sounds terribly criminal, don't you agree? I think of it as routine maintenance. After all, gentlemen, 'tis a wobbly orb we live on, and why should anyone object if a little grease must be applied now and then to keep it spinnin' smoothly?"

"Why indeed," said Holmes with a smile. "But allow me to make proper introductions. I am—"

"You are Sherlock Holmes, of course," said the man, as though this were patently obvious, and then, turning to me, he added: "And you must be Dr. Watson. 'Tis a pleasure to meet the both of you."

"You flatter me, sir," said Holmes coolly, "but I fear you have made a mistake. I am John Baker of London, and this is my associate, Peter Smith. I have not yet had the pleasure, however, of learning your name, sir."

The man flashed a dazzling smile. "Well, now, I guess you haven't. Rafferty's the name, Shadwell Rafferty. Most folks, though, just call me Shad. And don't you worry none, Mr. Holmes, I won't reveal your secret. If you want to be known as John Baker or the king of Ruritania, why, that's fine with me. But I do know who you are, and that's a fact!"

Under other circumstances, Holmes might have continued to contest our identities, but there was something so confident in Rafferty's manner that further argument seemed useless.

"Very well, Mr. Rafferty, you seem to have us at a disadvantage," Holmes said. "I shall not deny that I am indeed Sherlock Holmes and that this"—he nodded toward me—"is Dr. Watson. I should be very curious to know how you discovered our identities."

"Ah now, that would be a trade secret," replied Rafferty, wagging a finger at us. "Let us just say that I had the best of reasons for reachin' the conclusion I did. 'Tis not important anyway. What is important is that you're here, Mr. Holmes. You see, I'm hopin' you'll be able to lend me a hand in this ice palace business. The whole thing's fishier than the Fulton Market, if you ask me."[9]

"Then am I to take it," asked Holmes, "that you are investigating the disappearance of young Mr. Upton?"

"Why, of course I am," said Rafferty, as though we had somehow been expected to divine this fact. "Been at it since the lad vanished, but it's been a hard row in rough waters, if you must know. I've turned this town upside down and inside out lookin' for him, and so far I've nothin' but sore feet to show for my labors."

"And tell me, sir, are you with the St. Paul police?" Holmes asked.

"The police? Oh no, it's been many a moon since I worked for Bull O'Connor," Rafferty replied. He then began rummaging through his coat pockets until he found a small card, which he handed to Holmes. "Here. This will explain my present situation."

The card, which I have kept to this day, said: SHADWELL RAFFERTY, BARTENDING AND DISCREET INVESTIGATIONS, RYAN HOTEL, ST. PAUL.

"A most unusual combination of professions," said Holmes as he inspected the card, "but not without certain advantages, I would imagine."

"True enough," said Rafferty. "A man will tell more to his bartender than to his wife, and that's a fact."

Holmes studied the card a bit longer and then asked: "Who is your client in this case, Mr. Rafferty?"

" 'Tis someone with a deep interest in the affair, Mr. Holmes. Beyond that, I cannot say at the moment."

"I see. But may I ask why you have come here to the ice palace?"

Rafferty chuckled. "Why, for the same reason you and Dr. Watson have. This was the last place young Upton was seen alive, and so I'm wonderin' if there might be a clue here that the coppers overlooked. Besides, I've been studyin' the account of the guard on duty that night—Melander's his name, as I recall—and it's led me to consider certain strange possibilities."

"How interesting," said Holmes, not revealing the fact that he had been thinking along similar lines. "Then perhaps we should have a look around, for as you say, the police may have missed something. I should be especially interested to see the rotunda, where the wedding was to have taken place."

"Funny, that's just where I was headin'," said Rafferty. "Come along and we'll all have a look."

The ice dome enclosing the rotunda formed the south half of the palace. A long, high wall rose to the rear and served as the base for a series of towers and pinnacles. Atop the wall was a large crew of men, busy hoisting blocks into place to create its picturesque battlements, but there was little activity around the dome. As a result, no one appeared to notice as Holmes, Rafferty, and I slipped through the broad arched doorway leading into the rotunda.

Nothing in my experience could have prepared me for the eerie grandeur of this room. Bathed in a soft greenish glow caused by light passing through its translucent walls, the rotunda possessed an otherworldly aura that was at once cool, silent, and mysterious. As I glanced up at the curving walls of ice, I was astonished to see, at the top of the dome, a small oculus. This circular opening, which on clear days must have admitted a stream of sunlight, was located directly above the only object in the room—the altar where Jonathan Upton and Laura Forbes were to have exchanged vows.

"Well, now, they've cleaned things up a bit, I see," said Rafferty as we walked toward the altar, which was made from a long slab of ice laid atop big blocks on either end. Bold geometric ornament—done in the coiling Celtic manner and carved with much skill—adorned the front edge of the altar, which stood on a broad podium nearly three feet high.

"Last time I was in here," Rafferty continued, "the workmen were still about their business. Tools, small blocks of ice, and whatnot were scattered hither and yon. But I guess the altar is finally finished. All that's needed now is a groom."

"Indeed," said Holmes, whose ears had perked up at Rafferty's mention of his earlier visit to the rotunda. "And just when were you here last, Mr. Rafferty?"

" 'Twas Monday, Mr. Holmes, the day it became apparent that young Upton had vanished with the wind. But a lot of people were millin' about in here, and there wasn't much to be seen."

Reaching the podium, we walked up three steps to the altar, which both Holmes and Rafferty found quite fascinating. The two of them circled it like a pair of cats stalking their prey, although I could not imagine what they expected to find. At one point, Holmes took out his magnifying glass and went down on his knees to examine a red speck—which turned out to be nothing more than a tiny bit of wool cloth—that lay beneath the altar.

Something else had caught his eye, however. "Do you see this?" he said, pointing toward a block of ice which formed part of the podium directly beneath the altar. The block, about two feet square, appeared to have been wedged in at a slight angle, so that one end rose an inch or two above that of its neighbor.

"Sloppy work," said Rafferty, who had with some effort gotten down on his knees to take a look. "I'd say somebody just jammed it in there, like they were in a hurry."

"So it would seem," agreed Holmes. "Moreover, the block appears damaged—note its ragged edges and pitted surface. The blocks around it, by contrast, are very precisely cut. And unless I am mistaken, there is something else unusual about this particular block."

I could not tell what Holmes meant, but Rafferty caught on immediately. "Its color and texture are different from the others'," he said, rubbing one hand over the top of the block. "Why, it looks and feels so dirty I'd guess it's a block of river ice."

"River ice? What do you mean?" I asked.

To my surprise, it was Holmes who answered: "He means, Watson, that this block probably came out of the frozen Mississippi, whereas those around it—which are much clearer—undoubtedly were harvested from one of the many lakes near St. Paul. Am I correct, Mr. Rafferty?"

Rafferty nodded. " 'Tis true. Mississippi ice is usually dark and full of sediment, but it's cheap and easy to get, so the palace builders use it for interior walls and the like. But the altar and podium, as you can plainly see, are made of a much better grade of ice. That ice comes from Lake Vadnais, where I've caught some nice pike in my day, and it's as clear and clean as a diamond."[10]

"Then why—?" I began.

Holmes interrupted to complete my question: "Why has this block of river ice been inserted where all the other blocks are lake ice? A good question. Do you have any theories, Mr. Rafferty?"

Rafferty stroked his beard, which had turned white with frost from his breath. "My guess is that somebody took out the block that was originally here and replaced it with the one we see. I don't know why somebody would've gone to all that trouble, but I'd like to find out."

"So would I," said Holmes, standing up and wiping bits of ice from his knees. "Tell me, Mr. Rafferty, do you suppose there would be any great objection if this block of ice were to be temporarily removed from its setting?"

Rafferty grinned. "Perhaps, but only if anyone were to know about it. Let me go outside for a moment to reconnoiter the situation. I may even be able to lay my hands on some tools. I'll be back shortly."

True to his word, Rafferty returned within a matter of minutes, carrying a sturdy crowbar in one hand and a pair of ice tongs in the other. "Well, let's have at it," he said. "If you gentlemen will stand aside, I propose to do a little excavatin'."

Rafferty went to his knees again, his head touching the underside of the altar, and used the crowbar to pry up one side of the block, all the while refusing our offers to help.

"Spent a summer once diggin' rock out of a Nevada silver mine," he said between grunts. "A little block of ice is child's play in comparison." He soon succeeded in prying one end of the block up several inches and then got the tongs around it. The block must have weighed two hundred pounds, but it was no match for our newfound friend. Taking a deep breath, he grasped the tongs with both hands and pulled the block out from its setting as easily as I might have plucked a blade of grass from the ground.

"Well, now, that wasn't so ba—" he began, looking down into the hole left by the block.

Then the tongs dropped from his hands and his body jerked backward, as though he had suddenly touched something blazingly hot.

"Holy Jesus," he said in a stark, stricken voice, and that was when I saw the severed head in its tomb of ice.

It lay faceup and perfectly preserved inside one of the ice blocks which formed the bottom layer of the podium. The head was that of a young man, with short brown hair, a well-kept beard, and regular features except for small black eyes which popped grotesquely out of their sockets, as though staring in wonderment at the world of the living. A tangle of nerves, sinews and blood vessels were visible at the base of the neck, which had been severed just below the Adam's apple. I noticed something else as well: a large gold pin encased in the ice directly above the head.

I took this all in within a mere moment, for the sight was too horrible to dwell on.

Holmes, however, looked upon this monstrous scene with his usual scientific detachment. He looked at Rafferty and said: "Is it . . . ?"

"Oh yes," said Rafferty, anticipating the question. "'Tis poor young Jonathan Upton. And I must tell you, Mr. Holmes, I am already wonderin' where the rest of him has gone to."

3

I NEVER SEE HIM LEAVE

I t occurred to me that the police must be summoned at once, but Holmes would not hear of the idea.

"No, Watson, we must first look and think. This will surely be our best opportunity to examine the scene of the crime. We cannot afford to let it go to waste."

Rafferty agreed. "Mr. Holmes is right. Once the Bull and his coppers arrive, they'll make a fine mess of things. You can bet your last dollar on that."

Holmes by this time had gotten back down on his hands and knees so that he could thoroughly examine the ice block holding the spectral head, which resembled a bizarre piece of statuary encased in glass. He carefully went over every inch of the block with his magnifying lens before crawling out from under the altar.

"I am especially interested in the little pin which the murderer has so kindly left behind for our consideration," he said. "Unless I am mistaken, it is of gold—no less than twenty carats—and it depicts an animal which appears to resemble the American beaver."

"No, 'tis a muskrat," said Rafferty, peering down at the pin.

"Young Mr. Upton was a member of the Muskrat Club, here in St. Paul."

"As I recall, that fact was mentioned in the newspapers," said Holmes. "What can you tell us about the Muskrat Club, Mr. Rafferty?"

"The Muskrat Club, officially at least, is a social organization open to all young unmarried gentlemen of the city," Rafferty said. "Its membership includes a few real workin' men—Mr. Riley, the palace superintendent, belonged for a while—but mostly the club is a hangout for rich young swells like Upton and Forbes. The members rent a clubroom on Sixth Street and do what all young men of leisure do in this city, which is to say they drink, gamble, and whore. Indeed, its members are rumored to be particularly fond of the latter activity, to the point that they are, let us say, on intimate terms with many of the scarlet sisters who inhabit this poor old river town. And since the city's finest bawdy house, Miss Clifford's place, is but a stone's throw from the clubrooms, the young men have little trouble findin' female companionship."[1]

"But is not prostitution illegal in St. Paul?" I asked.

Rafferty shrugged. "I suppose so, but there is one thing you must always remember about St. Paul, Dr. Watson. 'Tis a city where privilege is everything and money counts above all else. And if a rich young rooster wants to have his run of the henhouse, well, there's nobody who'll stop him."

Holmes now asked: "Do you know of any particular reason, Mr. Rafferty, why young Upton's murderer might have gone to the trouble of placing a pin from the Muskrat Club beside the severed head?"

"No," replied Rafferty, the hint of a smile conspiring to form at the edges of his mouth, "but I'm assumin' it's a clue."

"I think that would be a safe assumption," Holmes said dryly.

Rafferty's next comment caught both Holmes and me by surprise. "By the way, am I correct in thinkin' that the poor lad was dead before he lost his head, so to speak?"

Holmes gave Rafferty a long, appraising stare. "You are a most observant man, sir. Yes, it is quite obvious that decapitation occurred after death."

" 'Tis a simple enough matter," Rafferty agreed. "If you look at young Upton's neck, you'll notice right off that there's no blood where it was severed. And the cut itself, well, it's as clean and sharp as can be. There's not a piece of dangling skin or gristle to be seen. Which means—"

Holmes interrupted: "Which means that the body was well frozen by the time the head was cut off."

"Oh yes, he was frozen, all right," said Rafferty. "My guess would be that the deed itself was done with a good, fine-edged saw—a hacksaw perhaps. It would have been simple enough, what with the body hard as a rock."

The image of someone neatly sawing off young Upton's head in the dark of night was too fantastic to contemplate, and I protested to Rafferty that cutting off a man's head could hardly have been as easy, or as tidy, as he supposed. Moreover, I saw no reason why the murderer could not have used an ax or some other bladed instrument to accomplish his grisly business.

Rafferty gave a vigorous shake to his head. "Oh no, Dr. Watson, 'twas not an ax that did this. Let me ask you, have you ever seen a frozen body? Mind you, I don't mean a body that's just cold or a bit chilly. I mean one that's frozen as hard"—here he pounded his fist on the top of the altar—"as this slab of ice."

I confessed that I had not.

"Well, Doctor, I've seen plenty of 'em. In my days patrollin' the streets for Bull O'Connor, I'd come across frozen bodies—'extra stiffs,' we coppers called 'em—every winter. 'Twas always the same story. Some poor blighter would be out drinkin' and carousin' and havin' himself a gay old time, and then after the saloons closed he'd start toddlin' on home to his nice warm bed, not realizin' that he's drunk as a skunk. Pretty soon the liquor and the cold would do their ugly work, and he'd pass out in some dark doorway, or behind a snowbank, or in the empty lot where he'd taken a shortcut. And if it happened to be one of those brutally cold winter nights—say ten or twenty or even thirty below zero—well, by mornin' he'd be frozen so stiff you'd need a team of horses just to pull his arms apart, and that's a fact! That's why I'm sayin' an ax couldn't have done this to poor Upton. It'd be like goin' at a thick piece of oak or an iron pipe and tryin' to cut clean through in one whack. No, 'twas a saw that did this job."

Holmes listened attentively to this remarkable speech and said: "I salute your analytical powers, Mr. Rafferty, but I do not think the issue of whether the young man's neck was severed with a saw, an ax, or—for that matter—by a guillotine freshly imported from the French Republic, is of crucial importance at the moment. We can worry about such questions later. Our immediate task is to examine this room to see what other evidence may present itself."

"Before we do so, I must confess that there is one thing about this affair which puzzles me greatly," I said.

"And what is that?" asked Holmes.

"Well, perhaps I have overlooked something, but I am curious as to how young Upton ended up back in the ice palace after the guard saw him leave. Do you suppose he came back later that night or even that the murder was actually committed elsewhere and the head later hidden in the ice palace, for whatever reason?"

"I suppose none of those things," said Holmes.

"But how . . . ?"

Rafferty, I could see, was prepared to offer an answer, and Holmes, with a slight bow toward the big man, said: "Go ahead, sir, let us hear your theory."

"Thank you, Mr. Holmes," Rafferty said. "Well, I don't know what you're thinkin', but I'm thinkin' that Mr. Upton was murdered right here, or somewhere nearby. You see, I doubt he ever left the ice palace on the night in question."

"You mean the guard is lying?" I asked.

"No, I see no reason why he'd be tellin' fibs. What I am sayin' is that the man the guard saw leavin' this rotunda, a man dressed in Jonathan Upton's clothing, was probably the murderer. Remember, Dr. Watson, what the guard told the newspapers. He said the man he took to be Upton wore a scarf around his neck and chin, which more or less disguised his face. The man also walked past the guard in a big hurry and said nothin' when the guard greeted him. Instead, he just gave a wave and kept walkin'. So that's why I'm thinkin' it could have been the murderer who left and not Mr. Upton. Do you agree, Mr. Holmes?"

"It is an intriguing theory, Mr. Rafferty, and quite possibly true," said Holmes. "We shall find out more, I'm sure, when we talk to the guard, as we must do as soon as possible. In the meantime, I suggest we concentrate on the task at hand, which is to search for evidence."

"Is there anything in particular we are looking for?" I inquired.

"Blood," said my two companions simultaneously.

❊   ❊   ❊

Our hunt for blood or other evidence proved futile, even though Holmes insisted upon trying to scour every square inch of the rotunda, a task which consumed well over an hour. Both Rafferty and I cautioned Holmes that the longer we stayed, the more likely it was that someone would stumble upon the scene, but he paid no heed to our warnings. I was thus hardly surprised when a workman at last wandered in through the doorway and asked what our business was. Rafferty, whose golden tongue I had come to appreciate, managed to put the man off with some incredible story, but it was nonetheless apparent that our presence had created suspicion.

"He will be back with some of his fellows soon enough," said Holmes, who had finally regained his senses, "and I would rather not be here when they return. Mr. Rafferty, I would like to ask a favor of you."

Rafferty nodded, and there was something like a mischievous twinkle in his blue eyes when he said: "Let me guess, Mr. Holmes. You and Dr. Watson would like to evaporate quietly from the scene, leavin' me to summon the good officer out yonder and report our awful discovery, makin' sure, of course, to omit your role in the matter entirely. Is that what you would like, Mr. Holmes?"

The man had cheek, I must say, and I was beginning to suspect that in the rather outsized person of Shadwell Rafferty, Holmes was up against a more agile mind than he had encountered in many years. Holmes could do nothing but concede the point.

"You are a most perceptive man, Mr. Rafferty. Of course, if you would prefer that Dr. Watson and I provide a statement to the police, then naturally we shall do so without protest."

"No need for that, Mr. Holmes. I can handle the coppers, though the Bull will no doubt want a piece of me poor hide once the news gets out. Well, then, go along, and I will take charge of things here. There are, however, two favors which you can do me in return."

"Name them," replied Holmes instantly.

Rafferty tugged at his frosty beard and said: "First, I would be grateful if you would not inform young Upton's father of what has happened here. 'Tis my duty to talk to him, since I am acquainted with the gentleman. The death of a son is the hardest thing a man can endure, Mr. Holmes, and I do not wish George Upton to learn the bitter news from a stranger."

I had not taken Rafferty to be a man of deep sensitivity, but I now began to think otherwise, for his concern seemed genuinely heartfelt.

"Very well," said Holmes. "And, pray, what is the second favor?"

"Only this: Please notify our mutual friend Mr. Pyle of our discovery here. 'Tis certain he will appreciate havin' a scoop, even if it won't last long, for the *Globe*."

"It will be done," replied Holmes. "Incidentally, you can do one more favor for me as well."

"Be happy to," said Rafferty.

Holmes smiled and said: "Then please give my regards to Mr. William Best, who I have reason to believe is an occasional patron of your saloon. Indeed, unless I am mistaken, it was Mr. Best who notified you this morning that Dr. Watson and I were in St. Paul."

Rafferty smiled in return and said: "Ah, you've found me out, you have. I guess there's no foolin' Sherlock Holmes."

"No indeed," said Holmes, "though many have tried. Good luck to you, Mr. Rafferty, and I have no doubt we shall see you again soon."

Leaving Rafferty to compose his story, which I suspected would be both colorful and convincing, we slipped quietly from the rotunda, proceeded to the south gate, and then—unseen by the policeman, who was occupied in a noisy argument with a delivery boy—walked across the street to our waiting sleigh.

Upon our return to the Hill mansion, Holmes proved as good as his word. He immediately placed a telephone call to Pyle, giving him a brief and somewhat bowdlerized account of our horrendous discovery at the ice palace. Then Holmes said: "You shall have more details, Mr. Pyle, as soon as I am able to provide them. In the meantime, I would like you to look up an address for me. There is someone I need to talk with at once."

Not long thereafter, we were again bundled up in Hill's sleigh, on our way to a corner of the city known as Swede Hollow. It was there, Pyle had told us, that we would find the residence of Lars Melander, the guard who had stood watch at the ice palace on the night of Upton's disappearance.

The snow had stopped and sunshine was breaking through the clouds, making our sleigh ride not at all unpleasant despite the cold. Our route took us back through the downtown district, and as we passed within a few blocks of the ice palace, along streets still gaily decorated for the Winter Carnival, I was overwhelmed with images of the terrible discovery we had made only hours earlier. The thought of that ghastly severed head—locked into its crystalline crypt, eyes bulging, the mouth agape in a frigid rictus of death—so affected me that I could not suppress a shudder, which Holmes mistook for a reaction to the cold.

"Do you need another blanket, Watson?"

"No. It is not the weather which is sending a chill down my spine."

Holmes understood at immediately. "Ah, I see you have been thinking about our rather grotesque discovery. Well, my dear Watson, do not let it haunt your dreams. Young Upton is dead and gone, and there is nothing we can do for him now except find the man who murdered him. And that is why it is imperative that I talk to the guard. I wish to know everything that gentleman saw and heard on the night in question. Everything!"

As Holmes spoke, I noticed that we had left the commercial center of the city and were now traveling on a busy street which ascended toward a line of high bluffs to the east. About halfway up this long hill, our driver swung to the north along another well-traveled thoroughfare. Shortly thereafter, we turned off on a small street and then, to my surprise, entered a short, curving tunnel. Descending through this portal, we crossed a pair of railroad tracks and found ourselves in a deep, narrow ravine carved out by a fast-flowing brook which tumbled down toward the Mississippi.

"Welcome to Swede Hollow," said our driver, a stout and talkative fellow who appeared to know the neighborhood well.[2]

At the head of the hollow stood a picturesque pile of red brick buildings, the tallest of which culminated in a dome and cupola. This, I soon learned, was the home of St. Paul's largest brewery—a fact readily confirmed by the sweet heavy odor of malted barley which permeated the atmosphere. But the most magnificent structure in view was a splendid brick and stone house which occupied the crest of a steep hill overlooking the brewery and the valley below. No other houses were visible around it, and in its commanding splendor the mansion reminded me of some ancient ducal palace lording over its domain below.

"That would be Mr. Hamm's house," said the driver. "He owns

the brewery, and I guess he likes to keep a close eye on business. Or maybe he just likes to watch all those poor folks struggling beneath him."³

Indeed, the contrast between the mansion on the hill and the dwellings in the valley could not have been more pronounced. The destitute people of the hollow—mostly recent immigrants, according to Pyle—lived in small wooden houses strewn haphazardly to either side of the rushing creek amid piles of waste lumber and other debris. These bleak abodes—many of them little more than shanties— were of the simplest possible construction and showed no evidence of paint or other attempts at adornment. Here and there rickety footbridges crossed the stream, which—judging by the number of outbuildings perched above it—also served as the community's sewer. Well-worn paths through the heavy snow provided the only "streets" in this impoverished squatters' village, which seemed quite literally to be the bottom of the world.

Holmes took in these sights with a look of indifference and then told the driver: "It is not Mr. Hamm I wish to see. I am looking for a Swede by the name of Lars Melander, who I assume occupies rather less grandiose quarters than the brewer."

"There ain't no rich men in the hollow," the driver agreed. "Ain't no addresses either, so we'll have to ask somebody where to find this fellow you're looking for."

A young girl walking along the road soon provided the help we needed, directing us down the road to a shack which was dilapidated even by the modest standards of its neighbors. And there, in a tiny room wallpapered with copies of the *Globe*, we found the one Swede in the hollow whom Holmes wished to meet.

Melander was a tall, slender, sandy-haired man in his early thirties, with a pale, blotched face and wary blue eyes which suggested that he had seen enough of the world to know that it could never be trusted to serve him well. Still, he did not seem averse to having guests, particularly after Holmes greeted him with a salutation in what I took to be Swedish. During his travels, especially after the incident with Professor Moriarty at Reichenbach Falls, Holmes had picked up bits and pieces of several languages, but until this moment I had not known that Swedish was among them.⁴

Melander was so pleased by Holmes's foray into the Swedish

tongue that he invited us to sit around a sputtering woodstove while he went to another room to retrieve a welcoming libation. This turned out to be a rather dirty-looking bottle of that peculiar Scandinavian liquor known as *akvavit*. Although varnish might have offered a more pleasant drinking experience than this wretched intoxicant, Holmes—who seemed immune to even the most poisonous forms of alcohol—pronounced the beverage "quite refreshing" and took a second glass from Melander without protest.

By this time, the conversation had switched to English, in which the Swede proved to be fairly proficient despite having been in America, as he told us, for barely three years. Moreover, the *akvavit* appeared to have a liberating influence on Melander's tongue, for the stolid Swede became quite voluble as he described his generally miserable experiences in the New World.

In time, however, Holmes was able to direct the conversation along more productive lines. He explained that he had been engaged to investigate Jonathan Upton's disappearance—he did not mention our grisly discovery—and that he would be most grateful for any information which Melander could provide.

Melander considered this request for a moment, smiled in a rather odd sort of way, and said: "*Ja*, that's good, but a man I think should be paid for his time."

Holmes, with a small smile of his own, removed a ten-dollar gold piece from his pocket and placed it on the table. As Melander eyed the coin hungrily, Holmes replied: "Indeed, a man should, but only if he provides something of value with his time. Can you do that, Mr. Melander?"

As it turned out, he could, for over the next hour Melander proved to be a font of information, although what he told Holmes seemed, if anything, to further cloud the circumstances surrounding Upton's murder. Melander began by acknowledging that he had not seen the face of the man who emerged from the palace's rotunda and whom he had assumed to be Upton. However, he could provide nothing in the way of a description of the figure, other than to note that the man's coat and scarf matched those worn by Upton when he had passed through the gate. Nor did Melander hear any sounds of a struggle, or note any other irregularity, after Upton had gone inside the rotunda.

Holmes nodded, then moved to an avenue of inquiry which was to prove much more fertile. "As I recall, Mr. Melander, you indicated in a newspaper interview that you had had a 'busy time of it' that night at the ice palace. What did you mean by that?"

Melander shrugged and downed another small glass of refreshment. "I mean there were many people out, that's all I mean. It's usually quiet at night and I can take it easy, unless there's some *barn*"—"children," Holmes quickly translated—"trying to sneak into the grounds. *Ja*, don't you know that's why I guard all night, to keep out the people. But as I am saying, on that night many people come and go before the young fellow Mr. Upton arrives."

Holmes cocked his head to one side and considered this revelation. "Did you know these people?"

"*Ja* sure I did."

"How intriguing," said Holmes, whose eyes now took on that eager glow which always testified to a moment of extreme interest on his part. "Perhaps you would be so kind as to identify these visitors?"

"I guess I can do that. Well, Mr. Riley, the big construction boss, he is there just after nine o'clock. Says he must look at the palace because it is so warm. You see—"

"You say it was warm," Holmes broke in, with more than a hint of eagerness in his voice. "Exactly how warm?"

"Why, it is—the numbers I am not too good at—*trettiosex* at midnight."

"Thirty-six degrees. How do you know that?"

"There's a *termometer* by the gate. It is so warm, Mr. Riley and the others, they are afraid the palace will melt. But it is still there, so I still have my job. That is good, don't you think?"

"Very good," said Holmes, who gave no indication as to why he had suddenly become so fascinated with the weather. "Now, Mr. Melander, you indicated that the ice palace had a number of visitors that night. You have already mentioned Mr. Riley. Who else did you see?"

"Well, Mr. Forbes and Mr. Upton—the older Mr. Upton, I mean—they are there for sure."

Holmes's eyes were now positively gleaming with excitement. "You mean Cadwallader Forbes and George Upton?"

"*Ja*, the both of them. They come in big sleighs."

"When was this?"

"I think maybe about ten o'clock. They are meeting with Mr. Riley."

"Did you speak with them at all when they passed through the gate?"

Melander drained another glass of *akvavit*—it was at least his fourth, and the effects showed—then looked at Holmes with a dumbfounded stare. "Speak with them?" he finally echoed. "Does a nobody like me speak with such mighty men? Ha! Oh, I say 'good evening,' but people like that, they don't speak to my poor kind unless there is something they want. *Ja* sure, I am nothing to them, don't you know. The rich men, they don't care—"

Holmes cut in with his usual impatience: "Spare me the socialist lecture, Mr. Melander, for I do not propose to pay you for your political views. Is that understood?"

"*Ja,* I understand you and your kind," said the Swede, pouring another shot of his dreadful libation. "All right, then, what else is it you want?"

"To begin with," said Holmes, "I should like to know where these two gentlemen went after they passed through the gate."

"Into the big ice room. That's where Mr. Riley goes too."

"You are referring to the rotunda, I take it."

"*Ja,* I guess that is what they call it."

"Now, did anyone else come through the gate before midnight?"

Melander scratched the back of his head, paused to examine his glass, and said: "Well, the big copper, he is there."

"Do you mean Mr. O'Connor, the chief of detectives?"

"Well, now, who else do I mean?" replied Melander, leaning across the table to address Holmes in a familiar way, as he might confide in some boon drinking companion. "And it is queer, don't you know. I never see him leave."

CHAPTER

4

I SAW A LIGHT

This latest revelation from the increasingly loquacious Swede left Holmes in such a state of high excitement that his cheeks took on a reddish glow, as though responding to some intense inner fire. He immediately pressed for more details.

"Mr. Melander, now you are beginning to intrigue me. Let us begin with the matter of Mr. O'Connor's arrival at the ice palace. When was that?"

"He comes a little after the others, I think."

"And did you speak with him?"

"I say 'good evening' and ask him what is the problem, because he is there only if something is wrong. That is what I think anyway."

"And what was his reply?"

Melander downed another shot of *akvavit* and licked his lips. "Oh, he is like the rest. He tells me to mind my own god--ned business, that's what he tells me, sure enough."

"What happened next?"

"He goes into the ice room with everybody. There is a big meeting in there, I think."

"Why do you say that?"

"Well, I hear voices, very loud sometimes. *Ja,* they are arguing in there, all right."

Holmes, I believe, now felt himself on the brink of some enormous discovery, for he leaned across the table and looked at Melander with such a penetrating stare that the Swede immediately turned to his bottle for support. Holmes said: "You overheard conversation, did you? Tell me every word you heard."

Melander looked down at the floor, like a child caught in a lie, and said: "Well, now, I don't hear very much. The wind is blowing, don't you know, and the words I don't hear so good. Rich man's business is not for me. It's just trouble for a poor man, that is what I say."

"And you will find even more trouble, sir, if you don't tell me what you heard," said Holmes in a manner so menacing that I could see the fear flashing in Melander's watery eyes.

The Swede gulped and said: "Well, maybe I hear a few words. I think one man, he says something like 'You owe me.' There is talk of money too. I hear that."

"What sort of talk about money?" Holmes asked.

"A big number, that's what I hear. Big dollars. It is—how do you say it?—ten and thousands of dollars, I think."

"Do you mean *tiotusen* dollars?" Holmes asked, again surprising me with his command of the Swedish tongue.

"*Ja, tiotusen.*"

"That is indeed ten thousand," Holmes said for my benefit. "A considerable sum of money. You are doing much better, Mr. Melander. Now, do you know who spoke these words about the *tiotusen* dollars?"

Melander shook his head vigorously. "*Nej.* The voices I do not know. That is God's truth."

This answer appeared to satisfy Holmes, for he abruptly switched to another subject: "You've said you did not see Mr. O'Connor leave. What of the other gentlemen? Did they return through the gate?"

"Mr. Forbes, he does for sure. I say to him, 'Good evening, sir,' as he goes by, but he says nothing to me. He is not happy, that I know. A man like that, with all his money, I think he must be happy. But I guess not."

"What about Mr. Upton?" Holmes inquired, ignoring the Swede's latest commentary on the privileged class.

"*Nej,* I don't see him go."

Holmes folded his fingers together and bowed his head, as though praying for knowledge. After a moment, he looked up and peered into Melander's weak and, at this point, none too well-focused eyes. "All right, what about Mr. Riley? Did he leave at some later point?"

Melander scratched his head again, perhaps in hopes of stimulating his memory. It did not seem to work, however, for he said: "I don't know about Mr. Riley. Maybe he goes out later, that's what I think."

Holmes put his elbows on the table, rubbed his eyes, and said softly: "What you are saying, in other words, is that you really didn't notice Mr. Riley leave. Nor, as you have already told us, did you see Mr. O'Connor or Mr. Upton on their way out. The question I now must ask, Mr. Melander, is what am I to make of your testimony? Am I to assume, for example, that these three gentlemen stayed in the rotunda for some reason after Mr. Forbes had gone?"

"*Nej,* I am thinking they go out the back way," Melander said matter-of-factly.

Here was yet another piece of new information, and Holmes's eyebrows arched in surprise. "You mean there is another entry to the palace grounds other than the two main gates?"

"*Ja* sure. There's a little gate off to the west side. There's a lock, but some of the men, like Mr. Riley, they have keys. The big copper, he has one too, I bet."

"Is this gate visible from your station at the front gate?"

"*Nej.* I tell you, elephants, they could go through, and I don't see them."

Holmes sighed and slowly shook his head. "Evidence of the elephants will no doubt present itself at any moment," he said acidly, "since every other living creature in St. Paul seems to have been at the ice palace that night. Very well, then, let us continue with this parade of nocturnal visitors. Tell me, Mr. Melander, who else was on the scene besides the four gentlemen you've already named? The city council perhaps? A marching band?"

Melander ignored Holmes's mocking tone and contemplated his glass of *akvavit* as though gazing at a crystal ball. "I am thinking that's all. Oh, wait. The man from *Italien,* he is there. But that is every night, of course."

"Of course," echoed Holmes wearily. "And who would this Italian gentleman be?"

"Giuseppe Dante, that is his name. He is the big carver of ice for the palace."

"Very well. And when did you first notice him?"

Melander shrugged. "As I say, he is at the palace all the time. At night, he does his carving often."

"On the night in question, did you see Mr. Dante enter or leave the grounds?"

"*Nej.* But he has a key, I'm sure, to the side gate."

"Now think carefully. Was there anyone else at the ice palace on the night in question?"

Melander furrowed his brow and otherwise made a studied show of cogitation, a process that cannot have been aided by the large quantity of *akvavit* he had been consuming. Nonetheless, he finally shook his head and said: "That is all."

Holmes rubbed his eyes again and began massaging his forehead as though in terrible pain. He then observed: "You are a most reliable witness, Mr. Melander, for which I am truly appreciative. But I fear that you have now complicated this investigation enormously."

"Funny, that's just what the other one says a couple of days ago," the Swede remarked.

Holmes, like a man who has climbed a lofty mountain only to discover that someone has preceded him to the summit, let out a groan of disappointment. "You have talked with Mr. Rafferty, I presume."

"*Ja,* he is the one. How do you know?"

"A wild guess," said Holmes. "But let us move on to more important matters. For example, I am curious as to why you failed to mention any of these late-night visitors in your interview with the *Pioneer Press.*"

"They do not ask," Melander replied succinctly.

Holmes smiled. "Mr. Melander, you are indeed a barrister's dream. But what of the police? Did you discuss the visitors with them?"

"They do not ask either. At least, the big copper they call the Bull, he does not speak of it. But I guess he already knows, because that night he is there, isn't he?"

"Indeed he was," said Holmes, "and I shall be most interested to hear his account of what went on in the rotunda."

Holmes now took the ten-dollar gold piece off the table and proffered it to Melander. "You have been most helpful, sir, and I wish you well."

The Swede, who despite Holmes's threatening manner did not lack for brazenness, looked at the coin and announced: "The other one, he gives me twenty."

If Holmes was taken aback by this blatant attempt at extortion, he did not show it. Instead, he stood up, grinned, and dropped the coin on the table. "Is that so? Well, Mr. Rafferty appears to be a most ingenious man, but I am inclined to think that in your case, sir, he spent twice as much as he need have. Oh, and did I mention that the severed head of Mr. Jonathan Upton was found today in the ice palace? I am sure the police will be talking with you soon, since I would imagine they must regard you as a prime suspect. Have a good day, Mr. Melander."

"Take us to the ice palace," Holmes told our driver when we returned to the sleigh.

"Why are we going there?" I asked.

"To find an Italian," Holmes said. "I should very much like to speak with Mr. Giuseppe Dante."

When we reached the palace grounds, I was not surprised to see that a large crowd was milling around outside the south gate, no doubt drawn by the news of our awful discovery just a few hours earlier. A line of policemen guarded the gate, keeping out the curious, while inside, other men in blue could be seen walking about the grounds, presumably in search of clues. The palace itself, bathed in the soft raking sunlight of afternoon, was more beautiful than ever, even if it had now become a bridegroom's tomb.

"I do not see how you will find Mr. Dante amid all of these people," I told Holmes after our driver had dropped us off.

"You forget, Watson, that finding people is something detectives do," replied Holmes, scanning the crowd. His gaze soon settled on a group of men in heavy jackets, who stood near the gate. "Ah, here are some men who look familiar, for unless I am mistaken, they are among the workers we saw near the rotunda earlier today. Perhaps they can help us."

Presenting himself as a stranger to the city with an interest in construction, Holmes had no trouble striking up a conversation with the men, who indeed turned out to be masons from the palace's building crew. Naturally, the initial topic of discussion was Upton's severed head, with several men theorizing that only a cuckolded husband would have been angry enough to perform such a heinous deed. But under subtle prodding from Holmes, the talk soon turned to ice blocks, scaffolding, joinery, and other details of the palace's construction. It was only then that Holmes finally brought up the subject of the ice sculptures adorning the palace.

"The carvings are quite wonderful," he said, drawing nods of agreement from the men. "I would like to meet the artist someday, as I am thinking of commissioning some sculptures myself. I believe his name is Giuseppe Dante. Do any of you know where I might find him?"

A tall, rugged man who appeared to be the leader of the group spoke up: "You'll have no trouble, sir. He's around here every day. And he lives in those apartments"—here he pointed toward a large brick building at the southwest corner of the park—"right over there."

After a few more perfunctory inquiries, Holmes thanked the men. Moments later, we were knocking at the door of Dante's apartment.

The man who answered our knock was small and swarthy, perhaps fifty years of age, with dark glittering eyes, a long Roman nose, and short-cropped black hair heavily flecked with white particles which I soon learned were marble dust. He wore a long green smock, also covered with white dust, and in one hand he held a heavy iron chisel.

"Yes, what is it you want?" he asked, with a heavy Italian accent.

"Mr. Dante, I presume," said Holmes with a smile, offering his hand. "It is an honor to meet you, *signore*. I am John Baker of London, and this is my friend Mr. Smith. We should like to talk with you about the art of ice carving, among other things. I must tell you that I greatly admire your work."

Dante looked at us in disbelief. "You would like to talk about my art, you say? *Bene!* That is a thing no one in this miserable city ever wishes to discuss. Money, now that is different. Everyone, they wish to talk about that. Please, sirs, come in, come in," he said, shaking Holmes's hand and then mine. As he did so, I could not help but notice the tremendous strength of his grip, which was no doubt the result of his artistic labors.

The sculptor's apartment, although small and poorly furnished, was quite remarkable, for it was so crammed with *objets d'art* that I felt as though Holmes and I were entering a museum. Paintings, mostly portraits in oil, covered nearly every inch of the walls, while the floor was strewn with marble busts, small bas-relief panels, plaster and clay models, and even a few virgin blocks of stone awaiting the master's hand. There was also a single large statue—an exquisite image of a nude male, which stood alone in one corner as though guarding the lesser artworks around it. The immediate object of Dante's labors, however, appeared to be a half-finished bust of a young woman. It rested in a circle of marble chips atop a long workbench, which was positioned so as to receive ample light from a large bay window overlooking the park.

"You will do me the favor of excusing the mess," our host said rather sheepishly, "but to create a sculpture, it is not easy to be neat, I am afraid."

"There is no need to make apologies," said Holmes, whose omnivorous eyes made a quick tour of the room and its diverse artistic contents. "You are a most prolific man, Mr. Dante. Do you have a studio as well?"

"A studio I cannot afford," Dante replied with a sad shrug of the shoulders, as he directed us to an old sofa which appeared to provide the room's only seating. "Thus, I must work here. But it is all right, you know. These sculptures and paintings, they are my only children now, and I like to have them near me."

"An admirable sentiment," said Holmes, stopping to run his fingers over the bust of an elderly man with a wrinkled face so perfectly rendered that the figure seemed ready to spring to life at any moment. "Carrara marble," Holmes noted. "Michelangelo's stone."

"The best," agreed Dante. "It is the only stone fit for the image of God."

"Indeed. And yet now you spend your days working with a far less permanent material, or so I have been told."

"You have seen the palace, then," Dante said eagerly. "Tell me, what do you think of my work?"

"It is, if I may say, *splendido*," said Holmes, who always enjoyed showing off his linguistic skills. "I never imagined such effects were possible with ice."

"That is most kind of you, sir," said Dante. "Yet I must admit that I, too, have been surprised by the ice. It can be . . . unforgiving, just like stone, but what wonders it does with light! I do not mind telling you that to be an artist in this city, it is to be nothing in the eyes of the big bosses. They do not care about the beautiful. But I am here now, and I try to bring what little beauty I can to this place. At least, that is my dream, sirs! And yet you are right about the palace. It is a wonderful thing—not even Florence has ever seen its like—but it will be gone soon enough, I fear."

"Though not forgotten, I should imagine," said Holmes, who seemed in no hurry to make the inquiries which I knew had brought him here. Instead, he now mentioned one of the paintings on the wall, and soon he and Dante were avidly discussing the art of portraiture. There was even something of an argument over the relative merits of the artists Giotto and Martini, with Dante defending the former and Holmes taking the side of the latter.[1] Meanwhile, Dante had brought out a bottle of white wine, a Soave from the "old country," as he called it, and this excellent refreshment helped the minutes go by quickly as I waited until Holmes, uncharacteristically, got slowly to the point of our visit.

"I should imagine good wine is not easy to find here," Holmes observed after taking one sip of the Soave, which tasted like the nectar of the gods compared to the foul liquor we had consumed at Melander's residence.

"You have spoken the truth, sir," said Dante. "But I have a friend at the Ryan Hotel who always finds something nice for me from his cellars."

"Would that friend be a big Irishman by the name of Shadwell Rafferty?"

"Yes. Do you know him?"

"Oh yes," said Holmes, "we know him."

As the wine began to flow more freely, Holmes finally steered the conversation toward his real subject of interest, which was the murder of Jonathan Upton. Rising from his seat and walking over to the bay window, Holmes remarked: "Would you look at that crowd by the ice palace! I suppose you have heard the tragic news by now, Mr. Dante."

"Oh yes," the Italian said, bowing his head in a gesture of mourning. "It is a terrible thing. People are talking of nothing else."

"Tell me, did you by chance know the poor young man? I ask only because I heard somewhere that his father has been much involved in the ice palace project."

"That is true. Mr. George Upton, he is quite the big man in this city. A very hard man, too, who does not like paying the bills which I give to his committee. All the time, he complains I am too expensive! But the son, I do not think I ever met him."

"I see. So I take it he was not a regular visitor to the palace before that night when he disappeared."

"No, I do not believe so. But who can say? There are many people at the palace every day."

"And even at night, from what I hear. I suppose you have had to work there at night sometimes."

"Oh yes, many times. You see, if it is a very sunny day, the ice it becomes soft and does not respond as it should to the chisel. But at night it is always cold. Always. And with the big electrical lights at the palace, I can see what I am doing no matter how dark it is. It is very quiet at night also, so I can be alone with my work."

"How very interesting," said Holmes, turning away from the window to examine the bust on the worktable. "Tell me, were you by chance at the palace on the night young Mr. Upton vanished?"

Dante reacted to this question with one of his own. "May I ask, Mr. Baker, why it is you are interested in that night? Perhaps you are an agent of the police. If so, you are wasting your time."

"No, Mr. Dante, I am not with the police," said Holmes, who showed no surprise at the Italian's sudden display of suspicion. "But since you have been so forthright with me, I shall extend the same courtesy to you. I have been engaged by one of St. Paul's leading men to investigate the murder of Jonathan Upton, and I would be most grateful for any help which you could give me. But I should add that this fact does not in any way affect the sincerity of my earlier compliments regarding your skill as an artist."

This last observation clearly pleased Dante, who smiled and said: "Very well, I will be most happy to assist you in any way I can. But there is little I can tell you which I have not already told the police. I was working at the palace that night, as you must know, but I left before the unfortunate young man arrived."

"What part of the palace were you working on?"

"I was finishing the sculptures around the entry to the rotunda."

"And how long were you there?"

"I came at about six o'clock, when all the workers had left. I went first, of course, to my workroom, which is behind the rotunda. There

I keep my tools and I also have a small stove for warming my hands. It was about half past six when I went to the doors of the rotunda to carve."

"Did you see anyone in or near the rotunda while you were there?"

"No one, except, of course, my friends King Borealis and Vulcanus Rex."

"Ah, the carnival figures. I have read about them."

"Yes, they are at the center of the carnival legend. One is the ice king, the other the fire king. It was their images I was carving around the doorway to the rotunda."[2]

"Of course," said Holmes. "And what fine carvings they are! The Vulcanus Rex is particularly remarkable. Indeed, it reminds me of a character from your namesake's *Inferno.* Now, *signore,* could you tell me what time you left the palace grounds?"

"It was around nine o'clock."

"And did you go out the front gate?"

"Oh no, I used the gate on the side. I have the key, and it is but a short walk from that gate to here."

"Do many other people have keys to that gate?"

Dante, who like all of his nationality was most voluble in his speech and manner, raised his palms in a show of uncertainty and said: "I do not have the only key, I am sure, but as to those who have the others . . ."

"I understand," said Holmes. "But tell me this: Did you see anything, anything at all, that night which aroused your suspicions? Please think."

Dante's expressive face now took on an agitated appearance, as though he were struggling with some terrible doubt. "Very well, sir," he finally said, "I will tell you something which I did not tell the police. But I must beg you and your friend to keep my name — how do you say? — in confidence, because I do not wish to become anyone's enemy."

"You may trust absolutely in our discretion," Holmes assured him. "Now, what is it you wish to tell us, Mr. Dante?"

"Only that there is something I saw that night. Something which I think now was strange. You see, I saw a light in the rotunda that I had never seen before."

Holmes perked up like a hunting dog on the trail of a fresh scent.

"Really, that is most intriguing, Mr. Dante. Pray, tell us more about this mysterious illumination."

"It was at half past eleven—I remember because I had just taken out my watch to rewind it—that I happened to look out my big window, toward the palace. At once I saw the light. It was shining right through the walls of the rotunda, which as you have seen is easily visible from my window. It was curious, this light, for it was small and bright, and it moved all about like a dancing white ball. I could not take my eyes off the light, because it was so beautiful the way it pierced the walls of ice. Then, suddenly, it went out."

"And what did you make of all this?" Holmes asked.

Dante shrugged his shoulders in dramatic fashion. "I thought at first that it was only the night guard looking for something with his lantern. But as I was about to turn away, I saw a man coming out of the side gate."

"A man, you say. Who was it?"

"The distance, it was too great for me to see a face, even though there is a streetlight near the side gate. But I could see well enough to tell that the man wore a long fur coat of the kind . . ."

Here, Dante paused, much to Holmes's unhappiness, and looked at him in a beseeching manner.

"Go on," Holmes prodded.

"I do not know if I should tell you this, sir . . ."

"Tell me," Holmes fairly shouted.

"Well," said Dante with great reluctance, "the coat, it looked just like one which I have often seen Mr. George Upton wear."

CHAPTER 5

HE GOT ONLY WHAT HE DESERVED

P yle was waiting for us in the library of Hill's mansion when
we returned from Dante's apartment. Although it was not
yet five o'clock, night had already clamped down like a vise,
and a powerful wind howled and rattled at the windows. Holmes's
mood — dark and restless — matched the weather. He had gone off to
make a telephone call immediately after our return, and the news he
received must have been unsatisfactory, for he now sat glumly in
front of the fireplace, furiously smoking one pipeful of tobacco after
another and muttering to himself.

The editor of the *Globe*, by contrast, was nearly bursting with excitement over the events of the day. Upon receiving Holmes's telephone call after our discovery at the ice palace, Pyle had begun work
at once on a special edition, a copy of which he now laid before us.
The headline across the top of the front page did not err on the side
of understatement. SEVERED AT THE NECK, screamed a bold block of
type, followed by a stack of smaller headlines: GHASTLY FIND IN ICE
PALACE — HEAD OF JONATHAN UPTON IN BLOCK OF ICE — REST OF
BODY NOT FOUND — BARMAN RAFFERTY MAKES AWFUL DISCOVERY —
NO CLUES AS TO MURDERER — POLICE SWARMING OVER SITE — UPTON

LAST SEEN MIDNIGHT SUNDAY—WAS TO HAVE BEEN MARRIED IN
PALACE TO MISS LAURA FORBES—FAMILY AND FIANCÉE IN SHOCK—
CARNIVAL MAY BE CANCELED.

"We have beaten the competition by a good hour," said Pyle enthusiastically as Holmes paused from his endless pacing long enough
to glance through the special edition. "I cannot tell you how grateful
I am for your telephone call."

"You do not have me to thank," Holmes replied. "It is your friend
Rafferty who insisted that I call you. Speaking of the Irishman, have
you seen him this evening?"

"He is still at police headquarters, I believe."

"Where he is no doubt spinning out a marvelous tale," said
Holmes. "But not even Mr. Rafferty's perfervid imagination can
match the reality of this matter. I have never before seen its like, Mr.
Pyle. Indeed, I am beginning to regret that I ever set foot in this ac-
cursed city! What a d--nably miserable affair this is!"

In my long acquaintance with Sherlock Holmes, I have become a
more than fair judge of his moods and manners, and I could see he
was now approaching a state of high dudgeon. Although Holmes
was the most fearless of men in the face of physical danger, his extraordinarily keen and active mind sometimes got the better of him,
and he could work himself into veritable furies of contemplation, like
a chess master obsessed with envisioning every conceivable move. In
such situations, Holmes became a kind of one-man hurricane, full of
wild and anxious energy, entirely unpredictable, and prone to those
destructive bouts of behavior which had sometimes caused me to
fear for his sanity. Yet there was no stopping him once the thunder-
clouds had gathered in his head, and I knew that Pyle and I could do
nothing but sit in our chairs like two ships at anchor and ride out the
storm of words which was about to buffet us.

Pyle soon provided the catalyst which touched off the explosion I
was dreading. "I am surprised to hear you so upset, Mr. Holmes," he
said. "Dr. Watson has told me that you had a most productive interview with the guard from the ice palace. Surely that will help put
you on the trail of the murderer."

"Ha!" Holmes replied, so loudly that the poor editor was startled.
"So that is what you think, is it? Well, sir, that is nonsense plain and
simple! No, Mr. Melander has been no boon to me. Rather, he is the

source of my troubles, the man who has left me adrift on a vast ocean of possibilities. Confound him!"

"I'm afraid I don't understand," Pyle admitted.

"Then let me explain," said Holmes, an urgent edge to his voice. "You see, if Mr. Melander is to be believed—and I see no reason why he should not be—then we are presented with a situation so perfectly and completely muddled, so rife with potential lines of inquiry, that we are like travelers in a strange city who have come upon a gigantic circus and can only wonder which of the many radiating avenues will lead us home. Will it be this one or that one? Should we go north or south, left or right? Well, the fact is that I have no idea, no idea whatsoever. I have looked down every avenue as far as I can see, but I perceive no end to any of them. I need something which will put me on the right road, Mr. Pyle. Otherwise, I fear, I shall spend my days chasing the wild goose, as you Americans like to put it."

"I hardly think it is that bad," I interjected, hoping that a few soothing words might put Holmes's mind at ease. "It seems to me that we have quite a few clues to work with."

"Oh yes, we have clues, Watson," said Holmes, spewing out words with the speed of a Gatling gun. "We have sufficient clues for a dozen investigations. Indeed, clues are springing up like weeds in a drought, and that is precisely the problem. For example, on the night Jonathan Upton was last seen alive, five people—all of whom have possible connections to the case—appear at the ice palace. What were they doing there? Why did they pick that particular night to be at the scene? And where did they all go afterwards? We know Cadwallader Forbes left through the front gate, but we cannot account for the others. And yet—if Mr. Dante's suspicions are correct—we also know that George Upton returned for a second visit to the rotunda. What was he doing there with that bright light? Did he hope to see his son? If so, what was to be the reason for their meeting? Or was the person seen by Dante in fact another visitor to the palace, perhaps even the murderer himself, preparing for his ghastly work?"

Holmes paused long enough to relight his pipe before continuing: "And what of the others—Mr. Riley, Mr. O'Connor, and Mr. Dante himself? We have only the latter's word as to what he did and saw that night. And why was he so busily carving at the palace on a night which was unusually warm and therefore not conducive to his work?

As for the other two, we are completely in the dark, for we know nothing of their movements after the meeting in the rotunda ended. Did one or the other, or both, stay behind, perhaps to lie in wait for young Upton? If not, did they see anything suspicious? Or did they leave at once by that side gate conveniently located in a place where it could not be seen by Mr. Melander? All of these questions have yet to be answered. However, accounting for the movements of these people on the night in question is but the beginning of the problem."

"What do you mean?" Pyle asked.

Holmes began fiddling with his pipe, as though trying to calm himself by resorting to a mundane task. Then he said: "What I mean, Mr. Pyle, is that many other questions buzz like angry bees around this case. There is the matter of the pin found with the head. Why was it left there? Was it merely an oversight or accident (which I doubt), or does it have some deep significance? If so, what are we to make of it? Will it lead us to the murderer, or is it a false clue designed to deceive, a distinct possibility in view of the careful planning that obviously went into this crime?"

Pyle appeared dumbfounded by these observations. "You say there was a pin found with the head, Mr. Holmes? What sort of pin?"

I had forgotten that Holmes, when he first telephoned Pyle, had not mentioned our discovery of the pin from the Muskrat Club. Holmes now described what we had found and then, to my surprise, pledged Pyle to absolute secrecy about the matter—at least for the time being.

"As for the many other questions which haunt this affair," Holmes continued, "one of the most troubling has to do with exactly when and where young Mr. Upton lost his head, so to speak."

"But I thought you had concluded he was killed on the night he disappeared?" I protested.

"And I still believe that, Watson. But I am far less certain as to when the decapitation occurred. Don't you see the problem? On the night in question, the temperature was well above freezing and stayed so until the next day, when much colder weather set in. This was confirmed by the telephone call I just placed to the offices of Mr. Pyle's *Globe*, which maintains daily meteorological records for St. Paul."

"Why is the weather of such importance?" Pyle asked.

Holmes turned to me. "Why indeed, Watson? Please enlighten Mr. Pyle in this regard."

Fortunately, I had been thinking about this very matter and was thus able to proffer an immediate answer: "I believe the temperature is significant because the murderer needed subfreezing weather in order to remove Mr. Upton's head as neatly as he did. Warmer temperatures would have made his task far more difficult."

"My lands, Watson," declared Holmes, "but you have surprised me. I shall never underestimate your deductive skills again."

"I see no reason why my statement should have come as a surprise to you," I replied with some asperity. "I am as well able to observe the obvious as the next man."

"Indeed you are," Holmes said with a smile, "and I would be the last to suggest otherwise, my dear Watson."

I took this as an oblique apology and bowed slightly toward my friend, who nodded in return. Holmes then stood up and went to the window, where the wind shook the glass like a thief trying to enter in the night. Gazing out into the cold darkness, Holmes continued his remarkable analysis of the peculiar circumstances of young Upton's murder:

"What a bizarre situation this case presents!" he resumed, still speaking at a rapid clip. "Not only do we have a surfeit of potential suspects, but we must also account for the murderer's singular and astonishing behavior. Consider: He lures young Upton to the ice palace (a fact I deduce from the careful way in which subsequent events unfolded), murders him (by means as yet unknown), hides the body somewhere within the confines of the palace (at least initially), dons the dead man's coat and hat, and then calmly walks out the front gate past the night guard. These facts alone indicate that we are dealing with a most cunning and resourceful killer.

"Ah, but this is only the beginning of our murderer's activities. For on the next day, or the day after that, or even yesterday for all we know, he returns to the scene of the crime, lops off the cadaver's head (or perhaps brings it with him, having previously removed the body to some more discreet location and done his nasty work of severance there), inserts the head into a large block of ice (which he undoubtedly had readied in advance), and finally installs the block and its ghastly cargo beneath the altar of the rotunda.

"What are we to make of this extraordinary sequence of events? Indeed, who could invent such a scenario, which would be too fantastic to contemplate were it not for the inconvenient fact that it actually happened? And, of course, the greatest question of all — the question upon which any hope of solving this case will surely depend — is this: Why was Upton's head cut off and placed beneath the altar? Why did the murderer go to so much trouble, and take what must have been terrible risks, in order to achieve this peculiar effect?"

Pyle now put forth an intriguing idea: "I cannot presume to answer these questions, Mr. Holmes, but I must say that there is something like a symbolic quality to this whole business. It is as though the murderer wished to present the world with a certain image, or whatever you might choose to call it, of Jonathan Upton. What I am saying, I suppose, is that it was not enough simply to kill the poor lad, but that — from the murderer's perspective — he had to be killed in a particular way."

Holmes turned away from the window and said excitedly: "Mr. Pyle, you are wasting your talents in the newspaper business. Instead, you should consider a career in the detective trade, for you have hit upon the essential point in this strange affair. It is exactly as you say. Young Upton's head has been presented to us — think of Salome and John the Baptist — as a statement. But of what? In other words, how are we to interpret the message which the killer has left for us?"

"Well," said I, "it would certainly seem to suggest that the killer bore some deep grudge against young Upton."

Holmes responded with a dismissive wave of the hand, then said: "My dear Watson, it is obvious that a terrible hatred motivated this crime. And for that reason, it must also be assumed that the killer knew Jonathan Upton, possibly quite well. But what was the source of this hatred? What happened to drive our murderer to such grisly and dramatic means of revenge? The specific motive still eludes us. In our present situation, I fear we are like Champollion when he first contemplated the mystery of the Egyptian hieroglyphics, struggling to make sense of something entirely alien and obscure. That is why we must find the Rosetta Stone of motive.[1] Otherwise, we shall never be able to decipher the murderer's message."

"And yet you have some initial theories about motive, do you not?" asked Pyle.

Holmes began pacing to and fro, his teeth clamped down so hard on his clay pipe that I thought the stem might snap off at any moment.

"Oh, I have many theories, Mr. Pyle, many theories. Far too many of them, in fact. Which is why — although dinner still awaits us — I now propose to retire to my room for what promises to be a night free of the burden of sleep. But I will tell you this: One way or another, I intend to get to the bottom of this matter. I particularly wish to speak with everyone who attended that mysterious gathering in the ice palace, beginning with Mr. Cadwallader Forbes. I would appreciate it, Mr. Pyle, if you could arrange for a meeting with that gentleman tomorrow."

"I will try to do so."

"Good. Oh, and one more thing. If Mr. Rafferty shows up, please notify me at once. There are a few questions I should like to put to him as well, for I have a suspicion that our Irish friend knows far more about this business than he has led us to believe."

"What leads you to that conclusion?" I asked.

"A number of things, Watson. Mr. Rafferty, for example, did not mention to us that he had already talked to Melander, the guard. Nor would he reveal for whom he is working, if in fact he has a client other than himself. And, as I am sure you and Mr. Pyle have noticed, he is much more than the amiable saloonkeeper he presents himself to be. He is a thinker, Watson, a deep thinker, and such a man always bears watching."

With these tantalizing remarks, Holmes bade us good evening, saying he would not be down for dinner. "I wish to work on the *America*. The foremast presents a tidy little problem, and while I am dealing with that, perhaps I shall let my mind wander over the much greater problem of how Jonathan Upton came to have his head cut off."

Pyle had to return to his newspaper, and so I was forced to dine alone, feeling like the lord of some remote and isolated manor as Hill's staff of servants hovered around me. I was just about to retire to the library, when one of the servants announced a "most urgent" telephone call from Rafferty. I sent the servant to fetch Holmes and then took the call myself, not wishing to leave Rafferty waiting on the other end of the line.

"Come quick," the Irishman told me as soon as I picked up the receiver. "She's here at the police station, and this may be our best chance to talk with her."

I quickly learned that the "she" in this case was none other than Laura Forbes, whom the police had called in to give a statement regarding her fiancé's murder.

"We can catch her on her way out if we move fast," Rafferty said. "Tell Mr. Holmes he must come at once. I'll meet you outside."

After giving me directions to the central police station, Rafferty abruptly hung up, just as Holmes was coming down the front staircase. I relayed the message, and Holmes immediately sprang into action, ordering a sleigh and sending a servant to get our coats.

"Mr. Rafferty seems to have a certain knack for being in the right place at the right time," Holmes noted as we waited for our sleigh to be brought around to the front of the house. "Now let us hope that the lady does not give too cursory a statement."

Fifteen minutes later, we arrived at the police headquarters, a grim pile of gray limestone which occupied one of the unsavory streets near St. Paul's infamous red-light district.[2] Rafferty was waiting for us in a nearby alley.

"Evenin', gentlemen," he said, stamping his feet in a futile attempt to ward off the biting cold. " 'Tis a fast trip you made. Even so, standin' around on a night like this is no picnic, I'll tell you that. You're in time, though, for the lady is still talkin' to the coppers. I was lucky enough to see her go by just as I was leavin'. That's her sleigh over there," he added, pointing to an elegant brougham parked across the street.

"I was not aware you knew Miss Forbes," Holmes said.

"Why, I've known her since she was a little girl. I used to do odd jobs for her father back in the old days."

"Is there anyone in St. Paul with whom you are not acquainted?" Holmes asked in a bemused tone.

"Probably not," Rafferty admitted. "I get around."

As the two of them talked, I could already feel the dense, cold air creeping through my coat, for the temperature had plunged well below zero.

"Perhaps we should wait inside the station," I suggested, not relishing the thought of a prolonged vigil in such frigid weather.

"No, we'd best not," Rafferty said. "I don't want the coppers askin' me any more questions. I've had enough of those today."

"I imagine the police gave you quite a going-over," said Holmes sympathetically. "I must state again how grateful Dr. Watson and I are that you kept our names out of this affair."

" 'Twas a pleasure to be of help to you, Mr. Holmes. But I have to tell you that I got a hotter grillin' from St. Paul's finest than the saints got from the Romans. Indeed, were it not for certain salutary connections I maintain with the political leadership of this city, I don't doubt the coppers would have brought out their hoses and done a little nasty work about my person, and that's a fact!"

"I can't believe the police would think you had anything to do with the crime," I protested.

"No, even Bull O'Connor knows that murderin' men in cold blood ain't my line of work. But the Bull thinks I know more than I am sayin'. He is right, of course, and if there is one thing a copper like the Bull hates, it is knowin' that he can't get at a man in his usual tender way. And he was none too pleased when I turned the tables and asked him just what he was doin' at the palace on the night Johnny Upton vanished."

"Ah, Mr. Rafferty, I see your recent conversation with Mr. Melander was most productive," said Holmes. "Pray tell, how did the chief respond to your impertinent inquiry?"

"Same way he does whenever a question is raised about his conduct. Told me 'twas none of my godd--ned business. The chief ain't exactly a font of information."

"So I gather. Well, Mr. Rafferty, I should be interested to hear of your adventures with the police. Have the men in blue reached any conclusions regarding this tangled affair?"

"Hard to say. The Bull ain't talkin', at least to me. The truth is, the coppers seem as baffled by this business as everybody else. But I will tell you this, Mr. Holmes: They are lookin' for somebody to hang it on, the quicker the better."

"And is there a likely candidate for the role of sacrificial lamb?"

"Not that I know of. But I promise you the Bull will find one soon enough. You see—oh, oh, there she is," Rafferty said, excitement rising in his voice, "comin' out the door. Now's our chance."

We followed Rafferty across the street, reaching the brougham a step ahead of Laura Forbes.

"Why, Miss Forbes," Rafferty said in his most amiable manner. "Fancy meetin' you here. I just wanted to extend my condolences in your hour of grief. 'Tis an awful thing that happened to your fiancé, an awful thing."

The carriage was parked directly beneath a streetlamp, and in its bright glow I could see the startled look on Laura Forbes's face. I could also see in an instant why she was the belle of the city. Tall and slender, she wore a long fur coat and a fur hat beneath which a luxuriant cascade of dark brown hair glistened in the light. But it was her radiant face, as perfectly proportioned as that of an artist's cameo, which drew my eyes. It was a face at once strong and sensuous—full lips, high cheekbones, a firm chin, and extraordinary violet eyes which sparkled like jewels. These eyes suggested that beneath her feminine facade lay a dense bedrock of determination and will. Her first words confirmed this perception.

Recovering from her surprise, she glanced at Rafferty and said: "Why, good evening, Shad. Thank you for your condolences. But you need have no pity for me, or for Mr. Jonathan Upton. He got only what he deserved."

I was astonished by this remark, coming so soon after the discovery of her fiancé's remains. Even Holmes, I think, was momentarily taken aback.

Rafferty, however, spoke up at once. "That is a hard thing to say about a man, Miss Forbes, especially a man you were about to marry. I am wonderin' what you mean by it."

She made no immediate reply, her fine face as smooth and impassive as a porcelain mask, but she did let Rafferty help her up into the sleigh. Once she was seated, she looked right at the Irishman and said: "You will learn what I mean soon enough, Mr. Rafferty. There is a sewer pipe which is about to burst in this city, and when it does, many are the men who will feel the taint of its foul contents. Great evil has been done, and the price must be paid for it. Now, if you do not mind, I shall be going. It has been a long day. All right, George," she said to the driver. "I'm ready."

During her brief conversation with Rafferty, she had paid no attention to Holmes or me, but this did not deter Holmes from asking one of those insolent questions for which he was famous.

"Tell me, Miss Forbes, why did you return your wedding dress before Mr. Upton's remains were discovered? It seems an odd thing to do, don't you agree?"

The question, I am sure, took her by surprise, and she turned to say something to Holmes, her violet eyes suddenly blazing, but then she thought better of it. Giving Holmes a withering look, she finally said: "I do not know you, sir, and I do not answer to you. Good night."

And with that parting comment, she was gone. We watched as her sleigh disappeared around the corner, and then Holmes said: "What an absolutely extraordinary woman! I shall have to talk to her again as soon as possible."

" 'Twill not be easy," Rafferty volunteered. "Cad Forbes likes to keep family matters to himself, and he's very suspicious of outsiders tryin' to meddle in his affairs."

"Well, he will just have to get used to my meddling," Holmes replied with his usual firmness, "since I do a good deal of it where murder is involved."

We returned at last to our sleigh, where I covered myself with blankets, for the bitter cold had penetrated to my skin. Holmes, by contrast, seemed hardly to notice the chill, and as we made our way along the quiet streets, he asked Rafferty if he could explain Laura Forbes's cryptic remarks.

"I am especially curious to know," Holmes said, "whether you have any idea as to the contents of the 'sewer pipe' which is about to burst on the good people of St. Paul."

Rafferty rubbed the thicket of whiskers on his face and replied: "I have only theories, Mr. Holmes, vague possibilities which flash in me tired old skull like little sparks of lightnin'. I can tell you that if there's a scandal brewin', 'twould be nothing new for this old river town, for St. Paul has always been awash in liquor and busy with sin. Yet I am inclined to think that whatever Miss Forbes knows, or thinks she knows, it goes well behind what happened to the Upton lad. The lady spoke the truth. There is somethin' evil and vicious in the air. I can feel it, smell it, almost taste it, and I do not mind tellin' you that I am fearful about what is to come."

"As am I," said Holmes solemnly. "This singular affair seems to grow wider and deeper by the minute, like a splash of acid burning into metal. And at the moment, I do not know how to stop the damage from spreading."

After dropping Rafferty off at his saloon, we went back to Hill's mansion, where I drank two glasses of hot brandy before happily retiring beneath the warmest covers I could find. When Holmes went to bed I do not know, but with both the *America* and the growing mystery of the ice palace affair demanding his attention, I thought it likely he would spend a sleepless night.

CHAPTER

6

THE FATHER, SON, AND HOLY GHOST

"I should like to see the morning newspapers."

These words, from Sherlock Holmes, were addressed to Joseph Pyle, at nine o'clock on the morning of January 25, our second day in St. Paul. Pyle and I were in the billiards room of Hill's mansion, enjoying a game of eight ball, when Holmes—blinking his eyes like a man newly emerged from the Stygian depths—appeared at the door and stated his request. One look at him—his eyes were red and droopy, his hair was disheveled, his suit badly wrinkled—told me that he had indeed been up all night.

"I have saved all the newspapers for you in the library," said Pyle. "As you might imagine, our local journalistic community was quite taken with yesterday's events. A regular blizzard of coverage, it was. Special editions all around, and the newsboys tell me they never made so much money in a single day. Sold out everything we could print. But I am proud to tell you that the *Globe* trounced the competition."

"How wonderful," said Holmes in a voice notable for its lack of enthusiasm. "Well, let us go see what sort of mischief the Fourth Estate has wrought."

We soon settled into comfortable leather chairs in the library, where a pot of strong hot coffee awaited us on the center table. Before long, a blue haze of tobacco smoke lingered pleasantly in the air as Holmes, puffing at his favorite pipe, rapidly perused each of St. Paul's four dailies.

I had, of course, already read the newspapers, which offered rather hysterical accounts of Upton's murder, along with the news — no doubt doubly depressing to the good people of St. Paul — that the Winter Carnival would be postponed (or possibly even canceled) out of respect for the victim's family. This announcement prompted much speculation regarding the future of the ice palace, which as word of the murder spread had quickly become a magnet for the morbidly curious from all corners of the city. Indeed, the *Pioneer Press* reported that the crowd converging on the palace grounds had become so large by midnight that police were forced to call in reinforcements to prevent damage to the structure.

The newspapers had also interviewed Rafferty at great length, and he told them all the same story, which was more or less true, although the Irishman did offer an embellishment or two. But there was no mention in any of these accounts that Holmes and I had been present with Rafferty in the ice palace. Like Holmes, Rafferty had kept his end of the bargain made the day before.

"Well," said Holmes when the last of the newspapers had been digested and tossed on the floor (an untidy habit which even the formidable Mrs. Hudson had been unable to reform), "I find one common feature of these voluminous accounts to be exceedingly peculiar, which is that none of them mentions the pin we found next to Mr. Upton's head. I suppose you may take solace from this, Mr. Pyle, since your correspondent was not alone in missing so salient a detail."

Pyle now made an interesting observation. "Perhaps my man did not miss it at all," he said. "Perhaps he never saw it, because the police believed it to be too important a clue to make public. After all, I have often known them to withhold crucial information in investigations."

"As have I," replied Holmes. "Yet the newspaper articles offer so many precise details — right down to the color of Mr. Upton's eyes and the exact position of his head within the block of ice — that a reasonable reader might conclude that reporters had been permitted to view the crime scene. And if this was indeed the case, then why did none of these enterprising journalists take note of the pin? I would like you to put this very question to your man at the ice palace, Mr. Pyle, and let me know his answer."

"I shall do so as soon as possible," Pyle promised.

"Good. Now I wish to point out two other newspaper items of interest, both of which—please observe, Mr. Pyle—happen to be in the *Globe*. The first is the rather mawkish profile of poor young Upton which appeared on page one of today's edition. In this reverent account, the late Mr. Upton is depicted as being only slightly less handsome than Apollo and slightly less saintly than Francis of Assisi. Indeed, I am surprised it was not also mentioned that he contributed vast sums to the relief of crippled orphans, tenderly petted all puppies within his purview, and rescued baby birds from drowning."

"Really, Holmes," I said, "I see no reason why the newspapers should not speak kindly of the dead."

Holmes, whose mood again seemed to be growing as black and bitter as the coffee he drank, replied: "My dear Watson, you are a hopeless romantic. Nonetheless, I am aware of no law which states that a man, simply by virtue of having shuffled off this mortal coil, must therefore be accounted more righteous than those who remain among the living. You see, I have been thinking about young Mr. Upton, and I have reached at least one conclusion, which is that decent and honorable men do not generally end up with their sawed-off heads in a block of ice! I shall be very surprised, in other words, if Mr. Upton proves to be a candidate for canonization. In any event, time will tell. For the moment, however, I am far more interested in another article in Mr. Pyle's newspaper, which is devoted to the thoughts of Chief of Detectives O'Connor. The chief, and I quote, says he 'intends to make an arrest shortly.' Yet he does not in any way account for this rather remarkable profession of optimism."

"Perhaps he has learned something we do not know," I said.

"That is possible," Holmes acknowledged. "Another possibility— one which Mr. Rafferty advanced when he stopped by early this morning—is that the chief of detectives is simply lying in order to placate his superiors, who must be under tremendous pressure to solve the murder quickly."

I was surprised to hear that Rafferty had talked with Holmes again. "I did not see him here this morning," I said.

"That is because you maintain regular hours, Watson. It was

about three o'clock when Mr. Rafferty paid me a visit, and we had a most interesting discussion of the case. He has some intriguing theories as to who might be responsible for Mr. Upton's demise, theories to which I am not yet prepared to subscribe. He also agreed to accompany us on our interview with Cadwallader Forbes. Speaking of which, have you made suitable arrangements yet, Mr. Pyle?"

"I have. Mr. Forbes will be pleased to meet with you at half past ten at his offices in Lowertown. On the other hand, he says a meeting with his daughter is, and I quote, 'absolutely out of the question.' I understand from Dr. Watson, however, that you've already talked with the lady. Quite a beauty, isn't she."

"A most fascinating beauty," Holmes replied, "and a most formidable one as well. I am disappointed to hear that her father will not permit an interview. We shall have to find a way around that little problem. As for Mr. Forbes, I find it surprising that he is at work today, given the shocking news of his future son-in-law's murder. Under such circumstances, I should have thought the gentleman would remain at home, tending to family matters. A heart-to-heart talk with his daughter, for example, might prove particularly enlightening."

"With Cadwallader Forbes, business always comes first," said Pyle. "Always. Now, if you don't mind, Mr. Holmes, I should be most interested to hear more about what you and Mr. Rafferty discussed at three in the morning."

"You shall, in good time," replied Holmes, leaning back in his chair and gazing up languorously at the ceiling. "Suffice it to say that Mr. Rafferty has a defiantly Celtic imagination and is thus inclined to see rich and swirling patterns in human events. He sees just such patterns in this affair, and he may be right. Then again, he may not."

"I should not underestimate Mr. Rafferty," said Pyle.

"Have no fear of that, although you should note that I do not propose to overestimate him either. In any case, now that he has insinuated himself so readily into this affair, I should like to learn more about the man. You appear to know him as well as anyone, Mr. Pyle. Pray, tell us all you can about Mr. Shadwell Rafferty."

"Well, I don't quite know where to begin, Mr. Holmes," said Pyle, taking a sip of coffee and producing a long cigar from his coat pocket. "But I can tell you this: Rafferty is an absolutely extraordinary character, though you couldn't tell it by looking at him. I suppose that's his secret, you know. People see a jolly fat fellow who owns a saloon and they assume he's just another genial, if none too swift, Irishman. But he's sharp as a January wind, and tough as old leather to boot. I remember the time—"

"Mr. Pyle," said Holmes impatiently, "I cannot afford digressions at the moment, however entertaining they may be. Please confine yourself to the basics. Perhaps you might begin by telling me what you know of his background—the kind of family he comes from, where he was born, what sort of education he has, and other such pertinent matters."

"Very well," Pyle responded with a look of disappointment, for he no doubt had many wonderful stories to tell about Rafferty. Be that as it may, Pyle without further delay began his recitation of the facts of Rafferty's life, as best he knew them, in a kind of clipped narrative style which I have paraphrased below:

Rafferty was born in Boston in the early 1840s. One of several children. Father an Irish immigrant and schoolteacher. Mother a dreamy, artistic Englishwoman said to be a descendant of Thomas Shadwell, poet laureate of England in the seventeenth century but best known to posterity as a prominent target of Dryden's satire.[1] Parents died when Rafferty was a boy ("might have been cholera," Pyle said), and he was adopted by a Boston Brahmin family for whom his mother had worked as a domestic. The family were ardent abolitionists ("as is Rafferty," Pyle noted, "and you should be warned that he is very passionate on the issue of Negro rights").

The young man received a good private school education in Boston ("Rafferty told me once," said Pyle, "that it was the Jesuits who taught him the 'two essential skills of logic and lying' "). Left Boston at age sixteen to see the world. Found his way to the frontier city of St. Paul in 1860. Worked along the levee for a year or so, where he befriended, among others, a young clerk named James J. Hill. Then the War Between the States broke out in 1861. Rafferty immediately enlisted as a private with the First Minnesota Volunteers ("the very first regiment offered to President Lincoln after the attack on Fort Sumter," Pyle informed us) and went east to fight the Confederacy.[2]

Pyle now abruptly halted his narration, much to Holmes's disappointment.

"Well, go on," Holmes prodded. "I should be curious to hear of Mr. Rafferty's war record."

" 'Tis not a matter I choose to discuss, as Mr. Pyle well knows," said a familiar voice. I looked up to see Rafferty, dressed in a white suit, standing at the doorway to the library. "But I am pleased to hear, Mr. Holmes, that you take such interest in the meager facts of my life."

"I should not describe them as meager, Mr. Rafferty," said Holmes. "Rather, it would seem you have led quite a colorful existence."

"I have seen a thing or two," Rafferty acknowledged, "though I am sure my experiences pale in comparison with yours, Mr. Holmes. But enough of this talk. 'Tis Cad Forbes you are interested in, is it not?"

"It is."

"Well, then, we best be on our way, as it's already past ten o'clock, and 'tis not wise to be late for an audience with the father, son, and holy ghost."

As we rode toward Forbes's offices, in the warehouse district, Rafferty explained his odd reference to the Trinity.

"You should know, Dr. Watson, that Cad Forbes occupies a special place in the religious life of this community. But it ain't church-goin' I'm talking about. Oh, Cad's a pious old bird, to be sure, and you can find him in the front pew every Sunday at First Baptist, shoutin' his hallelujahs. That's all right, I suppose, though if you ask me, religion—like good whisky—is best taken in small doses."

Rafferty paused to pull up the blanket around his lap—even with the morning sun, the temperature had hardly climbed above zero—before continuing: "Be that as it may, you have to understand that Cad's real religion is money, which is what the men of this city worship above all else. And Cad's their holy father, the man they all adore, because he's the fellow who first figured out how to make a fortune by takin' what was waitin' here to be took. He's our original Yankee money machine, he is, with a mind attuned by nature to the infinite calculus of the dollar. Why, 'tis said he can compute compound interest in his head, and if he don't have the first dollar he ever earned tucked away in his pocket, he can surely tell you where it is, and maybe loan it to you at twenty percent! Oh yes, he's our holy capitalist. Sure, Jim Hill's got more money now, but Cad was the one who led him, and a lot of others, to the promised land."

Holmes paid no attention to Rafferty's impromptu lecture, having apparently heard it already during their early-morning meeting. But I was much taken with Rafferty's tale and could not resist asking him about "the son."

"That would be Frederick, or Freddie, as most folks know him," he told me. "Cad didn't get around to marryin' till he was almost fifty, and Freddie's his only son. The lad's got a sharp head for figures, just like his father, but there's one problem. You see, Freddie has no interest in the business. Gamblin' and drinkin' and carousin' are more to his taste, much to the old man's disappointment. Oh, the boy's a real dandy, he is. But I've heard he does show up at the office every day and pretend to take an interest in the ledger books. He'll probably be there this morning if he ain't too hung over."

"That leaves the holy ghost," I said. "Who might that be?"

"Ah, that would be Jedediah Lapham. He is Mr. Forbes's factotum, confidant, adviser, and all-around handyman."

"And why do you call him the holy ghost?"

"Well, now," said Rafferty with a mischievous grin, "some people call him that because he's so pale and thin—a regular wraith, he is—and 'twould be a wonder to discover that a morsel of food has ever passed down his gullet! But there's also the fact that he is a most mysterious and shadowy figure, just like the Holy Ghost. You see, in my school days with the Jesuits, there was always some question about the third member of the Trinity. What, exactly, was the Holy Ghost's line of work among the immortals? Even the Jesuits, who could count angels on the head of a pin and perform similar miracles, weren't so sure about the Holy Ghost. He was a presence without a clear purpose. Well, the same is true of Mr. Lapham. He's always hoverin' around Mr. Forbes, but no one seems to know precisely what he does or how he does it. I guess you could say that he is a man who takes care of unseen things."

Rafferty turned and looked out the window of our carriage. "Ah, here we are, Dr. Watson. You'll see the holy ghost soon enough, I imagine."

Forbes & Son occupied the front of a small brick building overlooking a square in the heart of St. Paul's busy warehouse district. I had expected a rather grand office, but instead we found Forbes working at a plain wooden desk at the center of a small, high-ceilinged room. A dozen or so employees labored at nearby writing tables, and had it not been for the scratching of pens and an occasional hushed word, the room would have been as silent as a tomb. There was nothing personal or distinctive about this hive of activity except for one item prominently displayed on a table near Forbes's desk. It was, of all things, a very large and intricate ship in a bottle. Holmes went to it immediately and began inspecting it much as an appraiser might examine a fine work of art.

As Rafferty came forward to make introductions—we were simply identified as English friends of Hill with some experience in criminal investigation—Forbes stood up, and only then did I appreciate his stature, for he easily towered over Holmes. He was also lankier than Holmes, with spindly arms and legs, a prominent Adam's apple protruding from his long neck, and a thin, bony face beneath a shock of snow-white hair. Forbes's clothes—he wore a starched white shirt, dark pants, and a long brown frock coat, which was as muted as his surroundings—served to reinforce the notion that here was a man who had little time for finery. I guessed him to be well into his seventies, but it took only one look into his probing gray eyes to realize that he was still a man of formidable vitality.

Once the introductions were complete, Rafferty offered the appropriate condolences regarding Jonathan Upton's death, after which we all took seats around Forbes's desk. I expected Holmes to begin his interrogation at once, but instead he told Forbes: "I must compliment you, sir, on your ship in a bottle. It is a remarkable piece of work. Quite remarkable. All models of the *Mayflower* are conjectural, of course, but yours is as fine a one as I have seen. Did you build it yourself?"

"I built it with my son, years ago," Forbes replied, a faint note of wistfulness evident in his voice. "One of my ancestors came over on the *Mayflower*, or so family tradition holds. Freddie, like most boys, was a great model builder."

" 'Tis a fine pastime," Rafferty agreed, "though I never had the patience for it myself. Speakin' of young Freddie, I take it he is not in the office today, for I see his desk is empty."

"He never comes in on Saturday," Forbes said in a tone that left little doubt he was not pleased with his son's indifference to duty. "In any event, I understand from Mr. Pyle that you wished to speak with me regarding the matter of Jonathan Upton's murder. It is a most tragic business, gentlemen. Most tragic. But I do not know that I can be of any assistance to you."

Holmes said: "Since it was your daughter who was to be married to the victim, we naturally thought your family might have information of value to our investigation. But perhaps it would be best if we could talk to her first."

"That is impossible," Forbes replied brusquely. "The poor child has suffered enough. Besides, what little information I and my daughter possess—which I assure you is of minimal importance to this matter—has already been shared with Chief of Detectives O'Connor, in whom I have complete confidence."

"I am pleased to hear that," said Holmes, "for I have been told, perhaps wrongly, that the chief has a somewhat unsavory reputation in this city."

"Mr. O'Connor has enemies, like everyone else, but I have no doubt he will get to the bottom of this matter. Now, gentlemen, I must ask you to get to the point. Time is money, and I do not like to waste either."

"Very well," said Holmes. "Let us, as you say, get to the point. I should like to know what you were doing in the ice palace on the night Jonathan Upton disappeared and very probably was murdered. Please tell me when you arrived, whom you met in the rotunda of the palace (I would be especially interested to learn why Mr. O'Connor was on hand), what the purpose of this meeting was, what time you left, and where you went afterwards. I would also like to know whether you saw Jonathan Upton in the ice palace that night. Finally, I would ask for the names of any persons who can verify your whereabouts between the hours of eleven and one o'clock on the night in question. I trust, sir, that you will regard none of these questions as a waste of your time."

Forbes, who clearly was not used to being cross-examined in so blunt a fashion, gave Holmes a stony stare before replying: "Those are impudent questions, sir, and I do not propose to answer them."

I noticed that the rows of clerks behind us had stopped their incessant writing and appeared to be listening with rapt attention to our conversation. Forbes observed this lapse of discipline as well, and one stern look from him was enough to send the clerks back to their labors.

Holmes said: "I do not think my questions impudent at all, Mr. Forbes. I am merely trying to get at the truth. Surely you must have the same desire. And, of course, there is that matter of the missing ten thousand dollars."

At the mention of this sum, a pained expression appeared on Forbes's pinched face, and for a moment I thought he might speak frankly with us. But this proved to be an illusion, for the old man now said: "I will not tolerate intrusions into my business affairs, not from you, sir, or anyone else. The missing money is none of your concern. Now I bid you good day, sir."

Holmes was not to be denied, however. "So you admit that ten thousand dollars is missing. Tell me, Mr. Forbes, who stole it? Was it Jonathan Upton, by chance?"

Forbes, his patience all but gone, was about to reply to this latest provocation, when a voice from somewhere behind us said: "I would not excite yourself too much, sir. If you wish, I will be happy to deal with these individuals."

I turned around and saw a small man in a gray pin-striped suit walking toward us. Despite the quiet of the room, I had not heard him enter. As he approached, Forbes let out a tiny smile—or perhaps he was simply ungritting his pointy brown teeth—and said: "By all means, Jed, deal with them."

Without another word, Forbes rose from his chair and, with the aid of a cane, slowly made his way over to one of the clerks, whom he began berating for an improper ledger entry. Meanwhile, the man in the pin-striped suit reached Forbes's desk and stood perfectly erect beside it, as though guarding a sacred shrine from an invading band of infidels.

Rafferty, who was in the chair adjoining mine, nudged me with an elbow. "The holy ghost has arrived," he whispered. "We are in for a time of it now."

Jedediah Lapham, I must confess, hardly looked the part of a guardian, for he was—as Rafferty had described him—a wisp-like and almost childish figure, though I judged him to be at least fifty years of age. His fine features suggested a kind of feminine delicacy, but his round ashen face—furrowed with wrinkles beneath the palest blue eyes I had ever seen—was as cold and lifeless as a withered flower. Yet Lapham immediately proved himself to be very much alive, despite the deathly pallor of his appearance. Looking at Holmes, he said:

"Perhaps I can be of assistance to you gentlemen. However, you should know that it is Mr. Forbes's long-standing policy not to discuss business or family matters with strangers, however well-intentioned they might be." His voice was smooth and soft, like balm being applied to a wound.

"I take it that you are Jedediah Lapham," Holmes said with equal smoothness. "I have heard much about you from my friend Mr. Rafferty."

Lapham turned his gaze toward the Irishman and said: "How nice to see you, Mr. Rafferty. I trust you have spoken well of me, for what could be finer than to be held in high regard by a saloonkeeper."

I wasn't sure what to make of this ambiguous and possibly sarcastic statement, but Rafferty took it as an insult. "Why, you little —" he began, before Holmes cut him off:

"Mr. Rafferty, I believe, was about to take umbrage with your remark. But as it so happens, I am not interested at the moment in the merits of saloonkeeping as a profession. I am, however, interested in knowing why Mr. Forbes went to the ice palace on the night in question and what he did there. Am I to assume, Mr. Lapham, that you speak for your employer? If so —"

"I speak for myself," said Forbes, walking back toward us. He had picked up a ruler from one of the clerk's desks and now waved it in Holmes's face, like a magician trying to make something disappear with his wand. "Where I was or what I did is none of your business, sir. None of your business at all."

"Perhaps not," said Holmes, "but as you and George Upton were heard to be engaged in a heated argument over a matter involving Mr. Upton's son and a debt of ten thousand dollars —"

"That is a d--nable lie," thundered Forbes. "Jonathan Upton had nothing to do with the money or the argument —"

Lapham neatly stepped in to finish the answer: ". . . Which, if I may say so, Mr. Forbes, concerned business matters that bear no connection to young Upton's most untimely demise." Putting his arm on the old man's shoulder, he continued: "Isn't that what you were going to tell these gentlemen, sir?"

"Exactly," said Forbes, who seemed to grow calmer under his assistant's touch.

Holmes now detonated a surprise question. "Since you refuse to discuss your meeting in the ice palace, Mr. Forbes, perhaps you could clear up another small mystery: Why did your daughter hate the man she was supposed to marry?"

Forbes's face turned an apoplectic purple. "Why, why . . ." he sputtered, and for a brief moment I feared that he actually might try to throttle Holmes.

But Lapham, his unearthly blue eyes registering no trace of emotion, once again came to the rescue. Massaging the old man's shoulders, he said softly: "Pay no heed to this provocation, sir. Pay no heed to it at all. And don't you believe as well, sir, that the time has come for these men to leave? There is much work yet to be done this morning, and time is wasting. And I know how much you hate to waste time, sir."

"I do," Forbes agreed, the blood beginning to drain from his face. "Very well, Jed, escort these men out the door and make sure they never bother me again."

"Of course, sir," said Lapham in his most unctuous manner.

Holmes tried to press forward with more questions, but he met with an impervious wall of resistance from Lapham, and so we soon found ourselves back out on the icy streets, waiting for our carriage to pull up.

"Well," said Rafferty to Holmes, "that was a clever bit of work in there, and you might have gotten someplace if the holy ghost hadn't interfered when he did."

Holmes shook his head in disgust. "You are right, Mr. Rafferty. I nearly had the old man on the run with that story about an argument over a debt owed by Jonathan Upton. If only I knew it to be true! Still, we have learned much of value."

"And what exactly have we learned?" I asked as our carriage arrived.

"We have learned, Watson, that Miss Laura Forbes is hiding something from her father, that there was indeed an argument of some kind in the ice palace, and that Mr. Cadwallader Forbes is hiding something from us. We have also learned that Mr. Lapham may well know what both of the Forbeses are hiding. Now all we need do is find a way to share in their little family secrets."

"And how do we accomplish that?"

Rafferty provided the answer: "We must talk again with Miss Laura Forbes, and the sooner the better."

_____

YOU KNOW NOTHING OF MY SUFFERING

After our interview with Cadwallader Forbes, Rafferty went back to his apartment, while Holmes and I returned to Hill's mansion. Holmes immediately shut himself in his room—no doubt to ponder his next move—and I took the opportunity to enjoy a welcome nap. At about four o'clock, Pyle came around for a visit, by which time Holmes had emerged from his self-imposed isolation and was trying his hand at the magnificent pipe organ in Hill's large art gallery. Although Holmes preferred the violin above all else, his musical talent was such that he could improvise upon almost any instrument. He was working vigorously at his own set of variations upon a Bach toccata when Pyle and I, drawn by the music, found him in the gallery.

"Ah, Mr. Pyle," said Holmes, turning his head to greet us while he continued to improvise at the keyboard, "it is good to see you. I have always found music to be an aid to contemplation, although Dr. Watson will readily acknowledge that he is not always grateful to hear my scratchings upon the violin. Indeed, I am beginning to think I should concentrate my attention on an instrument such as this. What do you say to that, Watson?"

"I would not object," I said, "though I imagine Mrs. Hudson might, given your habit of making music at three o'clock in the morning!"

"Well, we shall have to see about that," said Holmes as he brought his composition to an end with a flourish of thundering chords. He then joined us on one of the long benches which provided an ideal place to contemplate Hill's collection of pastoral French paintings.[1]

Holmes, however, did not have art on his mind. "Well, Mr. Pyle, I should like to hear the latest news, if there is any."

"I believe I have one item which will interest you," replied Pyle. "I talked this afternoon with Mr. Parry, our reporter at the ice palace. He tells me that he and the other newspapermen of the city were indeed permitted to look at Upton's severed head yesterday while it was still in the block of ice. And he is absolutely positive that the block contained no pin or piece of jewelry of any kind. There was just the head, he told me, and nothing else."

Holmes nodded. "It is just as I expected. Someone removed the pin."

"But who would do such a thing, and why?" I asked.

"My guess is that Mr. O'Connor, the chief of detectives, took the pin. But as to why he did it, well, that remains a mystery."

Holmes would say nothing more on the topic, and the conversation soon turned to more recent events, as Holmes recounted for Pyle our singular meeting with Forbes and his assistant.

Pyle was surprised by what he heard. "Mr. Forbes, I will admit, is a difficult man, but I cannot believe he would deliberately withhold information regarding young Upton's murder. Surely he must wish as much as anyone else to bring the murderer to justice."

"Perhaps," said Holmes. "But if that is the case, his quest for justice is taking a most peculiar course. It appears that the gentleman's daughter has a far different view of the matter. We must talk with her again."

"Then you will have to find a way around her father," Pyle said. "I have made some discreet inquiries. Miss Forbes, I am told, is in mourning at her father's house and will receive no visitors."

Holmes gave a contemptuous snort. "What rubbish! Given her comments to us at the police station, I rather doubt that Miss Forbes has donned mourning apparel. But if she is indeed at her father's house, we must find a way to communicate with her at once. Her testimony could be the key to this entire matter. Perhaps—"

Before Holmes could complete his thought, a servant appeared at the door to the gallery and announced a telephone call for "Mr. Baker."

Holmes went out into the hallway to take the call. When he returned, there was a troubled expression on his face. "Come along, Watson," he said. "Our work this day is not yet finished. We shall need our coats."

"Where are you going?" Pyle asked as I rose from my chair.

"To see Mr. George Upton," said Holmes. "Something very odd has happened."

George Upton, like nearly all the merchant princes of St. Paul, resided on Summit Avenue, in a large rambling house which Pyle informed us was but a few blocks from Hill's mansion. Despite the frigid weather, Holmes insisted upon walking to Upton's residence, remarking that "a bit of fresh air will do us good."

Our walk proved to be more of an ordeal than a tonic, however, and I was chilled to the bone by the time we reached Upton's mansion—a monumental but dolorous pile of dark brick and stone set well back from the avenue, behind a tall iron fence.[2] I had tried to engage Holmes in conversation as we trudged through the cold, darkness already dropping around us like a black curtain, but he was not in a talkative mood, although he did mention that the telephone call had come from Rafferty.

I therefore was not entirely surprised to find the Irishman waiting for us when we were ushered into the main hall of Upton's house. The hall, brightly lit by huge crystal chandeliers, was splendid in a rather vulgar sort of way. Gilt-edged mirrors lined the pink and white walls, which were animated by swirling rococo plasterwork, while overhead an array of plump cherubs and other painted figures cavorted upon an elaborately vaulted ceiling.

Gazing upon this ornate if overwrought scene, Holmes remarked: "It is a pity, is it not, my dear Watson, that knowing how to make money and how to spend it are entirely different talents, not often found in the same individual."

I could not disagree with this sentiment, although it seemed to me that the hallway served its purpose, which was to attest to George Upton's wealth and magnificence.

Emerging from a small anteroom, Rafferty greeted us with his usual graciousness: "Ah, 'tis good to see both of you again. Mr. Upton is in the front parlor and will see us shortly, I trust. But first we must talk."

After a servant had taken our coats, Rafferty led us into the anteroom and carefully closed the door. "Now then," he began, "I suppose you're wonderin' what this is all about."

"There is no need to wonder," replied Holmes. "Indeed, it has been obvious for some time that you are working for Mr. Upton. It therefore was he who hired you to investigate the disappearance, and what we now know to be the murder, of his son."

Rafferty scratched the back of head and gave Holmes a conspiratorial smile. "Well, you've got me again, Mr. Holmes," he admitted. "You're right, of course. I've known Mr. Upton for many years and have helped him now and again with certain delicate business matters. So 'twas natural enough that he hired me to find his son, though I wish it was happier news I could have brought him yesterday."

"And just how did he receive the news of his son's death?" I asked.

"As well as any man could, I suppose, though he was shocked beyond all consolation, I fear, when I told him how young Johnny had died. 'Twas clear he was all broken up inside, and I left him to his grief soon enough, for he wished to mourn alone. And that's why what happened here today was so strange."

"And what exactly did occur?" asked Holmes. "You were rather vague over the telephone."

"My apologies, Mr. Holmes, but I thought it best to explain the situation to you in person. What happened was this: About an hour ago, as I'm gettin' ready to go down to the saloon, who should telephone me but Mr. Upton himself? His grievin', it appears, is already over and done with, for the voice at the other end of the line is cool and composed as can be. I'm instructed in no uncertain terms to come to his house, for Mr. Upton has something urgent to tell me. And under no circumstances am I to talk to the coppers in the meantime. Naturally, I do as I'm told, since Mr. Upton is payin' the bills. But when I arrive here, I discover that the 'urgent' matter he wishes to discuss is my dismissal! Imagine that. I am finished. Done with the investigation for good and not to say a word to anyone about anything. Well, I don't mind tellin' you I was a bit taken aback. But when I ask him why I am to be sent packin', he says—and these are his exact words—'I will take care of this business myself.' Now, what do you make of that?"

"I am not sure what to make of it," admitted Holmes, his interest clearly piqued by Rafferty's story. "However, I am inclined to think that Mr. Upton knows, or believes he knows, who murdered his son, and therefore wishes a free hand to, as he said, 'take care of' the matter himself."

" 'Twould be a reasonable assumption," Rafferty agreed, "though other interpretations are possible, I'm sure."

"I can think of five or six offhand," Holmes replied casually, "but that is beside the point. I should like to speak with Mr. Upton."

Rafferty smiled again. "I figured you would, which is why I made the phone call. Trouble is, Mr. Upton, I'm quite certain, does not wish to speak to you. Or to me either. In fact, to be perfectly honest about the situation—"

"Which in your case, Mr. Rafferty, would no doubt be a novel experience," broke in Holmes, "but, pray, do continue."

It was not like Holmes to make so unkind a remark, especially to a man who had been such a great help to us. Yet I think Holmes, for the first time in many years, felt from Rafferty the pressure of a true competitor. Always a keen judge of character, Holmes had understood almost at once that behind Rafferty's shambling facade there resided a mind of great power and sophistication. This presented Holmes with a challenge, as it were, to his authority. Lestrade and the other detectives of Scotland Yard, while competent enough, were never in Holmes's class, and he was able to dominate whatever investigation he undertook. Rafferty, however, was clearly a much more formidable rival, a situation which Holmes, initially at least, found difficult to accept.

Fortunately, Rafferty's temperament was such that he took no umbrage at the occasional jabs which Holmes threw his way. Thus, he simply ignored Holmes's attempt at a *bon mot* and continued with his story: "As I was sayin', the fact is that Mr. Upton doesn't even know we're here. I took the liberty of stayin' for a bit after being dismissed, in the hope that you, Mr. Holmes, might be able to bring the man to his senses, perhaps by surprisin' him with one of those devastatin' attacks of logic and deduction for which you are so famous."

Holmes, who never made a habit of underestimating his own

abilities, was as susceptible to a well-delivered piece of flattery as the next man, and Rafferty's words had their desired effect.

"You may be right," Holmes said after a moment's consideration. "Very well, sir, lead the way, and we shall see soon enough what sort of information can be extracted from the reluctant Mr. Upton. Incidentally, I should like to check—"

"—the front coat closet," said Rafferty as Holmes opened a small door off the entry hall and peeked inside. "I already have, and as you can see, it contains a very nice fur coat, just like the one Mr. Dante mentioned to you."

I must confess that I did not feel comfortable with Holmes's intentions. George Upton had only a day before learned of the death, in most hideous fashion, of his son, and now Holmes and Rafferty were prepared to "ambush" the poor man in his own home and no doubt pillory him with hard questions.

"Is this really wise?" I said. "Surely Mr. Upton deserves some consideration at this most difficult time. Tomorrow—"

"Tomorrow may be too late," Holmes snapped. "Murder is not a matter for the social niceties, Watson. If Mr. Upton has some knowledge of this dreadful business, then we must find out what he knows and how he knows it."

We left the anteroom and returned to the front hall, where the servant who had admitted us was still hovering about, in what appeared to be an agitated state.

Rafferty summoned the man, whom he seemed to know, slipped a coin into his hand, and told him that we would "be most grateful" to see the master of the house, whereupon a voice behind us said in a sharp, hostile voice:

"I thought you were gone, Mr. Rafferty. What is it you want, and who are these men?"

Such was our introduction to George Upton.

My image of the American tycoon had been formed by James J. Hill, whose craggy features and broad torso evoked an overwhelming sense of power, rather like one of the massive locomotives which had helped make his fortune. Upton, though I knew him to be a notable entrepreneur in his own right, possessed a far less imposing presence. He was, in fact, a rather small and frail-looking man, with a round, owlish face beneath a dusting of thin white hair, and he was slightly stooped at the shoulders, as though worn down by the cares of the world. Had I not known his station in life, I might have mistaken him for a clerk or bookkeeper—an impression enhanced by the green visor he wore atop his head. His blue eyes, however, told a different story. They were keen and unyielding, and they now fixed themselves on our friend Rafferty.

"Well, sir," he said before Rafferty could launch into one of his charming deceptions, "I am waiting for an explanation."

"And you shall have it," replied Holmes, stepping forward to return Upton's gaze. "I am John Baker of London, an acquaintance of Mr. Rafferty's, and this"—he nodded in my direction—"is my friend Mr. Smith. We are here to help you find the person who so cruelly murdered your son."

The sheer bravado with which Holmes announced our purpose left Upton temporarily speechless, and he stared at us with a kind of alarmed fascination, as though we were some noxious breed of pest which had crawled suddenly out of the walls.

"Is that so?" he finally said. "Well, gentlemen, when and if I am in need of assistance, I shall ask for it. But as that is not the case now and will not be the case in the near future, I must ask you to leave."

"That is your right, of course," replied Holmes evenly. "Still, I should be curious to know two things before I leave: Just what were you and the other gentlemen—including Chief of Detectives O'Connor—arguing about in the ice palace on the night your son disappeared? And why did you come back to the rotunda at half past eleven that same night?"

Upton reacted to these brazen questions with outrage. "My affairs are none of your business, sir," he said harshly.

Cadwallader Forbes had responded in much the same way to Holmes's questioning earlier in the day, and I now began to realize that the business tycoons of St. Paul were not used to having their motives, or their movements, scrutinized.

Holmes, however, gave no ground. "Murder is everyone's business," he told Upton. "And it is especially the business of a man whose own son is the victim."

The mention of his dead son seemed only to increase Upton's fury. "You will leave at once," he told us. "Mr. Yates"—here Upton motioned toward the servant, who had moved a discreet distance down the hall—"escort these gentlemen out the door. And if they give you any trouble, summon the police and have them thrown out!"

Without another word, Upton turned around and began to walk away down the hall.

One of Holmes's supreme gifts was his ability to keep a man talking. He seemed to know, in some purely intuitive way, precisely the question or remark that would elicit a response from even the most reluctant of witnesses. Indeed, on at least one occasion—while investigating the strange affair of Gottfried, the German forger—Holmes's ability to maintain a prolonged conversation against all odds had saved him from a fate too horrible to contemplate.[3]

My friend now demonstrated his skill once again, albeit in unpleasant fashion, when he remarked loudly: "I must say, Mr. Rafferty, your friend here is quite amazing. If it were my son who had been discovered dead only a day ago, his body most horribly mutilated, why, I doubt that I could control my anguish. But Mr. Upton apparently has done his mourning already—"

These cruel words produced their desired effect. Upton stopped instantly, spun around, and in a furious, anguished voice shouted at Holmes: "How dare you, sir! How dare you speak that way! You know nothing of my suffering, nothing of the agony I have felt at losing the only son I will ever have!"

Tears were forming in the old man's eyes, and I am inclined to think that had Upton been armed with a deadly weapon at that moment, things might have gone badly for Holmes. As it was, Holmes saw the opportunity open before him and exploited it ruthlessly:

"And that is why you must have your vengeance, is it not, Mr. Upton? That is why you intend to hunt down the killer yourself, without interference from the police or anyone else."

"Indeed I will, sir. I intend to bring the traitor who killed my son to justice if it is the last thing I do on this earth."

Holmes pressed on. "And what of this killer, Mr. Upton? You know him, don't you, or think you do. And you know as well why this horrible deed was done. Tell me, how did you learn the murderer's identity and motive so quickly? Or did your suspicions about this individual begin even before your son disappeared? Or perhaps it was something you learned that night at the ice palace."

Upton, wild-eyed and inconsolable, stared at Holmes for a moment and then suddenly blinked, like a man emerging from darkness into bright sunlight, and in that instant I knew that the door which Holmes had so brutally pried open, if only a few inches, was now once again shut and barred.

"I have nothing more to say to you, either now or in the future," Upton declared, enunciating each word with icy precision. "Now, for the last time, all of you, leave my house immediately!"

"I think we'd best go," Rafferty agreed. "We've got what we came for, though I don't much like the price we paid."

"Murder is not a sentimental matter, Mr. Rafferty," Holmes replied, "and cannot be treated as such. Still, you are right. Mr. Upton will tell us nothing more today."

As we left, Holmes surprised me by opening the door to the coat closet and briefly going inside for a second time. This earned him a sharp rebuke from the servant escorting us. Holmes immediately apologized, explaining that he somehow had forgotten that the servant would retrieve our coats.

"All right, Mr. Holmes, just what were you lookin' for in there?" Rafferty asked once we had left the house and stepped out into the night's deep chill.

"Let us just say that I found what I needed to find," Holmes replied. "Ah, this clean, cold air is positively bracing, don't you think?"

" 'Tis a regular tonic," Rafferty agreed, "if you happen to be a polar bear. In any case, you've done it now, Mr. Holmes."

"What do you mean?"

"Mr. Upton still owes me one hundred dollars for my work on his behalf, but I do believe that in light of your tender questionin' of the gentleman, I'll see Jehovah himself before I see any of that money, and that's a fact!"

As we neared the front gate of Hill's mansion, Holmes announced that he intended to take a walk. "I have always found pleasure in strolling at night," he said to Rafferty. "But you and Dr. Watson may as well go in, since I shall be a while."

"Suit yourself," replied Rafferty. "But just don't walk too far or too long. This ain't no damp, easy English sort of cold you're dealin' with, Mr. Holmes. This is the genuine article, straight from the North Pole, and it can creep up on a man before he knows it."

"I am not the sort of person who is easily crept up on," said Holmes, his breath turning to icy fog with every word. "I assure you I do not intend to freeze to death. But if you would be so kind, please have a hot brandy waiting in the library when I return."

"We can manage that, I suppose," said Rafferty, opening the gate. "Well, let's go inside, Dr. Watson. It appears that mad dogs and Englishmen—yourself excluded, of course—not only walk out in the noonday sun but also enjoy goin' for a stroll when it's ten below zero! Bein' Irish, I've got more sense than that!"

While Holmes took his solitary constitutional, Rafferty and I awaited his return in the library. But when Holmes had not come back after more than an hour, I could see that Rafferty was growing worried. He went over to the window, drew the curtains, and looked out across Hill's front yard toward Summit Avenue.

"Well, Dr. Watson," he said, "the world's greatest consulting detective is nowhere to be seen. If he stays out any longer, he'll freeze that big brain of his, he will. I think we'd best go out and find him before he keels over in a snowbank and we have to pry his eyelids open with a crowbar."

I quickly agreed, knowing that Holmes, when lost in thought, tended to be oblivious to even the most extreme kinds of weather. After piling on as many clothes as possible, I followed Rafferty out into the night. Once we reached Summit, Rafferty suggested that I go to the right for several blocks while he went a like distance to the left, the thought being that one of us would find Holmes soon enough. Summit was an exceptionally well lit street—its wealthy residents had been among the first to petition the city for the newest incandescent streetlamps—and I had barely turned to begin my search when I was relieved to see Holmes walking toward me. He was a block or so away, but I could not mistake his silhouette—the lanky profile, the distinctive forward momentum of his walk, the heavy fur hat atop his head.

"I see him," I told Rafferty, intending to wait for Holmes's arrival. But then I saw something else—a figure lying on the sidewalk, about midway between Holmes's position and mine.

Rafferty, coming up to join me, also spotted the figure. "Looks like somebody's taken a tumble on the ice," he said. "We'd better go help."

Holmes must have had the same idea, for he began to walk rapidly toward the figure, whose unmistakably feminine cries of distress I now heard. "Oh, help me, sir, please help me," said a high, plaintive voice.

Holmes reached the woman before we did, and I heard him say, "I am here to help," as he began to reach down toward her. What happened next left me wide-eyed with astonishment.

Running past me like a big horse at full gallop, Rafferty shouted to Holmes: "Stay away!"

Startled, the woman—who had been facing Holmes—began to turn around, only to receive a terrific kick from Rafferty. This blow was delivered with such force that it knocked her scarf and bonnet off. Before Holmes or I could protest this brutal behavior, Rafferty leaped upon the poor woman and pinned her to the ground.

"My God, Rafferty," I said, rushing up behind him. "What have you done?"

Only then did I notice that the "woman" had a long, perfectly waxed handlebar mustache.

"What I have done," said Rafferty, holding one hand to the man's throat and pinning his right arm with the other, "is to save your friend from a knife in the ribs.

"Well, now," said Rafferty as he straddled the man, who wore a long brown dress beneath a wool coat, "if it ain't Billy Bouquet. It's a little cold to be out in ladies' clothes, don't you think, Billy?"

"Get off me, you fat mick," came the reply in a husky voice. "I ain't doing nothing to bother nobody."

Rafferty responded by tightening his grip until the man began to choke. "Watch your tongue, Billy, or I may have to remove it for you. Understand?"

The man, gasping for breath, gave a weak nod.

"Good," said Rafferty, who then made a formal introduction of sorts. "Gentlemen, meet Mr. Billy Bouquet, one of St. Paul's most infamous footpads. Billy is a most unusual fellow, as you can see by his attire. Seems he likes to dress up like a lady, pretend to be hurt, and then—when some unsuspectin' Samaritan comes by—undertake a little robbery at the point of a knife."[4]

"And I take it I was to be that unfortunate Samaritan," said Holmes.

"You were. Therefore, the first thing we must do is to relieve Mr. Bouquet of the knife in his coat pocket. Lend me a hand, would you, Mr. Baker?"

"Certainly," said Holmes, reaching down into the right pocket of Bouquet's coat and emerging with a wicked-looking stiletto.

Rafferty glanced at the dagger and smiled. "Ah, Billy, me boy, I see you have lost none of your talent for mayhem. Now, Mr. Baker, please examine Mr. Bouquet's right shin, if you wouldn't mind."

Holmes did so and found a second knife, held in place by a strap. "Mr. Bouquet does not appear to suffer from a lack of well-honed weaponry," Holmes observed as he tested the knife's razor-sharp edge.

"Nor does he mind carvin' up a man when he gets the chance," said Rafferty, who began pulling Bouquet to his feet. "All right, Billy, up you go. I think we need to have a nice little talk."

"I got nothin' to say," growled Bouquet, who turned out to be a slender man with small, dark eyes, a prominent chin, and a wide, battered nose which was strangely askew, as though someone had once tried to twist it off his face. I also noticed that he was missing his left ear.

I was about to comment on this peculiarity when Bouquet, with a sudden lunge, broke free from Rafferty's grasp, shouldered me out of the way, and began running down the street.

"Hold it!" Holmes shouted, and turned to give chase, but Rafferty held him back.

" 'Tis no use," he said. "You will never catch him, Mr. Holmes. Billy's the fastest man on foot between here and Chicago."

"We should at least notify the police," I said. "I'm sure they could track him down."

"They could," Rafferty agreed. "But they won't. You see, Billy's got a protector in the department. It's been that way since he came up from Chicago a few years ago."

Holmes watched as Bouquet turned the nearest corner and disappeared into the night, then said to Rafferty: "Chicago, you say? Why did he come to St. Paul?"

Rafferty shrugged. "I'm not sure. But I've heard he was in the Star Cleaners there and things got a bit too hot for him after an alderman was stabbed and robbed on the streets one night. 'Tis said Billy did a little pimpin' in his day too, though robbery is his specialty."

The mention of Chicago's most notorious gang further piqued Holmes's interest. "How curious," he said, "for I spent some time studying the Star Cleaners on our recent visit to Chicago. I shall have to send a telegram to our friend Mr. Wooldridge, to see whether he has ever run across Bouquet. There is something else about this little episode which is even more curious, however."

"What do you mean?" I asked.

"Just this, Watson: It is a hardly a good night for footpads to be out roaming the streets, since, in this bitter cold, strollers such as myself are few and far between. Indeed, I would wager that on a night such as this, one could expect to walk anywhere in St. Paul without fear of molestation, since even the sturdiest strong-arm men must of necessity be warming themselves at the home fire like everyone else. And yet Mr. Bouquet nonetheless picks this particular night to take up a position on an unusually well-lighted avenue in hopes of finding a victim. Does that make sense?"

"No sense at all," said Rafferty before I could answer. "No, Mr. Holmes, I fear Billy was waitin' on just one person—you."

CHAPTER 8

I THINK EVERYBODY HAD
BEST *SETTLE* DOWN

Upon our return to Hill's mansion, Holmes showed no inclination to discuss our encounter with Bouquet, other than to thank Rafferty for his assistance. Nor did Holmes make mention of our singular interview with George Upton. Instead, after making a telephone call, he returned once again to his room, where I assumed he would spend yet another long night in anxious, solitary thought. Rafferty, meanwhile, had gone off to tend to business—"A tavern," he remarked, "is like a garden, for both are full of livin' things which require constant replenishment"—but not before inviting Holmes and me to visit his establishment anytime it suited us.

Much to my surprise, Holmes did not stay in his room for long. Just before eleven o'clock, as I was preparing for what I hoped would be a pleasant night of rest, Holmes came down to the library.

"Ah, Watson, I am pleased to see that you are still awake," he said. "I have just solved a most vexing problem with the topgallant sail of the *America*, and I do not think it will be long before she is ready for her final resting place in glass."

"You seem quite preoccupied with that miniature ship of yours," I noted. "I am surprised that you would continue with such a project, especially in the midst of a case as demanding as this one."

"Why should you be surprised, Watson? Building such a ship is a matter of discipline — discipline of the mind and discipline of the body. It is also a matter of foresight and anticipation, both of which are virtues no good detective can afford to be without. In any case, now that the *America* is once again sailing in smooth waters, I have a mind to visit our Irish friend at his saloon. Would you care to join me?"

"Very well," I said, despite the lateness of the hour and the weariness I felt from the relentless press of events. Indeed, thinking back on those recent occurrences — from our gruesome discovery in the ice palace to our potentially lethal encounter with Billy Bouquet — I could scarcely believe that we had been in the city for little more than thirty-six hours. Holmes, who in the late afternoon had looked so haggard and melancholic, now seemed as chipper as a schoolboy on holiday, and I could only conclude from this sharp change in demeanor that he had made a breakthrough of some kind in the case, just as he had with his model ship.

My impression was soon confirmed, for Holmes began to whistle — a "trifle" from Mozart, he told me — as we waited for our sleigh to be brought up. Then he said: "My dear Watson, I think I am beginning to see the first dark contours of this affair, the lines from which a complete and beautiful map will ultimately emerge. And I have the recalcitrant Mr. George Upton to thank for stimulating my vision."

"Was it something specific he said?" I asked, trying to recall all the particulars of our recent interview with the dead man's father.

"Indeed it was," said Holmes with a sly smile, just as our sleigh appeared in the driveway. "Ah, here is our driver and team now. Come along, Watson. Let us see just what sort of establishment Mr. Rafferty operates."

Rafferty's saloon, identified simply as SHAD'S by a large lighted sign over the front door, was not what I had anticipated. My expectation was that Holmes and I would find it to be a rather "rough and ready" place, as the Americans say. Instead, the saloon — located on the ground floor of the Ryan Hotel, St. Paul's largest and most popular inn — turned out to be, with one exception, a surprisingly elegant establishment.[1]

Rafferty, dressed in a white shirt with frilled cuffs and a bartender's apron, saw us at once and rushed forward to greet us.

"Welcome, gentlemen, welcome," he said, grabbing Holmes and me by the arms and escorting us toward the bar, as though ushering a bridal party to the altar. All the while, he offered a running commentary on the wonders of his establishment, which was by far the largest saloon I had yet seen in America. Its decor was that of a comfortable gentlemen's club, with oak-paneled walls ("taken at great expense from an old estate in County Cork," Rafferty claimed), a polished marble floor, and gleaming brass trim. Lining the walls were large photographs depicting what Rafferty described as "historic St. Paul," which appeared to consist of any building more than ten years old. Small tables, each set out with white linen, occupied the center of the room. Rafferty made much of these seating arrangements, assuring us that he didn't run "some cheap stand-up joint for rummies and dehorns."[2]

The heart of the establishment was a richly carved mahogany bar, which extended a good thirty feet along the back wall. Behind this massive fixture, between a pair of glass-fronted cabinets well stocked with liquor, was the room's centerpiece—an oversized nude portrait of a rather fetching older woman said to be one of the city's most celebrated madams. Rafferty explained that this lapse of taste by remarking that "there's nothin' like the sight of a naked woman to make a man thirsty."

The saloon was noisy, crowded, and thick with cigar smoke, and the mere sight of Rafferty coming out from behind his usual station at the bar seemed to intensify the din. Men rose from their tables to pat Rafferty on the back or seek a quick word with him. He acknowledged each of these customers by name, returned their good-natured gibes with his own, but still managed to keep us moving toward the bar, which was presided over by a massive bald Negro and two much shorter assistants.

"You appear to have quite a following, Mr. Rafferty," Holmes remarked.

"So it would seem," responded Rafferty. "Of course, the fact is that if it's appreciation a man wants, there's no easier way to get it than by openin' a good saloon."

Rafferty had hardly finished these words when a small brown and white bulldog suddenly bounded out from behind the bar and leaped into his arms.

"Hey, big boy, how are you?" said Rafferty, rubbing the excited beast on the chest. "Gentlemen, meet John Brown. He's the coproprietor of this establishment and my chief assistant when it comes to ejecting unwanted guests and otherwise maintainin' law and order. Come on, big boy, show us those teeth."

The dog instantly bared its canines and emitted a growl sufficiently menacing to give any troublemaker second thoughts.

Holmes, who had always been fond of dogs, was quite taken with this display and took the liberty of rubbing the throat of the animal, which instantly quieted under his hand.

"Well, now," said Rafferty, " 'tis not just any man John Brown will cotton to so quickly. I do believe he likes you, but that is no surprise, for he is a fine judge of character."

"Which I am sure accounts for his devotion to you," said Holmes with an unexpected touch of gallantry.

" 'Twould be nice to think so," replied Rafferty with a smile, "but I am of a mind that John Brown's devotion is based more upon the considerations of his stomach. You see, 'tis dinnertime."

The sound of these last words caused the dog to jump from Rafferty's grasp, race around to the side of the bar, and bark furiously until the Negro bartender produced a large plate of meat scraps.

While the dog devoured its meal, Rafferty introduced us to the bartender: "This is George Washington Thomas, best barman in the Northwest. Been with me for years, through thick and thin. Wash, I'd like you to meet Mr. Baker and Mr. Smith, visitors from England. Whatever these gents want, it's on the house."

"Pleased to meet you," said Thomas in a sonorous voice. "Any friend of Shad's is a friend of mine. What'll you have?"

Holmes ordered a glass of brandy, while I selected one of the local pilsner beers.

"Coming right up," said Thomas, and then—with a barely perceptible nod of his head, which I took to be some kind of private signal—attracted Rafferty's attention.

"Why don't you take a seat?" said Rafferty, pointing us toward a vacant table near the bar, "and I'll make sure Wash lays his hands on the best brandy in the house."

We took our seats and watched as Rafferty and his employee engaged in an animated conversation, their words drowned out by the raucous sound of revelry from nearby tables. When Rafferty joined us a few minutes later, Holmes said:

"Is there some trouble, Mr. Rafferty? I trust the bottle of brandy which you and Mr. Thomas discussed at such great length has not been misplaced."

Rafferty shook his head. "There's no trouble, Mr. Holmes, at least not at the moment, though it may be on the way, and quite soon."

Before Holmes or I could ask Rafferty what sort of "trouble" he expected, the bartender appeared with our drinks. To my surprise, Rafferty had ordered nothing for himself except a glass of water.

" 'Tis an ironclad rule of mine," he explained. "No liquor before midnight. Keeps the mind clear, if you know what I mean, though I admit a sip of good Irish whisky would be most welcome after the unpleasant events of recent days. Now, what would you gentlemen like to talk about?"

"I have been thinking about our recent interview with Mr. George Upton," said Holmes, taking a sip of brandy. "Tell me, Mr. Rafferty, was there anything you found particularly odd about his comments?"

A big smile lit Rafferty's face. "Ah, so you caught it too, did you. As I have said before and will no doubt say again, there's no gettin' a thing past Sherlock Holmes, who will find not only the needle in the haystack but the thread that goes with it too, and that's a fact! It was Mr. Upton's peculiar use of the word 'traitor' that caught your attention, was it not?"

"It was," Holmes acknowledged. "You know Mr. Upton better than I. Why do you suppose he used that word?"

"I have been ponderin' that very question most of the evenin', Mr. Holmes, and have a sore brain to show for my efforts. Still, I can come to only one conclusion in the matter, which is that Mr. Upton believes the murderer is someone he knows well, someone who has 'betrayed' him, as it were, by taking his son's life. But, of course, I am open to different interpretations."

"Your idea has great merit, Mr. Rafferty," said Holmes, "and I have considered it myself. Still, the word 'traitor' has distinct connotations—it refers above all else to someone who has violated a great trust. But why would George Upton have entrusted the very life of his son to some other person? That seems unlikely. Therefore, I am inclined to think that the traitorous act Upton had in mind may not have been his son's murder but rather some previous occurrence which in turn became the motive for the crime. Do you follow my reasoning?"

"Perfectly," replied Rafferty. "But I can tell you nothing as to what this betrayal might have been. Certainly, Mr. Upton never hinted of such a thing to me. But then he did not share his secrets, not with me or anyone else, I suspect. Why, it was only after I talked to the guard that I learned that Mr. Upton had been at the ice palace on the night of his son's murder. Yet he never bothered to mention this crucial fact to me. Imagine that!"

Rafferty paused to take a drink of water before continuing: "There is something else you should know about George Upton, Mr. Holmes. He is a decent enough man of his kind—no worse, to be sure, than the other hard-crusted merchants in this city—but he has always been prone to seein' shadows where there are none, if you get my drift."

"You are saying, I take it, that Mr. Upton has the sort of temperament which leads him to believe, against all evidence, that others— business competitors, for example—are conspiring against him."

"You have stated it better than I could," said Rafferty. "Mr. Upton is a believer in cabals and other organized mischief, I fear. 'Tis just as well he is not Irish, for he would probably attribute every business reverse to the malign influence of leprechauns!"

Even Holmes found this remark amusing, and said: "Perhaps you might invoke the little people to help us, Mr. Rafferty, as I fear we shall need all possible assistance in resolving this case. And speaking of the Irish, though of a decidedly larger variety, I should like to learn more about Mr. O'Connor, the chief of detectives. What do you think he was doing at the ice palace on the night of young Upton's disappearance?"

Rafferty slowly shook his head. "I don't know, but he was up to somethin' no good, you can count on that. You have to understand, Mr. Holmes, that the Bull is a man who hires himself out to the highest bidder in exchange for the best policin' money can buy. And since there were only two rich men—George Upton and Cadwallader Forbes—at that cozy little meetin' in the ice palace, my guess is that one or the other was payin' the Bull for services rendered. Trouble is, I haven't figured out yet just what those services might have been."

"Nor have I," said Holmes, "though I intend to put the question to Mr. Forbes when I talk with him again. In the meantime, I simply must speak at great length with his daughter. Mr. Pyle has been busy trying to arrange an interview but reported no success when I telephoned him earlier this evening. Therefore, I may have to resort to more irregular means."

"And just what might those be?" Rafferty asked. "Nothing too illegal, I trust."

"I do not intend to kidnap the lady, if that's what you think," Holmes replied. "I merely wish to talk with her, which means I must be in a position to speak with her the minute she steps out of her father's house. And in light of her earlier remarks to us, I do not believe she spends the entire day weeping in her room. She must go out now and then."

Rafferty rubbed his chin and said: "I take it that you're lookin' for a man to watch the house."

"I am."

"I know just such a man for the job, and I will set him to work in the morning. His name is—"

Rafferty abruptly stopped and turned his head toward the front of the saloon, where a large man in a black suit and black bowler hat stood motionless just inside the door. What appeared to be a bright silver badge was pinned to his chest. A hush instantly settled over the room, as though every occupant had just learned of a death in the family.

Holmes briefly regarded the bulky figure at the door and then broke the silence. "Am I to presume," he asked Rafferty, "that the Bull has arrived?"

"Oh yes," came the reply, "he is here, and I would advise the both of you to be very, very careful."

Chief of Detectives John J. O'Connor stood for a few more moments at the door, sweeping the room with his eyes. He was tall, wide, and powerfully built, and he held himself with the kind of easy physical confidence which only the largest and strongest of men enjoy. His quarry soon became clear, for a harsh grin contorted his features when he spotted Rafferty. The saloon was now as quiet as a churchyard at three in the morning, but this anomaly did not seem to bother O'Connor in the least. After carefully removing his hat and placing it on a peg near the door, he strode toward us—past the tables of silent, staring men—like some mighty dreadnought steaming through a fleet of rowboats, powerful beyond all thought of challenge.[3]

As O'Connor reached our table, he paused to take one last look around the room, as though issuing his final statement of authority over all the silent, cowering men. His broad, splotchy face was nested with wrinkles, and the redness of his nose and cheeks identified him as a man well acquainted with the companionship of the bottle. There was, however, no hint of weakness or indulgence in his small, deeply set eyes. A mysterious cloudy green in color, these eyes suggested a malign mixture of intelligence and cruelty, and looking at them, I had the sense of gazing into the depths of a poisoned well.

After completing his unhurried inspection of the premises, O'Connor turned toward Rafferty and said: "Well, I see the usual riffraff have wandered in to drink your adulterated liquor. But it's a quiet crowd, ain't it, Shad?"

"No doubt they are simply awestruck by the presence of so distinguished a visitor," said Rafferty in a cool, level voice. "To what do we owe the pleasure of your company, John?"

"Cut the crap," snarled O'Connor. "You know why I'm here." Having uttered this cryptic statement, he took a seat at the table next to Holmes and across from Rafferty, all the while paying no attention whatsoever to Holmes or me.

Holmes, however, never took his eyes from O'Connor, regarding the chief of detectives with a look of fascinated curiosity, as though he had just come upon some amazing specimen from the Cro-Magnon era. I thought Holmes—who feared no one—might have a word with the man, if for no other reason than to upbraid him for his lamentable lack of manners. Instead, my friend seemed content to keep his silence and watch events unfold, which they soon did in spectacular fashion.

Rafferty, on the other hand, was more than willing to engage the chief in conversation. "I don't know why you've come to my humble establishment, John, but I can guess," he said, returning O'Connor's stony stare with one of his own. "You have been to see Mr. George Upton, I imagine, and you are unhappy as a result."

O'Connor pounded a fist on the table. "You're d--n right I've been to see him, but the man ain't talking. Not a word. Seems he's got his own ideas about this business and would just as soon leave the police out of it. The man's hiding something, of course, and I have no doubt you put him up to it. So what's your game, eh, Shad? You got some scheme to separate the poor distraught man from his millions?"

"I have no game," Rafferty replied calmly, "nor have I any influence over George Upton. As to what, if anything, the gentleman may be hidin' from the excellent police of this city, I can't tell you, because I don't know. Sorry I couldn't be of more help, John, for I am always willin' to assist the police in their lawful endeavors. So why don't you sit back, enjoy a glass of beer, and I'll introduce you to my friends here —"

O'Connor cut in, his voice so loud that it could not help but be heard by everyone in the saloon: "I don't care who your godd--ned friends are, Rafferty, and they can go to hell as far as I'm concerned. What I care about is a cheap, swindling son of a b---h such as yourself sticking his filthy nose into my investigation. I won't have it."

These were fighting words, and O'Connor knew it. Although it hardly seemed possible, the saloon suddenly grew even quieter, as a kind of breathless, expectant silence enveloped the room. I became aware of a clock ticking behind the bar and the insistent hiss of the gas lamps which lighted the room. Outside — in the dark, frozen night — I could hear horses clopping by on the street, oblivious to the drama unfolding before us. All eyes were now fixed on the two big Irishmen, who sat across from each other as rigid and unyielding as statues. I turned to Holmes, with a silent plea in my eyes that he step in to separate the combatants, but he gave a slight shake of his head, and I realized that, like everyone else in the room, he wondered how Rafferty would react to O'Connor's blatant provocation.

The answer came soon enough. Regarding O'Connor as he might some especially vile species of reptile, Rafferty leaned back in his chair, folded his arms, gazed without fear into those poison-green eyes, and said in a soft but forceful voice: "You had best watch your words, Chief, or you may regret them. And if there is any swindlin' that's been done hereabouts, you'd be better acquainted with it than I, since 'tis well known you take your filthy cut from every crooked transaction in this city."

The events of the next few seconds resembled something out of a Wild West show. Bellowing like a wounded animal, O'Connor pushed back the table, rose to his feet, and reached inside his coat, presumably for a weapon. Rafferty was equally quick, grabbing the table as it came toward him and crouching behind it, a derringer miraculously appearing in his hand as he did so. Meanwhile, men all around us began diving for the floor, in the apparently well-formed

belief that bullets were about to fly. Having seen the sanguinary results of several barroom brawls during my service in Afghanistan, I
now thought it wise to do the same.

I was just dropping to the floor when I heard, above the commotion, a loud metallic clank, a noise which caused Rafferty and O'Connor to instantly freeze, as though suddenly inoculated with some
paralyzing drug. What had stopped them in their tracks was the menacing sound of a shell being chambered in a pump-action shotgun.

Looking up, I saw Thomas, the bartender. He had come out from
behind the bar, big Winchester in hand, and his resolute manner suggested to one and all that he would not be afraid to use the weapon.[4]

"I think everybody had best settle down," he said, his resonant
bass booming across the room like a clap of thunder.

Hardly had Rafferty's faithful bartender spoken these words
when another, and quite unpredictable, actor entered the scene.
John Brown came racing out from behind the bar and, with a ferocious growl, threw himself at O'Connor. The dog briefly managed to
get hold of one of the chief's legs, and undoubtedly would have done
his best to chew it off had the opportunity presented itself. But the
plucky beast proved no match for the big man, who with a powerful
kick sent the animal crashing headfirst into the brass rail at the foot
of the bar. The dog whimpered, then lay still.

Turning to Rafferty, O'Connor spit at him and scowled: "It's just
like you, Shad, sending a dog and a nigger to do your dirty work."

Rafferty responded to these ugly words by picking up the over-
turned table in front of him and, with a tremendous show of
strength, using it to batter O'Connor to the floor. It now seemed to
me that a full-scale brawl—or worse—was about to break out. I
knew that Rafferty was armed, and I could only assume that O'Connor was as well. Meanwhile, Thomas appeared quite prepared to use
the shotgun, which he began to level in O'Connor's direction.

It was at this moment of maximum peril that Sherlock Holmes,
the coolest man I have ever known in a tight situation, came to the
rescue. He did so by uttering only one word—"Stop!"—but in a
voice so commanding that it seemed to mesmerize everyone in the
saloon. I have seldom had occasion to comment upon the incompara-
ble quality of Holmes's voice, which was remarkable not so much for
its timbre—that of a dry baritone—as for its tone. Whether he was
speaking to a friend in an intimate, convivial whisper or addressing a

crowd of the most hardened men, Holmes's voice was an instrument of domination, for it always expressed the full force of his iron will.

After he had secured everyone's attention, Holmes got up from his chair and, talking as calmly as though he were reporting the results of a game of whist, said:

"Mr. Thomas, the bartender, has made an excellent suggestion. It is time for you two gentlemen"—a reference to O'Connor and Rafferty—"to go your separate ways, as I do not think an exchange of gunfire would be a lasting benefit to either of you."

O'Connor, who lay on the floor beneath Rafferty and the table, pushed himself free with an angry grunt and scrambled to his feet. As he did so, I caught sight of a pearl-handled pistol holstered beneath his coat, and for an instant I thought he might try to use it. But the chief was no fool—he knew Thomas was behind him with the shotgun—and he kept his hands in plain view while turning to face Holmes.

"And just who the devil are you?" he asked.

Rafferty, who stood next to Holmes and whose blood obviously was up, tried to say something, but Holmes interrupted him: "I will do the talking here from now on, Mr. Rafferty, and you will do me the great favor of shutting up."

Turning to O'Connor, Holmes said: "I am merely a visitor to your fair city who is trying to keep the peace. But since you are here, Chief, perhaps you could tell me what you were doing at the ice palace on the night Jonathan Upton was murdered."

Mouth agape, O'Connor stared at Holmes, astonished that anyone would dare ask so provocative a question. But the chief now proved that, despite his ire, he had not lost complete control of himself.

"Well, now," he said, "you must be the limey who's been nosing around here of late. I've heard about you. And now that I've seen your ugly English face, I won't forget it."

"You haven't answered my question," said Holmes, ignoring the insult.

"You and your question can both go to hell," O'Connor growled. Then he glanced at Rafferty, smiled in a venomous sort of way, and said: "So I see you've got yourself an English master, Shad. Ain't that sweet."

"Why, you . . . ," Rafferty began, but then—no doubt out of respect for Holmes—he somehow managed to hold his tongue.

O'Connor, meanwhile, had turned his attention back to Holmes: "I think I'll be leaving now, if that's all right with you. But I'll be back, and I'll bring along a few friends. And then you and me, and Mr. Rafferty and his colored boy, we'll all have a nice little talk down at the jail. A nice little talk."

"You will do no such thing," Holmes said curtly.

O'Connor let out a bitter, mocking laugh. "Is that right? Who's going to stop me? You?"

Holmes looked into O'Connor's menacing eyes without flinching and said: "I am exactly the man who will stop you. Understand this, sir. One word from me, and you will be finished in this town. If you think I am bluffing, then go ahead—walk out the door and play your hand. But I guarantee you, it will be the last hand you ever play as chief of detectives in St. Paul."

O'Connor, however, would not back down. "We'll just see who plays the last hand in this town," he said. "We'll just see. But I'll give you and your friend Rafferty some advice. From now on, wherever you are, you'd best watch yourself. St. Paul's full of criminals who prey on men just such as yourselves in the dark of night. So be careful, be very careful."

"Thank you for the kind advice," said Holmes. "Indeed, we have already met one of St. Paul's most notable footpads, a certain Mr. Billy Bouquet. I understand he is a friend of yours. Please give him my regards and tell him how much I look forward to seeing him again."

O'Connor made no reply to this taunt other than to give Holmes one last contemptuous look. The big man then turned around, walked past the tables of still silent men, retrieved his hat, and went out the front door, slamming it behind him.

As if by signal, the entire room instantly exploded into the babble of a hundred rapid and excited voices.

"Well," said Rafferty as John Brown—a bit bruised but otherwise none the worse for wear—came over and nuzzled up against his legs. "I guess we've got a world of trouble now."

In fact, as the next few days would demonstrate, our troubles were just beginning.

9

HE WAS QUITE HEARTBROKEN

S unday is normally accounted a day of rest, but Holmes and I were to enjoy no leisure on the Sabbath which followed our tumultuous encounter with O'Connor. Indeed, the day proved to be so ripe with developments—the last of which left even Holmes in a state of stunned disbelief—that I can recall few others quite like it in my long association with the world's greatest consulting detective.

The day had begun with a telegram from Hill, our absent benefactor, who expressed shock at the news of Jonathan Upton's death and informed us that he would be returning to St. Paul at once to offer personal condolences to the victim's father. Naturally, Hill also wished to know every detail of our investigation.

"Mr. Hill will derive little satisfaction from what we have learned thus far," Holmes remarked as he wrote out a quick reply to the Empire Builder. "We are still mariners in the fog, searching for an elusive shore."

"And yet you noted only yesterday that you were beginning to distinguish the first contours of the case," I reminded Holmes.

"That is true, Watson. But these contours are as yet vague and shadowy, no more than dark wisps of possibility. What I need at the moment are hard facts. And I shall go out and get them, one way or another!"

A servant now appeared and announced a telephone call for Holmes.

"It has to be Rafferty," Holmes said as he left the breakfast room, where we had been talking. "Perhaps Miss Forbes is on the move at last."

Holmes was gone only briefly, but by the time he returned, his features had taken on a solemn cast. "There is no end to this matter!" he said with disgust. "No end! Well, we must go out again, Watson."

"Are we to speak with Miss Forbes?"

"No, we are not, though that was indeed our favorite saloonkeeper on the telephone. It seems he returned to his apartment just moments ago, to find a rather frantic young man waiting for him. The man happens to be Frederick Forbes, Laura's brother. According to Mr. Rafferty, the young man is 'just about scared right out of his britches.' "

"What is he so afraid of?"

"That," said Holmes, "is what I intend to find out. But from what Mr. Rafferty tells me, it appears that young Forbes is quite convinced that he will be the murderer's next target."

We found Frederick Forbes seated at the dining room table in Rafferty's spacious apartment suite at the Ryan Hotel. A fire crackled in a large hearth at one end of the room and cast a flickering glow over Forbes's features. He was thin, melancholy-looking, and yet undeniably handsome, with dark brilliantined hair, a long, angular face, and soft brown eyes of the sort women are said to find "soulful." Judging by the smoothness of his slightly olive-toned complexion, I put his age at about twenty-five. He sat with a pronounced slouch—whether out of indifference or weariness it was hard to tell—and managed only a wan smile when Rafferty, who hovered over him like a mother hen, introduced us rather coyly as "English gentlemen with considerable experience in criminal matters."

"Well, I guess that's all right," replied Forbes, taking a hefty gulp from a glass of brandy, his hand shaking noticeably as he did so. He was dressed foppishly in a long mauve jacket, dark slacks, and a perfectly starched white shirt with gleaming ruby cuff links. His shirt collar and tie had been loosened, however, and he appeared to be sweating profusely, even though the room was hardly overheated. It was also quite obvious that he had been drinking heavily.

Holmes, of course, took in all these details at a glance as we seated ourselves across the table from Forbes. Without any further introduction, Holmes then inquired—much to the young man's astonishment—whether he had been "in a hurry" when he left his "lady friend" to visit Rafferty's apartment.

"How in heaven . . . ," began Forbes, but before he could continue—or, for that matter, before Holmes could provide one of his beloved demonstrations of deductive legerdemain—Rafferty spoke up:

"Ah, Freddie, me boy, did I not tell you that Mr. Baker here is a most ingenious man. A regular Sherlock Holmes, he is, and that's a fact! Mr. Baker no doubt noticed the long strand of red hair clinging to your shirt, and, of course, he could not fail to spot the smudge of lipstick—'tis a lovely cinnamon red, by the way—on your collar. And since the top of your shirt is unbuttoned, well, Mr. Baker probably surmised that you had come here in something of a hurry."

Holmes was impressed. "Very nicely done, Mr. Rafferty," he said with a slight bow, "though you might also have mentioned the aroma of perfume—a Parisian scent, if I am not mistaken—which can be detected on Mr. Forbes's person. A gift for the lady, no doubt."

Looking at Rafferty and Holmes as though he had just stumbled into a nest of madmen, Forbes said: "Well, I don't see how any of this is your d--ned business."

"It seems as though everyone today is telling me to mind my own business," Holmes remarked, staring at Forbes, "and the more they do so, the more interested in *their* business I become. So let us therefore discuss your business, sir. You have come here, I am told, because you fear for your life. I should like to know why."

Forbes removed a silk handkerchief from his coat pocket and slowly daubed perspiration from his forehead. "Very well, show him," he finally said, looking up at Rafferty. "I guess it doesn't matter."

Rafferty nodded, went to a small table near the fireplace, and took from its drawer a single sheet of paper, which he unfolded and handed to Holmes. " 'Tis this which has the young man so upset," he said.

The sheet was blank save for a brief but chilling message: BE WARNED MY VENGEANCE IS NOT COMPLETE. The words themselves consisted of letters which had been cut out from a publication of some kind and then pasted onto the paper. This peculiar and laborious means of construction somehow added to the sinister quality of the communication.

"It is a rather vague message," remarked Holmes, inspecting the document carefully with his magnifying glass. "And yet it seems to have inspired within you, Mr. Forbes, a quite marked degree of fear. Tell me, sir, why is that?"

Forbes took another drink of brandy, and there was something like terror in his eyes when he told Holmes: "I have good reason to be fearful, for Johnny Upton received a similar message the day before he disappeared!"

Holmes showed no immediate reaction to these words, though I could tell by a slight quivering of his nostrils that he was surpassingly interested in Forbes's revelation.

"You say it was similar. What were the message's exact words?" he asked.

"I know them by heart," replied Forbes grimly. "It said: 'You will be punished for your sins.' "

"And were the letters pasted onto the paper in the same way?"

"Yes, of course," came the reply, with a touch of irritation. "I saw it with my own eyes. Johnny showed it to me the night he got it."

"And that would have been . . . ?"

"Last Saturday night. Johnny had found it under his door at the Costanza that afternoon. But he was not at all concerned about it. He told me it must be the work of some prankster, and even said he had a 'good idea' as to who might have sent it. I remember he said, 'I shall have to look up the fellow and make his life difficult,' or words to that effect. It was all a joke to him, you see."

"And did you also take the message as a joke?"

Forbes shrugged. "Why not? If Johnny thought it perfectly harmless, then there was no reason for me to worry about it."

Rafferty now posed an intriguing question. "There's one thing that puzzles me here, Freddie, if you don't mind my askin'. I get the impression that you never mentioned this threatenin' note to the police when they came inquirin' as to young Upton's whereabouts. Am I right?"

Forbes nodded and then hung his head, as though feeling the

weight of his own guilt. "You are right, Shad. I didn't mention it to the police at first. But don't you see, I had no reason to believe the message was important, especially since Johnny made such light of it. I can see now that I was wrong. Good God, Johnny might still be alive if I hadn't been so stupid!"

These last words were delivered with desperate intensity, and I was beginning to fear that Forbes might be on the verge of a breakdown.

Holmes, however, wasted no time on sympathy.

"What is done is done," he said matter-of-factly, "and there is no point dwelling on it. At the moment, we must concentrate on the situation at hand, beginning with this latest message."

Placing the paper on the table, Holmes carefully flattened its edges and went over it again with his magnifying glass. He then held it up to the light before returning it to Rafferty.

"The paper itself is quite ordinary and no doubt comes from one of the local five-and-ten-cent stores," Holmes said rapidly, as though dictating to some invisible amanuensis. "As for the type which forms the message, it is a variety of Roman, and almost certainly from a newspaper or other periodical."

"You are right about that, Mr. Baker," said Rafferty. "In fact, unless I'm mistaken, the typeface is Garamond, which is the same kind used by Mr. Pyle's *Globe*."

"Mr. Rafferty, you are a veritable font of information, if you will pardon the play on words," said Holmes. "Unfortunately, the typeface does not tell us anything of value, since anyone could have cut the letters out of the newspaper. Tell me, Mr. Forbes, how was this singular document delivered to you?"

"Found it under the door of my apartment early this morning, just the same way Johnny got his message," Forbes replied in a shaky voice. The glass of brandy in front of him had now been emptied, and Forbes drummed his fingers nervously on the table. "I could use another drink," he announced.

"Ah, Freddie, I think you'd best wait a bit for that," Rafferty said kindly. "You need to keep you head about you at the moment."

Rafferty realized at once that his choice of words had been less than apt. "What I mean, Freddie—"

"I know d--ned well what you mean," Forbes said. "And you're godd--ned right I'd like to keep my head. Now get me that drink."

"I think not," said Holmes. "What Mr. Rafferty was trying to tell you in his rather inelegant way is that you must try to remain calm. Only then can we—"

But Forbes, whose rising sense of panic was almost palpable, could no longer contain himself. His eyes darted wildly about the room, as though looking to the walls for consolation, and I could see tears welling in his eyes. "For God's sake, can't anybody tell me what's going on?" he burst out. "Who has killed Johnny, and why does he want to kill me? I have done nothing to injure any man."

Holmes fixed his sternest gaze on Forbes and said in a commanding tone: "You sir, will settle down and conduct yourself like a man. We cannot help you if you go to pieces. Now, can you be more specific as to when the message was placed under your door?"

Rafferty, returning Holmes's stern look with one of his own, sat down beside Forbes and put an arm over his shoulder. "There, there, Freddie, just take a minute to gather yourself. I know what you're feelin', because I've felt it many a time myself. Fear's a terrible thing, me boy. 'Tis like a wild horse stompin' through your head. But there's only one thing you can do, and that's to master it. Now take a deep breath and answer Mr. Baker's question, for he means well."

"My apologies," Forbes said, beginning to compose himself. "It has been a trying day, as you must imagine. Very well, I will answer your questions as best I can. As to when the message arrived, I can only say that it must have been between midnight and eight o'clock this morning."

"And how do you know that?" Holmes asked.

"Because when I returned to my apartment at the Hotel Barteau at midnight with, as you have suggested, a friend, the message most certainly had not been delivered. It was only at eight o'clock, when I left to escort my friend home, that I found it on the floor."[1]

"Is it possible anyone might have seen the person who delivered the message?"

Forbes thought for a moment. "It is possible. But the Barteau is a large building. People come and go at all hours, and no one pays much notice."

The next question came from Rafferty, who had gotten up from the table and begun to wander aimlessly around the room like a big, curious cat. "Tell me, Freddie, why do you suppose someone would send threatenin' messages to you and young Upton? 'Twas no joke, that is now all too certain. 'Tis obvious the author of these little missives has a grudge, and a murderous one at that. Were you boys shaggin' another man's wife or some such thing?"

Forbes's cheeks instantly flushed. "Absolutely not," he said with all the firmness he could muster. "I do not claim to have led a blameless life, Shad, but I know of nothing I have done that would make anyone wish to harm me."

"And yet," observed Holmes, lighting a cigarette and watching the smoke curl up toward the room's ornate ceiling, "you have noted that Mr. Upton appeared to have at least some idea as to who might have sent the message to him. I find it very curious that you, by contrast, are completely in the dark upon this subject."

Forbes bowed his head and took a deep breath before looking up at Holmes. "All right, I will be completely honest with you. I do have an idea about who might have sent the message. But you must realize that I have no proof whatsoever, and I do not wish to accuse any man of wrongdoing without solid evidence."

"Finding evidence is my job," said Holmes impatiently, "and you need have no concerns that I shall persecute the innocent. Now, sir, whom do you suspect?"

"Well," Forbes said with a sigh, "it is no secret that Michael Riley, who is the construction superintendent of the ice palace, had a terrible crush on my sister, Laura. He was quite heartbroken when she decided to marry Johnny."

Holmes considered this intriguing piece of information for a moment, then said: "And you think this Riley might have sought revenge against the man who stole the girl of his dreams?"

"The thought has occurred to me, I must admit."

"But why should he also seek vengeance against you?"

Forbes paused, and a hint of fear came back into his eyes when he told Holmes: "Well, if you must know, it was I who persuaded Laura that Riley was not the right man for her. And I don't think he will ever forgive me for it!"

Over the next half hour, Holmes interrogated Forbes at great length about Riley and his relationship with Laura Forbes. We learned that Riley had come to St. Paul in the 1880s from New England, working initially as a laborer but soon rising by dint of his resourcefulness and intelligence to ever more responsible positions in the local construction industry. He was especially well known as a builder in ice, a skill he had mastered while working on one of the early Montreal ice palaces. In St. Paul, he had helped build the ice palaces of 1886, 1887, and 1888, and his expertise was such that there had been no doubt he would be hired to superintend the huge palace now standing in frozen solitude in Central Park. Planning for the palace had begun the previous summer, and it was then — when Riley had come to the Forbes residence to discuss preliminary drawings—that he met Laura Forbes.

"If you believe in love at first sight," said Forbes, who obviously did not, "then I guess that is what it was. I was there with Father, and we both remarked afterward how Mr. Riley had gazed at Laura like a moonstruck puppy. It was almost comic, I must say."

"And what was your sister's reaction to Mr. Riley's attentions?" Holmes asked.

Forbes allowed himself a small chuckle. "Let me put it this way to you, sir: Laura adores being adored, so I am sure she was flattered by the attention. But what she could see in that brawling sort of Irishman is quite beyond me," Forbes added disdainfully.

Rafferty took exception to this remark. "Nothin' wrong with a good brawl," he observed.

"As you have most recently demonstrated to us," said Holmes. "But let us return to the subject at hand. I take it, Mr. Forbes, that your sister was not yet engaged at this time to Jonathan Upton?"

"No. She was still toying with Johnny, and I think she liked the idea of having two suitors," Forbes said, before adding with a shrug: "But who can fathom the ways of women?"

"Who indeed?" echoed Holmes, who was himself prone to bafflement when confronted with the wiles of the fair sex. "Now, you said, Mr. Forbes, that you convinced your sister to end any relationship with Riley. How did you do so?"

"I simply took her aside one day and informed her that she must do the proper thing and become engaged to Johnny. I told her that Riley was a good enough fellow but that he would hardly be an appropriate match for someone of her social standing. She agreed and shortly thereafter became engaged to Johnny."

Rafferty now broke in: "And that was all it took, was it, Freddie? Just a word from you, and the lady saw the error of her ways. You'll pardon me for sayin' so, but in my experience, affairs of the heart do not generally settle themselves in such a tidy fashion. Tell me, do you think your sister loved Riley as he apparently loved her? He is, after all, a rather bold and handsome fellow, even if he is a brawler."

"Oh, she may have been infatuated, I suppose," Forbes replied, as though the question were hardly important, "but I'm sure it was nothing more than that."

"And what of Johnny Upton?" Rafferty asked. "Did she love him?"

Forbes's answer was quite revealing. "I am sure she would have learned to love him," he said.

"In my experience, lovin' is a hard thing to learn if it don't come naturally, especially for a woman," Rafferty observed.

"Let us return to Mr. Riley, if you don't mind," said Holmes. "How did he take the news that Jonathan Upton had won your sister's hand?"

"He was furious, at Johnny—whom he never liked, or so I have been told—and at me. We had a big row down at the Muskrat Club, and when it was all over, he stomped out, saying he was through with us and the club forever. Later that night, he came to my apartment— he also lives at the Barteau—and berated me for so long that I finally had to shut the door on him. And, of course, we nearly came to blows in Shad's saloon just a couple of weeks ago. Do you remember, Shad?"

" 'Tis true," Rafferty said, turning to Holmes. "But the both of them were drunk as skunks, so I would not make too much of their little disagreement."

"And just what prompted this 'disagreement'?" Holmes asked Forbes.

"I will be honest with you, sir. I do not precisely recall, for I admit that I had overindulged. But I know the subject of Laura came up and that before long Riley and I were shouting at each other. As I told you, he was a very bitter man, especially as the wedding drew near. I suppose the fact that he was building the very structure in which Laura would be married to another man made the situation especially painful for him."

"I see. Now, is there any other occasion you can recall on which Mr. Riley overtly threatened you or Jonathan Upton?"

Forbes rubbed his forehead and said: "I seem to recall once he said something about 'getting even,' or words to that effect, but I am afraid I don't recall the exact circumstances. Johnny had a couple of run-ins with him too. But Johnny never told me much. I think he just felt bad about the whole situation."

Holmes nodded, stood up, and walked across the room, where—his back turned to Forbes—he appeared to become absorbed in studying the intricate Lincrusta pattern which covered the walls. Then he spun around and asked a question which caught all of us by surprise:

"What can you tell us about the Muskrat Club, Mr. Forbes?"

The young man blinked and stared dumbly at Holmes, as though he had just been asked to solve a quadratic equation.

"Come now, Mr. Forbes," said Holmes impatiently. "The question cannot be that difficult. You moved in the same social circles as Jonathan Upton. You must be familiar with the club."

"Well, yes, I know about it. I was a member for a while but quit, let's see, a couple of months ago. I found myself too busy to make use of its facilities. What has all of this got to do with anything?"

"Do me a favor, Freddie, and humor the man," said Rafferty. "He has his reasons for askin'."

"Thank you, Mr. Rafferty," said Holmes. "Now, Mr. Forbes"— Holmes had approached the table and bent down so that he could look directly into the young man's frightened eyes—"I shall ask you once again: What can you tell me about the Muskrat Club?"

Forbes paused to wipe more perspiration from his brow and finally said: "It is just a club for young men to get together and have a good time. There is a small bar, which has been known to serve drinks on Sunday when all the taverns are closed, so I guess that makes it a popular place for some of the fellows about town. There is also a card room, where, I will admit to you, gambling sometimes takes place. But the same could be said of almost every men's club in St. Paul. The club also sponsors a uniformed marching group for the Winter Carnival parade. That is about all I can tell you. It is a very ordinary sort of club."

"And how many members does it have?"

"I suppose there might be fifty or so, most of whom come from the better families of the city."

Holmes, whose eyes had been riveted on Forbes, now backed away from the table and let his gaze wander toward the ceiling. When he at last spoke, his voice had dropped almost to a whisper. "In other words, what you are telling me, sir, is that the Muskrat Club is, in so far as you know, a perfectly innocent and legitimate organization. Is that right?"

"Yes. But I do not see—"

"You do not see why I am bothering you with such an insignificant question," said Holmes, his voice suddenly much louder. "Very well, then, Mr. Forbes, perhaps you will be interested to know that one of the club's rather distinctive pins turned up next to Mr. Upton's severed head. Presumably, it was placed there by the murderer. Does my question seem more significant now?"

"I . . . I did not know this," said Forbes, sounding thoroughly flustered. "I cannot imagine why anyone, that is, why the murderer would have done such a thing, unless he . . ."

"Unless he had a grudge of some kind?" prompted Holmes.

"Well, yes, that does seem possible, doesn't it. Mr. Riley had been a member of the club for several years, but after the business with Laura, as I said, he quit in a huff."

"And did he turn in his pin when he left?"

"I . . . I'm not sure," Forbes admitted. "But I don't think so. Members buy the pins with their own money, so there is no requirement to turn them in."

"How interesting," said Holmes. "Now tell me this: In your experience, did Jonathan Upton often wear his club pin?"

Forbes furrowed his brow in thought. Then he said: "Yes, I believe he did like to wear it. But I cannot say whether he had it on all the time."

"I see. And now I have but one more simple question: Where were you, Mr. Forbes, on the night Jonathan Upton disappeared?"

Startled by this sally from an unexpected direction, Forbes looked over at Rafferty, as though uncertain of what to do next. Rafferty's only response was a shrug.

"Well?" said Holmes. "Where were you?"

"Why, I was . . . I was in Minneapolis with friends," Forbes finally stammered. "There are dozens of witnesses, if you must know. But surely you don't suspect that I had anything to do with Johnny's death? He was my dearest friend."

"I did not say I suspected you of anything," Holmes replied evenly. "I merely asked where you were at a certain time. And now you have told me. Therefore, I have no more questions for you, Mr. Forbes. I suggest you go home and get some rest."

"But what about that threatening message?" Forbes asked, panic now edging back into his voice. "How do I know I won't be murdered just like Johnny was?"

Rafferty said to Holmes: "The young man has a good point. His life may well be in jeopardy."

"You are right," said Holmes, who then told Forbes: "Take a room here in the Ryan tonight. To be doubly safe, I suggest you occupy a room other than the one you have been assigned. I am sure Mr. Rafferty, with all of his influence at this hotel, can make such an arrangement."

"That I can," Rafferty vowed, helping Forbes up from his seat. "All right, come along, lad. I'll get you checked in. Don't worry, you're in good hands now."

"Well," I said after Rafferty and his charge had gone out the door, "it would appear that we now have at least one prime suspect in this matter."

"So it would seem," agreed Holmes. "I think the time has come to have a long talk with Mr. Michael Riley."

As it turned out, however, we were not able to talk with Riley that day, for the simple reason that we could not find him. No one answered the door at his apartment, where we went after leaving Rafferty. Nor, we discovered, had Riley been seen at the ice palace grounds. By early afternoon, upon our return to the Hill mansion, Holmes had enlisted Pyle's aid in the search. But even our enterprising newspaper friend, with the numerous resources at his command, could not locate Riley. Laura Forbes also remained beyond our reach, for the man sent by Rafferty to watch the Forbes residence had nothing to report all day. The lady, it seemed, was staying home.

Then, just after dark, Pyle came bursting into the library, nearly breathless with excitement.

"I have just gotten word," he said. "They have found him, down by the Upper Levee."[2]

Holmes, who had been reading the Sunday newspapers, jumped to his feet. "Good work! Let us go talk to the elusive Mr. Riley at once."

A look of vast confusion rolled across Pyle's features like a passing cloud. "Riley? Oh no, Mr. Holmes, it is not Riley I mean. It is Jonathan Upton. They have found his body at the city dump. There is something else you should know. Michael Riley is not the only missing person in St. Paul. It seems Laura Forbes and George Upton have also vanished."

10

I INTEND, *SIR*, TO COMMIT A CRIME

With a look of profound disgust, James J. Hill tossed aside the latest edition of the *Globe* and turned his good eye, which could bear down on a man like the barrel of a rifle, toward the slender figure of Sherlock Holmes.

"Well, Mr. Holmes," said our patron, "I trust you can tell me what the devil is going on here!"

Hill, freshly arrived from New York City and impatient for answers, spoke these words at nine o'clock on Monday morning in the library of his mansion, where he and three others—Rafferty, Pyle, and myself—had gathered to hear Holmes's thoughts about the case. Outside, snow had begun to fall, swirling down like hard white dust amid the stately mansions of Summit Avenue. Gazing out at this frigid scene, I felt a growing sense of desolation. Even the remote, parched pineries to which Holmes and I had ventured in the summer of 1894 seemed to me less forbidding than this city gripped so cruelly by the unrelenting hand of winter. I found myself wishing— not for the first time since our arrival in St. Paul—that Holmes and I could flee home to damp, green England and be done with this arctic madness.

Yet I knew all too well that Holmes would not leave now. His blood was up — he had taken George Upton's unexpected disappearance as a personal offense, an insult, as it were, to his genius — and he would not rest until he had seen the case to its conclusion. The harsh reality, however, was that the events of the previous evening had taken Holmes by complete surprise. Indeed, he had speculated only hours before the discovery of Jonathan Upton's headless corpse that the body was "probably dragging along the bottom of the Mississippi and already halfway to New Orleans." The news of George Upton's disappearance had come as an even greater shock to Holmes. "It was," he admitted to me, "a possibility which never entered into any of my calculations."

Curiously, the news that Laura Forbes had also been reported missing seemed not to concern Holmes in the least. "Do not fear for her," he had remarked upon receiving word of the lady's disappearance. "I cannot tell you where Miss Forbes is, but I am certain she will turn up soon enough, as will Mr. Riley."

Now, however, with Hill demanding answers, Holmes could not afford to be so cavalier. Sitting glumly in a large armchair, one hand resting on his chin in the pose of Rodin's *Thinker*, he told Hill: "What is going on, sir, is indeed devil's work, but I cannot tell you who this particular devil might be or what additional mischief he may have in mind. Nor do I have any good ideas as to the whereabouts of your friend George Upton. As for Miss Forbes . . . well, her situation, I believe, will become clear in due time. Unfortunately, the industrious journals of this city, including your own *Globe*, appear to know more at the moment than I do!"

Holmes was not exaggerating in this regard, since all of our efforts to learn more about the peculiar events of the previous night had been thwarted. After Pyle's startling announcement, we had rushed down to the garbage dump — a loathsome, stinking hole surrounded by St. Paul's most fetid slum. The headless corpse, lodged in a large pile of garbage, had been found by a young Bohemian girl searching for food amid the mass of corruption. She immediately informed the police, who by the time Holmes and I arrived had already removed the corpse. They had also disturbed the site to such an extent that there could be no hope of finding any clues.

We had then gone to George Upton's mansion to investigate the circumstances of his disappearance. Here again, the supposed forces of law and order stood in our way, for we were not allowed inside the house, much to Holmes's displeasure. So angered was Holmes by this police barricade that at one point he threatened to thrash a beefy police sergeant guarding the front door. The sergeant in turn suggested that my friend might benefit greatly from a dunking in the frozen Mississippi. But imprecations, pleas, and even attempts at bribery all proved useless, and so we had gone back to Hill's house, with Holmes in as foul a mood as I had ever seen him. By this time, Rafferty had also made an appearance, reporting similar difficulties with the police. "The coppers are bein' a pain in the rear," he informed us, "and you can bet 'tis all the Bull's dirty work."

Holmes's state of mind did not improve when he read the morning newspapers, which seemed to have had no trouble acquiring information from the police and other sources. The *Globe*'s long article ran beneath a screaming banner headline — THE DEAD AND THE MISSING — of the size normally reserved for the outbreak of war. Despite wide yellow streaks of sensationalism, the story contained many "intriguing and useful details," as Holmes put it.

The salient facts regarding George Upton's disappearance were these: At about ten o'clock on Saturday night, he had gone downtown in his sleigh to the Minnesota Club, of which he was a prominent member.[1] Upton's driver told the police that his employer seemed to be in "an anxious frame of mind" and carried a small briefcase, as though intending to conduct some business. Upton informed the driver that he would sleep over at the club, where he maintained an apartment. However, by five o'clock the next afternoon he had not returned home. One of his servants then telephoned the club, only to receive the "shocking news" that Upton had not been seen at the club either Saturday night or Sunday.

At this point, the police were notified. Fearing Upton might have suffered an accident of some kind in the extreme cold, the authorities made a thorough search of the commercial district and checked with the local hospitals, but found no trace of him. Business associates and friends were also interviewed, to no avail. No one, it appeared, had seen George Upton since the time his driver had let him off by the club.

The circumstances regarding Laura Forbes's disappearance were equally mysterious, or so it seemed to me, although Holmes clearly did not share my belief. The *Globe* reported that she had last been seen "retiring to her room" in her father's house at about nine o'clock Saturday night. As she was often a late sleeper, her household did not think it unusual when she failed to appear for breakfast or lunch the following day. It was not until three o'clock Sunday afternoon that her father finally entered her room, where he was "shocked to find absolutely no trace of his beloved daughter." The *Globe*'s story went on to say that "a valise and several items of apparel were missing from the room, leading the police to speculate that Miss Forbes may have left of her own accord. However, Mr. Forbes firmly believes otherwise and is said to be 'most fearful' that his daughter has been abducted."

The only other portion of the long story which drew Holmes's attention was a comment attributed to Chief of Detectives O'Connor. The chief, it was said, "hinted strongly that he has a suspect in Jonathan Upton's murder, though the name of that person cannot now be made public. However, the suspect in question is well known in St. Paul, and his arrest, should it come, would undoubtedly create a sensation."

Our gathering in the library had begun on an amicable note — coffee and rolls were served while Holmes regaled Hill with tales of our adventures in Chicago. But it was not long before the Empire Builder had discarded his morning newspaper and gotten in his usual forthright way to the matter at hand. Hill clearly expected the usual series of dazzling deductions from Holmes, and so he reacted with disbelief to my friend's admission that he had gleaned most of what he knew about George Upton's disappearance from the newspapers.

"Is that really all you can tell me, Mr. Holmes?" Hill asked in an almost plaintive voice. "Surely you must have some theories about what has happened to Mr. Upton."

"I wish that were so, Mr. Hill, but at present I have only vague and half-formed notions which hardly qualify as theories."

"I see," said Hill in a tone of voice which suggested that he in fact did not. "Perhaps you are not aware of it, Mr. Holmes, but George Upton is one of my oldest and dearest friends. We worked on the levee together as young men, served with the same volunteer firefighting company, spent Christmas holidays together with our families, and have been neighbors either here or in Lowertown for almost thirty years. His disappearance is not a matter which I take lightly."

"I understand," said Holmes, who sat still as a sculpture in his armchair, a cigarette dangling from one hand, "and if he is to be found, I shall find him, in one way or another. Now, since you know Mr. Upton so well, I should like to ask you a few questions about the gentleman."

Hill, who had begun puffing at a long cigar, gave a quick nod of assent. But I doubt he was ready for the first question Holmes put to him: "Was Mr. Upton in any financial trouble?"

The query earned Holmes a cold, puzzled stare from the Empire Builder, who nonetheless promptly answered: "Not that I know of. Why do you ask?"

"I am merely curious about that sum of ten thousand dollars which was mentioned during the argument in the ice palace. Perhaps it was a debt owed to or by someone. Would it be a significant sum to a man of Mr. Upton's means?"

"Ten thousand dollars, whether it is a debt owed or awaiting collection, ought to be of importance to any man, regardless of his means," said Hill. "But knowing Mr. Upton as I do, I am inclined to doubt that the sum would be an overdue debt, for he has always been most prompt in meeting his obligations."

"Very well, then, let me ask you this, sir: Was Mr. Upton subject to fits of despondency or other mental disturbances?"

"Never," said Hill firmly.

Rafferty, whom Hill appeared to hold in high regard, now joined the conversation for the first time. "Yet is it not possible that the death of his son unhinged the poor man? To have a child murdered, especially in so terrible a way, would test the well-being of any man, no matter how strong his character."

"I suppose it is possible," Hill acknowledged, "but you should know that Mr. Upton has seen terrible tragedies in his life before. His two elder sons both died of diphtheria as small children, and he lost his wife to influenza some years later. Though he may not look it, he is not a man to give in to anything."

"I agree with you," said Holmes quickly. "I am not inclined to think that your friend wandered off aimlessly into the night after losing his mind to grief. The reason for his disappearance, I fear, lies elsewhere. Now, if you please, Mr. Hill, tell me this: Were Mr. Upton and Mr. Cadwallader Forbes on good terms?"

Another look of mystification spread across Hill's features, but again he made an immediate reply. "I do not believe they were close friends, Mr. Holmes, but neither do I have any knowledge that they were enemies."

"And in so far as you know, the two of them worked well together on the committee which planned and financed the ice palace?"

"Yes, though I have paid little attention to the palace this year. It is a frivolity which, in my opinion, the people of St. Paul can ill afford."

I could see that Hill was growing irritated at Holmes's seemingly tangential questions, and I wondered whether we might soon witness one of those volcanic displays of temper for which the Empire Builder was legendary. As though reading my mind, Holmes next posed a question so odd and far afield that it seemed certain to detonate just such an explosion in Hill.

"I have recently come into possession of a membership list of the Muskrat Club," he said to Hill, "and I note that neither of your older sons, both of whom must be accounted as among the most prominent young men of St. Paul, are members of this organization. Can you tell me why?"

"What in God's name—" Hill began, and the room would certainly have shaken with his thunderous wrath had not Rafferty deftly come forward to rescue the day. Cutting off Hill before he could work himself up to a state of fulmination, Rafferty said: "I assume you've posed this most peculiar question, Mr. Holmes, because you are curious as to the club's reputation. The fact that its membership does not include the two most distinguished young gentlemen of the city naturally suggests that the club may have an unpleasant odor to it. After all, if the Muskrat Club were completely on the up-and-up, there's no doubt Jim Hill's boys would be its preeminent members. 'Tis a very clever question, sir, as I'm sure Mr. Hill appreciates."

Hill was more than intelligent enough to know when he had been outflanked, and he could only shake his head in amazement at Rafferty's impromptu exercise in diplomacy. In any event, Rafferty's soothing words had their desired effect, for Hill—his anger subsiding—finally agreed to answer Holmes's rather impertinent question. "I do not like dragging my family anywhere near this tawdry affair," he told Holmes, "but I will tell you that, yes, I have heard unsavory stories about the Muskrat Club. And that is indeed why James and Louis are not members, though they both wished to join."

"Could you be more specific about these stories, which—"

"No," Hill said, in a manner which left no room for appeal on Holmes's part. "But I will be specific about this, Mr. Holmes: I am a man used to getting things done, quickly and correctly, and I expect the Upton case to be resolved in just such a manner. I am well aware that the murder of Jonathan Upton must now be the chief concern of the police. However, the fact remains that the young man is dead and there is nothing to be done for him now. But it may yet be possible to save George Upton from whatever fate has befallen him. That is why I expect you to use every means at your disposal to locate my friend. It must be your priority. Whatever you need—money, men, materials—it is yours for the asking."

Holmes was quiet for a moment and then replied: "I will, of course, do everything possible to locate your friend, Mr. Hill. But the circumstances of his disappearance are most ominous. There are peculiar features to this case which make it as difficult as any I have ever encountered."

"Please, explain yourself," said Hill, who obviously did not wish to hear of any difficulties.

Holmes bestirred himself from his chair and went to the library table, where a huge jigsaw puzzle—a favorite pastime of the Hill family, Pyle had informed me—lay partly completed. Scanning the puzzle, which depicted a French pastoral scene, Holmes quickly picked up one of the scattered pieces and inserted it in its proper place. He then looked over at Hill and said:

"It is commonplace, Mr. Hill, to use a puzzle such as this to describe a criminal investigation. The detective gathers the pieces of evidence, organizes them according to various criteria, and finally assembles them into the finished picture. It is all supposed to be very neat and straightforward. But this case is unique, Mr. Hill, because I do not yet know even the dimensions of the puzzle. Its boundaries elude me. I do not know when or how it really began, nor do I yet see where it will end. And until I locate these edges of time and circumstance, I cannot fill in the middle pieces. Unfortunately, Mr. Upton's disappearance is almost certainly just such a piece."

This short speech provided, I thought, a most remarkable insight into Holmes's way of thinking. Hill, however, was not impressed.

"I do not propose to talk of puzzles, Mr. Holmes," he said, a hardness to his voice. "I propose to find George Upton, a man for whom I have the deepest affection and respect. Therefore, I would like to know what you intend to do next."

We all waited to see how Holmes would respond to this challenge. He said nothing at first, preferring to fiddle with his cigarette case, opening and shutting it repeatedly as though fascinated by its simple mechanism. But when Holmes finally looked up, I saw in his eyes something I had not seen in the last two days—that bright sparkle of hope which is always a detective's most valuable ally.

Turning to Hill, Holmes replied with a smile: "I intend, sir, to commit a crime."

My friend's declaration came as no surprise to me (Hill, on the other hand, was quite appalled), since Holmes had long been accustomed to operating on the margins of legality. Indeed, he had on more than one occasion crossed so far beyond the divide—as in the strange affair of Lady Carrington's codicil,[2] where his talents as a master forger came to light—that I could not help but think that his natural genius lay in criminal enterprise. Holmes invariably justified his illicit excursions on the grounds of necessity, once remarking to me that "if the means do not justify the end, then I am inclined to think that nothing does." Yet there can be no doubt that he also loved the sheer audacity of breaking the law. Holmes himself often remarked upon what an excellent criminal he would have made, and society may account it a good fortune that he only rarely acted upon his felonious instincts.

Be that as it may, I had always tried to discourage Holmes from violating the law, believing that he had become entirely too casual about it. But I had no opportunity in this instance to dissuade Holmes from his criminal intentions, for the simple reason that he refused to discuss them in advance. In keeping with his love of mystification, Holmes would reveal nothing of his plans to me or anyone else during our meeting with Hill, although the railroad titan pressed him for details.

"I cannot be specific," he told Hill. "Suffice it to say that under these circumstances, 'ignorance is bliss,' for the less you know of my intentions, the more protection you will have should anything go wrong."

Only Rafferty, a mischievous twinkle in his eyes, appeared to have some idea as to Holmes's intentions. "Your friend will do well in his criminal enterprise," Rafferty said to me as he put on his coat before venturing out into the snowstorm. "He has the mind for mayhem, and the nerve. But I must tell you, Dr. Watson, that your Mr. Holmes is about the most exhaustin' fellow I've ever met."

"What do you mean?"

"Oh, don't get me wrong," Rafferty said, noting my look of concern. "I like Mr. Holmes just fine. The problem is that all of that thinkin' of his gives me a headache. 'Tis like tryin' to keep up with a runner who never gets winded."

"You seem to be holding your own in the race, Mr. Rafferty," I observed.

"Thank you kindly. For a fat man, I guess I run well enough. Still, we'll just see how I do now that the situation is beginnin' to get hot. Well, good day to you, Doctor, and Godspeed."

"And to you as well," I said as Rafferty went out the door.

Holmes by this time had already retired to his room "to make preparations," as he told me. These proved to be quite befuddling. He began by spending more than an hour on the telephone. Next, he sent one of Hill's servants to the county courthouse on an undisclosed mission. Then came a brief meeting with Frederick Forbes (who had spent an uneventful night at the Ryan under Rafferty's watchful eye). Finally, at about three o'clock in the afternoon, Holmes ordered a sleigh and went for what he described as "a little jaunt." When he returned three hours later, he announced that his preparations were complete.

"Now we must simply wait for the appointed hour," he said.

"And when will that be?"

"Eleven o'clock," Holmes said. "In the meantime, Watson, I suggest you get some rest. We could be in for a very long night."

"Wake up, Watson! It is nearly time to go," said Sherlock Holmes, shaking me out of a most curious dream, in which I found myself staring through a crystalline sheet of ice at a dim figure floating in a pool of green, cloudy water. "Make sure to dress warmly."

"Where are we going?" I asked as I reluctantly rolled out of my comfortable bed and consulted my watch. It was a quarter to eleven.

"For a walk. I should like to make a visit to Mr. George Upton's house," replied Holmes, who had taken a seat by the dresser in my bedroom. "Now be quick about it, and make sure to bring your revolver."

As I got into my clothes, I puzzled over the purpose of our impending visit to the Upton mansion and could come to only one conclusion. "I take it you expect to find Mr. Upton there," I said.

"No, Watson, but I do expect to find something that will tell us where he may be and who murdered his son."

"But how — ?"

"Did I reach this conclusion?" Holmes asked, anticipating my question. "Very well, Watson, since it appears you will require some time to make yourself presentable, I will tell you. All of my deductions in this instance are drawn from Mr. Upton's behavior over the past week. Consider: When his son vanishes, Mr. Upton initially acts as the understandably worried parent. He first notifies the police. Then, apparently unsatisfied with their efforts, he hires Mr. Rafferty to make further investigations. Unfortunately, his son's head is discovered a few days later in the ice palace. It is a terrible shock, of course, and the old man goes into mourning. But on the very next day, his behavior changes radically. First, he calls off Rafferty and the police. Then he tells us in a stone-cold voice that he intends to find on his own the 'traitors' who murdered his son. Now, what are we to make of Mr. Upton's sudden transformation?"

"That he had found something out?" I ventured. "Something that he didn't know before?"

"Watson, you are growing more insightful by the day," said Holmes with a broad smile. "You are exactly right. Sometime between our discovery of his son's severed head and our interview with him the next day, Mr. Upton learned something so extraordinary, and perhaps so damning, that it caused him to take matters into his own hands. Ah, but what, exactly, did he find out? I asked myself that question but could arrive at no immediate answer. So I considered another question: How and where might Mr. Upton have made his crucial discovery? I spent much of yesterday pondering possible answers. But it was not until early this morning, before our meeting with Mr. Hill, that I had—if I may say so—an inspiration, and so I placed a telephone call to Mr. Thomas Greene."

"I'm afraid you have lost me," I confessed as I pulled on my heaviest wool sweater. "Who is Mr. Greene?"

"Mr. Greene, my dear Watson, is the proprietor of the Costanza Apartments, where Jonathan Upton lived."

I now remembered seeing Greene's name in an early newspaper story. But I still failed to see why Holmes had called him.

"I telephoned Mr. Greene for one very simple reason, Watson. I wanted to know whether George Upton had visited his son's apartment on Friday or Saturday. Mr. Greene readily confirmed my suspicion that this had indeed been the case. At about noon on Saturday, George Upton came to the Costanza, asked for and received the key to his son's apartment, and spent more than two hours inside. He may have gone simply to collect some of his son's belongings, or he may actually have been looking for clues. In either case, he must have found something quite revealing."

"But hadn't the police already searched the apartment?"

"Certainly. But I suspect their search was perfunctory, since they had no real idea of what to look for. Mr. Upton, on the other hand, knew. Moreover, there can be no doubt that he found something, since he left with a bag full of items, according to Mr. Greene."

I began to see the picture. "And you believe, Holmes, that whatever evidence Mr. Upton found, he took home with him."

"Yes. Naturally, there is no way of knowing for certain that the evidence remains in his house. But Mr. Upton is not a rash man— one does not make a fortune by failing to exercise foresight—and that is why I believe it to be very likely that he put the evidence in a safe place, where I intend to find it."

"So it is to be another burglary," I said, thinking back to our recent act of breaking and entering at Caulfield Gardens.[3] "I must tell you that I do not like the idea."

Holmes shrugged and stood up. "Really, Watson, by now I should think you would be quite used to a life of crime. Oh, and bring your stethoscope. I may need it."

11

I THOUGHT WE MIGHT FIND YOU HERE

Not long thereafter, I found myself crouched in the darkness behind one of the massive stone posts which anchored the iron fence surrounding George Upton's mansion. Holmes stood to my rear, and from our hidden vantage point we could see a policeman guarding the front door. Another policeman, Holmes told me, patrolled the rear of the house.

"Mr. O'Connor is taking no chances," Holmes whispered, "so we must be very careful."

We waited in silence for several minutes, Holmes giving no indication of how he intended to gain entrance to the house. Fortunately, the night was quite pleasant, with new-fallen snow sparkling in the streetlights and no wind to sharpen the cold. By half past eleven, the situation had not changed, and I finally asked Holmes what we were waiting for.

"We are waiting for trouble," he replied, drawing my attention to a pair of unsteady figures walking along Summit toward the gate, "and unless I am mistaken, it is about to arrive."

The two figures, dressed in long coats, stopped at the gate. Their deep, raucous voices identified them as men, while their slurring of words left little doubt as to how they had spent the evening.

"Hey, you, open the gate!" one of these drunken vagabonds shouted at the policeman. "We want to look for the missing millionaire."

"Oh where, oh where, is the millionaire?" sang the other man, who sounded just as intoxicated as his companion.

"Maybe he fell in his gold-plated bathtub and drowned," said the first man, causing his friend to break out in cackling laughter. "What a pity! We must search the bathtub, that is what we must do." He then screamed at the policeman: "Come along, now, you pig, open the gate, or . . ."

"Or what?" demanded the policeman, who had come up to the other side of the gate, all the while slapping his hickory stick in the palm of his hand. "Go on, move along, you dehorns, or I will open your thick skulls for you."

"Ooh, I'm scared to death," taunted the first drunk. "This copper's a fighting man, he is, brave as can be, standing behind that fence. Well, open up, you filthy cur, and I will teach you some manners."

"And I will assist," chimed in his comrade.

"Is that so?" said the policeman contemptuously. "We'll just see about that."

He swung open the gate, causing his mockers to back away, their desire for a taste of hickory apparently not as strong as it had once been. Still, they continued to insult the officer in the foulest terms, and before long, he had had enough. Raising his nightstick, he went after the men, who turned and fled. The policeman soon got hold of the two scoffers, however, and began beating them with his stick, as they wailed and begged for mercy.

I was so caught up in this small drama of crime and punishment that I hardly noticed when Holmes slipped by me and began walking rapidly toward the gate, which was no more than twenty feet from our hiding place. He turned back to me and said sharply: "Do not dawdle, Watson. This will be our only chance to get into the house."

With the policeman busy pummeling his inebriated opponents, we had no trouble slipping through the gate and up to the front door, where Holmes surprised me by producing a key which fit the lock perfectly.

"How in the world did you get that key?" I asked once we had gotten safely inside.

Holmes said nonchalantly: "It was easy, Watson. I stole it. You see, that is why I went back into the cloakroom, on the premise of looking for my coat, after our recent visit with Mr. Upton. I saw a large key hanging on a hook and guessed it must be for the front door. So, with the idea that the key might prove useful someday, I made a quick impression of it with the block of wax I always carry for just such an emergency. Later, a locksmith of Mr. Rafferty's acquaintance made a duplicate for me."

"My God, Holmes," I protested. "I should not be surprised to hear next that you have taken to robbing men at gunpoint in the street!"

"Robbery is far too primitive a crime to appeal to me," Holmes replied as he bent over to light a small kerosene lantern he had brought along. "I am disappointed, Watson, that you would even suggest such an idea."

"Well, you have already admitted to theft, and we are now in the process of burglary," I noted. "So I do not think my suggestion was entirely unfounded. Incidentally, if those two topers hadn't shown up, how did you intend to get past the police? It was most fortunate that the pair of them came along."

"Oh, but there was nothing fortunate about it, my dear Watson. It cost me fifty dollars this afternoon to hire those two gentlemen of leisure, whom I found in one of the local watering holes. Once their skulls have healed, I should imagine they will be pleased to buy a round of drinks for their many thirsty friends."

"All right," I said, "you have demonstrated your infernal cleverness once again, Holmes. But now that we are in Mr. Upton's house, where do you expect to find the evidence you are looking for?"

"Why, I expect to find it by cracking a safe," said Holmes, as we crept along the front hallway. "Mr. Upton undoubtedly has a vault somewhere in the house."

"And I suppose you are prepared to spend all night looking for it," I said, "even if the police—"

"Shh!" Holmes admonished. "We must be as quiet as possible. One of the servants—Mr. Yates, the butler—stays over in the house. I am assured he is a sound sleeper and that his room is located in a distant part of the third floor. But one can never be certain, and I do not wish to be heard. As for locating the safe, Watson, I can assure you that I do not intend to spend much time looking for it, since I have already deduced where it must be."

With Holmes leading the way (and making sure to keep the yellow light of his lantern close to the floor so that it would not be seen from outside the house), we soon reached the main staircase. Holmes moved quickly up the steps, while I followed behind. A wooden tread soon creaked beneath our feet. Holmes, whose sense of hearing had always been exceptionally acute, paused at once to listen for any sign that we had been detected. There was none, and only a clock ticking away somewhere in the darkness interrupted the eerie silence of the huge, nearly empty house, from which George Upton had so unaccountably disappeared. When we reached the top of the stairs, Holmes moved confidently along another large hallway, before stopping at the third door on our left.

"Mr. Upton's room," he whispered. "You will be pleased to hear, Watson, that I do not have a key for this door, and if it is locked we shall have to discover some quiet way to break it down."

I knew of no "quiet" way to accomplish such a task, since the door — of heavy oak construction — appeared likely to withstand even the assaults of a battering ram. But we did not have to resort to such means, for when Holmes turned the ornate bronze knob, the door swung open, smoothly and silently. Only then, as my heart leaped into my throat, did I see (and smell) the end of a large cigar burning in one corner of the pitch-dark room.

"Good evenin', Mr. Holmes," said a familiar voice. "I figured you and Dr. Watson would be along soon enough, and I ain't too proud to admit that I'm most glad to see you, because I've had a devil of a time tryin' to open Mr. Upton's safe."

"Rafferty!" said Holmes, pronouncing the name with that mixture of exasperation and admiration he had once reserved for another Irishman, Professor Moriarty. "I thought we might find you here."

"Did you now?" replied Rafferty, in a tone which suggested he did not for a minute believe Holmes. Neither did I, but I knew that Holmes would never admit to being outwitted by a mere saloon-keeper. "Well, now that you're here," Rafferty continued, "I will show you the problem which confronts us."

Rising from the chair in which he had been so patiently awaiting our arrival, Rafferty ignited his own lantern and directed the beam toward a section of richly carved oak paneling to either side of a four-poster bed. "The safe is there," he said, indicating with his light a solid-looking panel about four feet above the floor, "nicely hidden behind a little slidin' door. I figured Mr. Upton for a man who likes sleepin' close to his money, so findin' the safe was a simple enough matter. Openin' it, however, has proved a bit more of a challenge."

Without a word, Holmes went over to the panel and quickly slid it open to reveal the steel door of the wall safe. He studied its combination locking mechanism for several minutes, using his magnifying glass to examine the workmanship. He also listened to the lock's tumblers with the aid of my stethoscope. Finally, he turned to Rafferty and said:

"Since I see no tool marks around the tumblers, I must assume you tried to pick the lock."

"That I did, Mr. Holmes. But as I told you, I had—"

"No success," Holmes interposed. "Nor would you ever be likely to have any, Mr. Rafferty, since a modern safe of this type—which was manufactured by the excellent Diebold firm of Canton, Ohio— is virtually immune to 'picking' by amateurs such as yourself, or even by a professional cracksman, for that matter."[1]

Holmes, I could see, was now beginning to enjoy himself, for he finally found himself at an advantage over his unlikely rival. Naturally, Holmes could not let such an opportunity go by without a lecture, which he now delivered at some length, apparently indifferent to the fact that our risk of discovery increased with every extra moment spent inside Upton's house.

"It is commonly supposed," began Holmes, "that the picking of a modern combination lock is an easy thing. Indeed, the more sensational detective literature will often depict a cracksman, equipped with the usual paraphernalia of his trade, breaking into a safe in a matter of minutes or even seconds. The truth is far different, as my recent monograph on the subject demonstrates.[2] In fact, the modern safe—especially if it is the product of a reputable manufacturer and employs a combination lock with at least three tumblers—is quite resistant to 'picking' or 'cracking.' The tumblers rarely give away their secrets to the stethoscope or other listening device, which explains why brute force—the use of punching tools or even explosives—is now the preferred method of even the best class of safecrackers.

"But since we do not have the luxury of employing such noisy means, we must find some other way of opening the safe. Any random attempt to discover the combination would, of course, be entirely useless. A three-tumbler lock such as this"—here, Holmes shone his light on the safe's black dial—"has something on the order of one million possible combinations, a sufficient number to test the patience of Job—"

"Or the longevity of Methuselah," Rafferty broke in. "Speakin' of which, I do not plan to live another nine hundred years, Mr. Holmes, and while your speech is marvelously informative, I am wonderin' if we might just move along a bit and get down to brass tacks. You wouldn't be rubbin' my big red nose in the dirt unless you were pretty sure you could open this safe. I am willin' to be impressed if you will be so kind as to do the deed before I drop dead of old age."

"Come now, Mr. Rafferty, it is not as bad as all that," said Holmes defensively. "But as you seem to be in a hurry, I will do as you ask. The secret to opening this safe is right in my pocket."

I expected Holmes to pull out some novel gadget similar to those he was always testing for his brother, Mycroft, who had ready access to all of the latest devices used by espionage agents.[3] But what Holmes actually took from his pocket was nothing more than a piece of plain paper on which a series of seemingly random numbers had been scribbled.

I handed the paper to Rafferty, who studied it while Holmes launched into yet another speech:

"As we all know, George Upton is an elderly man, which means that his memory—though apparently still quite good—cannot be as sharp as it once was. Therefore, he very probably worried that he might forget the combination to his safe. The simplest expedient, of course, would have been for him to write it down. Yet I do not think he would have done so. He is a cautious man, living alone in a house full of servants, and he would quite naturally worry that any written combination might fall into the wrong hands. Thus, I think it far more likely that he resorted to a mnemonic aid of some kind. Now, the easiest way for him to keep the code in memory would be to use a combination consisting of familiar numbers."

"Such as his street address or telephone number," said Rafferty, who had been listening intently to Holmes's dissertation.

"Exactly. But it must also be assumed that Mr. Upton is too intelligent a man to use his street address or telephone number for such a purpose. Nor would he use his birthday, another obvious possibility. Instead, he would pick a sequence of numbers whose significance no one outside his immediate family would be likely to appreciate."

Rafferty handed the paper to me and said: " 'Tis a very clever notion you have, Mr. Holmes. Very clever. And just what numbers did you come up with?"

"I have written down twenty-five possibilities," Holmes said. "Some have a fairly obvious provenance. The first sequence, for example, is the birth date of Upton's wife. The second marks the day she died." I looked down at the first two numbers on the paper — which Holmes had jotted down as 06–12–33 and 12–23–75 — and saw at once what he meant.

"But what of some of these other numbers?" I asked. "A sequence like forty-four, nineteen, and twenty-seven, which I see here, cannot refer to someone's birthday."

"Those are numbers taken from the legal description of this property," Holmes said. "One of Mr. Hill's servants, a very bright young fellow, did a bit of research for me earlier today. By combing through county and city records, old newspapers, and other pertinent documents, the young man was able to develop quite a numerical profile, as it were, of Mr. Upton."

"Well, then, let's give these magic numbers of yours a try," said Rafferty. "We've done enough jabberin', I think."

While Rafferty and I stood behind him and directed our lights toward the safe's dial, Holmes tried his numbers, one after the other. It was tedious work, for the dial had to be spun very precisely, and Holmes tried each combination three times so as to be certain he had not missed a number. The late Mrs. Upton's birth and death dates yielded nothing. Nor did other Upton family birthdays provide the right combination. Numbers derived from legal descriptions also failed, as did certain combinations relating to Upton's early business ventures.

After half an hour, Holmes had gone through twenty-two of the numbers on his list, all to no avail.

"Well," I told Holmes, "perhaps Mr. Upton is a more clever man than you think. Or perhaps he was content to memorize a random combination."

"Perhaps, but I do not think so. There are still three numbers left, and one of them must work!"

Rafferty, who had been holding the list and reading off the numbers to Holmes, now announced the next set: "Zero nine, fourteen, fifty-five. Another birthday, Mr. Holmes?"

"In a way," Holmes said as he began to spin the dial. "It is the date on which Mr. Upton's present company was founded."

I watched, by now rather indifferently, as Holmes quickly spun the dial left, right, and then left again, until it rested at 55. He then gave the handle beneath the dial a firm pull, as he had twenty-two times before. To the amazement of both Rafferty and myself, the door of the safe swung open.

Inside the safe, amid a clutter of business documents and a large ledger book, we found a voice from the grave, one which would ultimately lead us to the astonishing denouement of the ice palace mystery. The voice, that of Jonathan Upton himself, was recorded in a leather-bound diary he had kept sporadically since his twenty-fourth year. Holmes, hardly able to contain his excitement, opened the diary immediately and began poring over its contents, which consisted of several hundred pages of prose rendered in a crabbed, untidy hand that was by no means easy to decipher. Rafferty, meanwhile, took a deep interest in the ledger, examining its columns of figures with the practiced eye of an accountant.

I had no doubt that the two detectives, now thoroughly engrossed in their work, would have been content to spend the rest of the night in Upton's mansion, oblivious to the danger of discovery. Indeed, I had come to see that Holmes and Rafferty, despite their disparate personalities, were identical in one vital respect, which was that both possessed what might be called a command of circumstance. By this I mean that both saw themselves as being firmly planted at the center of the world, and so were not prone to the nagging apprehensions of lesser men. "Coolness under fire" is what soldiers call this quality, and it is not so much courage as it is a kind of unshakable optimism, a refusal to accept the possibility of failure. And so, while I nervously watched, fearing a hundred ways in which we might be discovered, Holmes and Rafferty calmly went about their reading, indifferent to my repeated requests that we leave.

It was only after an anxious hour that I finally managed to

persuade the two of them that we should make our escape from the mansion so as to avoid the ever growing chance of being detected by the police outside the house or the servant within. The question, of course, was how to leave without being spotted.

" 'Tis not a problem," Rafferty assured me as he closed the ledger book and stuffed it inside his huge wool topcoat. "I have an escape plan."

"Let us hear it," said Holmes, who—it now occurred to me—had made no mention of what our means of egress was to be. "I trust it does not entail climbing down ropes or other gymnastic feats."

Rafferty laughed and said: "I'm too fat for climbing ropes, Mr. Holmes, and too old to turn somersaults. What I have in mind"—he took a large metal whistle from his pants pocket—"is this. You see, this whistle got me in and it will get us out. 'Tis a special whistle, Mr. Holmes, one that you or I can't hear but which is most audible to my friend and associate John Brown. When I blow on it, Mr. Brown— who can be a most annoyin' fellow—will proceed to create a mighty ruckus out back, just as he did earlier this evenin.' Oh, the coppers will not be happy to see him again, I can assure you. While they're busy with Mr. Brown, we will take the opportunity to make a quick exit."

This plan, I must admit, sounded rather far-fetched. Still, having seen Rafferty's dog go after O'Connor in the saloon, I could not doubt that the beast would indeed stir up plenty of trouble for the two policemen outside the house.

Holmes, who always liked the idea of a novel adventure, offered no objections. Putting the precious diary in one of his coat pockets, he said: "Very well, Mr. Rafferty, let us see what that bulldog of yours can do."

After Holmes had carefully closed the safe and restored the sliding panel to its original position, we went back downstairs. Rafferty led us through the front hallway to the dining room and then into a large kitchen, where a door opened out onto the back yard. Peering through a window, I caught a glimpse of the second police officer, who stood near the mansion's carriage house, smoking a cigarette.

"All right," said Rafferty, putting the whistle to his mouth, " 'tis time to let loose the dog of war."

I could hear nothing as Rafferty blew the whistle, but outside, the response was instantaneous. John Brown, as though shot from a hidden cannon, came flying into the yard, growling and barking so ferociously that the poor policeman dropped his cigarette.

"Go away! Go away!" the officer shouted, swinging his club at the beast. But the dog was relentless, leaping and snarling as though perfectly rabid, and the policeman soon retreated toward the front of the house, no doubt to seek help from his comrade.

"Time to go," said Rafferty, and a moment later we were out the door and running along a path which led to the carriage house. We made our way around the carriage house to a narrow alley, and from there it was an easy walk back to Summit Avenue. All the while, we could hear John Brown at work, yelping so loudly that the whole neighborhood must have been awakened.

Once we were out of sight of the house, Rafferty blew his whistle a second time, and John Brown—who to my surprise was clad in a wool sweater—soon came bounding up to his master.

"You have a most valuable dog, Mr. Rafferty," Holmes observed, "though I am surprised he did not get shot."

"The coppers know better than that," said Rafferty in an unusually harsh voice. "The man who hurts this dog will have to deal with me."

And dealing with Shadwell Rafferty, as we were soon to learn, could be very dangerous indeed.

I THINK I AM FINALLY READY TO DIE

We read the entire diary immediately upon our return to Hill's mansion. Holmes ordered sandwiches from the kitchen, while I drank coffee in an effort to stay awake. Rafferty, meanwhile, had found a bottle of "tolerably good Irish medicine," as he put it, and poured himself a liberal dose of the whisky.

The diary seemed at first to be an entirely unremarkable record of the hopes and aspirations of a young man beginning to make his way in the world. There were accounts of numerous social and athletic events—concerts, parties, masked balls, iceboating expeditions to White Bear Lake, and, in the summer, regattas—along with frequent references to the tedium of working for the firm of Upton & Son. There were also lists of books to be read, regular vows of self-improvement, descriptions of items purchased for one collection or another, and the usual tales of courtship, love, and loss. Jonathan Upton rendered these diverse experiences and ideas in the intense, painfully self-aware manner so common to the young, and I must confess that I felt it highly improper to be reading what had clearly been intended as a private diary.

Holmes and Rafferty suffered from no such scruples, however, and the two of them pored over the journal like a pair of gleeful pirates in possession of unprecedented booty. Their disappointment was palpable as the early pages of the diary revealed only the most mundane of secrets. But the tone of the document changed dramatically in the spring of 1895, as Upton wrote of his involvement in various immoral or illicit activities. Unfamiliar names—Spider was one, O'Reane another—also started to appear at this time. The entries which proved to have a significant bearing on the ice palace affair began in April 1895, as the following excerpts indicate:

April 16: Went to the club at 10 p.m. Spider there, introduced me to Mr. O'Reane, a rough-looking fellow he'd met in one of the gambling dens on St. Peter.[1] Spider has many strange friends, so I didn't think much of it at first. Drank, played cards with the boys till two in the morning, then Spider took me aside and told me of a most incredible idea for picking new flowers of a kind we have never had before. Said O'Reane can get whatever we want, though it will cost us plenty. When I asked how much, Spider just laughed and said rich men like us could afford whatever we wanted. It all seemed risky to me, but Spider said not to worry, O'Reane is very discreet and has all the right connections in St. Paul. Nobody would ever know. Told him I would think about it. Spider laughed and said I would do it in the end. He is right. I probably will. God help me!

April 22: We did it yesterday, picking the first new flower. A terrible thing—I feel unclean—but I could not help myself. Spider got the flower to the club just after 4:30, and O'Reane's "secret potion" worked as advertised. God, but it was a thrilling thing to see—the flower all ours, every secret open to us. Spider went ahead in his rough way, taking his terrible pleasure, and then he watched me, smoking and laughing all the while. The flower knew nothing and we were never seen, I am sure. How can so much gratification come from something so cruel? Surely I will pay the price one day, but I cannot go back now. After deed was done O'Reane demanded $200.00, but Spider said he would have to do better to earn such money. Settled for $100.00. Am fearful the man will expose us, but Spider says he would not wish to lose such good customers. I pray he is right. Still, I wonder: Am I throwing my life away?

May 5: Picked another flower last night. All went smoothly, O'Reane there with his little bottle of magic. Have never known such rapture and yet I hate myself. Why is that? I know I must stop, but I also know I cannot. Spider understands. "Once a man has got the taste," he says, "it never leaves him." I dream of it now day and night. Papa must never know or I am ruined.

May 18: I have never been so fearful as I am today. The newest flower was most beautiful yet but could not be easily picked because O'Reane's "magic potion" did not work as it should. Worse, I am almost sure I was seen, though Spider insists all will be forgotten. There was an awful row afterwards and Spider, who is crueler than I ever imagined, did terrible things. O'Reane wants even more money and is threatening to go to the police, though Spider insists he is too much a part of our business to do so. Besides, he says the police already know about what goes on here. I hope he is right, yet I cannot help but feel that judgment day is near at hand, hanging over my head like a sharp sword.

This was the last entry of note for more than four months—a gap which was explained by the fact that Upton had gone to Europe in late May for "a grand tour." Temporarily free of his difficulties in St. Paul, the young man was content to devote his journal to his experiences on the Continent. But not long after his return to St. Paul, in early September of 1895, Upton's problems began anew:

September 15: Have made up my mind to tell Spider that there must be no more flowers. The risks are too great and it is only a matter of time before we are found out. The scandal would kill Papa. So I must become a respectable man again and stay away from Spider and his evil friends. I can only pray that Laura F. does not learn of my improprieties.

September 16: Met Spider at his house late p.m. Told him of my intentions. He shrugged and said that was my business.

Then came the big surprise. He wants a "loan" of $1,000.00. Said he has already stolen all the money he can and that he has debts which must be paid "or else." I said I did not have $1,000.00 because Papa is always tight with his money. Spider then said: "Get it if you do not wish people to discover what you have been doing in the dark of night." Spider's face told me at once that he was not joking. I reminded him that my ruin would be his as well. He said: "Go ahead, then, either get the money or ruin the both of us. It does not matter one way or the other to me." It was only then that I began to understand what a dangerous and devious man he is. So now I am being blackmailed and have two weeks to produce the money or face humiliation! Strangely, I have stopped worrying. I now think of myself as already a dead man and live accordingly.

September 29: Got the money for Spider and thereby compounded my crimes. I am now a thief in addition to my other offenses, but I no longer care. Everything has spun out of control and I can only hang on till I crash to the ground or, more likely, perish. . . . I see now that there is no end to this terrible business and doomsday must surely await me. . . . Went to Kennedy Bros. and bought a nice .44 pistol. Will use it if necessary.[2]

After this there occurred an unexplained hiatus in the diary, lasting until early January, when a series of increasingly desperate entries began:

January 2: The new year is no different from the old, though I continue to act as though my life is in perfect order. Went to New Year's Eve party with Laura F. Everyone was having a gay time and I drank champagne and celebrated as though the happiest of men. Yet the truth is that I feel perfectly trapped now, a mad little rat in a cage, waiting to be crushed by the iron hand of fate. I dare not tell Papa of my situation, of course, and my only hope is that he will die before the dishonor I have brought to his name becomes known.

January 4: Laura F. has found out something, I am sure, for I do not sense our old affection for each other. But I cannot back out now. Too many "reputations" are at stake. What a sham it will be. . . . Have locked away the pistol lest I be tempted to use it. . . .

January 6: Spider asking for more money. Wants $2,000.00 now for ever mounting debts. Told him I have nothing and can steal no more, as I would surely be caught. Papa is already suspicious, and I have no doubt his accountants will soon discover what I have done. Spider, of course, cares nothing about my problems and says I must get the money. What am I to do?

January 7: . . . Early this morning, after another sleepless night with fearful dreams, I took the pistol from its locked case, cleaned and loaded it, spun the cylinders, and put it to my temple. I tried to pull the trigger, knowing it would be my salvation, but I couldn't do it. No courage, which has always been my problem. I wish I had the strength to do what needs to be done. Perhaps tomorrow . . .

January 10: I have never felt so sick, so tired of everything. Went to House of Hope and prayed, but I wonder if He heard. Some crimes, I fear, cannot be forgiven. It is hard living without hope. . . .[3]

January 14: I have decided that I have no choice but to laugh harder and harder, every day, at my absurd circumstances. The latest source of misery is O'Reane, who has joined Spider in asking for more money and threatening dire consequences if I fail to pay him. I actually laughed at him—it is wonderful what complete indifference to my fate has done for me—and told him to do whatever he wished. He grabbed me by the throat and threatened to kill me then and there. I told him to go ahead, that it would be a relief. He then left, thinking no doubt that I have gone mad. Perhaps he is right.

January 16: I am now drinking a quart of whisky a day and taking laudanum, seeking the solace of oblivion. . . . The pistol remains loaded. When will I have the courage to use it and end this farce?

January 18: I awoke this morning at 9 a.m., thinking that at the least my situation—Spider and O'Reane demanding money, Papa's men soon to discover my frauds, Laura F. cold with suspicion—could not possibly grow worse. But it has, for one of the flowers has come back to haunt me. A man called me on the telephone and said he knows what happened and wants a payoff. He wouldn't say how much but insisted we meet tomorrow night in ice palace. Otherwise, he says, I will be ruined just like the flower. He does not know that I am already a house without foundation, waiting for the walls to collapse. As for the money, I told him this poor turnip has long since been bled dry. He did not believe me and still demanded that we meet to discuss "arrangements." I agreed— what difference does it make, after all?—but if he is looking for a pot of gold he will just have to take his place in line with all the other harpies tearing at my worthless flesh. . . .

The final entry, of course, was recorded on the day Jonathan Upton disappeared and, presumably, was murdered:

January 19: Will this be the day when my life comes completely apart at last? I will welcome the unraveling, glory in my destruction. God knows I deserve nothing less for my sins. The man has set the meeting for midnight—an odd time, but I suppose he has his reasons. And why the ice palace, of all places? So I will go and add yet another scene to the ridiculous farce my life has become. I have no hope of persuading the man to forget the matter, and I have no money to make him forget, so I will leave it to him to decide what to do, since the "honorable solution" is, for obvious reasons, out of the question. I cleaned the pistol again this morning and have kept it loaded by my bedside. I think I am finally ready to die.

"A most strange and remarkable document," said Sherlock Holmes as he finally closed the diary at nearly three in the morning.

"Young Mr. Upton was not, as I suspected, quite the saint he was made out to be in the newspapers."

"Then there is no doubt in your mind what he meant by 'picking flowers'?" I asked.

Holmes responded with a grim smile. "I do not think, Watson, that Mr. Upton and his friend Spider were conducting experiments in horticulture. Although our diarist has been rather coy, the 'flowers' he refers to must be virginal young women, whom it appears he and his friend regularly violated in the most cruel and unspeakable manner imaginable."

"Good God, it is rape, then, and nothing less," I said. "But did not the women report these violations to the police? They must have, and I fail to see why young Upton and his fellow brutes were not arrested, tried, and them promptly hanged. That is what they all deserved, in my opinion."

Rafferty, who had been sitting silently with his head cupped in his hands, now spoke up, though in an uncharacteristically quiet voice: "Rich men don't get hanged, Dr. Watson, not here and not anywhere else that I know of. Poor men and Negroes—they are the only ones this most kind and just society chooses to dangle by the neck until dead. As for the unfortunate victims, the shame alone would keep them away from the police. Besides, if young Upton's diary is to be believed, the women may not even have known what happened to them after they were lured to the scene of the debauchery."

"That is entirely possible," Holmes agreed, "for there can be little doubt that drugs were used to subdue the victims and perhaps even cloud their memories afterwards. The 'secret potion' provided by the man identified only as O'Reane was undoubtedly some sort of knockout drop, perhaps hydrate of chloral or one of its relatives. As you may recall from our encounter with the notorious Mickey Finn in Chicago, such drugs are readily available to the criminal element."

Rafferty let out a vast sigh and slowly shook his head. "This is a far more horrible business than I ever dreamed it could be," he said. "Far more horrible. Oh, I have heard tales of private clubs in London, Paris, and other such faraway places where degenerate noblemen drug and violate young women for their perverse amusement. But never have I heard of such a thing here in St. Paul, where men have always satisfied their lusts by buyin' their pleasure in the old-fashioned way. And to think that Johnny Upton would be part of such a thing, well, 'tis almost beyond belief. What is the poor world of ours comin' to? What a pity!"

"Indeed," replied Holmes, who seldom bothered with pity or the other sympathetic virtues, "but the more immediate question is what we are to make of the clues this document provides. Who, for example, is the mysterious Spider? And who is the person with the curious name of O'Reane? And, of course, who is the man Upton went to meet in the ice palace on the night he was murdered?"

"Could it have been his father?" I asked, recalling that the senior Upton had been seen late that night in the palace.

"Don't seem likely," said Rafferty, taking a sip of whisky. "Johnny referred to his father as 'Papa' throughout the diary, so it would be odd if he suddenly switched to callin' him something else. No, I'm thinkin' it must have been somebody else Johnny linked up with that night."

"Any ideas as to who this man might be?" I asked.

Staring into his glass of whisky as though it held deep secrets, Rafferty said: "Well, it's obviously a relative—a father, an uncle, a husband, even—of one of the young women who were violated. But since we don't know who these women were, we're still in the dark, as far as I can see."

"I fear you are right," said Holmes. "But what about the mysterious Spider? Have you any ideas as to that gentleman's identity, Mr. Rafferty?"

"I probably have the same ideas you do, Mr. Holmes. There's only one man I know of in this affair who might readily be likened to a weaver of webs."

"Jedediah Lapham," I volunteered.

"Indeed," said Holmes, "he is the obvious candidate. Mr. Lapham, the shadow who hovers behind the Forbes family, a man who is the very model of modesty and decorum, is now revealed to be a procurer of the vilest sort, or so it would appear."

I could not let this observation pass without comment. "Well, it seems to me that you and Mr. Rafferty are both jumping to conclusions. What evidence do you have that Lapham is the Spider? I have heard none."

"You are right, Dr. Watson," Rafferty admitted. " 'Tis only speculation, though I cannot disagree with your friend. Pimpin', after all, is what Mr. Lapham does for a livin', only it ain't of the fleshy variety. 'Twould come as no surprise to me if that starched little man, who presents himself to the world as the front-pew type, is secretly involved in such a business as this. But provin' it will not be easy, and that's a fact!"

"Perhaps it will not be as difficult as you think," said Holmes, removing a sheet of paper from his jacket pocket and carefully unfolding it. "I have here a list of members of the Muskrat Club, courtesy of Mr. Frederick Forbes. All are well-off young bachelors, with one signal exception. That exception is none other than Mr. Jedediah Lapham, who is not merely a charter member of the Muskrat Club but also wrote its bylaws and is, according to county records which I have consulted, the owner of the club's building."

Holmes, after taking several volumes from Hill's library along with him, finally retired to his room at four in the morning, though I knew he would not sleep, for he was obsessed with the diary and its mysteries. Rafferty, meanwhile, had turned his attention to the ledger book removed from Upton's safe. Using the library table, he laid out the book—which also contained a manila envelope filled with receipts, bills, and the like—and studied it with great interest. After a good half hour of scrutiny, he said:

"Well, Dr. Watson, it seems Mr. Holmes is so enchanted by young Upton's diary that he's forgotten all about this ledger, which also has secrets to tell."

"Really?" I said, trying to stifle a yawn, for the hour was absurdly late and I had been without sleep for far too long. "Was there some irregularity with Mr. Upton's accounts?"

"No, but there was plenty wrong with the buildin' of the ice palace. You see, this ledger book is for the expenses incurred in connection with that project, which Mr. Upton and Mr. Forbes organized and promoted. But lookin' at these numbers and comparin' them with the actual bills and receipts, I can only conclude that somebody has been a regular chef with the account books. They're baked, boiled, fried, and otherwise cooked to an amazin' degree, as Mr. Upton must have discovered."

Rafferty now had my complete attention. "How do you know that?" I asked, for ledgers had always been a complete mystery to me.

" 'Tis all here in black and white," Rafferty replied, gazing down at a column of figures. "Or perhaps I should say red and white, given the amount of money which seems to have bled away. You must remember, Dr. Watson, that bookkeepin' is a fine and creative art, and the man who knows its intricacies can do most anything he wants and make it look just as sweet as can be."

"Are you saying there was fraud?"

Rafferty shrugged. "Call it what you will. But from what I can tell, Cadwallader Forbes made a killin' on the palace, which was never intended to be for private gain. Take the matter of the ice itself. This ledger indicates that the Ice Palace Committee paid a harvester just over ten thousand dollars to deliver thirty thousand ice blocks to the palace site. But the actual bill submitted by the harvester—a Mr. Michael Defiel of St. Paul—comes to just over nine thousand dollars. That bill was paid in full by Mr. Forbes, who acted as the committee's treasurer. Naturally, this raises a simple question: What happened to the missing one thousand dollars?"

"You obviously believe it went into Mr. Forbes's pocket."

" 'Twould seem that way. And from what I can tell, other contracts—for labor, for security, even the architect's fee—were treated in the same fashion. Mr. Forbes took a cut off the top of everything, and no one was the wiser. All told, I'd guess there's a good ten thousand unaccounted for."

This figure had a familiar ring to it. "Ten thousand dollars was the amount mentioned during the meeting in the ice palace on the night young Upton disappeared," I said. "That means—"

"That George Upton already knew by then that the Ice Palace Committee had been defrauded," Rafferty said with a nod. " 'Tis most interesting, ain't it. I understand now why Mr. Upton felt betrayed, as he told us."

"But how does this all connect with Jonathan Upton's murder? After all, he was not directly involved with the ice palace, as far as we know."

"That's true enough, Dr. Watson. Still, it's possible there may be a connection we're as yet unaware of. Or maybe the cookin' of the books had nothin' whatsoever to do with young Upton's murder. Alas, two of the men who could answer our questions—Mr. Upton and Mr. Riley—have inconveniently vanished. And the third, Cadwallader Forbes, ain't talkin', at least not to us."

"So what should we do?"

"Get some rest," said Rafferty, closing the book and putting it under his arm. "Maybe we'll see things more clearly in the mornin' light."

CHAPTER

13

I WAS LOOKING FOR A BACH FUGUE

Despite my weariness, sleep came only fitfully, and by eight o'clock in the morning I could stay in bed no longer. Once I had dressed, I knocked at Holmes's door, but his only reply was "Not now," delivered with such vehemence that I knew he must be in the midst of crucial deliberations. With nothing better to do, I went downstairs to enjoy an unhurried breakfast of eggs, toast, bacon, and hot cereal. Thus fortified for the morning, I determined to take a long walk, since the weather, I was assured by one of the servants, had warmed so suddenly that "forty degrees will not be impossible by afternoon."

The servant had not deceived me, for the morning was indeed delightful, with soft sunlight washing across the fresh snow and shining through the long icicles which hung in dramatic clusters from the high eaves of every building. A quarter hour of vigorous walking put me in the heart of the commercial district, which was bustling with all the energy of the vibrant young city. I was following no particular course, though I had in mind paying a call on Pyle at the *Globe* and then perhaps stopping in to chat with Hill, who had issued a standing invitation for Holmes and me to visit him at his offices in Lowertown.[1]

This was not to be, however, for as I turned a corner off St. Peter Street I happened quite by chance to spot Rafferty, or at least a man who looked very much like him. He was just entering a church, which I soon learned was the Cathedral of St. Paul. I shouted to him, but as he was some distance away he evidently did not hear me, for the door closed and he was gone. Still fairly certain it was Rafferty I had seen, I followed him up the steps and into the church, which was a rather crude structure of gray limestone that bore no resemblance to its splendid namesake in London. Inside, I found a surprisingly pleasant and serene place of worship, with simple whitewashed walls, a vaulted ceiling, and two long balconies extending the length of the nave. There was, however, no sign of Rafferty.[2]

Indeed, the church appeared empty—the morning mass obviously was over—and my footsteps echoed as I made my way down the long center aisle toward the ornate altar. I was just nearing the altar rail when, near the end of a short transept to my left, I saw a man kneeling before a small table upon which glowed a row of votive candles. He had heard my approach, and when he looked up I saw at once that it was Rafferty.

"Dr. Watson," he said in a startled voice, "what are you doin' here?"

"I just happened to catch sight of you going into the church," I explained, suddenly feeling embarrassed, for I sensed that I had interrupted a private moment. "But I do not wish to disturb you. Pray, continue with your worship, and I will—"

"No, no, I am finished here," Rafferty said with his usual amiability. " 'Tis just a thing I must do every day, and now I have done it." He offered no further explanation, and I did not ask, knowing that if Rafferty had wished to tell me more, he would have done so.

"Well, then," he said as we walked out the side door and into the sunshine, "how is Mr. Holmes farin' with that diary of young Mr. Upton's? Got it all figured out, I suppose."

"I don't know. I have yet to see him this morning. He was not in the mood for company when I knocked on his door."

"Ah, so he is locked up in his room, he is, thinkin' and plottin' like a madman," said Rafferty with a smile. "Well, maybe I can be of some assistance. Do you have a piece of paper on you, Doctor? And maybe a pencil too?"

I produced the small notebook which I always carried, along with a pencil, and watched as Rafferty quickly scribbled out a message. He then tore out the piece of paper, folded it twice, and handed it to me.

"Now, I don't want you peekin' at this," he said. "Just give it to Mr. Holmes when he finally comes out of his room. Tell him it's a little gift from Shadwell Rafferty. Will you do that for me?"

"Of course," I replied. "But may I ask —?"

Rafferty cut me short. "No, you may not. But you can ask me if I'm hungry, and I will tell you that my stomach is growlin' like a angry bear in a cage, and that's a fact! So, Doctor, can I interest you in some breakfast? They serve a mighty fine mornin' plate at the Ryan."

"I'm afraid I've already eaten, Mr. Rafferty. Besides, I should like to get back up to the house. I have a feeling Holmes will be looking for me."

"You're probably right. All right, then, have a good day," Rafferty said, shaking my hand before he turned to go. "And don't forget to give that message to Mr. Holmes."

Hardly had I walked through the front door of Hill's mansion when the butler, a somber and dignified gentleman whose face was normally a model of polite impassivity, greeted me with uncommon enthusiasm.

"Ah, Mr. Smith, I am so happy to find you," he said, sounding greatly relieved. "Your friend Mr. Baker has been looking for you and has been raising quite a ruckus, I'm afraid. Quite a ruckus. You will find him in his bedroom."

I went upstairs at once and knocked, for the second time of the morning, on Holmes's door. "It is Dr. Watson," I said.

"Come in, come in," Holmes replied. I opened the door and was greeted by a state of chaos which even by Holmes's standards of untidiness was quite extraordinary. On a large table in one corner stood what was to be the *America*, only it resembled less a model ship than miniature piles of flotsam and jetsam — pieces of wood and paper, wires, threads, bottles of paint, and jars of glue, all in such disarray that it was a wonder how Holmes could ever expect to finish the project. His bed and the floor around it, meanwhile, were littered with scraps of paper, books and pamphlets, and various discarded items of apparel.

"I have it!" Holmes exclaimed excitedly, ignoring my looks of disapproval.

"Well, I hope whatever you have is not contagious," I observed, a remark which Holmes found quite amusing.

"Ah, Watson, I see you have lost none of your Attic wit," he said, sitting down on the bed and thrusting a small notebook under my nose. "Well, take a look! I have discovered the true identity of Mr. O'Reane, the procurer mentioned in the diary."

I looked but could distinguish nothing except a mass of letters, arranged every which way into a series of what appeared to be non-sensical words.

"I am afraid you will have to explain all of this," I said, handing the notebook back to Holmes. "It looks like the work of a messy child to me."

"Code breaking is not a tidy business, my dear Watson," Holmes replied agreeably, for it was clear that no amount of grumpiness on my part could dampen his enthusiasm.

Holmes, of course, was endlessly fascinated by substitution and numerical codes, figurative ciphers, anagrams, cryptograms, and all other forms of secret communication. Indeed, he had only recently completed (though not yet published) his famous monograph entitled "Twenty-five Kinds of Ciphers and How to Solve Them."[3] As it turned out, however, Holmes's encyclopedic familiarity with the many forms of secret writing had actually proved to be a disadvantage when he began pondering young Upton's diary.

"My task was harder than it should have been," he informed me, "because the secret to Mr. O'Reane's identity was in fact extremely simple. I was looking for a Bach fugue, something intricate and sinuous, but all that young Upton had to offer in the end was an almost childish anagram."

"I see," I lied. I then asked Holmes to explain his triumph of code breaking, since I could tell he was anxious to do so.

"After wasting much time looking for complex transpositions and other sophisticated coding devices, I finally did the obvious thing, which was merely to look at the letters in the name O'Reane," Holmes said. "You will agree, Watson, that it is a very queer name.

Indeed, I borrowed several books on Irish history from Mr. Hill's library but could find no mention of the name or anything close to it."

"It *is* strange-sounding," I admitted.

"That is because it is entirely made up," Holmes replied. "You see, it is possible to rearrange the six letters in this name to form two very simple words. Would you care to guess what they might be?"

"No," I said. "I have never been good at guessing games."

"My lands, Watson, but you are being a bit of a pill today," Holmes complained. "Very well, then, I shall tell you the two words whether you wish to hear them or not. They are 'one' and 'ear.' Do these words suggest anything to you?"

"Good Lord! The procurer must be Billy Bouquet, the man with one ear."

"So it would seem," said Holmes, a note of triumph in his voice.

"Your ingenuity, as always, beggars description," I told Holmes. "But are you absolutely sure Bouquet is involved in this business?"

Holmes responded by removing a small piece of yellow paper from his shirt pocket and waving it in my direction. "Some hours ago, while you were still napping, I sent a telegram to Mr. Wooldridge in Chicago. I have here his reply. He informs me, among other things, that Bouquet, when he worked in Chicago for the Star Cleaners, was known to frequent Mickey Finn's tavern. That suggests how he came upon the 'magic potion' mentioned in the diary."

It suggested something else to me, for if Bouquet was indeed linked to the murder in the ice palace, his attack on Holmes took on a sinister new meaning.

"This must explain why Bouquet attempted to waylay you," I said. "But how did he know your identity here in St. Paul?"

Holmes took a seat on one of the bedroom's richly carved mahogany side chairs, lit his pipe, and exhaled an elegant coil of smoke toward the ceiling. "I fear our presence in St. Paul is all too well known, Watson. Mr. Rafferty, for example, had no trouble learning our identity, and it would be foolish to expect anything less from the industrious criminal element of this city. These are dangerous days, Watson, and we must be eternally vigilant. From this point forward, carry your revolver with you at all times."

"I shall. Incidentally, I have something for you from Mr. Rafferty," I said, remembering the folded note in my pocket. I gave

Holmes the message as I recounted my chance meeting with Rafferty at the cathedral.

Holmes read the message and burst out laughing.

"What is so funny?" I asked.

"See for yourself," he said, handing the paper back to me. "Our Irish friend, as I have said more than once, should not be underestimated."

The note, scrawled in Rafferty's broad, looping hand, read: "O'Reane = One Ear = Billy Bouquet. Do you agree, Mr. Holmes?"

I did not see Holmes again until the afternoon, when he mentioned, almost casually, that he had spoken with Jedediah Lapham on the telephone and that we were to meet that gentleman at two o'clock at the Muskrat Club.

"Shall I notify Mr. Rafferty?" I asked.

"No, I think not, Watson. Mr. Rafferty and Mr. Lapham seem to share a mutual distaste for each other, and I do not wish to waste time with pointless unpleasantries. We will deal with Mr. Lapham on our own."

The Muskrat Club occupied a small brick structure of nondescript appearance in a mixed neighborhood of houses and small commercial buildings almost directly below Hill's mansion. Two of the club's namesakes, carved in red sandstone, gamboled atop columns flanking the front door, but there was otherwise nothing to identify the building's use. We rang the bell, and Lapham himself appeared to greet us.

He was wearing, as he had at Forbes's countinghouse, a gray pinstriped suit over a perfectly starched white shirt, and a silk tie. This restrained wardrobe, however, had been augmented by one unexpected flourish—a bright-red boutonniere, which lent a certain dapper charm to Lapham's otherwise staid appearance. His round, chalky, almost juvenile face was as impassive as ever as he shook our hands.

"Welcome to the Muskrat Club," he said with no great warmth. "Please come in and have a seat."

We followed him into a well-appointed room furnished with Oriental carpets, dark leather chairs, heavy oak tables, and brass reading lamps. Newspapers and other periodicals could be seen atop the tables, while to the rear was a small bar. I had expected to find the club quite busy, but the room was empty except for us, although I could hear the faint sounds of a billiards game in progress elsewhere in the building.

Lapham must have noticed my look of surprise, for he said: "We are mostly a young men's club, Mr. Smith, and young men do not tend to congregate until well into the evening. If you were to come back at, say, ten o'clock tonight, you would find this room very busy indeed."

We took seats near a heavy stone hearth, where a fire burned vigorously, and soon found our insides warmed as well with excellent glasses of cognac provided by our host.

"Now, gentlemen, as I understand it, you are interested in learning more about the Muskrat Club," Lapham said. "I am at your service."

"We are indeed interested in the club," Holmes replied, "though it was only recently we learned that you are its guiding force. I trust I will not offend you by observing that it is, as I understand it, a club for young men and yet you are, Mr. Lapham, perhaps a bit past that magical time of life."

Lapham's slit-like eyes gave no indication that offense had been taken. He said: "I am indeed no longer young, Mr. Baker, but I look upon myself more as the club's sponsor than as an active member. The fact is that I have always taken, shall we say, an interest in younger men, and when the opportunity arose some years ago to purchase this building at a modest price, I did so. My idea was to create a lively but respectable establishment where young men of means might gather for social and business purposes. No such place existed at that time in St. Paul. The club was an immediate success, so much so that in recent years I have had to limit membership. I am curious, however, as to why you are so interested in this humble establishment."

"It is merely part of my normal procedure," said Holmes, who excelled at the art of being disingenuous. "I thought that since Jonathan Upton was a member of the club, there might be something useful here I could learn about the unfortunate young man. How active a member was he?"

"I would describe him as typical," Lapham replied. "He had many friends here and usually came in two or three times a week."

Holmes now posed one of those quick, out-of-the-blue questions which were a hallmark of his interviewing style. "Was one of those friends the Spider?"

Lapham showed no reaction to this unexpected thrust. His face a perfect picture of repose, he said: "I'm afraid I have no idea what you're talking about, Mr. Baker. Who is this Spider of whom you speak?"

"It is a name I have come across in connection with my investigation," Holmes said. "But as you apparently are not acquainted with such a person, I will not bother you further with the matter. What about the name Billy Bouquet? Is he known to you?"

Lapham stifled a yawn, as though Holmes's questions were of little interest, then said: "The name is vaguely familiar. Mr. Bouquet, I believe, is one of the city's criminal characters. If you are asking whether I know the man personally, the answer of course would be 'no.' I do not traffic with street ruffians and their ilk."

"I see. Would you therefore be surprised to learn that there is good evidence Mr. Bouquet has been seen in the Muskrat Club?"

"Most certainly. Indeed, I would be appalled if what you say is true. Naturally, I should like to hear more specifics."

The interview had now reached a critical point, and I could see that Holmes was debating how best to proceed. The question was how close to the vest he should play his cards, and it soon became apparent that he had decided to play them very closely indeed. He said: "The specifics, I imagine, will become apparent to you before long. For the present would it be accurate to say that Mr. Bouquet, to your knowledge, has never been associated in any way with the club?"

"It would be," Lapham said.

"And would it also be correct to state that you know of no illicit, immoral, or other questionable activities occurring at the club over the past year?"

"Certainly. But what is the point of these rather ridiculous questions? I suppose that any moment now you will be asking me whether, as a rule, I avoid beating animals and small children. For the record, I do."

It was, I must admit, a clever sally, which even Holmes admitted: "Your point is well made, Mr. Lapham, and I apologize for inconveniencing you." Holmes, however, was not through with his odd series of questions, for he now asked: "May I inquire, Mr. Lapham, whether you are married?"

The sphinx at last began to show some pique. "No, Mr. Baker, I am not married. Are you?"

"No," said Holmes with a smile, "but my friend Mr. Smith has ample experience in that regard."

"How nice," Lapham replied with unconcealed sarcasm. "Now, if you have no further questions —"

"Only one," Holmes interposed. "I am curious if you could tell us exactly what it is you do for Cadwallader Forbes."

Lapham, I thought, would give only a perfunctory answer to this question, since he clearly had grown tired of Holmes's impertinent inquiries. To my surprise, however, Lapham appeared to relish the opportunity to explain his work.

After pausing to adjust the knot of his tie, he said: "Others have asked the same question, Mr. Baker, and the answer I give is always the same: I am simply the lubricant which helps keep the company of Forbes and Son running smoothly. My duties are many and varied. I write and respond to business letters, schedule meetings, seek out new sources of capital, dun creditors when necessary, and hire and fire in accord with Mr. Forbes's express wishes. There is, in short, no great mystery about what I do."

"I see. Incidentally, do you handle the account books as well?"

"Not on a regular basis. We have bookkeepers for that."

"Of course," said Holmes. "Well, sir, you have given me a most helpful explanation of your duties. You are right, however, in supposing that others find your position with the firm somewhat puzzling. Indeed, I have heard it said that you are a fixer, a puppetmaster, a kind of invisible hand behind everything the firm does."

Lapham smiled for the first time, though in such a tight and unnatural way that his face seemed almost contorted by the effort. "You make me sound like a rather sinister character," he said.

"Are you?" shot back Holmes.

It was a question so blunt and brazen that Lapham, whose poise was almost eerie in its perfection, surrendered control for an instant, as evidenced by a slight quivering of one of his facial muscles. By the time he responded, however, his face was once again a blank.

"I suppose every man has a sinister side," Lapham said, coolly looking Holmes in the eye. "Nonetheless, I have always suspected that detectives, with their constant immersion in the world of crime, must be quite the most sinister people of all, although I am sure you are the golden exception to that rule, Mr. Baker."

"I would not count on it," said Holmes.

Both men now stood, signaling that the interview was over. Lapham escorted us back to the front door, where Holmes paused and said: "Well, sir, I thank you for your time. I always enjoy meeting a clever man such as yourself. Still, I would offer you one piece of advice. Do not make the mistake of believing that your cleverness is without limit. I have sent several men to the gallows who made that error."

Returning Holmes's unflinching stare, Lapham then offered some remarkable advice of his own: "I have found that detectives may also be prone to error, Mr. Baker. They can be deceived by appearances as much as the next man. I have spent much of my life watching the human animal in all its vast imperfection, and I have learned that the man to fear most is the man who wears a mask. Perhaps there is even as we speak such a man among us, and you would do well to find him before further blood is shed. Now, sirs, I bid you a good day."

Once we reached the street, I turned to Holmes and said: "I must tell you, that man makes my skin crawl."

"He is something less than warm-blooded," Holmes agreed, "but most interesting nevertheless. And unless I am mistaken, he has just given us a clue."

"A clue? What sort of clue?"

"I am not sure," Holmes admitted, "though I have no doubt it is an important one. But let us put Mr. Lapham out of our minds for the moment and take a little stroll. I should like to see the ice palace again."

"Is there something in particular there you're looking for?"

"Luck," Holmes said with a knowing smile. "I shall be looking for luck."

Much later, when Sherlock Holmes came to reminisce on our remarkable adventures in St. Paul, he would always describe the ice palace case as "a perfect demonstration of the art of being lucky." By this it might be supposed Holmes meant that only by dint of good fortune was he able to at last solve the tangled affair. Yet Holmes never saw luck and chance as one and the same.

"We do not come by luck," he once told me. "Luck comes to us, but only if we are ready and willing to receive it. I have known many men who protest their ill fortune whenever events work against them. But one might as well complain that the sun rises or that the tides ebb and flow to the rhythm of the moon. Fortune favors him who knows where to find it. Indeed, I have often thought of luck as a beautiful flower which can be grown in the garden of the mind. A man must cultivate the soil with foresight, seed it with intelligence, fertilize it with the power of his will, and water it with hope. Only then will luck bloom."

As for myself, I have always been inclined to think that the luck Holmes claimed to cultivate was in fact a mysterious gift from the heavens, a kind of uncanny long-sightedness which only a very few men are selected by providence to possess. With his gift, Holmes was unfettered by the limitations of the horizon—he could see beyond the curve to distant prospects hidden from lesser mortals. I do not mean to suggest that he could predict the future, for Holmes never denied the role of blind chance in human affairs and his vision was hardly infallible (as subsequent events were to show). Still, he saw more than other men and so was often able to anticipate the forward flow of events—what he would call being in a position to receive luck. And in the extraordinary days which were to bring the ice palace affair to its conclusion, Holmes's luck—or gift, as I prefer to think of it—was to display itself time and again.

14

GOOD LORD, DO YOU SEE THAT?

The day now seemed almost balmy, with the temperature pushing well above thirty degrees, and as we strolled toward the commercial district I thought of how cold such weather would have felt in London and the bitter complaints it would have engendered from the shivering populace. In St. Paul, by contrast, even the slightest upward movement of the mercury was cause for celebration, so that the streets were crowded with smiling people, some of whom had already shed their topcoats and mufflers in order to enjoy the unusually mild air.

Although Holmes had said our destination was the ice palace, we first made a stop at the offices of the *Globe*, since he wished to have a talk with Joseph Pyle. We soon reached the newspaper's building—a tall brownstone structure with a lookout tower surmounting one corner and a polished granite globe mounted above the main entrance. Inside, we found an enclosed, skylit court served by a pair of those remarkably fast elevators which are a distinctly American invention, and we fairly flew up to the *Globe*'s headquarters on the eighth floor. Having visited the offices of several Fleet Street newspapers over the years, I was not in the least surprised by the atmosphere of barely contained pandemonium which greeted us in the *Globe*'s crowded newsroom.[1]

Copy boys rushed about with stacks of paper, telephones rang incessantly, wire machines clattered and clicked, while a group of beleaguered-looking men whom I took to be reporters pounded madly at their typewriters, as though trying to destroy the poor machines with the power of their words. We had hardly entered upon this chaotic scene when a terrible yelling could be heard above the din.

The source of this uproar was an office set at one end of the room, behind panes of frosted glass. I could see only a silhouette beyond the glass, but the deep bass voice belonging to the shadowy figure within was instantly familiar.

"Da-- it all to hell," Joseph Pyle shouted after first releasing a torrent of colorful oaths which might have caused a sailor to blush. I was surprised to hear such language from Pyle—I had always found him to be a perfect gentleman—though I supposed that the nature of his work was such that politeness must sometimes be sacrificed.

"How did this happen?" Pyle went on, still in a rage. "Were you sleeping again, Peterson? Is that it? Well, you're finished here. Do you hear me? *Finished*."

This last word was pronounced with such terrible force that it brought the entire room to a silent standstill, as all eyes focused on the unfortunate Peterson, a small, jittery man in a blue suit who now came slinking out of Pyle's office like a dog that had just been caught eating its master's dinner. Pyle was right behind him, no doubt ready to heap additional verbal abuse on the poor fellow, when he caught sight of us.

"Why, Mr. Hol—I mean Mr. Baker and Mr. Smith—I did not know you were here," he said apologetically. "Please, come into my office."

The newsroom, having observed its moment of silence for the departing Peterson, quickly went back to business and was its usual clamorous self by the time we took seats in Pyle's small, paper-strewn office.

"It appears as though someone missed a scoop," Holmes said, referring to the scene we had just witnessed.

"He certainly did," Pyle replied, still looking rather hot under the collar. "Last night, the city council decided to change the entire scavenger system, which has been the source of much public dissatisfaction and not a little corruption. I know it must sound like a minor matter to you, Mr. Holmes, what with the ice palace affair, but the collection of night soil is a big issue here.[2] In any event, Mr. Peterson, who apparently had had a hard day, chose to sleep through the council meeting. The reporter for the *Pioneer Press*, on the other hand, was very much awake, and so we were scooped. I do not like it at all when that happens. But enough of my problems. Is there something I can do for you?"

"I hope so," said Holmes. "I should like to know more about Billy Bouquet and why he appears to operate with such impunity in this city. Am I to take it that, as you Americans like to say, 'the fix is in'?"

"That would be a fair statement," Pyle replied, "though you would find few people of authority in St. Paul who would admit as much. Still, there has been much whispering over the years that O'Connor, and many of his men, accept money from criminals in exchange for protection from arrest. Unfortunately, no one has ever been able to prove these allegations."

"Why is that?"

"Because everybody fears the Bull, nobody more so than the criminals of this city. The crook who tried to rat on O'Connor would be found floating toward New Orleans shortly thereafter, and he wouldn't be on a boat. It's happened before, or so I've been told."

"But if O'Connor is so blatantly corrupt, why do the city fathers not replace him?" I asked.

Pyle smiled and said: "Ah now, that is a very good question, Dr. Watson, a very good question indeed. I can't say for certain that I know the answer, but it's long been rumored that the chief has 'the goods' on several prominent civic leaders and that he also knows where twenty years' worth of political skeletons are buried. I suppose you could say he's like a big, nasty spider at the center of a huge web. Kill the spider, and lots of unpleasant dead things start dropping out of the web, things which a number of important people in this city would just as soon forget about. At least, that's the story I've heard."

Pyle's likening of O'Connor to a spider naturally caught our attention, but Holmes made no comment, presumably because he was not yet prepared to advise Pyle of our "discovery," if that is the right word, of the diary.

I now said: "I still find it hard to believe that a bully like O'Connor could operate this reign of terror without anyone opposing him."

Pyle shrugged. "As I said, everyone's afraid of him, except, of course, for Rafferty. Speaking of whom, I must tell you that I am getting worried about Shad."

"How so?" asked Holmes, who — though he would be reluctant to admit it — had grown very fond of the big Irishman.

"Well, I talked with him just this morning on the telephone, and he said strange things have been happening since he had that run-in with the Bull a few nights ago. That incident, by the way, has been the talk of the city, for you may imagine there are many people who would like nothing better than to see the Bull get his comeuppance."

"I can readily understand why," Holmes said. "Did Mr. Rafferty tell you what these 'strange things' were?"

"He mentioned a couple of them. Last night, somebody broke into the apartment of his bartender, Mr. Thomas. The whole place was torn up, and there were vicious threats scrawled on the walls."

"What sort of threats?"

"Threats that Mr. Thomas would be lynched if he didn't get out of town, that sort of thing. Perhaps luckily for him, Mr. Thomas was visiting a lady friend until about two in the morning. I've known George Thomas almost as long as I've known Shad, and he's a man who doesn't scare easily. But he was plainly frightened by what happened last night, and I don't blame him. Shad came over to stay with him the rest of the night, just to be on the safe side."

"Has Mr. Rafferty been threatened as well?"

"Not exactly. But he does think he's being followed, probably by one of O'Connor's men, and he's convinced the Bull is plotting some sort of revenge. It's a dicey situation, Mr. Holmes, and that is why I'm so worried. O'Connor is capable of anything, and he has plenty of men to do his dirty work for him."

This news clearly disturbed Holmes, whose instinct for danger was usually unerring. "Perhaps Mr. Rafferty ought to stay with us for a few days," he suggested. "I'm sure Mr. Hill would have no objections."

"Shad would never do that," Pyle responded. "You see, he's absolutely fearless. When you've seen what he has seen in his life, then I suppose that is the way you must be."

This remark piqued Holmes's curiosity. "Pray, tell us more if you would, Mr. Pyle. Much of Mr. Rafferty's past is a blank to me, and I should like to have it filled in."

Pyle got up from his chair and went to the office's only window, which offered a panoramic view of St. Paul's smoky skyline. Gazing out across the ranks of tall office buildings, he said: "Shad would have a fit if he knew I was talking about him, bit I think you deserve to know just how remarkable a man he is. He's always been reluctant to talk about his experiences in the great war, but it's not because he has some awful secret to hide. It's just the opposite, in fact. You see, Shad was in the First Minnesota Regiment of Volunteers, from 1861 to 1863. Do you know anything of the First Minnesota's history, Mr. Holmes?"

"I fear I do not."

Pyle returned to his chair and pulled out a well-thumbed book from a shelf beside his desk. "Well, it's all here in the regimental history. All you need to know is that there was probably no finer regiment in the Army of the Potomac than the First. They fought in almost every big battle in the early part of the war. They took forty-nine dead at First Bull Run and were the last Union regiment to leave the field that bitter day. They fought on the Peninsula and at Antietam, which Shad in his cups once told me was the worst battle he'd ever seen. They were at Fredericksburg and Chancellorsville and, of course, at Gettysburg, the biggest battle of them all."

"And a great Union victory," I noted.

"Oh yes, but the First paid for that victory with its blood. You see, they were in reserve behind Cemetery Ridge on the second day of the battle when an entire Rebel brigade—a thousand men at least— suddenly came out of the smoke and right toward a huge gap in the Union lines. Win Hancock was the Union general on the scene, and he saw at once what had to be done. He needed time to bring up reinforcements, and so he sent the First Minnesota, which had only about three hundred men, charging right into the Rebel brigade. It was suicide, but the boys from the First didn't hesitate. They slammed right into the Rebels, bayonets drawn, and stopped them in their tracks for fifteen minutes until Hancock could call up his reinforcements. He got them just in time, and the Rebels were finally beaten back. But when the fighting was over, eighty percent of the men in the First Minnesota lay dead or wounded. The regiment was all but destroyed."[3]

"What an extraordinary story," said Holmes. "Was it at Gettysburg that Mr. Rafferty acquired that distinctive scar on his forehead?"

Pyle laughed. "No. Believe it or not, he acquired that memento after the war, in Nevada, where he had gone to try his luck at silver mining. Another miner slashed him with a bowie knife during a robbery attempt. Shad shot him dead on the spot and later remarked to me"—here Pyle did an excellent job of mimicking Rafferty's style of speech—"that ' 'tis never wise, me boy, to bring a knife to a gunfight.' "

"Advice well worth remembering," Holmes said with a smile. "But I am still waiting to hear why Mr. Rafferty is so reticent about his war experiences."

"I'm getting to that," Pyle replied, "but first you should know that what was left of the First Minnesota—'shattered lightning,' one general called the regiment—were also in the thick of the third day's fighting at Gettysburg, when Pickett made his famous forlorn charge against the Union lines. It was during this frenzied fight that Rafferty captured the regimental colors of the Twenty-eighth Virginia in hand-to-hand combat. But Shad won't talk about how he got the flag, nor will he tell you that he won a Medal of Honor for his valor that day."[4]

"My God," I said, "isn't that the highest medal a man can receive in the American armies?"

"It is," Pyle confirmed. "And yet I've never seen it. I don't even know if Shad has it anymore."

"Fascinating," Holmes observed. "You have put Mr. Rafferty in a whole new light for me. But I am still waiting—"

"To hear the end of the story," Pyle cut in. "I know. All right, you shall have it, but promise me first that you will never let on to Shad what I am about to tell you, or he will never speak to me again."

"You have our word," Holmes said solemnly.

Taking a deep breath, Pyle now resumed: "The First Minnesota's last battle, in October of 1863, was at an obscure little place in Virginia called Bristoe Station. A. P. Hill was commanding a Rebel corps that day and thought he had a chance to strike a blow at the Union Third Corps. What Hill didn't know was that the Second Corps, where the Minnesotans served, was also on the scene. Now, these troops were the cream of the Army of the Potomac, as fine a body of fighting men as there was in the world, and they were entrenched behind a railroad embankment, with plenty of artillery to back them up. So when Hill, who had a lot of green recruits from the Carolinas, made his charge, his boys had no chance. They were outnumbered and outgunned, and they got cut to shreds. It was a regular turkey shoot. When the slaughter ended, the Confederate dead littered the field, while the First Minnesota had lost only one man — a sergeant struck in the forehead and killed instantly by a minié ball in the very last minutes of the fighting."[5]

Pyle paused, and I could see that he was nearly overcome by emotion. Then he said: "The sergeant's name was Shamus Rafferty, Shad's older brother. Think of it. The two of them had somehow come through the worst battles in the history of this continent, and then just as their regiment is about to celebrate its last and greatest victory, Shamus is killed right before Shad's eyes. After that, Shad was through with war forever, and to this day he will tolerate no talk of its glory. You see, war for him is nothing but a lost brother lying in a distant grave."

Hearing this tragic tale, I had a sudden thought. "I happened to see Mr. Rafferty today at the cathedral," I told Pyle. "He was lighting a votive candle, I think. Was that perhaps in memory of his brother?"

Pyle slowly shook his head. "No, Dr. Watson, the candles he lights every day are for his wife and infant son. You see, Shad got married when he returned to St. Paul after the war. I have never seen a picture of his wife — her name was Mary, I think — but it is said she was quite a beauty. A couple of years after their marriage, she died in childbirth, as did the baby. Shad was devastated, of course, and he never remarried. He told me he wouldn't take another wife because he didn't want to see anybody else he loved die."

As I considered this melancholy story, I could not help but wonder how Rafferty had managed to maintain such an effervescent spirit. "How can that be," I asked Pyle, "after all that he has suffered."

"It's interesting that you should ask that, doctor, because I put the very same question to Shad once. And do you know what he told me? He said he decided to be happy in order to spite the gods."

"How remarkable," said Holmes, shaking his head. "How absolutely remarkable. We are in your debt, Mr. Pyle, for sharing this information with us."

"I just wanted you to know the kind of man Shad is. I would do anything for him."

"As, I think, would we," said Holmes, rising from his chair and putting on his hat. "Well, we must be on our way to the ice palace, Mr. Pyle. Again, I thank you for your help, and I can only pray that Mr. Rafferty does not have to go back to war before our business is done here."

"War?" Pyle asked incredulously. "With whom?"

"With Mr. O'Connor," said Holmes. "And if that happens, I do not like Mr. Rafferty's chances."

It was but a fifteen-minute walk to the palace, which we reached at about four o'clock. Although the grounds remained closed, with police stationed at the gates to keep out any bold curiosity seekers, the great domed structure had lost none of its appeal to the people of St. Paul. As we neared the south gate, we could see scores of strollers making their way around the low perimeter wall of the grounds. There were young lovers holding hands, prim matrons in high bonnets, and knots of noisy boys out on an after-school lark.

"I did not expect to see so many people," I remarked as we joined this circumambulating mass of humanity.

"Nor did I," said Holmes, surveying the crowd. "But there is only one person I am interested in at the moment, and that is George Upton. I believe he may be here."

"You mean you think he is somewhere in this crowd?"

"Not exactly, Watson. But unless I am badly mistaken, we can expect to find him nearby."

"And how did you reach that conclusion?"

"In the usual way, by thinking the problem through."

Offering no further explanations, Holmes set a course toward the northwest corner of the palace grounds, where a four-lane toboggan slide—yet to be used—began its downhill run. A large platform, built up from blocks of ice, was to have served as the top of the slide. The discovery of Jonathan Upton's severed head and the subsequent closing of the palace grounds had brought a halt to all work, and the platform was thus unfinished. Behind it stood a large, ragged pile of ice blocks, which I assumed had been set aside for constructing the platform. Dusted with snow and looking rather like gigantic sugar cubes, these blocks stood just within the perimeter wall and so were in plain view of strollers circling the palace.

"I find the toboggan slide quite interesting," Holmes said as we approached it. "Indeed, it might be a convenient place to hide something, if that is what a person wanted to do. Don't you think so?"

I looked at the big pile of ice blocks. "I suppose it would be," I said. Only then did it dawn on me what Holmes had in mind.

"But don't you think the police would already have conducted a search?"

"Relying on the police of this city is not, I think, an especially wise idea. It is hard to know what they do, other than to cause mischief for our friend Mr. Rafferty. Ah, we are almost there, Watson. Look sharp."

A strolling couple was just ahead of us, and they stopped to examine the toboggan platform and the pile of ice blocks beside it. The blocks glistened with moisture under the warm rays of the late-afternoon sun, but their thickness was such that they were in no imminent danger of melting away.

I suppose I should have been prepared for what happened next—it was, after all, merely another example of Holmes's famous "luck"—but even today I still find myself amazed at our opportune arrival upon the scene. For just as we approached, something caught the eye of one of the strollers who had paused to look at the blocks. This man—a dapper fellow wearing a long coat and a black bowler hat—pointed down between the blocks and said to the woman standing beside him:

"Good Lord, do you see that, Mollie? Am I having visions, or is that a man's hand?"

These words galvanized Holmes, who rushed up just as the woman let out a small scream and turned her head away.

"Why, it is a hand!" said her companion. "My God, we must notify the police." The man now noticed us and eagerly pointed to his find. "Do you see that? There's a man's hand wedged between those blocks. My wife and I just now spotted it."

"Oh dear, you are right," said Holmes, doing his best to feign horror. "Well, there is but one thing to do. You and your wife must go around to the south gate as quickly as possible and notify the officer in charge. We will keep watch here until you return."

"Very well," said the man, who had begun to flush with excitement. "Come along, Mollie."

Hardly had the couple left than Holmes leaped over the low perimeter wall to make a closer inspection of the hand, which lay at the bottom of a snow-filled crevice formed by a gap between the blocks. A beam of brilliant sunlight illuminated the hand, as though some heavenly power had mandated its discovery. In a way it had, for without the melting caused by this shaft of light, the hand might have remained hidden for many more days beneath its obscuring blanket of snow.

The snow was nearly waist deep in parts of the long crevice, which ran perpendicular to the perimeter wall, but Holmes waded through it with all the gusto of an Arctic adventurer on his way to the pole. When he reached the hand, which was perhaps ten feet back from where I stood, he bent down for a quick look and then began furiously to excavate the snow around it.

"What are you doing, Holmes?" I asked as he dug into the snow like a hound in search of a buried bone. "You are making quite a scene."

Alas, the reason for Holmes's frenzied excavation quickly became apparent, for within moments I saw the face which went with the hand. George Upton, like his son, had met death on the grounds of the ice palace, though I was relieved to see that he had not lost his head in the process.

Only an hour after we returned from the palace, with Holmes at once stirred and saddened by our discovery, Pyle delivered the day's second piece of sensational news. Michael Riley and Laura Forbes, our newspaper friend told us, had been found together in a hotel in the city of Red Wing, about fifty miles south of St. Paul. They were quite alive and quite married, the ceremony having been performed by a judge in Minneapolis over the weekend. It seemed doubtful, however, that their union would prove to be a long and fruitful one, for Michael Riley had been arrested on a warrant from St. Paul, where the authorities intended to charge him in the morning with the murders of Jonathan and George Upton.

CHAPTER

15

THERE ARE FIVE SIMPLE QUESTIONS

To the newspapers, of course, these startling developments had much the same effect as a side of beef tossed to a starving mastiff, and by the time the Fourth Estate had finished its meal, there was little left, as Holmes observed, except "the bare bones of fact, which are always more interesting than the speculative meat upon which the gentlemen of the press so vigorously chew."

The first extra edition, from the *Pioneer Press*, appeared at ten o'clock that night, and the other dailies, including Pyle's *Globe*, quickly followed suit. Holmes read these sensational dispatches immediately and pronounced them "not without certain features of interest." As far as I could tell, however, the stories offered little in the way of new information regarding the discovery of George Upton's body, which was attributed by the *Globe* to a "Mrs. and Mrs. Edward Fitzgerald of St. Paul."[1] There was, however, an intriguing reference to the role played by Holmes and me:

> One curious aspect of the affair is that two men—whom Mr. Fitzgerald did not know—came almost immediately upon the scene and offered to stay with the body while he and his wife went

to notify the nearest policemen. Upon their return, the Fitzgeralds were surprised to see that the site had been disturbed. Snow had been cleared from the victim's face and there were footprints around the body. The two men, however, were gone. The police are uncertain what to make of this but have promised a thorough search for the mystery men, who at the least may face charges of disturbing the repose of the dead.

"Well, Holmes, it looks as though we are now officially fugitives from justice," I observed. "The police do not seem to have taken kindly to your examination of the body."

"I did not expect that they would, Watson, though I see by the newspapers that the coroner has already confirmed what I found, which is that Mr. Upton died instantly from a knife wound to the heart. Still, I had no choice in the matter, since it was imperative to examine Mr. Upton's body before the authorities arrived."

Holmes's brief scrutiny of the corpse had indeed proved fruitful. In the space of no more than a minute, he examined Upton's face, torso (where he noted the stab wound), and hands, and even scraped samples of a black substance from beneath one of the victim's fingernails. After our return to Hill's mansion, Holmes went immediately to his room to "study the evidence," as he put it. Not long thereafter, he emerged to inform me that George Upton had been killed elsewhere and his corpse then transported to the ice palace grounds. To my astonishment, Holmes went on to say that he knew "exactly what sort of vehicle was used to move the body." In keeping with his usual secretive manner, he declined to expand upon these observations.

Larger events soon interceded, however, for it was then that Pyle rushed in with word of Riley's arrest and his secret marriage to Laura Forbes. I was stunned by this news. Holmes, on the other hand, was not.

"It has been quite obvious for some time," he told us, "that Miss Forbes's real affection was not for her fiancé. After all, she returned her wedding dress as soon as Jonathan Upton vanished, thereby indicating that his fate was a matter of no importance to her. Then, after his death, she made those startling comments that he had gotten what he deserved. Therefore, when she disappeared, I could only assume she had gone off with Mr. Riley, the man she truly loved but whose social station made him an unsuitable groom in the eyes of her father."

Holmes did admit that Riley's arrest had been unexpected. "Naturally, he was a suspect," Holmes remarked, "but only one among many. I shall be curious to see just why the police have arrested him."

The answer was in the newspapers, which suggested that the evidence against the young man — evidence that Holmes, for the most part, had been unaware of — was very strong indeed. The best account of Riley's arrest and the formidable array of evidence against him appeared in the special edition of the *Pioneer Press*, and I include excerpts here:

MICHAEL RILEY TO BE CHARGED WITH UPTON MURDERS — ELOPEMENT INTERRUPTED — ARRESTED IN RED WING WITH NEW BRIDE — HAD WED LAURA FORBES IN MINNEAPOLIS — RILEY BATTLES POLICE AND PROCLAIMS INNOCENCE — INCRIMINATING ITEMS FOUND IN APARTMENT

Perhaps never in the history of St. Paul has there been more astonishing news than that which occurred today, when word was received that Michael Riley stands accused of the murders of George and Jonathan Upton. Riley, who is thirty-one years of age and is well known to the citizens of St. Paul as the construction superintendent of the ice palace, was taken into custody at about five o'clock this afternoon in a hotel in Red Wing. Equally astonishing are the circumstances of his arrest, for Riley was found in the company of Miss Laura Forbes, who was Jonathan Upton's fiancée at the time of his murder.

The police say they have "incontrovertible evidence" that Riley is the man who murdered and decapitated Jonathan Upton last week and then, only a few days later, added to this horrendous deed by stabbing the young man's father to death. Riley was to be returned to St. Paul late tonight and lodged in the county jail. He will be charged tomorrow with two counts of first-degree murder.

Evidence Discovered
The murder of Jonathan Upton and the disappearance of his father had baffled the police for several days, for there was an absence of any clues. Early this afternoon, however, an anonymous

telephone call directed police to Riley's apartment at the Hotel Barteau. There, after gaining access with a passkey, detectives found a blood-stained knife, which, it is believed, was used to kill George Upton. A gold watch with George Upton's name on it and a wedding ring inscribed with the name of his late wife were also recovered. Further search revealed a valuable diamond pin thought to have belonged to Jonathan Upton. Several account books which may have a bearing on the case were also confiscated.

"A Ferocious Fight"

Convinced now that they had found their man, the police launched an immediate search for Riley, only to learn that he had not been seen in St. Paul for several days. Chief O'Connor was about to put out an alert, when the anonymous tipster called again to report that Riley might be found in Red Wing. Instantly, telegrams went to the authorities in that city, who soon located Riley, and Miss Forbes, in a large suite at the popular St. James Hotel.[2]

Capt. Thomas Gray of the Red Wing police said Riley put up "a ferocious fight" when four officers arrived to take him into custody, and it was only with the judicious use of the hickory stick that he was finally subdued. All the while, Riley protested his innocence in the loudest manner possible. "This is a set-up," he told the officers. "I have murdered no one."

Meanwhile, Miss Forbes, whom police found in a somewhat scanty wardrobe, was also taken into custody, though it is not yet apparent whether she will be charged with any crime. Train tickets found in the couple's possession indicated that they intended to travel to New York and, from there, possibly overseas. . . .

A Brief Elopement

It appears the couple were married in Minneapolis Sunday night by a judge, the ceremonies occurring less than twenty-four hours after George Upton's mysterious disappearance from the vicinity of the Minnesota Club. This elopement apparently came as a complete surprise to the bride's father, who was unwilling to talk publicly about the matter this evening. . . .

More Than One Motive Possible

Chief O'Connor said the elimination of a rival for Miss Forbes's affection may not have been the only motive for the murders. The chief noted that documents found in Riley's apartment suggest "financial irregularities" may have occurred in connection with the building of the ice palace. Declining to be more specific, O'Connor warned reporters: "Don't jump to any conclusions just yet, boys. There is still much we don't know about this sorry business." Yet if Riley did indeed commit some manner of fraud in building the palace, this would suggest a strong motive for the slaying of George Upton, who was a prominent member of the committee which oversaw the palace's construction.

"There are five simple questions I should like to have answered," said Sherlock Holmes, digging into a large bowl of rice pudding and then waving his spoon before us like a symphonic conductor summoning a crescendo. "First, who was the anonymous caller who told the police to search Michael Riley's apartment and later suggested where he could be found? Second, why was Mr. Riley so meticulous about planning and executing the murder of Jonathan Upton but so slovenly when it came to the killing of his father? Third, why did Mr. Riley go to all the trouble of transporting George Upton's corpse to the ice palace grounds after murdering him? Fourth, is it likely that a man known as a hot-tempered brawler could be nicknamed Spider? And finally, why was Jonathan Upton decapitated? I shall be interested in any theories which you gentlemen may care to advance."

This intriguing set of questions was posed early on the morning of January 29, the day after Riley's arrest. Five of us—Holmes and myself, along with Hill, Rafferty, and Pyle—had gathered for breakfast at Hill's mansion to discuss the case. Holmes first briefed Hill and Pyle on the contents of Jonathan Upton's diary, without mentioning how we had obtained it. He then described our discovery of George Upton's body on the grounds of the ice palace, adding that he was "absolutely certain the murder occurred somewhere else."

By this time, we had already read the morning newspapers, which reveled in the lurid details of the case, especially those relating to Laura Forbes's attire at the time of her husband's arrest. The *Globe*'s story in particular seemed to suggest that the young lady had been close enough to stark naked to embarrass the arresting officers, and I promptly took Pyle to task for wallowing in such salacious mire.

But he insisted that "facts are facts" and stood firmly on the "First Amendment," the prop used to justify every wretched abuse of American journalism.

For his part, Holmes took no interest in our argument, remarking to me: "I care not one whit what the lady was, or was not, wearing. The real problem with today's batch of stories, Watson, is that they contain a dearth of new information regarding Mr. Riley's arrest and incarceration."

The press did provide us with one important piece of news, however, which was that Miss Forbes would not for the moment be charged as an accessory to her husband's alleged crimes. Nonetheless, it was suggested that she could face charges at a later date, pending further police investigation.

This revelation touched off a surprisingly heated exchange between Hill and Rafferty, who expressed opposing views of the feminine psyche. Hill accepted fully the notion that Miss Forbes had been deceived by Riley and was purely a victim of love. Rafferty, who had the advantage of knowing the lady in question, took a much different position.

"I am not sayin' the woman is guilty of anything," he told Hill, "but 'twould be unwise, in my opinion, to think of her as an innocent lamb led down the garden path by her blackguard of a husband. I know the woman, Mr. Hill, and she is just as likely to lead as to be led."

"Nonsense," retorted Hill. "It is well known that a woman in love is the most suggestible of creatures and will allow her judgment to be clouded in ways that men such as ourselves can only view with amazement."

Rafferty remained skeptical. "I have found that women have more iron in their blood than we men give them credit for, Mr. Hill. Miss Forbes has a powerful mind of her own, which is why—"

"—we must talk to her again at the first opportunity," interposed Holmes smoothly. "For the time being, however, there are more pressing matters before us, beginning with the question of how we should proceed in light of Mr. Riley's arrest."

"There is no question that I can see," said Hill, who shared Holmes's enthusiasm for the pudding and was busily at work on a bowl of his own. "The only issue as far as I'm concerned is how long it will take to get a noose around Mr. Riley's neck and give him the hanging he deserves!"

"So there is no doubt in your mind as to his guilt?" asked Rafferty.

"None whatsoever," replied Hill with his usual firmness. "It is an open-and-shut case. Do you agree, Mr. Holmes?"

Holmes spooned down the last of his pudding, carefully wiped his mouth with a linen napkin, and said: "Oh, it is shut, all right, much like the lid of a coffin. But I am not sure quite yet that it has closed on the right man."

It was then that Holmes propounded his five questions. There was an uncomfortable moment of silence before Hill, who had obviously expected a different response, said: "So in effect you are telling us, Mr. Holmes, that the police have the wrong man. I find that difficult to believe."

"Do not misunderstand me, Mr. Hill. I am not proclaiming Mr. Riley's innocence. I am merely suggesting that the case against him is by no means airtight. As I said, I should be interested to hear any answers you gentlemen may have to my questions."

"I will give it a try," volunteered Pyle, who was always eager to match wits with Holmes. "As for your first question, I would answer it by identifying Jedediah Lapham as the anonymous tipster. Mr. Lapham seems to know everything which goes on in the Forbes family. If anyone would have known of the planned elopement, he would be that person."

"You could be right," Rafferty said. "Then again, if I were Miss Forbes and were plannin' to run off with a man, I'd take great pains to make sure Mr. Lapham was kept in the dark, what with his reputation for findin' out other people's secrets."

"Your objection is duly noted," Holmes told Rafferty with a smile, "but Mr. Pyle has nonetheless put forth an interesting theory. Let us assume that Mr. Lapham is indeed the man who fingered Michael Riley. It is easy to see how he might have learned of the elopement— such things are usually well known to the servants of a house, if no one else. But how did he happen to know of the incriminating items which Mr. Riley so foolishly left in his apartment?"

"He probably received a tip from someone else," Pyle said. "Mr. Lapham, after all, is renowned for his ability to collect information."

"And who might this subsidiary tipster have been?" Holmes inquired.

Pyle thought for a moment, then said: "How about Billy Bouquet? We know from the diary that Bouquet tried at one point to blackmail Jonathan Upton. Failing that, he may simply have carried out his threat to inform on the young man."

"There's another possibility, of course," said Rafferty, "which is that Mr. Lapham knew about the incriminatin' items because he put them there himself."

"Oh, come now," said Hill irritably. "Mr. Lapham may not be a well-liked man in St. Paul, but that hardly makes him a murderer! Besides, what possible motive would he have?"

Holmes leaned back in his chair and looked out the window toward the snow-covered bluffs of the Mississippi. "I can think of several possible motives. If he initiated the kind of activity which I believe occurred at the Muskrat Club, then he might have done whatever was necessary—up to and including murder—to avoid being found out. In any case, Mr. Rafferty is correct. We must consider the distinct possibility that the evidence so conveniently found in Mr. Riley's apartment were planted there in order to 'frame' him for the crimes."

Hill shook his head, and I could see a vein throbbing on his massive brow. "This is all quite ridiculous, the stuff of dime novels," he said to Holmes. "Why not face the facts? Riley was caught red-handed. But instead of admitting the obvious, you prefer to make allegations of some vaguely sinister 'activity' at the Muskrat Club. I should like to know exactly what you are referring to."

"I am not prepared to be specific at this point, Mr. Hill. However, I expect to know more very soon."

"I would prefer a better answer today," Hill replied, leaving no doubt as to his unhappiness with Holmes. "However, as it does not appear I will get one, let me reiterate that I see no evidence here of any kind which would suggest that Jedediah Lapham is a calculating murderer, and you would be wise, Mr. Holmes, to keep such thoughts to yourself."

Holmes took this dressing-down with surprising calm. "You may count on my discretion, Mr. Hill, but you also must realize that I deny no possibility to my mind. I would otherwise be a failure as a detective. In any event, let us consider question number two. Why did Mr. Riley perform so brilliantly in his first crime, which was as carefully choreographed as a ballet, and then—after murdering for a second time—leave behind evidence that even the village idiot would have seen fit to destroy?"

Pyle had a ready answer to this seeming conundrum. "I think Mr. Riley simply got careless and let his mind wander to other things. After all, the prospect of running off with a woman as beautiful as Laura Forbes . . . well, I believe it would be enough to make any man lose his . . . his . . ."

"Composure?" Holmes suggested.

"Yes. That is what I mean."

Rafferty, who was seated next to Pyle, let out a great guffaw and slapped the editor on the back. "By God, you've made your case, Joseph, for you seem to be tongue-tied yourself by the mere mention of the lady."

Pyle's face turned deep red. "I am sure I have no idea what you mean," he said with as much conviction as he could muster.

"Well, Mr. Pyle," said Holmes, who could not resist a smile himself, "let us accept your idea that Riley was simply moonstruck, a veritable puppy in love. Why then did this singular illness not affect him while he was so skillfully carrying out the very complicated murder of Jonathan Upton? Why was it only after George Upton's murder that Mr. Riley became so suddenly disabled by stupidity?"

Pyle by this time had regained his equipoise. He said: "I can only assume, Mr. Holmes, that as the day of his elopement grew near, Mr. Riley became preoccupied in a way that he had not been earlier."

"Perhaps you are right. But there is another, and I think far simpler, explanation for the differences between the two murders."

"You mean, of course —" Rafferty began.

"I mean not to discuss the matter further at the moment, if you please, Mr. Rafferty, though I have no doubt you are thinking along the same lines as I am. So let us now turn to question number three, which deals with the movement of George Upton's corpse. I must tell all of you again that I am absolutely convinced that this gentleman was not murdered on the grounds of the ice palace, for reasons which I shall not explain at present. Why was his body then taken to the palace grounds and dumped there? What purpose did this serve?"

"Symmetry," said Pyle without hesitation.

"And just what in blazes do you mean by that?" demanded Hill, directing a stern look at the editor. Holmes, by contrast, said nothing but indicated with a sympathetic nod that Pyle should expand upon his singular observation.

Braving Hill's imperious gaze, Pyle forged ahead: "I merely meant to suggest that if Mr. Riley's motive for murdering the Uptons was indeed revenge for various 'wrongs' which he thought had been committed against him, then leaving both bodies in the ice palace would achieve, from his point of view, a pleasing symmetry. After all, it was in the palace that Jonathan Upton was to have married the woman Mr. Riley secretly loved. As for George Upton's murder, the police seem to suspect that the motive, in part at least, may have been to cover up fraud related to the construction of the palace. Thus, the palace can be seen to have had great symbolic significance, as it were, for Mr. Riley."

Rafferty, who had been busy peeling an orange but who had obviously followed Pyle's every word, raised an immediate objection. "If symmetry was Mr. Riley's goal, why didn't he murder George Upton right in the palace? Why kill him elsewhere and lug the body all the way up to the grounds?"

Pyle was ready for the question. "I can only assume that with so many police officers stationed around the palace after the first murder, Mr. Riley found it impractical to strike again in the same spot."

Holmes shook his head and said: "As it so happens, Mr. Pyle, I have made it a point to check how many police officers were on duty at the palace grounds on the night George Upton disappeared and, presumably, was murdered. There was, it seems, only one officer on duty that night between midnight and dawn, along with the customary guard. No, Mr. Pyle, I do not think security measures prevented George Upton's killer from committing his dark deed in the ice palace."

"Then what did?" I asked.

"I cannot say with any certainty," said Holmes. "But I will tell you this: The symmetry of which Mr. Pyle speaks is not readily apparent to me. No, I think something else explains why George Upton's corpse was taken to the ice palace."

Holmes now glanced over at a large grandfather clock which stood in one corner of the dining room and said: "I see that it is approaching eight o'clock, and there is much yet to do today. Therefore, I would like to move quickly to a consideration of my fourth question, which concerns the mysterious Spider mentioned in the diary. Would a man such as Mr. Riley really have so inappropriate a nickname?"

Pyle once again took the floor. "Nicknames are a funny thing, Mr. Holmes. I played amateur baseball in my younger days, and we had many nicknames which seemed to make no sense. The largest, fattest man on the team we called Slim, while another fellow, who was rather slow of mind, became known to one and all simply as the Professor. What I am saying is that I would not find it surprising if a blunt and two-fisted man like Riley was known as Spider precisely because he does *not* seem the sort to spin webs of intrigue."

For once, Holmes had no answer to an argument. Instead, he raised one hand to his forehead in a sort of salute. "Mr. Pyle, you are a genuine, invaluable resource! You are right, of course, and you make a point which I had failed to consider. Nicknames cannot be taken literally. Indeed, they are often assigned in jest and therefore may be deliberately deceiving as regards a man's true appearance or character. I shall have to reassess my thinking on this point. In the meantime, let us conclude with the last and, I believe, most troubling of my five questions: Why was Jonathan Upton decapitated?"

There was to be no immediate answer to Holmes's question, however, for a servant appeared at the door to announce that a lady wished to speak with us on a "most urgent and sensitive matter." Her name, we were informed, was Mrs. Laura Riley.

CHAPTER

16

IT WAS THE LOOK OF A MAN
BOUND FOR HELL

At first I did not realize that our caller was in fact Laura
Forbes, the woman who seemed to be at the very center of
the ice palace mystery. Even Holmes, I think, was startled
to hear her announced by her married name.

"By all means, let us speak with the lady," he told the servant. "After
all, it is not every day that one has an audience with Helen of Troy."

Hill, who was about to leave for his office, with a reluctant Pyle in
tow, found this remark amusing. "I just hope that I do not find a
large wooden horse at the front gate!" Turning to Pyle, he added:
"Now, come along, Joseph. I do not wish to see you waste your time
mooning over unrequited love. Mr. Holmes will give us a full report
of his interview this evening."

A few minutes later, Holmes, Rafferty, and I were ushered into the
drawing room, where Mrs. Riley stood waiting for us with obvious
impatience. Although Holmes's comment about Helen of Troy had
been made in jest, it proved to be, if anything, an understatement, for
Laura Riley, as she now had to be called, looked even more radiantly
beautiful than the first time we had seen her. It was easy to see why
men had fought—and perhaps even died—for the right to her hand.

With her slender and elegant figure, she reminded me of one of those captivating women depicted by the popular illustrator Charles Gibson.[1] Instead of a flowing gown, however, she wore a long brown jacket with leg-o'-mutton sleeves and braided felt trim, a matching pleated skirt, and a lacy white blouse. She wore no jewelry of any kind, suggesting that her very appearance was the most precious gem of all. On her face was that same look of determination we had observed during our brief interview with her near the police station, and as we approached, her violet eyes took us in with a kind of feline intensity.

Stepping forward to meet us, she gave Rafferty a quick smile and said: "I have come to see Mr. John Baker, who I am told is a detective of great skill and daring. If that is indeed the case, then I wish to hire him at once."

Taking her gloved hand in his and kissing it in a suave continental manner, Holmes said: "I am Mr. Baker, and I trust you will not think ill of me as a result of our first, rather hurried meeting. I also trust that you will find my abilities a match for your high expectations."

If she recalled the question about her wedding dress that Holmes had hurled at her outside the police station, she gave no evidence of it. Instead, she said: "I can only pray, sir, that your abilities are indeed as advertised, for I am at the moment in need of a miracle. Are you up to miracles, Mr. Baker?"

"Minor ones perhaps," said Holmes without hesitation. "But before any loaves are multiplied or water turned into wine, allow me to introduce my associate, Mr. Peter Smith." I gave a slight bow, and as I lifted my head I briefly caught Mrs. Riley's gaze. I am not ashamed to say that I felt at that instant as though I had looked into the eyes of an angel.

"Now then, Mrs. Riley, what is it we can do for you?" asked Holmes after we had all taken seats by the fireplace.

"What you can do, sir, is to shine the light of truth upon a dark and terrible lie!" she said with great force and passion, in a rich velvety voice of the kind which can have an almost hypnotic effect on the male of the species. "I have come to you, Mr. Baker, because a great injustice is being done and you, I have been informed, are the man who can right it. My dear husband, Michael Riley, is in jail for crimes he did not commit. It is all a set-up. I implore you to talk to him at once. His very life may depend on it. Will you do this for me? I will pay whatever you ask."

"I am always interested in justice, Mrs. Riley," said Holmes. "I am therefore at your service. You may be assured that I will speak with your husband as soon as possible. As for my fee, give it no thought."

"That is very kind of you, sir."

"Well, then, Mrs. Riley, let us talk about this 'great injustice' being done to your husband. I am rather well acquainted with the case against him, and I should like to hear why you believe, contrary to all the evidence gathered by the police, that your husband does not deserve to hang!"

If Holmes had expected his harsh question to provoke an emotional outburst from Mrs. Riley, he was to be disappointed. Sitting ramrod straight on a small settee, her every feature taut with resolve, she stared unflinchingly into Holmes's magnetic eyes and said: "My Michael will not hang for crimes he did not commit. I will see to that, in one way or another. If you cannot help me save him, sir, then I will find someone who can."

Holmes said: "You seem very certain of your husband's innocence. And yet, if you will permit me to say it, a woman in love can sometimes be blinded to painful truths."

Mrs. Riley reacted to this provocative comment with a short, bitter laugh. "I have stars in my eyes, is that what you think, Mr. Baker? I'm just a poor, swooning thing deceived by my heart? Then let me tell you something, sir. I know men. I know what they want and what they will do to get it. I know their dark wiles and their petty deceits and their brutal yearnings. I have watched them my whole life, because that is all I have been permitted to do in this wretched, suffocating city. I have seen the lust in their eyes and heard their sweet, insincere whisperings. 'Oh, Laura, I love you,' they say, when what they really desire is the one thing I will not give them. Oh no, Mr. Baker, I have no illusions about men. That is why I believe a woman who cannot judge men is as bound for trouble in this world as a horse breeder who cannot judge stallions. When I chose Michael—and make no mistake, it was I who did the choosing—I knew exactly what I was getting, which was a good, kind, and honorable man, and certainly not a man who would commit cold-blooded murder. If you think otherwise, then you are a fool."

This remarkable speech, delivered with a bluntness of language which I was unaccustomed to hear from a member of the fair sex, left Rafferty and me—and even Holmes, it appeared—in a state of wordless wonder. For the first time, I began to fully appreciate what a fortunate man Michael Riley was, even if he did sit languishing in the county jail.

Holmes maintained his silence for a moment, no doubt reconsidering his strategy, and then said: "Very well, Mrs. Riley, let us trust to your judgment. Let us assume your husband is entirely innocent of the charges against him. What evidence do you offer that testifies to this? Can you, for example, provide him with an alibi for the nights on which the two Uptons were murdered?"

"I was not with Michael on the night Jonathan Upton died, so I have nothing to say in that regard," she replied. "But as you well know, Mr. Baker, George Upton disappeared on the same night Michael and I eloped. Michael came for me just before midnight, and we were together thereafter until the police—who are little better than thugs, in my opinion—burst into our room in Red Wing. Now, if the newspapers are to be believed, George Upton was last seen at around ten o'clock Saturday night. Presumably, he was murdered about that time and his body then taken to the ice palace grounds—"

Holmes jumped in to interrupt: "Why do you assume the body was moved after death? I do not recall reading any such thing in the newspapers."

"Mr. Rafferty told me," she said, turning toward our friend with a sweet smile. "He has been a pillar of strength for me since this nightmare began. We had a long talk last night, and it was he who suggested that I seek your help, Mr. Baker."

Holmes could only sigh. "Well, Mr. Rafferty, I see that you have been talking to the coroner about Mr. Upton's death."

"We did have a chat down at the saloon," Rafferty acknowledged. "Dr. Morrison's a regular. He's also a garrulous fellow when he gets a little whisky in him, so it didn't take me long to learn that Mr. Upton wasn't killed at the ice palace."

"I think I have the picture," said Holmes dryly. "Now, Mrs. Riley, pray continue."

"All I wish to say, Mr. Baker, is that Michael met me at about a quarter to midnight. I do not see how he could have waylaid Mr. Upton, murdered the poor man, carted his body to the ice palace grounds, dumped it, covered it with snow, and then traveled to my house, all within the span of ninety minutes or less. The mere thought of such a thing is preposterous."

"And you told all of this to the police?"

"I did."

"What was their response?"

"They did not believe me. They think I am lying to cover up for Michael."

"Are you?"

Anger flashed in Mrs. Riley's eyes. "Of course not. I feel no need to lie for any man."

Holmes considered this answer for a moment, then said: "Yet you must realize, Mrs. Riley, that the police would seem to have good reason to be suspicious of your husband. For example, how do you account for the incriminating evidence found in his apartment?"

"I have no doubt it was planted there."

"By whom?"

"By the police, of course," she said, in a tone which suggested that Holmes had utterly failed to grasp the obvious. "Mr. O'Connor, who has the dirtiest hands in St. Paul, would know all about it, I'm sure."

"And why would the police do such a thing?"

"Is their motive not apparent? They are protecting the real murderer."

"And who might that be?"

"You are the great detective, Mr. Baker, not I."

"So you have no idea as to who actually committed these crimes?"

"I did not say that."

"Then perhaps you can enlighten us," said Holmes, displaying a hint of impatience. "I am especially eager to hear about the 'sewer pipe' you mentioned to us a few days ago. As I recall, you said this pipe was about to burst, spilling its foul contents on the city. I should like to know exactly what you meant by this."

"What I meant, Mr. Baker, is that there is a cruel, vicious secret at the heart of this sordid affair, and that there are men of influence in this city who know the secret and are trying at all cost to keep it. They have made my Michael their scapegoat, but they will not get away with their scheme if I have anything to say about it."

"Who are these men you speak of?" Holmes asked.

Mrs. Riley paused, making it clear she intended to weigh her words carefully. "I will admit I have no evidence," she finally said, "but I would be willing to wager every cent I have that Jedediah Lapham is the spider at the center of the web."

"Really? And just what makes you suspect Mr. Lapham?"

Holmes asked in the indifferent tone of voice he affected when trying to disguise his own excitement.

Mrs. Riley took a deep breath, folded her hands across her lap,
and said: "It is a long and disgusting story, Mr. Baker, one which
does honor to no man. But if you wish to know the awful truth of
what has happened in this city, then you must hear it."

"We will, I assure you, be most patient and appreciative listeners,"
said Holmes. "Please tell us everything you know."

The story which followed was indeed sordid to an almost unimag-
inable degree, and I still find my anger rising whenever I think of it.
Here is what Mrs. Riley told us:

In the early fall of 1895, one of the servant girls at her family
home had come to her with a frightening tale. Mrs. Riley always
maintained friendly relations with her servants—"it is the only way
to find out what is really going on in my father's house," she told
us—and so it was not unusual that the girl would confide in her. The
girl, whose name Mrs. Riley would not reveal, was in a state of fright
because she had just learned from a doctor that she was carrying a
child. Mrs. Riley tried to calm the girl, who was only nineteen years
old and quite beautiful, and then asked the name of the child's father.
It was at this point that the story grew curious. The girl insisted—
offering even to swear on her mother's Bible—that she had not
knowingly been intimate with any man.

"Naturally, I questioned her closely," Mrs. Riley said, "for I assumed she was simply deluding herself. She was quite adamant
about her chastity, however, and told me she would gladly identify
the father if she could. Only then did she tell me of a strange and
troubling incident that had occurred during the previous spring."

According to Mrs. Riley, the girl said she had received a telephone
call one evening in May from a man who identified himself as the proprietor of the Muskrat Club. The man, who seemed very friendly, said he
had been referred to her by a friend and that he was looking for someone to clean the clubrooms once a week. Would she be interested in the
job? As the pay being offered was exceptionally attractive, the girl said
she would. The man then asked her to come to the club on her day off so
that he could show her what needed to be done. When she arrived at the
appointed hour, the man—whom she described as "rough-looking, with
one ear all but gone"—let her in and took her to a small office.

Holmes, who had been sitting with his usual languid posture, instantly perked up. "Did the girl perchance say which of the man's ears was missing?" he asked Mrs. Riley.

"It was the left ear, I believe."

"Thank you," said Holmes, exchanging a knowing glance with Rafferty. "Please, go on with your story."

Mrs. Riley said the girl, although put off by the man's appearance, nonetheless continued the interview, since the job offered such excellent wages. After briefly describing what would be expected of her, the man offered the girl a glass of apple cider, which he said he had just made up himself. The girl was not especially thirsty, but the man insisted, saying it would be the best cider she would ever taste. She finally agreed, and found the cider to be indeed quite delicious.

"And that," said Mrs. Riley, "was the last thing she remembered with any certainty about her interview at the Muskrat Club."

"What do you mean?" I asked.

"What Mrs. Riley means," said Holmes, "is that the young girl was drugged, no doubt by our one-eared friend, Billy Bouquet. And unless I am mistaken, she awakened several hours later to find her clothes in disarray, but with almost no memory of what had happened to her. Am I correct?"

Mrs. Riley showed surprise for the first time, tilting her head to one side as though not believing what she had just heard. "How did you know this, Mr. Baker?"

"I will explain later. First, I should like to hear the rest of the girl's story."

Mrs. Riley confirmed that the girl had indeed awakened several hours later in the office. The man who had summoned her to the club told her that she had unaccountably fallen asleep. He then dismissed her, saying he would have to find someone who could "stay awake on the job." Still in a confused state, the girl left, but as she made her way back to the Forbes house she began to experience vague flashes of memory. She remembered loud voices, wild laughter, faces hidden by black masks. Other, more disturbing images also flickered through her mind, until she began to wonder whether the worst had happened.

"It is certain that she was violated," Mrs. Riley concluded matter-of-factly, "and that the child she now carries is the result of that brutal attack."

I saw now that there could be no doubt as to what Jonathan Upton and his friend the Spider had done at the Muskrat Club. The thought of it sickened me. "Did the girl report this assault to the police?"

"No, she was too embarrassed," Mrs. Riley replied. "But even if she had done so, it would have been to no avail. The police of this city exist solely to serve the interests of the rich and powerful. She would have been laughed out of the police station."

Rafferty, who had been silent during Mrs. Riley's gripping narration, now let out a vast sigh and slowly shook his head. " 'Tis all too true. The coppers would not have given her the time of day. 'Tis a dirty shame."

"Indeed," replied Holmes, "but the real shame would be if the men who did this go scot-free. One of the perpetrators, of course, has already paid with his life. Tell me, Mrs. Riley, how did you discover that your onetime fiancé, Jonathan Upton, was among the men guilty of this crime?"

Once again, Holmes had caught the lady unawares. Taking another deep breath, as though bracing herself for an especially painful experience, she said: "So you know of that as well. Mr. Rafferty was right. You are indeed a genius, sir."

"It took no genius to deduce that you had become estranged from your fiancé," Holmes said with uncharacteristic modesty. "The fact that you returned your wedding dress while Mr. Upton was still missing suggested that your ardor for him had long since cooled. Then, of course, there were your other comments to us at the police station, not to mention what we have learned from Jonathan Upton's diary."

"Diary?" Mrs. Riley repeated. "Jonathan kept a diary?"

As Mrs. Riley listened with a look of fascinated horror, Holmes described the contents of the diary, including Upton's account of the "items"—which we now knew for certain were innocent young girls—delivered to the Muskrat Club by Billy Bouquet. Holmes also mentioned how Upton had written at one point that his fiancée was "cold with suspicion."

"It is true," said Mrs. Riley. "I had begun to suspect him of terrible deeds."

"What prompted your suspicion?" Holmes asked.

"It was something the servant girl said, a few months after she first came to me. She was continually having nightmares about her awful experience. She would see grim faces hovering over her and hear the cruel laughter of her tormentors. She also heard, in almost every dream, a name being called out."

Holmes leaned forward in his chair, his eyes bright with anticipation. "A name? Whose was it?"

"Actually, it was a set of initials—J.T.—spoken as though referring to a person. And when I heard those initials, Mr. Baker, I must tell you it was as if a knife had been thrust in my heart. You see, Jonathan Upton was known to many of his friends as J.T. These initials began being used, I believe, when he was a child. The 'T' stands for his middle name, Thomas. His father had the same middle name, and people often referred to the two of them as G.T. and J.T."

Holmes sat back in his chair and thought for a moment. "This is most interesting, Mrs. Riley. But I find it hard to believe that the mere mention of these initials was sufficient to make you suspicious of your fiancé."

"It was not only the initials, Mr. Baker. Jonathan had begun to act strangely. He was nervous, short-tempered, distracted. Then one night—when I asked what was the matter—he told me that something terrible had happened and he felt 'doomed.' That was his exact word. He also told me that he was thinking of calling off our wedding because he did not wish, as he put it, 'to cause a scandal.' And that was when I truly began to suspect the worst of him."

"What did you do next?" Holmes asked.

"I went to talk to Michael and ask for his help."

"Then I take it you were still seeing Mr. Riley, despite your engagement to Jonathan Upton?"

"I will be honest with you, Mr. Baker. I never loved Jonathan Upton. But in a moment of foolishness—Michael and I had had a quarrel— I agreed to the engagement with Jonathan. Father, of course, was most pleased, since he always believed that Michael was beneath me. Yet I knew all along that I would return to Michael in the end."

"I see," murmured Holmes, though I suspect that in truth he did not, for the subtle operations of the female mind in matters of amour were always quite beyond him.[2] "Very well, then, tell me what you asked Mr. Riley to do."

"I asked him to help me investigate the servant girl's story. You see, Michael was at that time still a member of the Muskrat Club. Moreover, he and Jonathan had once been friends. I felt that if anyone could get to the bottom of what was going on at the club, it would be Michael. He became my own private investigator, as it were."

"How interesting," remarked Holmes. "And just what did this detective of yours learn?"

"Michael learned a great deal," Mrs. Riley said, somewhat defensively, "although it took him a while. He first went down and talked to a few of his friends at the club. They knew nothing of anything improper going on with young women, or so they told him. He also talked with Mr. Lapham, who as you may know owns the club's building."

"And what did Mr. Lapham have to say?"

"He denied any wrongdoing at the club, of course, and professed no knowledge of a man with one ear. That must be a lie, however, because Michael has told me that nothing at the club escapes Mr. Lapham's attention. Indeed, legend has it that he can tell just by looking at the bottles behind the bar whether someone has taken an extra shot of whisky and failed to pay for it."

" 'Twould not surprise me," said Rafferty with a chuckle, "for I've always had the impression that Mr. Lapham is a man with a fine eye for detail. If my eye were as good, I'd be a rich man by now, for the first law of saloonkeepin' is to watch your liquor."

Ignoring this brief digression, Holmes pressed Mrs. Riley for further details of her husband's investigation at the Muskrat Club.

"Michael did learn one very interesting thing," she told us. "He found out that a man with one ear had been seen idling about the club building on several occasions. Worse, this man—the one you have identified as Billy Bouquet—was seen at least once with Jonathan. It was only at this point that I began to fear that Jonathan was almost certainly among those who had so viciously assaulted my servant."

"What did you do next?" inquired Holmes.

"The only thing I could do," Mrs. Riley said with her usual resolve. "I confronted Jonathan and demanded to know if he had violated the girl, and if so, how he could live with himself. I will never forget the look on his face at that moment. It was the look of a man bound for hell. I knew then what he had done, and what I must do. I never spoke to him again."

"And yet the marriage plans went forward," Holmes noted. "Why was that?"

"That was Father's doing. I told him that I could not marry Jonathan under any circumstances. I also told him why. Naturally, he did not believe me and said he would not hear of calling off the wedding. I'm sure he thought I was just having hysterical fantasies, an idea which Mr. Lapham no doubt helped to implant, in that subtle, insidious way of his. In any case, Father proved absolutely impossible, and he even sent in my brother Freddie to try to 'talk some sense' into me, as he so insultingly put it."

"Was it not your brother who had convinced you to become engaged to Mr. Upton in the first place?" I asked, recalling our interview with the young man.

"Freddie is a fool and a layabout," she said with surprising contempt. "He fancies himself quite the expert in affairs of the heart. It does not surprise me that he would try to take credit for my decision to become engaged to his dear friend Jonathan. The truth is that Freddie had nothing to do with the matter. I have never gone to Freddie for advice about anything. Besides, he would never dare cross Father. So you see, I had no choice but to take my future into my own hands. I knew Michael was the man I had loved all along and that we must make our life together. And so we eloped."

What an extraordinary woman this was! My heart went out to her, and I now took it as an article of faith that her husband must be innocent of the charges against him. I vowed to myself that I would help the two of them in whatever way I could.

I was about to urge Holmes to do likewise, when a commotion erupted in the hallway outside the drawing room. There were raised voices—it sounded as though the servants were trying to intercept an unwelcome visitor—and then Frederick Forbes rushed headlong into the room, his features frozen in a mask of fear.

"Thank God I have found you, Mr. Baker," he said, a brace of unhappy servants trailing behind him. "I must talk to you at once. You see—"

He now caught sight of his sister, and his eyes widened in surprise. Still, he managed a slight nod in her direction as he reached inside his coat pocket and, with trembling hands, removed a folded sheet of paper. Holding the paper well out in front of him, as though it might explode in his face at any second, Forbes fumbled to unfold it and then handed it to Holmes.

"I . . . have received another . . . ah . . . another threatening letter," he said, stumbling nervously over his words, "and you also must know that someone . . . well, what I mean to say is that there is a man, and . . . you see, I believe he is following me!"

17

IT IS THE MIND OF A MASTER MANIPULATOR

S o gripped by fear was Forbes that I had to administer a glass of brandy and force him to take several deep breaths in order to calm him. Holmes, meanwhile, scanned the threatening letter and then passed it on to me without comment. Like its predecessor, the message was formed of individual letters cut from a newspaper or other periodical. It read: BE WARNED THE WORK OF VENGEANCE WILL CONTINUE. The sinister vagueness of this message, I realized, only served to intensify its effect, and I could readily understand how it might cause a man as high-strung as Forbes to become completely unnerved.

Mrs. Riley, however, showed no such sympathy. Looking at her brother with a kind of amused loathing, she at first could only shake her head at his unseemly display of trepidation. But when she finally spoke up, her words cut like the slash of a saber.

"Really, Freddie, you remind me of a scared rabbit," she scolded. "Be a man for once in your life."

"Oh, that is easy for you to say," he replied, stung by her remarks. "You have not had a maniac following you around and writing terrible letters. I wonder how brave you would be then!"

"Brave enough," she said coolly. "As for the man supposedly following you, I shall be happy to go outside and tell him to leave!"

She began to rise from her chair and would no doubt have done exactly as she promised, had not Holmes interceded. "Please stay where you are, Mrs. Riley," he said firmly. "I believe Mr. Rafferty would be more than willing to undertake that mission."

"I would indeed," said our friend, who went over to Forbes and gave him a consoling pat on the shoulder. "Don't worry, Freddie, me boy. If there's anybody lurkin' around outside, I'll make it hot for him."

Once Rafferty had gone, Holmes turned his attention back to Forbes, whose features still displayed the anxious look of a man approaching a date with the gallows. "Now, sir," said Holmes, "do not let fear get the better of you. Sit down, compose yourself, and tell us when you received this message."

Taking several more deep breaths, Forbes said: "I found it this morning. It was left under the door of my apartment, just like the first one."

"I take it you did not see the person who delivered the message?"

"No."

"And you still have no idea who the sender might be?"

Forbes looked at his sister and then said in almost a whisper: "I . . . well, what I wish to tell you is that after I received the first message, I thought it must have come from . . . you know . . . Mr. Riley, but—"

"That is a lie!" proclaimed Mrs. Riley, casting a venomous glance at her brother. "Michael is no sneak, and you know it. Mr. Baker, if you think—"

"What I think," said Holmes, cutting her off, "is not the issue at the moment. I should like to hear your brother's story, without interruption, if you would be so kind. You may rest assured that I shall be appropriately skeptical, madam. Now, Mr. Forbes, please go on."

The young man nodded, obviously grateful that he would not have to confront his sister's wrath, at least for the moment. "As I was saying, I thought the first message might have come from Mr. Riley, for reasons we discussed earlier. But this message, well, I suppose he could not have delivered it, since he is jail. So I am at a loss."

"Perhaps Mr. Riley has an associate," Holmes suggested.

Mrs. Riley bridled at this remark, but she held her tongue after I had indicated by a slight shake of my head that another outburst would do her husband's cause no good.

"I would not know about any associate," Forbes replied, glancing sheepishly at his sister. He then turned back to Holmes and added: "And I wish to emphasize, Mr. Baker, that I have never claimed Mr. Riley is guilty of anything."

"Nor have I," said Holmes impatiently. "Now, sir, let us consider the mysterious shadow you seem to have acquired. When did you first notice that you were being followed?"

"It was last night. I had left my apartment just after six to dine at Magee's Café in Lowertown.[1] As the night was so warm for this time of year, I decided to walk rather than take the streetcar. There were quite a few people about, and at first I didn't notice anything out of the ordinary. At Seven Corners, however, I became vaguely aware of a figure walking behind me, about half a block away. I turned around to look, but the darkness was such that all I could see was a shadowy presence."

"What caused you to notice this figure?" Holmes asked.

"I honestly do not know. It was just one of those things. I suppose you could say I began, in some strange way, to feel the person's eyes upon me. It was almost as if a chill ran down my spine and something inside me began to send out a warning."

I understood precisely what Forbes meant. In Afghanistan, I had known several soldiers who seemed to have just such a sixth sense in the presence of the enemy. Of course, Holmes himself also possessed this gift, to an exceptional degree.

Holmes now continued his questioning: "What did you do, Mr. Forbes, once you began to suspect that someone was following you?"

"At first I wasn't sure exactly what I should do, but then it occurred to me to start taking a roundabout route, just to be certain that I was indeed being followed. So I walked down Fourth Street, cut through Rice Park, took Fifth to Cedar, went up to Seventh, then came back down Minnesota to Third."

"And what happened?"

"The figure stayed right behind me, but always far enough away so that I couldn't see a face or other identifying feature."

"Very well. Did you eventually then go to Magee's?"

"Yes. I had my dinner, but I will not deny that I was so nervous that I had little appetite. I quickly downed a few morsels, put my coat back on, and then asked the waiter to show me out the back door, which opens into a long alley."

"You hoped by this means, I take it, to thwart the person following you?"

"Yes, that was my plan. I followed the alley to Sibley Street, almost in front of the Union Depot, where there were the usual crowds coming and going. I looked around, saw no signs of my shadow, and started up Sibley, thinking I was safe at last."

Forbes paused long enough to consider his empty glass of brandy. "Say, do you suppose I could get a refill?"

Holmes gave me a small nod and I poured another glass for Forbes, who reacted with a grateful smile. He continued: "In any case, once I got up to Sixth and Sibley, near the Ryan Hotel, I began to get that strange feeling again. I spun around, and sure enough, there the figure was, lurking a half block away, in the entrance of a building. I don't mind telling you I was quite afraid by that time."

"Did you consider confronting the person?" I asked.

Taking a large gulp of brandy, Forbes—whose courage appeared to be much fortified by alcohol—stared glumly at me and said: "I tried to do so. You see, I was afraid, but I was also angry. I am not the trembling coward some people think I am. So I turned around and started walking right toward the person."

"And what effect did this have?" Holmes inquired.

Forbes puffed up his chest, as though impressed by his own unlikely courage, and said proudly: "The person ran away the minute I started to approach! That is when I also noticed something most peculiar."

"And what was that?"

Forbes paused, scratched the back of his head, and said: "You will probably think me crazy, Mr. Holmes, but I am sure I saw a long skirt flaring out beneath the person's coat. I do not mind telling you that I was astonished, because the way the person ran, with a long and powerful stride, I'd swear it was a man!"

Holmes sat upright in his chair, gave Forbes a long hard look, and said: "I wish you to be very clear, sir. Are you telling us that the person following you appeared to be a man dressed in woman's clothing?"

Forbes blushed, as though the very idea of such aberrant behavior was an embarrassment to him. "I know how bizarre it sounds, Mr. Baker, but yes, that is how it looked to me. Is such a thing possible?"

"I have no doubt that it is," said Holmes. "Indeed, I think I can say with complete confidence that your shadow is a man by the name of Billy Bouquet, who is well known to both Mr. Smith and myself. Do you happen to know this gentleman, Mr. Forbes?"

"No, though I think I've heard the name. Isn't he a criminal of some sort?"

"He is, and a very dangerous one at that, despite his delightfully aromatic cognomen and his taste for women's apparel." Holmes then went on to describe Bouquet and our earlier encounter with him in some detail.

Mrs. Riley, who had listened attentively to Holmes, now posed an excellent series of questions: "Can anyone tell me why on earth this despicable man Bouquet would be following Freddie? Is he looking for something? Is he just being a nuisance? Or does he wish to do Freddie some harm? And if so, why?"

"I fear, madam, that I cannot at the moment provide a good answer to any of those questions," Holmes admitted, "but you may be assured that I intend to find the answers and to find them quickly. Tell me, Mr. Forbes, did this man-dressed-as-a-woman follow you this morning when you came to see us?"

"Oh yes. I guess that is why I was so, well, so upset. I am sure I caught a glimpse of him as I came up the hill toward Summit. It was broad daylight, of course, and this time he was much farther back. But I am positive it was the same person."

"Well, whoever your shadow is, Freddie, he ain't around at the moment," announced Rafferty, who had returned just in time to hear Forbes's last words. "I shuffled out onto Summit and did a little nosin' about. Went around to the back of the house too. Didn't see a thing, except for one of Mr. Hill's servants tryin' to steal a kiss from a rather saucy little maid out on the porch. I'll tell you this, though, Mr. Holmes: It must be forty degrees out there and heading for at least fifty unless I'm wrong. 'Tis a regular January heat wave, and if you're intendin' to solve this ice palace business, you'd best be quick about it. With that sun shinin' the way it is, the palace won't be standin' much longer, and that's a fact!"

"Thank you, Mr. Rafferty, for that meteorological update," said

Holmes with a grin. "Incidentally, while you were on the watch for spooning servants, we learned that the shadow trailing Mr. Forbes is your old acquaintance Billy Bouquet."

"Well, now, ain't that interestin'," Rafferty said. "That little weasel seems to have his paw marks all over this dirty business. I guess we'll just have to turn over whatever rock he's hidin' under these days and then squeeze what we can out of him."

"My thoughts exactly," said Holmes. "However, I do not think we need go looking under rocks for Bouquet. Instead, we shall let him come to us."

"What do you mean?" Forbes asked.

"That will become clear soon enough," said Holmes, walking over to the young man and gripping him firmly by the shoulders. "Now, sir, listen very carefully to what I am about to say, because your life may depend on it. . . ."

Half an hour later, Holmes and I were strolling down Summit Avenue, dodging icy pools of water which had formed at every intersection like tiny alpine lakes, fed by dirty gray "mountains" of melting snow. Holmes was in a talkative mood, for he had just set in motion a plan which he believed would bring us at last to the bottom of the ice palace mystery. After giving Forbes a detailed set of instructions for the night ahead and sending him on his way, Holmes had then repeated his promise to Laura Riley that we would visit her husband in jail.

Rafferty, who of course knew the sheriff of Ramsey County quite well, volunteered to arrange the interview. This was agreeable to Mrs. Riley, who said she would accompany Rafferty to the jail. First, however, Holmes had taken Rafferty aside and questioned him closely about the disturbing incident involving Thomas, his bartender. Holmes also expressed concern about the fact that Rafferty apparently was being followed.

" 'Tis all the Bull's work for sure," Rafferty told us. "But don't worry, Mr. Holmes, I have no fear of O'Connor. I don't think the Bull will come for me."

"Why is that?"

Rafferty, who could be as infuriatingly opaque as Holmes, said: "Let's just say the Bull is not stupid. He knows what it would cost him if he were to try to do me direct harm, and I don't think he's willin' to pay that high a price. Oh, he'll bark and growl like the mangy dog he is, and he'll try to terrorize my employees, as he did with Mr. Thomas, but I don't think he's got the nerve to go any further."

"I pray you are right," said Holmes, displaying more emotion than I was accustomed to seeing from him, "but if you need any assistance, Dr. Watson and I will not hesitate to stand beside you."

Rafferty gave us one of his big, glowing smiles. "That is mighty fine of you, gentlemen, mighty fine. Now take care, and I will see you again soon."

We then said our good-byes as Rafferty and Mrs. Riley went off to visit the sheriff, none of us realizing at that moment what terrors and wonders the next forty-eight hours would bring.

It was not long after Rafferty's departure that Holmes had suggested a walk, to which I readily assented. Rafferty, we quickly discovered, had not exaggerated the warmth of the morning air. Indeed, the day was even milder than the previous one, so bright and balmy beneath a soft blue sky that we did not require overcoats. The entire city seemed energized by this sudden January thaw, and along every street, pale, smiling people had emerged from their houses to bask in the sunshine and enjoy an unlikely furlough from their wintry prison.

"What a splendid day!" I observed as we detoured around an especially large and deep puddle. We were walking east, toward Rice Park and the city's main commercial district.

"Indeed it is," agreed Holmes. "I only wish that the problems before us would melt as readily as the snow!"

"But I thought you believed that a solution is near at hand. Is that not cause for optimism?"

"Optimism, yes. Certainty, no. You see, Watson, there are still two great unknowns at the center of this whole tangled affair. The first has to do with the very nature of the crimes themselves."

"I fear you will have to explain yourself, Holmes."

"Very well, I shall try," he said amiably. "I want you to think back to one of our experiences over a year ago in Hinckley, when we were hot—perhaps I should say *very* hot—in pursuit of the Red Demon.

Do you remember, Watson, how we learned that lumbermen in the pineries use special marks to identify their product, so that logs cut by one firm will not be confused with those of another?"

"Yes. As I recall, the lumber companies put a special stamp, or mark, at the end of each log before shipping it to the sawmills. But what does that have to do with our present situation?"

"I am merely offering an analogy, Watson, so I trust you will bear with me. Now, as to these log marks, what is important to note is that no two are alike. Each logging company's stamp, in other words, is unique. Well, it is just so with murder. Every murderer puts a personal stamp on his crime, a stamp different from that of any other killer. Of course, different stamps may look quite similar, as in the Cavendish Square murders. In fact, there were slight differences, notably in the techniques used to disembowel the victims, which ultimately gave the game away."[2]

"I remember that grisly case all too well," I said. "But again, what exactly is your point?"

"My point, Watson, is that we must be very careful in the present case so that we do not commit the detective's cardinal sin, which is to proceed on the basis of a fundamentally erroneous assumption. We must keep our minds open to all possibilities, for the very nature of these murders may be different from what we suspect."

"You are being rather enigmatic," I told Holmes.

"Do not despair, Watson. If our interview with Mr. Riley proves productive, and if all goes well tonight, then I am confident you will be enlightened in short order. If we are doubly fortunate, we may also find an answer to the second unknown—the identity of the mysterious Spider. And when we find this weaver of lies, we will almost certainly find a murderer as well."

"But I thought you were fairly certain that Jedediah Lapham is the man who fits this description."

Holmes paused to light his pipe, drew in the soothing smoke, and said: "As I have already told you, I am certain of nothing. Curiously, my uncertainty stems from the paradoxical fact that the more I seem to know, the less real knowledge I seem to possess!"

"Holmes, you are talking in riddles," I responded with some exasperation.

"No, I am merely stating the facts of the situation. You see, I feel at the moment rather like a prospector wandering in a field strewn with golden nuggets of evidence. They glitter everywhere before me, so bright that I cannot possibly ignore them. One by one I pick them up and put them in my sack, which is soon heavy with treasure. You would think under such circumstances that I should be the happiest detective in the world, overjoyed that so many riches have come my way. And yet I feel no such exultation. Rather, I feel like Midas, groaning under the burden of too much gold!"

Although Holmes was in many ways the most rational of men, a thinker for whom the iron laws of logic held supreme sway, he was not without a poetic side, as evidenced by this striking speech. Indeed, he once remarked that to him, the "perfect detective" would be a "combination of Aristotle and Keats, a man who could both know the truth in his mind and feel it in his heart." Holmes always accounted himself deficient in the latter regard, which may explain why he sometimes resorted to metaphor and analogy, for I think he regarded them as ways of releasing his imagination from the constricting chains of analytical thought.

Be that as it may, I have always found myself at something of a loss when Holmes slips into one of his metaphorical moods. That was certainly the case now, and I readily confessed to Holmes that I was unsure what he meant by his talk of prospecting for gold.

Holmes looked up at the brilliant blue sky, as though searching its vast expanse for answers, and said: "What I am trying to tell you, Watson, is that Mrs. Riley may well be right about her husband. Perhaps he was set up. Perhaps all of those glittering nuggets of evidence which threaten to send him to the gallows were indeed planted. And that is why there hangs about this whole strange affair a peculiar atmosphere of unreality."

"In what sense?"

"In the sense that I am never sure, at any given point, whether I am seeing the real thing or simply a mirage created for the express purpose of misleading me. You see, I am convinced that behind everything which has happened here in the last few days there is a cunning, diabolical, and utterly ruthless intellect. It is the mind of a master manipulator, a mind able to command large events yet also capable of perceiving the subtlest nuances of the human heart. So powerful is this mind that sometimes I can almost feel the weight of it bearing down on me."

"Really, Holmes, I think you are being entirely too melodramatic."

"Perhaps," Holmes admitted with a rueful smile. "Still, I have no doubt that I am facing one of the greatest challenges of my career, Watson. Someone out there is a murderer whose every move is calculated to deceive me by the subtlest means imaginable, for his ultimate aim is to create an environment in which I will, in the end, deceive myself!"

As Holmes spoke these foreboding words, we turned down Fifth Street and reached Rice Park. This little irregular square, dominated by the massive tower of a new federal building being constructed on its north side, had been decorated with numerous ice sculptures for the Winter Carnival.[3] In our previous visits to the park, Holmes had paid little attention to these sculptures, but he now made a point of stopping to examine the pensive, elegant carving of the young woman we had noted on our first day in St. Paul. The sun beat down remorselessly on this figure, and as her melancholy face began to melt away, it almost seemed as though she had broken into tears at last.

"It is quite a remarkable piece of work," I said. "Pity that it will be gone in a day or two if this thaw keeps up."

Holmes made no reply at first. Instead, he circled silently around the figure, carefully studying its details as though he were contemplating some great treasure in the Louvre. Then he said: "One does not have to be a connoisseur, Watson, to see that this sculpture is undoubtedly the work of Mr. Dante. His genius is evident in every feature. I should be most curious to know where its inspiration lay."

"Why?"

"Let us just say that I have had a passing fancy, Watson, a little idea whispering to me. Come along. I think we shall have to stroll up to the ice palace one more time. I wish to speak to the artist himself."

After a brisk walk, we reached the palace grounds, where we found far more men at work than we had the day before. The sun was doing its best to destroy the magnificent structure, while workers were doing their utmost to save it by draping huge sheets of canvas over its moist, sun-drenched walls. This frantic activity had the look of a losing battle, however, and I wondered how much longer St. Paul's great monument to chill could withstand the sun's devastating assault.

We came up to the front gate, where the inevitable policeman stood guard. I became worried that Holmes would now precipitate another clash with the forces of law and order. Fortunately, there was to be no trouble with the police, because hardly had we arrived at the gate when Giuseppe Dante, chisel and hammer in hand, spotted us from inside the palace's courtyard.

He was busy chipping away at his gigantic sculptures of King Borealis and Vulcanus Rex, but when he saw us he dropped his tools at once.

"Mr. Baker," he called out, rushing toward us. "I wish, if you please, to talk to you."

"Good morning," said Holmes as Dante came through the gate. "I trust all of your excellent work has not melted away."

"No, Borealis and Vulcanus and their friends, they will survive today, I am sure, but tomorrow"—he gave a dramatic shrug of his shoulders—"who can say?"

To my surprise, Dante then dropped his voice to a whisper and, at the same time, grasped Holmes by the arm and began leading him away from the gate. "You will pardon me," he said, "but there is something important I must tell you, and I do not wish the police to hear."

"Very well," said Holmes, who seemed amused by the Italian's almost conspiratorial manner. "Let us go for a short walk, and you can speak freely."

Once we had gotten well clear of the gate, Dante looked around to make sure no one else was near, and said: "Mr. Baker, I know you are a great detective, and that is why I have been thinking since yesterday of coming to you. But now the good Lord"—here Dante made a quick sign of the cross—"has seen to it that you have come to me."

"I am not sure the Lord deserves the credit, Mr. Dante, but I will take your word for it," said Holmes. "Now, what is it you wish to tell us?"

"Something for your ears only," said the sculptor, his eyes still darting in every direction as though he expected a police spy to appear at any moment. "It concerns Michael Riley, the man the police have arrested. You see, I know that he did not murder Jonathan Upton."

CHAPTER
18

I FEAR THAT HE HAS FINALLY
TAKEN HIS REVENGE

As it turned out, any hope that the Italian might possess some concrete and compelling evidence in Riley's favor was quickly dashed. Instead, all he could offer was what might be called the evidence of character.

"When I hear that Mr. Riley has been arrested, I cannot understand it," Dante told us, shaking his head in disgust. "I think, have the big bosses of this city gone mad at last? Why else do they wish to hurt so fine a gentleman? It is most terrible, I tell you, and the police, they should be ashamed. Mr. Riley, he is a man of great passion, a man who is not afraid to fight. But a murderer? *Mai! Mai!*"

"Never," Holmes translated for me.

Dante nodded and said: "Yes, that is what I say. Never could Mr. Riley do such a bad thing. His heart, it is too big and kind to be that of a killer. You must believe me when I say this."

"I respect your beliefs," said Holmes softly. "But you must understand, Mr. Dante, that your testimony would mean nothing in a court of law. To say that Mr. Riley could never kill because you have found him to be such a good man is not evidence, and it is evidence alone that will decide his fate."

Dante was unswayed by such legal arguments. Placing both hands on his chest, as though about to recite a sacred pledge, he said: "My heart, it is the only evidence I need! The only evidence! And my heart tells me that Mr. Riley would not sneak about in the night like some common criminal and murder men. He is a man of honor, a man of dignity. I would be proud for him to marry my daughter. That is how much I believe in him."

"You obviously are very fond of Mr. Riley," Holmes said sympathetically. "Has he done you favors in the past?"

"He has done me the best favor of all," replied Dante with great fervor. "He has shown me respect. I ask for nothing else in this world. Mr. Riley, he has been good to me in other ways also. The bosses, the big men with their fancy suits, they argue about money all the time, accuse me of bad things. Never was Mr. Riley like that. When the money disappeared, he did not come to me with blame in his eyes, the way the big men did. He—"

Dante suddenly stopped and put one hand to his mouth, like a child who has just blurted out a naughty word. It was too late, however, for Holmes had caught the blunder.

"Ah, now you have piqued my interest, sir. Tell me about the missing ten thousand dollars."

A look of painful astonishment overtook Dante's features. "But how . . . how do you know of that?"

"A better question, Mr. Dante, might be how *you* came to know of it. I am also curious as to why you made no mention of it previously."

Dante let out a long, sad sigh and cast his eyes to the heavens. Then he looked back at Holmes and said: "You are very smart, Mr. Baker. Too smart for a simple man like me. All right, I will tell you about the money, but you must promise you will not use anything I say against Mr. Riley."

"You have my word on that, Mr. Dante. Now let us hear about the money."

The sculptor glanced around again to make sure we could not be overheard. It was an unnecessary precaution, since we were standing a good fifty yards away from the front gate of the palace and there was no one nearby. Satisfied that we were safe from eavesdroppers, Dante began his story:

"It was about two weeks ago that this happened, before the Upton boy disappeared. Mr. George Upton, he comes to the ice palace one afternoon. He is very excited, very angry, and he wishes to talk to Mr. Riley at once. At least, this is what some of the workers tell me later. Me, I do not see Mr. Upton at all that day. I only hear him."

"Why is that?" Holmes asked.

"Because I was in my workroom behind the rotunda, sharpening my tools. I cannot see into the rotunda, but I can hear voices very well. The ice, you see, it does not hold sound the way it holds light, so I cannot help but hear what Mr. Riley and Mr. Upton are saying."

"I understand," said Holmes. "Now, what did you hear?"

"It is an argument, a very big argument over money. Mr. Upton, he has been checking the account books, and there is money missing. Ten thousand dollars, that is the number I hear. Mr. Riley, he says he knows nothing of such a thing. His accounts, he says, are in order. Mr. Upton, however, is not so sure, and the two of them, well, they have many angry words. I do not recall them all."

"But as you understand it, Mr. Upton at some point accused Mr. Riley of theft. Is that correct?"

"Yes. He is not the only one who stands accused, however. Mr. Upton, he even suggests I have been taking money. Do you know what he says?"

"Please tell us, Mr. Dante."

"He says: 'Watch that wop ice carver of yours, Mr. Riley. You can never trust a wop.'" Dante's features seemed to compress and harden under the painful assault of this bitter memory, and I could see he was near tears. "Imagine such hateful words! Imagine what I feel! At that moment, I decide I must go and tell Mr. Upton to his shameful face what I think of him. But I do not. I do not because Mr. Riley, he speaks for me. He says—and these are words I will never forget so long as I live—he says: 'I will tolerate no name-calling here. Mr. Dante is a fine artist and a gentleman, and I trust him absolutely.' That is what he says. So if you wonder why I wish to speak up for Mr. Riley, well, now you know."

I could not help but be moved by this extraordinary testimonial, and even Holmes appeared to be struck by the Italian's passion and sincerity. Still, there was business to attend to, and Holmes did not ignore it.

"You have told us, sir, how you reacted to Mr. Upton's allegations against you. But what of Mr. Riley? He, too, was accused of theft. What was his response?"

"What do you think?" Dante said with a shrug. "He is very upset. He says if Mr. Upton wishes to accuse him of anything, he must have his facts straight. Oh yes, he is very mad, and who can blame him?"

"Indeed. Did Mr. Riley say anything else?"

Dante thought for a moment. "Yes, there is one thing, and this, too, I remember exactly. He tells Mr. Upton: 'Maybe you should ask your partner for an accounting.' "

"Whom did he mean by Mr. Upton's partner?"

"I assume it is Mr. Cadwallader Forbes. He and Mr. Upton, they were the big men behind the ice palace."

"What did Mr. Upton say to this?"

"Oh, he becomes even angrier and says he will have Mr. Riley's job. And Mr. Riley, he says, 'You are welcome to it.' After that, Mr. Upton goes away. That is all I know."

"I see now why you did not mention this incident before," Holmes noted. "You assumed, rightly perhaps, that it would simply give Mr. Riley another motive for murder."

Dante admitted as much with a shrug, after which Holmes turned to an entirely different line of questioning: "There is one more thing, Mr. Dante. Am I correct in assuming that you carved the statue of the young woman in Rice Park?"

For the first time, suspicion showed itself in Dante's dark eyes. "Yes," he said slowly. "It is my work."

"I must say that it is quite magnificent and certainly unlike anything else I have seen at the carnival. Tell me, what prompted you to carve so tragic a figure?"

With a look of great reluctance, Dante told Holmes: "I do not wish to talk about it, Mr. Baker. That sculpture, it is something I was hired to do."

"Really? May I ask who your client was?"

"I cannot say."

"Why is that?"

Dante appeared to be growing more uncomfortable by the moment. "Please, sir, do not ask me more about that sculpture. It is a secret I am sworn to keep. The man who hired me, he insisted no one should know his identity. That is how it must be."

Naturally, Holmes tried to press the matter further, for his curiosity was now at an extreme pitch, but Dante remained resolutely tight-lipped. "I have told you all I can," he finally said. "Now I must go back to my job, and you must go to yours, which is to save Mr. Riley from the hangman. The sculpture, please believe me, it is a matter of no importance."

"I shall be the judge of that," Holmes said, after which we bade the suddenly taciturn sculptor farewell.

Upon our return to Hill's mansion, I again asked Holmes why he was so interested in the sculpture, but he would give no good answer. Instead, he turned his attention at once to a message left by Rafferty. The Irishman had "pulled a few reluctant strings," as he phrased it, with the result that we would be granted an interview with Michael Riley at one in the afternoon. The sheriff, however, would permit us only half an hour with the prisoner, a fact which Holmes immediately bemoaned.

"There are easily a day's worth of questions I could pose to Mr. Riley," Holmes said, collapsing into a chair and immediately assuming a posture of deep thought, his brow tightly knitted in concentration. "This is a case full of strange and complex entanglements, and Mr. Riley—in one way or another—seems to have been intimately involved in all of them. Think of it, Watson. Mr. Riley was at the mysterious meeting in the ice palace on the night Jonathan Upton vanished. He was, for a time at least, a member of the Muskrat Club. He once worked under the shadowy Mr. Lapham and knows both Cadwallader and Frederick Forbes quite well. I suspect he also knows something of Billy Bouquet. And, of course, he married the woman who seems to be at the center of the entire affair. Mr. Riley is the key, Watson, the man who can unlock for us the last secrets of this case, assuming, of course, that he is not a murderer."

"Come now, Holmes, surely you do not believe, after what Miss For—I mean Mrs. Riley—has told us, that he can be guilty of these murders. I think it obvious he is an innocent man!"

Holmes smiled, in that sometimes infuriating way of his, and said: "Watson, you are a man insensible to the wiles of the fair sex, as the lovely jack pine twins demonstrated not so long ago.[1] You believe Mrs. Riley because she is young and beautiful and full of passion and because you are inclined to view women as vessels of purity uncorrupted by the dark, wicked workings of this world. If only it were so! Mrs. Riley may, in fact, have been entirely truthful with us, or she may not. In either case, her husband has much to explain and little time to do it. You see, Watson, I do not assume innocence or guilt until all the facts are established. Only then will I know whether Mr. Riley must be saved from the gallows or sent to them!"

I was about to protest, but Holmes put one finger to his lips and shook his head. "Not now, my dear Watson, not now. I must make my preparations for our interview with Mr. Riley. Call me when it is time to leave."

"Very well," I said, knowing that Holmes wished to be alone. "Still, I am curious about one thing. What is the one question you would most like to put to Mr. Riley?"

Holmes's answer was quite unexpected: "I should like to know, Watson, how construction debris is removed from the grounds of the ice palace."

At precisely five minutes to one, Holmes and I arrived at the Ramsey County Jail after a brief but vigorous walk through the still gathering warmth of the day. The jail was a squat, graceless structure of dirty gray stone, which appeared to be among St. Paul's oldest buildings. Occupying a small plot of land at one corner of the much more grandiose city hall and county courthouse, the jail had the look of a poor stepchild long ignored by its parents. Bent and rusted window bars, crumbling stonework, great zigzagging wall cracks, and a roof which sagged noticeably over the front entrance all testified to an irreversible history of neglect. Indeed, so palpable was the sense of gloom and abandonment conveyed by this decayed wreck of a building that it seemed to suggest there could be no hope for its unfortunate occupants.[2]

We found Rafferty waiting for us within, looking as jolly as ever in a bright plaid suit and an almost incandescent red waistcoat. After receiving passes from the guard at the front desk, we were escorted down a long, dank hallway with cells to either side. Flickering gas jets and a few small windows provided the only light in this dreary passageway, and as we walked past inmates sitting dejectedly in their cells I was reminded of the grim confines of Dartmoor.[3] At the very end of the hall, our escort—a huge, surly guard with a fat ring of keys dangling from his belt—unlocked a heavy iron door, which led to a steep set of stairs going down to the basement. Here, we followed another dismal corridor, its ceiling arched in the manner of a catacomb, until we reached a second door, which was even more massive than the first. Only when this door was opened, creaking and groaning as though it had not been moved in ages, did we find Michael Riley.

Wrapped in an old blanket, he lay on a small cot, the only item of furniture in the tiny cell which had now become his unwelcome home. At the sound of the door opening, he came instantly to life, and when he saw Rafferty he broke out in a broad smile.

"God, Shad, it's good to see you," he said, springing to his feet and giving our friend a warm hug. "I'm going crazy in this place. Tell me, how is Laura?"

"Your wife is fine," Rafferty said, returning Riley's display of affection with a crushing bear hug of his own. "She thinks of you every minute, lad, and she's devoted herself to gettin' you out of this rat hole. That is why she's engaged these English gentlemen"—he gestured toward Holmes and me—"to help you."

Rafferty then made the appropriate introductions—Holmes was described simply as "a man with great experience in criminal matters"—after which Riley grasped our hands eagerly and promised he would tell us whatever we wished to know.

For some reason, I had formed an image in my mind as to Riley's appearance, thinking he would be one of those big, powerful Irishmen of the sort represented by our friend Rafferty and Chief of Detectives O'Connor. In the flesh, however, Riley looked nothing like what I had imagined. He was actually on the short side, with a compact and sinewy build such as one often sees in acrobats. He had a lean, angular face punctuated by full lips, a rather thick nose, and close-set eyes the color of pewter, all capped by an unruly mass of curly red hair. Despite his small stature, there was nothing soft or delicate about him. Rather, he reminded me of those tough, wiry cavalrymen I had known in Afghanistan—men who were quick to act, gifted with amazing endurance, and much stronger than their size might otherwise indicate.

It was easy to see why incarceration was causing him to "go crazy," as he told Rafferty, for the tiny cell in which he resided had the atmosphere of a medieval dungeon. Looking almost as though it had been carved out of bedrock, the cell could not have been more than eight feet on a side, and it had but one small window—heavily barred and set high up in one corner—to admit natural light. A single gas jet provided additional illumination, but it glowed so weakly that it was hardly of any use. The cell was also extremely damp and chilly, so much so that I found myself wishing I had brought my heavy coat. In such a cold, dim, and isolated environment, a man might quickly lose his hope and his nerve. Fortunately, Riley appeared to remain in full possession of both.

"I must tell you that I am absolutely innocent of all these charges," he said in a surprisingly deep voice. "I have been framed, as anyone who knows me must realize."

Holmes received this avowal without expression and motioned Riley, who was dressed in drab prison garb beneath his blanket, to sit down on the cot. Riley did so, all the while regarding Holmes with bright, expectant eyes.

"Let us get down to business at once," said Holmes, who now began to pace in his usual manner, though the cramped confines of the cell gave him little room to maneuver. "I accept your expression of innocence, Mr. Riley, but it means nothing in and of itself, nor will it mean much to twelve jurors good and true should they be asked to decide your fate. Therefore, what I want from you, sir, are specifics, and as we have but half an hour for this interview, I must ask you to answer my questions quickly and succinctly. Some of my questions may strike you as odd, but please believe me when I tell you that there is a carefully calculated purpose to every one of them. Now, are you ready to begin?"

"I am," said Riley, his face displaying a mixture of hope and anxiety.

Holmes started his interrogation with the most basic of questions: "Do you have an alibi, Mr. Riley, for the night Jonathan Upton disappeared, say from midnight to dawn?"

"I was alone in my apartment, sleeping," Riley replied. "I—"

"You have answered the question. There is no need to tell me more. And as for the night on which George Upton disappeared, you have as an alibi only the testimony of your spouse. Is that correct?"

"Why, yes, but—"

"Then I fear it is no alibi at all," said Holmes, "for it is commonly thought that a wife will think nothing of lying for her husband."

Holmes followed with a rapid series of questions, jumping so abruptly from one topic to another that Riley hardly had time to think. I knew, however, that there was a cunning method behind the apparent disorder of Holmes's interrogation, for he believed in keeping a subject "off balance," as he put it, to the maximum degree possible. In this regard, I will never forget what Holmes told me after the Masterman stock fraud case, which featured perhaps his most brilliant achievement in interrogation: "Lying, unless it is an inborn and carefully cultivated habit, requires perfect concentration and great anticipation. But if you keep a man off balance, he will almost always tumble into the truth, no matter how hard he tries to avoid it."[4]

Among other things, Holmes asked Riley about his relationship with Jonathan Upton ("I did not hate him, but I did not care much for him either"), his feelings toward Cadwallader Forbes ("I hold nothing against the man, but I believe he should have shown more respect for his daughter's wishes"), and his dealings with Jedediah Lapham ("We got along well enough, but I could never figure out exactly what he did or how he did it"). Holmes also inquired about Riley's "investigation," at the behest of his wife-to-be, into the horrible activities at the Muskrat Club ("I am still appalled by what I learned," he told us) and asked whether Riley knew anyone with the nickname of Spider (he did not).

There was nothing unexpected in any of these responses, as far as I could tell. It was only when Holmes switched to another line of inquiry and asked about the damning evidence found in Riley's apartment that we received a surprise. Riley, of course, insisted that he had been set up, but he then offered an interesting theory as to who might have planted the incriminating items.

"My guess is that it is the work of a man named Billy Bouquet," he told Holmes. "He is a vicious character, and he harbors a grudge against me."

"Why is that?" asked Holmes, who by a slight lifting of his eyebrows showed that he was quite intrigued by this revelation.

"It is a rather long story," said Riley.

"Then tell it quickly," Holmes prodded.

"Well, it all goes back to last fall. That's when I ran across Bouquet for the first time. He tried to run a protection racket on me while I was superintending a big construction project in Lowertown. Bouquet told me he represented a syndicate of men who would protect my workers from any 'accidents'—that was his word—on the job. He wanted two hundred dollars a month for this 'service,' as he called it."

"What was your response, Mr. Riley?"

For the first time during our visit, Riley became visibly angry. He said: "Why, I told Bouquet he'd rot in hell before he saw one red cent from me. I also told him that if he ever dared approach me again, he'd be sorry for it. I used some other words as well, but I would not wish to repeat them among gentlemen such as yourself."

"I see," said Holmes, who appeared to regard Riley with new respect following this display of righteous indignation. "What happened next?"

"Bouquet left, but not before warning me to be careful. I remember his words very well. He said: 'Accidents happen all the time to men who aren't careful and who don't pay up their insurance.' I took this as a direct threat and acted accordingly. I have a Colt revolver, and I began carrying it with me day and night, suspecting that Bouquet would seek to ambush me. Two nights later, up near Ninth and St. Peter, as I was on my way home, he tried to do just that. Coward that he is, he'd brought along a couple of friends, and the three of them attempted to knock me down and drag me into an alley. They intended to cut me — Bouquet had already drawn out a long knife — but I had the barrel of my Colt tickling his forehead before he could do anything. I told him his friends had five seconds to leave, or I would blow him to kingdom come."

Rafferty, who appeared to relish this story greatly, said with a big grin: "They must have left, Michael, me boy, because Bouquet is still among the livin'."

Riley nodded and even managed a small chuckle. "You're right about that, Shad. The two of them took off, so then it was just Billy and me, and I don't mind telling you that I was up for a fight. I took Bouquet's knife and threw it down a sewer drain, put my pistol back in my pocket, and told him that if he wanted to take me on, now was his chance. As it turned out, this was a foolish thing to do, because, quick as lightning, Bouquet whipped out another knife and came right at me!"

I recalled, of course, that Bouquet had also carried two knives during his aborted attack on Holmes, who now said: "I presume it was shortly thereafter that Mr. Bouquet lost his ear."

Riley gave Holmes a look of stunned disbelief. "How did you know that?"

"Let us just say that I had an encounter with Mr. Bouquet recently and noted that his missing ear was the result of a fairly recent misadventure."

"Well, you are right. We fought over the knife, and somehow or other, one of Bouquet's ears got sliced clean off."

"I suppose he was not a happy man at that moment," Rafferty observed.

"He was not," Riley confirmed. "He ran off, blood pouring down the side of his head, all the while screaming that he would 'get' me in one way or another. Now I fear that he has finally taken his revenge."

"Am I to conclude from this that you believe Mr. Bouquet murdered the two Uptons?" Holmes asked.

"Either that or he knows who did," Riley replied. "I'd bet on one or the other. And, of course, I know he was acquainted with Jonathan, because they were seen together at least once near the Muskrat Club."

Holmes nodded and said: "Your lovely wife mentioned that fact to us, Mr. Riley. Incidentally, did you ever report Mr. Bouquet's attack upon you to the police?"

"I saw no point in it. It's common knowledge that Bouquet is protected by the police and pretty much does what he wants in this city."

"So it would seem," agreed Holmes, taking out his watch and glancing at it. I did likewise and estimated that we had less than ten minutes left with Riley. Holmes said: "You have been most helpful, sir, and I shall trouble you with only a few more matters. First, let us return to the night of Jonathan Upton's disappearance. There was a meeting that evening in the ice palace, was there not?"

"There was."

"Who was at this meeting?" Holmes, of course, already knew the answer to this question, but I assumed that he asked it in order to test Riley's veracity.

Riley paused briefly and rubbed his forehead. "Let's see. I guess there were four of us. Myself, George Upton, Cadwallader Forbes, and Chief of Detectives O'Connor."

"Who called the meeting?"

"Mr. Upton. I saw him that afternoon, and he said he wished to meet at nine or so to see how the palace was standing up to all the warm weather."

"Did you find it at all surprising that he wished to meet at night?"

"Not really. You see, if you get a warm night where the temperature doesn't drop below freezing, that's when you start to worry with ice. On a warm day you naturally expect some melting, but if everything freezes that night, then you're usually all right. So I just assumed Mr. Forbes wanted to look over the palace to see how much melting had taken place and to talk about what, if anything, we could do about it."

"I see. Did you also expect Cadwallader Forbes and Mr. O'Connor to attend this meeting?"

"Mr. Forbes and Mr. Upton always worked closely together on palace matters, so I cannot say I was surprised to see old Cad. But I had no idea at first why O'Connor showed up."

Holmes instantly stopped his pacing, turned to look directly at Riley, and said: "You say 'at first.' I take it, then, that the reason for Mr. O'Connor's presence soon became apparent."

"It did. But I do not see —"

"Allow me to do the seeing, Mr. Riley, if you would," interrupted Holmes. "Your only job at the moment is to answer my questions. Now, why was Mr. O'Connor called to the ice palace that night?"

Riley glanced over at Rafferty, like a defendant appealing to a higher court, but he won no relief. Rafferty said: "Just answer Mr. Baker's question, Michael. He has good reason for askin' it, and believe me, he's not tryin' to incriminate you."

"All right, if you must know, O'Connor was there because Mr. Upton believed that Cadwallader Forbes had stolen ten thousand dollars from the ice palace construction fund."

19

SOMETHING TERRIBLE HAS HAPPENED

Riley's surprising disclosure must have incited in Holmes a tremendous stirring of interest, but he gave no evidence of his excitement. Instead, he gazed down at the floor, as though fascinated by its random pattern of stones, and said:

"That is most intriguing, Mr. Riley. But tell me, was Cadwallader Forbes the only person upon whom Mr. Upton's suspicion fell?"

I thought this an odd question, but I soon realized that Holmes must be once again putting Riley's honesty to the test. We already knew, from our interview with Dante, that George Upton had at one point accused Riley of stealing the money. Would Riley now admit as much?

To my relief, he did. "I will not mislead you," he told Holmes. "George Upton for a time thought that I had embezzled the ten thousand dollars."

"I see. What led him to suspect you?"

"I'm not certain. Perhaps he thought that because I dealt with so many subcontractors and suppliers, I must therefore be the person who was fiddling with the books. Of course, I told him at once that the very idea was absurd, since the final bookkeeping was not in my hands. I also pointed out that if I had been trying to skim away a bit of money, it would have been noticed immediately."

"By Mr. Upton?"

"No, by Mr. Forbes. You see, it was to his office that I sent all bills, invoices, and the like. Mr. Forbes then made payments as necessary from the ice palace fund. That was the arrangement from the very start of construction."

"To your knowledge, did Cadwallader Forbes personally handle these accounts?"

Riley, after a moment's thought, said: "I really can't say. I do know, however, that when I worked for Mr. Forbes on other projects, before the ice palace, it was Mr. Lapham who usually took care of the books. At least, he's the person who would come to me with questions."

"Most interesting," murmured Holmes, who had resumed his pacing, even though the size of the cell was such that he could go only about two paces in one direction before having to turn around. After a pair of these quick back-and-forth trips, he said to Riley: "In other words, you made it clear to Mr. Upton in every way you could that if there was fraud, it had to be occurring in Mr. Forbes's office."

"I'm sure I was not quite that blunt about it," Riley said, offering a slight smile. "But yes, I did let Mr. Upton know that he needed to look at his partner's books if he suspected someone had a hand in the till."

"Did that convince him to look elsewhere for the culprit?"

Riley sighed, shook his head, and said: "It did. Unfortunately, his next suspect was poor Mr. Dante, the ice carver. You see, George Upton, like many men of his class, distrusted all 'foreigners,' as he called them. I always had the feeling that he barely tolerated me simply because I was not born in this country. He especially disliked immigrants from the southern regions of Europe. To him, they were all lazy and shifty-eyed. I finally had to stand up and tell him that it was utterly ridiculous to point the finger of blame at Mr. Dante, who worked strictly for wages and would have had no means of embezzling funds."

"Good for you," said Rafferty, adding: "Young Michael's description of Mr. Upton's prejudices is all too accurate. If you weren't a jut-jawed Yankee whose forebears landed on the *Mayflower* and scraped their shins on Plymouth Rock, then you weren't to be trusted."

"And yet he hired you, Mr. Rafferty," Holmes noted with a grin.

"So he did," admitted our friend. "Maybe he thought I looked enough like a Pilgrim to be one."

This moment of levity coaxed a laugh even from Riley, who had found little enough amusement in recent days. Holmes soon returned to his interrogation, however, asking Riley: "Tell me if you would, sir, how Mr. Upton reacted to your suggestion that he should make inquiries of his partner regarding possible fraud?"

"At first he refused to even entertain the idea, for he had long enjoyed a close relationship with Mr. Forbes. The two of them, as I am sure you know, had had business dealings together for many years. But it finally dawned on Mr. Upton where the truth must lie."

"How do you know this?"

"Because of something he told me the day before the big meeting in the ice palace. He came up to me that afternoon and apologized for his accusation. I accepted his apology, though I was still rather hot under the collar about the whole business. I then asked what he intended to do next. He wouldn't tell me, but he did say that 'Mr. Forbes will have some explaining to do,' or words to that effect."

"Did Mr. Upton say anything else?"

"No. He was not the sort to share much information with a working man such as myself. It was not until the next night, in the ice palace, that I learned what his suspicions were."

"How did the matter come up?"

"Mr. Upton got right to it as soon as O'Connor put in his appearance. Indeed, I think the supposed reason for the meeting—to consider what to do about excessive melting of the palace—was nothing but a pretext. Mr. Upton really wanted to question Mr. Forbes about the missing money."

"And he did so, I take it?"

"Oh yes, and I don't mind telling you it got very hot between the two of them. Mr. Upton tried his best not to sound too accusatory and was very careful about how he stated his suspicions. But it didn't do him any good, because Mr. Forbes became so outraged at the merest hint of wrongdoing that he could scarcely control himself. Mr. Upton, who had quite a temper himself, then got his dander up, and that's when things got downright nasty. For a while I thought the two of them would pull a John L. Sullivan right there, which would have been pretty comical for men of their age."[1]

"No doubt," said Holmes. "Now, can you be more specific as to how Mr. Forbes responded to the allegations from his old friend?"

"Well, once he got over his urge to punch Mr. Upton in the chops, he said that his books were no secret and that Mr. Upton could examine them anytime he chose and even take them to an auditor if he wanted to. After that, Mr. Forbes said, he would expect an immediate apology, but in any event, their relationship was over. Mr. Upton said that was fine by him and he would come by the next day to inspect the ledgers."

"Which it appears that he did," Holmes noted, "although he may not have looked at the ledgers immediately, since his son disappeared that same day." Turning to another topic, Holmes now said: "I am curious about Mr. O'Connor's presence at the meeting. Did he have anything to say when Mr. Upton made his allegations?"

"Not a word. To tell you the truth, I think he would have preferred to be somewhere else. I imagine that from his point of view, Mr. Upton's accusation was nothing but trouble, with him standing square in the middle of it."

"I am still a bit puzzled as to why the chief was brought in," said Holmes. "Were he and Mr. Upton friends?"

"I don't think so. My guess is that Mr. Upton brought O'Connor along for display purposes, as it were, to show Mr. Forbes that he was serious about his allegations."

Rafferty now weighed in with a question. "What about Mr. Upton himself? Was he satisfied with Mr. Forbes's offer to let him inspect the books?"

"Not by a long shot," Riley said. "By that time, the argument had gotten so vicious and personal that Mr. Upton was out for blood. I remember he turned to O'Connor and told the chief he expected a complete investigation by the police."

"How did Mr. O'Connor respond to this request?" Holmes asked.

"As I said, the Bull didn't want a thing to do with the whole business. But he was in a corner, and he finally said he would agree to look into the matter if Mr. Upton wished to sign a formal complaint."

"And did Mr. Upton wish to do so?"

"He did. Or at least, he said he did. After that, Mr. Forbes went stomping out of the rotunda, looking like an angry bull ready to gore the first thing that got in his way. At that point, I figured there was no reason for me to stay any longer, so I got out of there as well."

"Did you also leave through the front gate?"

"No, I went out by the side gate," Riley said, confirming what the guard Melander had told us earlier. "I have a key."

Holmes's ears perked up at these words. "Who else, Mr. Riley, has a key to the side gate?"

Riley stopped a moment to think. "Let's see. I know several of my foremen and workers have them. Keys were also given to the night guard, of course, and to the police. I don't know if Mr. Upton and Mr. Forbes had keys, but they could have gotten them simply by asking."

"Very well. Now, let us go back one more time to the meeting in the ice palace. You have mentioned how you and Mr. Forbes left the grounds. What about Mr. Upton and Chief O'Connor? Did you see either of them leave?"

"No. I guess they must have stayed and talked awhile."

Holmes was about to pose another question, when we heard heavy footsteps coming down the corridor outside the cell.

"Must be the guard," Rafferty said. "If you've got anything else you want to tell us, Michael, now's the time."

"I only wish to restate my complete innocence," Riley said with what struck me as convincing earnestness. "I have murdered no one and will say so to the very end, even if they put the noose around my neck."

The footsteps stopped, and then we saw the guard's dull, beefy face through a small slot in the cell door. "Time's up," he said. "Riley, you stay on that bunk while I open the door, or there'll be plenty of trouble. All right, gentlemen, come out one at a time so I can see you."

After a moment of fumbling with his keys, the guard turned the lock, and the thick iron door slowly began to swing open.

"You two go first," Holmes said to Rafferty and me. "I still have one more question for Mr. Riley."

While Holmes asked his final question, Rafferty and I—after assuring Riley that we would do everything possible to establish his innocence—went out into the corridor.

The guard then summoned Holmes, who ignored him and continued to speak in hushed tones to Riley. Only after the guard had begun to make dire threats with his truncheon did Holmes finally go, leaving poor Riley alone again as the door shut behind us like the closing of a tomb.

I felt a tremendous sense of relief when we at last got back out of the dank miseries of the jail and into the afternoon sunshine.

"What was your last question to Riley?" I asked Holmes as the three of us began walking up Cedar Street.

"The question I mentioned to you earlier, Watson. I asked Mr. Riley how debris was taken from the ice palace while it was being built."

Rafferty said: "A good question, Mr. Holmes. I suppose you're wonderin' just how Johnny Upton's corpse got taken to the dump."

"You are correct, my friend, as usual," Holmes replied. "Mr. Riley told me that debris, including a large quantity of waste wood and the like, was usually taken out in large wagons. Canvas was placed over the piled debris to keep it from blowing or falling off the wagons as it was being transported. I would be willing to wager that it was in just such a wagon that Jonathan Upton's headless corpse was transported to the city dump. If so, we are in possession of a significant clue."

"Why do you say that?" I asked. "There must have been many wagons that hauled away debris."

"Undoubtedly there were," said Holmes. "Yet haulers, I would think, could not simply have come and gone as they pleased from the palace. The trade must have been regulated in some way. Indeed, I was trying to question Mr. Riley on this point when that thug of a guard intervened. Still, if we can find records of who hauled debris and when, then we may be able to discover exactly which wagon carried young Upton's corpse."

"I'll look into it," Rafferty said, adding: "There's another thing worth thinkin' about. If Johnny got taken away in a wagon from the palace grounds, then his murder almost certainly had to have been an inside job, if you see what I mean."

"I'm not sure I follow you," I said.

"What I'm sayin', Dr. Watson, is that whoever killed the lad had to have had regular access to the palace grounds, so that there'd be no suspicion if somebody saw him loadin' up a wagon there."

"You make a good point, Mr. Rafferty," said Holmes. "Unfortunately, it appears that just about every suspect in this affair had easy access to the grounds."

A startling idea, or so it seemed, now occurred to me. "Is it possible the elder Upton's body, after his murder, was transported in the same way as his son's?"

"Not exactly," Rafferty told me, "as I'm sure Mr. Holmes will be happy to explain."

He was. Said Holmes: "What Mr. Rafferty is too modest to tell you, Watson, is that he and I have come to the same conclusion in this regard, which is that George Upton's body was taken to the ice palace in an enclosed cart of the kind used for collecting and transporting night soil."

I could not help but react with revulsion to this revelation, for even after death a man deserves to be treated with dignity.

" 'Twasn't pretty," Rafferty agreed, "but it was simple and efficient. You see, Dr. Watson, city ordinance requires that all night soil removed from privy vaults or latrines must be transported in a completely enclosed cart so as to lessen odors and the possibility of a spill on the streets. My friend Dr. Morrison, the coroner, told me that traces of excrement were discovered on George Upton's body. Mr. Holmes noticed the same thing when the two of you found the poor man's corpse."

"Indeed, a night-soil cart is in many ways the perfect vehicle for the clandestine removal of a corpse," Holmes noted. "The carts are commonly seen about the city after dark, and no one pays them much heed. Equally important, no one—least of all the average policeman walking his beat—is at all interested in inspecting their contents."[2]

"Can't blame them," said Rafferty, holding two fingers to his nose. "In my days of poundin' the pavement, I always gave those carts a wide berth."

"A sensible decision," said Holmes with a smile. "Incidentally, I should mention something else Mr. Rafferty alerted me to. He tells me there has been a scandal in the scavenging business in St. Paul in recent years. There are allegations that criminals control the trade, which can be surprisingly lucrative since so few men aspire to such an earthy occupation. I think you can now understand why Mr. Pyle was interested in the topic when we talked with him yesterday. In any case, it is said that the criminals involved in scavenging have even resorted to bribing public officials. Watson, would you care to guess the name of one of the most prominent of these criminals?"

It required no great thought to provide the answer. "Billy Bouquet," I said.

"An excellent guess. Mr. Bouquet, it seems, has a habit of turning up wherever there is criminal activity in this city. Moreover, his connections to the scavenging business mean that he might easily have had access to the grounds of the ice palace."

We had now reached the corner of Sixth and Cedar Streets, which was only two blocks from Rafferty's saloon, and our friend said: "Gentlemen, I must be on my way. I've been absent from my business too long, and I don't want the honorable drinkin' men of St. Paul to think I've abandoned them in their hour of need. But rest assured, Mr. Holmes, I'll be at the appointed place tonight at eleven-thirty sharp."

"We will see you there," said Holmes, shaking Rafferty's hand. "Good luck to you, sir, and Godspeed." I shall always remember this parting, for in the perilous hours which followed, Rafferty was to become a changed man.

In almost every criminal investigation, there is what Holmes likes to call the "point of acceleration," the moment at which events begin to speed toward their conclusion, like a river approaching the head of a great cataract. Sometimes, Holmes could feel this torrent coming on, sensitive as he was to the subtle currents of circumstance. At other times, however, even he was taken unawares by the oncoming rush. When that happened, he once confided to me, there was nothing to do but "keep your eyes open and hang on as best you can."

So it was to be with the ice palace affair, for the dramatic events into which we were soon to plunge would lead us on a tumultuous course, ending with a solution that was truly one of the most extraordinary of Holmes's career. First, however, there was a period of calm. Holmes used this respite to make several telephone calls. He also held a brief meeting with Hill, during which he recounted our interviews with Laura and Michael Riley and then advised the Empire Builder of our latest plan. After this, he went to his room to, as he put it, "occupy my hands with the *America* and my mind with the events that are to come."

These events were to center around a complicated plan which Holmes had already worked out in detail with Frederick Forbes. At midnight, Forbes was to leave his apartment at the Hotel Barteau and begin walking downtown, following a carefully plotted course. Holmes, Rafferty, and I, meanwhile, would already be concealed outside the hotel, hoping that Billy Bouquet would show himself and begin trailing Forbes. We would then follow the follower, as it were, and when the opportunity presented itself get the slippery Bouquet in our grasp.

Holmes had decided on this approach because of Bouquet's reputation as a hard man to find. Like many of St. Paul's more notorious gangsters, he maintained no permanent address but instead moved from place to place, staying with various companions in crime.

"It will be much easier if, instead of trying to track Mr. Bouquet down in one of his lairs, we let him come to us," Holmes said. "And when we have him, we will make him talk one way or the other, for there can be little doubt he was involved, to one degree or another, in the two murders."

We had left Rafferty just before two in the afternoon, and as Holmes and I walked back to Hill's mansion in contented silence, I let my mind wander over the many remarkable events which had occurred during our brief stay in St. Paul. What struck me was how time seemed to have slowed down, as though even its remorseless march through the small affairs of men had somehow been retarded by the deep chill of winter. I felt as if I had already been in St. Paul for months, when in fact it was now only the twenty-ninth of January, which meant we had spent less than a week in the city. I was still marveling over this peculiar sensation a few hours later, when the dinner bell at Hill's mansion rang, as it always did, at six o'clock.

At almost the same instant I heard another ringing—a telephone call, which turned out to be from Joseph Pyle. Holmes took the call and, moments later, met me in the hallway outside the dining room, his face taut and blanched. "Something terrible has happened at Rafferty's saloon," he said. "We must go at once, Watson. Be sure to bring your bag."

At Holmes's request, Hill always kept a carriage and a team of horses waiting for us in the event of an emergency, and so we were on our way to the saloon within five minutes. As we descended the Selby

Avenue hill, the lights of the city shining before us, Holmes quickly told me everything he had learned from Pyle in their hurried conversation over the telephone. I was aghast at the news and only prayed we could reach Rafferty in time to prevent a great catastrophe.

Our driver, who was both highly skilled and utterly fearless, took us through the busy downtown streets at breakneck speed, and Holmes gave him a princely tip when we at last arrived in front of the saloon. On a normal Wednesday night, Rafferty's establishment would have been bright and noisy, alive with the gaiety of drinking men. On this grim evening, however, the saloon had a dark and funereal appearance, with only a single dim light visible through the broad front windows. Holmes pounded on the door until George Thomas emerged out of the dimness, holding his shotgun at the ready. After a quick glance up and down the street, he let us in.

"Where are they?" Holmes asked anxiously.

"In the office behind the bar," the Negro told us. "But you'd best be careful, gentlemen. Shad's been drinking steady for an hour, and he's getting crazier with every drop of whisky. He's put on the uniform, and that always means awful trouble. Mr. Pyle hasn't been able to talk any sense into him, and neither have I."

"All right," said Holmes. "We will do what we can."

Thomas stayed by the entrance while we made our way through the empty tavern, which seemed queer and ghostly in the faint, flickering light provided by the one gas jet which had been left to burn. Behind the massive bar was a paneled door leading to Rafferty's office. The door was closed, but Rafferty's booming voice could easily be heard through it, and his words were at once ominous and heartbreaking.

"They have killed him," he cried out. "The bas---ds have killed him, and by God, I shall have their blood."

20

HE IS COLD AND DEAD, GONE FOREVER

Holmes rapped lightly on the door, and we heard another voice—Pyle's—ask who it was.

"It is Sherlock Holmes and Dr. Watson."

"Thank God," Pyle responded, opening the door. He had the haggard, desperate look of a man at wit's end, his face drained of color, his eyes red and puffy. "Shad's in a terrible state. I scarcely know what to do anymore. He says he's going to war with O'Connor, for that is who he blames, and he insists no one can stop him. I have tried to reason with him, but it's hopeless. He's been drinking for at least an hour"—an empty bottle of whisky on the floor testified to this—"and if we don't stop him, God knows what will happen."

Holmes gave a somber nod, and we went past Pyle into the office. The scene which greeted us was at once pitiful and bizarre. The office itself—a small, windowless room lit by bright incandescent lamps and furnished with a heavy oak desk, a large wooden filing cabinet, and tall bookcases against one wall—was a shambles. File drawers lay open, their contents scattered everywhere, and books had been pulled from their shelves and tossed on the floor. A miscellany of other objects—pens and pencils, a glass paperweight, a box of shotgun shells, and even the stuffed head of a buck, which Rafferty had shot in the North Woods—added to the general litter, so that the room looked as though it had been struck by one of those cyclones so common in the American Midwest.

Nothing in the room, however, could compare with the heart-rending spectacle presented by Rafferty himself. Dressed in full military regalia, he sat on a stool in the center of the room, his shoulders slumped and his head hung low in mourning. The object of his grief—the valiant bulldog John Brown—lay motionless at his feet, swathed in blankets. The beast's front legs were contorted into an unnatural position, his eyes were glassy, and his menacing jaws were wide open, as though preparing for a final attack on his master's enemies. Alas, there were to be no more battles for John Brown. In the early morning hours, someone had broken into the saloon, entered the office, where the dog kept watch, and then clubbed him to death so viciously that the back of his head was all but obscured by a hideous mass of clotted blood. All of this Holmes had learned over the telephone from Pyle. Worse yet, it was Rafferty himself who had found his beloved pet, already rigid with death, not long after leaving us outside the jail.

Rafferty had broken down into sobs upon discovering the dog's battered body, but his grief—fed by large doses of whisky—had soon given way to promises of violent revenge. By the time Pyle arrived, after a worried call from Thomas, Rafferty was vowing to "go to war" and had already donned the military apparel he now wore.

Had the circumstances not been so tragic, Rafferty's appearance might have been regarded as comical. A blue soldier's cap, decorated with the insignia of the Union, was perched atop his massive head at an angle so precarious that it seemed likely to tumble off at any moment. His dark-blue military coat, which featured a high collar and a gleaming row of brass buttons, looked equally absurd, for it was several sizes too small for a man of his considerable girth, and I could only wonder how he had managed to squeeze himself into it. I soon realized that this ill-fitting coat was in fact Rafferty's old Civil War dress uniform, last worn long ago when he and the other brave young men of the First Minnesota had gone off to fight the Confederacy. A single gleaming decoration—undoubtedly the Medal of

Honor he had won on the bloody fields of Gettysburg—was pinned to the chest of the coat, which bore on its sleeves the double stripes of a corporal.

Far more worrisome than Rafferty's apparel was the musket he held across his chest. Long and heavy, with a bayonet attached to its barrel, this weapon (as we later learned from Pyle) was the very same Springfield rifle Rafferty had carried throughout the great war. Pyle was not sure whether Rafferty had managed to prime and load the musket, but we proceeded on the assumption that it was indeed ready to fire.

Beneath the rifle, folded over Rafferty's lap, was a blue and red flag with a large X-shaped pattern of stars. I surmised, and Pyle soon confirmed, that this was the battle flag Rafferty had captured from the ill-fated Virginia regiment at the culmination of Pickett's doomed charge up Cemetery Ridge.

Holmes, of course, took in the whole melancholy scene at a glance. Advancing a few steps, he bent down and rubbed his hand over the dead bulldog's back. Then he stood up and said gently: "I am so sorry, Mr. Rafferty. I know how much you loved your John Brown."

I will never forget the haunted expression on Rafferty's face as he gazed up at Holmes. Drawn from some ancient reservoir of Celtic desolation, it was a look which told of sorrow beyond all measure. Yet there was also in his eyes at that moment the steely chill of a man prepared to kill without hesitation or remorse.

In a thick, slurred voice, Rafferty said: "Oh yes, I loved the poor beast, and look what has become of him. Look! He is cold and dead, gone forever."

"Mr. Rafferty, I—" Holmes began, but he was soon drowned out by the Irishman's bellowing voice.

" 'Twas a cowardly act," Rafferty roared, as though he wished the God of us all to hear his angry protest. Using the musket to steady himself, he rose to his feet and said: "That murderin' son of a b---h O'Connor will pay. His polluted blood will flow into the sewers of St. Paul before this night is over."

He continued his denunciation of O'Connor, in ever more extreme and violent language, for several more minutes, and so great was his emotion that I feared he might rant on all night. To my surprise, however, he abruptly grew quiet after glancing down at the

floor and noticing the battle flag, which had fallen from his lap when
he stood to speak.

He stared at the banner for a long time, as though trying to decipher some hidden meaning in its pattern of stars, and then said to
Holmes in an almost wistful way: " 'Tis the flag of the Twenty-eighth
Virginia. Oh, they were brave lads, Mr. Holmes, brave lads. I can
still see them now, comin' up the ridge in the boilin' hot sun, fallin'
one by one in the tall grass, like flowers cut down before the scythe."

Overcome by this distant memory, Rafferty paused to gaze down
once again at the flag. Then, lifting his head and looking at Holmes
with blazing eyes, he said in a much louder voice: "Do you know
how I got that flag?"

"No, Mr. Rafferty, I do not."

"Well, then, let me tell you," he said, lowering the musket and
thrusting the bayonet forward, as though attacking some phantom
enemy. "I got it by killin' one of those Virginia boys. He was even
younger than I was, I'm sure, but he was hangin' on to that flag for
dear life, coming up with his regiment toward the bloody angle.[1] The
air was filled with the sound of shoutin' men and screamin' metal—it
was hell on earth, Mr. Holmes—but the boy kept comin', and when
he got near, his eyes wild with fear, I just jumped up and stuck him.
'Twas the easiest thing I ever did, because killin' is always easy if
you've got the stomach for it. The boy—he had blue eyes, I remember, and a babyish face—he just stared at me after I slid my bayonet
into his gut. He just stood there, he did, like a statue, for you see, he
had ceased to be real at that instant, and he knew it. Then he gave a
little cry, stumbled back, took a last look down at the life spillin' out
of his insides, and fell to the ground, dead and gone, dead and gone."

Rafferty pronounced these last words almost as though they were
the refrain of some old, sad song, and tears clouded his eyes—and
mine. He then fell silent, his head drooping toward his chest. I
breathed a sigh of relief, assuming he would soon pass out, which
would have been a blessing. Instead, his head jerked up, as though
he had suddenly returned from wherever his memories had taken
him, and I once again saw cold fury in his eyes. Staggering over to
the desk, he took a drink from a second bottle of whisky and then,
without warning, hurled the bottle against the opposite wall, sending
shards of glass spraying through the room.

"A pretty story, ain't it," he said, addressing no one in particular.

"Young Shad Rafferty is made a hero for killin' some poor lad who thought he'd find glory by marchin' off to war. Well, the lad earned his glory and I earned my medal, but in the dark of night 'tis often I wonder just who got the better of that transaction."

Rafferty was swaying on his feet now, caught in an alcoholic haze of guilt and anger, and he had a lethal weapon in his hands. I realized for the first time just how dangerous the situation was—for him and for us—and I glanced over at Holmes, hoping for guidance. He gave me a quick look in return, his eyes going down to the medical bag in my hand, and I understood at once what had to be done. I was just reaching into the bag for a syringe when Rafferty started roaring again, like a huge storm catching its second wind.

"There's a lesson here, Mr. Holmes, a lesson which you must learn. You see, I am the man who cannot be killed. 'Tis my genius and my burden. Bobby Lee and the Confederate Army couldn't kill Shadwell Rafferty, nor could the bushwhackers and highwaymen infestin' every miserable hellhole between Deadwood and Virginia City. They all tried, and here I am, the man who cannot be killed. And now I intend to find out if John J. O'Connor is up to the task of killin' Shadwell Rafferty, for if he does not kill me this night, then by God I will kill him."

Bringing himself to attention, the musket at his side, he thrust out his chest, stood as straight as he could in his condition, and favored us with his final announcement of the night: "Therefore, I must ask all of you"—he made a sweeping gesture with his right arm, as though addressing a vast multitude—"to stand aside. Stand aside, I say, stand aside! Sound the tocsin, let the trumpets blare! Double time now, double time, forward into the abyss! Give 'em lead, boys, till they run home to Virginia! There is killin' to be done this night, and Shadwell Rafferty is the man to do it."

It was an astonishing scene, and I had the eerie sensation that I was watching a performance on Drury Lane and that if Pyle, Holmes, and I would only give our heartfelt applause, Rafferty might bow deeply and exit the stage with a smile.[2] Yet I also knew that Rafferty, however absurd his appearance and intentions, was deadly serious and that under no circumstances could we allow him to leave the room.

Pyle obviously felt the same way, for he moved over to block Rafferty's path to the door. "Shad, you must calm down," he pleaded. "Nothing is to be gained by going after Mr. O'Connor tonight."

It was at this moment that, as Rafferty himself might have described it, all hell broke loose. Quick and powerful as a big cat, Rafferty pounced on the startled newspaperman, who was by no means a weakling, and with only one arm literally tossed him over the desk, much as a grizzly bear might dispose of an irritating mouse.

"Now, is there anyone else who wishes to stand in my way?" Rafferty inquired, pounding the butt of his musket on the floor.

"I'm afraid I must," said Holmes, stepping forward to deliver a hard and accurate kick, which knocked the musket from Rafferty's hand and sent it clattering to the floor. Rafferty looked up in amazement at Holmes and took a quick jab in the face for his trouble. The blow, however, succeeded only in making Rafferty more irate, and with hardly a pause he came straight back at Holmes, who now saw the wisdom of retreat and began backing toward the door, like a man trying to avoid the path of a charging rogue elephant.

With Pyle still out of commission, I knew that even Holmes and I together were no match for Rafferty, and it would have gone badly for us had not Thomas, hearing the commotion, chosen this opportune moment to come running into the office.

"We must stop him," Holmes shouted as Rafferty, growling like a wounded beast, prepared to attack.

"No one will stand in my way," Rafferty thundered as he lurched forward toward the door. But Thomas was an extraordinarily strong man in his own right, and with his head down, he smashed into Rafferty like a battering ram, knocking him back several paces.

The wild scene which ensued nearly beggars description. Rafferty, whose strength was uncanny, grabbed his loyal barman by the head, like a cowboy wrestling a recalcitrant steer, and flung him against one of the bookcases. The remaining contents of the case crashed to the floor, as did Thomas himself. Meanwhile, Holmes had leaped on Rafferty's back, no doubt in the hope of knocking him off his feet. This assault from the rear did not succeed, however, and Rafferty—whose earlier boast of invulnerability was starting to appear all too true—began to spin Holmes around like a whirligig. Holmes hung on as best he could, but I feared that at any moment he might lose his grip and go smashing into the nearest wall.

I saw nothing to do but enter the fray, and so I made a dive for one of Rafferty's legs, thinking I might at least slow him down. All I earned for my efforts was a hard kick to the chest, which sent me reeling. Fortunately, Thomas—who had quickly gotten back on his feet—came to the rescue. By means of a running tackle, he was able to bring Rafferty to the floor, while Holmes somehow kept his arms around the Irishman's neck. Pyle, too, was now able to rejoin the fight, and the three of them held Rafferty down long enough for me to retrieve my bag and inject him with a massive dose of barbiturates.

Rafferty gave a sharp cry of pain and continued to struggle for several minutes, and in was only with the utmost exertion that we managed to keep him on the floor. The drug, however, inexorably took its effect, until Rafferty at last slipped into a deep sleep.

"Are you all right?" Holmes asked Pyle, who had taken a nasty cut on the forehead during his sudden flight over the desk.

"I feel like I just stepped in front of a freight train," the plucky editor of the *Globe* replied with a grin, "but I guess I'll survive. How about you, Mr. Holmes? Any serious damage?"

Fresh from our battle with Rafferty, we were sitting at the bar, where Thomas had opened the best bottle of brandy in the house and joined us for a much-needed libation.

Holmes examined his coat, which was badly torn in two places, and told Pyle: "I fear my apparel has suffered fatal injuries, but otherwise I am fine, though for a moment I felt as though I had somehow gotten on a merry-go-round gone mad. What of you, Watson? Any wounds from the great battle?"

"None that I know of," I replied. "But I don't mind telling you that Mr. Rafferty is about as strong a man as I ever hope to meet."

"I will not challenge you on that point," said Holmes, who now raised his glass and said: "Before we go any further, I propose a toast to Mr. Thomas. I am most grateful, sir, for your assistance, most grateful. I fear Mr. Rafferty would have made his escape had you not come to our aid when you did."

Thomas, who was standing behind the bar, smiled and said: "When I heard all that banging in there, I figured right away what the trouble must be, so I came running. Shad's a bear when he's been drinking. Most of the time, he stays away from old John Barleycorn because he knows what it does to him, but when he found his dog all beaten to a pulp like that, well, I just knew we was in for a hard night. I called Mr. Pyle right away, but Shad was already tossing down the whisky like there was no tomorrow. It scared me. I didn't know what he might do with all that liquor in him, especially if he went out looking for the Bull."

"You did exactly the right thing," Holmes said, "and someday Mr. Rafferty will be grateful that you did. By the way, I have a question for you, Mr. Thomas. Was the office in disarray when Rafferty found his dog, or did he, shall we say, rearrange the furnishings himself?"

"Oh no, sir, it was all torn up when Shad got there. Somebody was looking for something, that's all I can figure, and poor John Brown got in their way."

Holmes nodded and raised his glass a second time to the loyal barman. "Mr. Thomas, you have the makings of a genuine detective, for your assessment of the situation is entirely reasonable. Nonetheless, there is another, more sinister possibility, which is that whoever broke into the office did so for the express purpose of killing the dog, and the manhandling of the room's contents was merely a cover, so that it might appear John Brown had interrupted a burglary in progress."

"Why on earth would anyone wish to do that?" I asked.

Pyle provided the answer: "If Mr. Rafferty's suspicion that O'Connor or one of his henchmen killed the dog is correct, then it would have made sense for the Bull to try to make the ugly deed look like a burglary, therefore diverting suspicion from himself."

Thomas now made a remarkably acute observation: "I guess you gentlemen know your business, but here's the way I look at it. Even if the Bull didn't kill John Brown, he had to know that Shad would blame him anyhow. So if I was the Bull, I wouldn't worry much about trying to cover my tracks. I'd just kill the dog and then wait for Shad to come calling. Don't you see, that's why we had to stop Shad. The Bull is expecting him, and I don't suppose he's waiting all by his lonesome. Shad would've been a sitting duck if we'd let him out the door."

Holmes could not refute this impeccable logic. He said: "Mr.

Thomas, I believe you are right. Therefore, we must conclude that whoever killed the dog was also looking for something in Mr. Rafferty's office."

"But what?" I asked.

Holmes said: "I am not sure. However, I suspect that the burglar was searching for any evidence Mr. Rafferty might have collected in connection with the ice palace case. Tell me, Mr. Thomas, do you recall seeing a large ledger book which Mr. Rafferty acquired only recently?"

"Yes. He told me it belonged to George Upton."

"Do you know where he kept it?"

Thomas thought for a minute. "Last time I saw it, I think it was on his desk. But I'm not sure where he might have hidden it away. Maybe in the safe, though I'm not sure it would fit in there."

Holmes nodded. "Then I think we must have a look for it."

We went back into the office, where Rafferty lay sleeping on the floor beneath a blanket, and searched for the incriminating ledger book taken from George Upton's safe. It was nowhere to be found in the ransacked office, not even in Rafferty's secret floor safe, which Thomas opened for us.

"Well, it appears that the burglar got what he was looking for," Holmes said. "I fear this is a bad business all the way around."

I now went over to check Rafferty's condition. He was breathing easily, his pulse was steady, and he appeared quite comfortable.

"Our friend Mr. Rafferty is sleeping the sleep of the just," Holmes said. "How long can we expect him to remain in this blissful condition?"

"Eight hours at a minimum, I should think," I said. "I administered as large a dose of barbiturates as I dared."

"Good. Let us then consider our plans for the rest of this already fateful night." Addressing Thomas, Holmes said: "If you have no objections, sir, I should like you to stay with Mr. Rafferty until he awakens. It is possible some threat may yet be made against him, and I can think of no one better than yourself to serve as his protector."

"Don't worry," said Thomas, cradling his big shotgun. "There's a load of buckshot awaiting the first man who tries anything."

"Bravo!" said Holmes, standing up and pumping the Negro's hand. "I knew I could count on you." Then he turned to Pyle and said: "Now I must ask you, Mr. Pyle, if you also are willing to undertake further adventures tonight. Mr. Rafferty was supposed to go along with us, but that will be impossible now."

"I am always ready to assist the great Sherlock Holmes in whatever way I can," said Pyle with his usual enthusiasm and resolve. "Lead the way and I shall follow."

"Good man! All right, here is what you must do. . . ."

A light fog had begun to infiltrate the wintry darkness when we arrived, at precisely eleven-thirty, at a prearranged meeting place two blocks from the Hotel Barteau. Although the trap for Billy Bouquet was not to be sprung for another half hour, Holmes wished to have everything in place well beforehand, in case Bouquet was already lurking in the vicinity.

Our meeting place—the recessed doorway of a small brick building which stood on a short, lightly traveled street near Seven Corners— provided a good view of the hotel, a massive brick and stone structure which rose above its modest neighbors. At the rear of the hotel, on the sixth and highest floor, Holmes pointed out a single window, lit dimly as though with a candle.

"That is Mr. Forbes's apartment," he told Pyle and me. "When the light goes out, it will be time for us to move. Are both of you clear about what is to be done?"

We were, for after leaving Rafferty in the care of his loyal barman, we had returned to Hill's mansion, where Holmes had spent over two hours drilling us in every detail of his plan, which would require a good deal of intricate maneuvering.

The plan was this: Once Forbes left the hotel, the three of us were to form what Holmes called "a box" around him, all the while watching for Bouquet to begin stalking his prey. Forbes was to take a route that would lead him down toward the darker parts of the city, near the river, and it was there Holmes believed we would have our best opportunity to get the slippery Bouquet in our grasp. I was to parallel Forbes's route one block to the north. Pyle would do likewise to the south, while Holmes would take up the rear. Both Holmes and Forbes carried a police whistle, to be blown when either felt the time was ripe to converge on Bouquet.

Although Holmes seemed to view his complicated plan as foolproof, I was not so certain. We had all brought along revolvers, which would appear to give us the advantage in any confrontation with Bouquet. However, the fact that the four of us — counting Forbes — would all be a block or more apart gave me cause for concern. The fog, which seemed to be growing thicker as the night went on, only added to my worries, for it would give Bouquet an additional means of concealment.

"Perhaps we should wait for a better night," I suggested to Holmes as the appointed hour grew near. "The fog will make it difficult to track Bouquet, don't you think?"

"I agree," said Pyle. "This business could get very dicey if the fog doesn't lift."

Holmes thought otherwise. "The two of you must learn to think positively," he chided. "The fog is our friend, not our enemy, for it will help us remain concealed from Mr. Bouquet."

"I trust you are right," I replied, looking out through the fog at the window which had now become the anxious focus of our attention. After staring at the window for what seemed to be many minutes, I fumbled for my watch, knowing I would have to strike a match in order to read the time. Before doing so, I glanced up again at the window.

The light was out!

"Come along, gentlemen," said Sherlock Holmes, stepping onto the sidewalk. "The game is afoot."

CHAPTER

21

I FEAR NOTHIN' CAN BRING HIM BACK

O nce the light had been extinguished in Forbes's window, the three of us separated to form the box. I went to the nearby intersection of Ninth and Fort Streets, where I was to await Forbes's passage a block to the south along Sixth. (I must pause to explain here that due to a unique and inexplicable quirk of St. Paul's street system, Sixth and Ninth Streets are but a block apart in certain parts of the city.) Although the weather remained unusually clement for late January, the streets were only lightly traveled, and I saw but one other pedestrian—a young man, who greeted me with a friendly "Good evening"—before reaching my appointed station.

The fog, which had continued to thicken, hung over the city like a vast shroud, reducing visibility to a block or so at best. Off to my north I could still see the lighted twin towers of a large German-style church.[1] Its slender steeples, which normally thrust like illuminated spikes into the night sky, were already lost to the enveloping mist. The view along the streets was not much better, for this portion of St. Paul remained gaslit, not yet having been fitted out with the new and much brighter incandescent lights found in the main commercial district. Despite the poor light, I was able to see the intersection where Forbes, if all went according to plan, would soon pass by.

Forbes was to distinguish himself by carrying a long umbrella, which could also be used for self-defense in the event Bouquet made a sudden attack. I stood at my corner, peering down toward Sixth Street, waiting for Forbes to appear. Under better weather conditions, I might also have been able to see Pyle, stationed another block to the south, but this was now beyond hope.

Holmes had told Forbes to walk at a leisurely pace, so that Pyle and I could move ahead of him from block to block and then mark his passage at every intersection. I therefore expected something of a wait, but as the seconds ticked away, with no sign of the young man, I began to grow anxious. What if Bouquet, hiding in the very shadows of the Hotel Barteau, had silently slipped a knife into Forbes's back before we had even formed our protective box? What if—

Then I saw him, a dark silhouette, umbrella in hand, strolling through the dim pool of light which illuminated the intersection. I waited in accord with Holmes's instructions to see if anyone— especially anyone looking like a woman—was trailing Forbes. No one appeared, however, and I quickly moved on to the next intersection, arriving only seconds before Forbes made his passage. Again I waited, and again I saw no one behind him.

This process was repeated without incident for several more blocks, until we reached St. Peter Street. Here, Sixth and its parallel numbered streets took a sharp turn to the northeast, and here, too, Forbes changed direction, turning south along St. Peter toward the river just a few block away. This part of the city contained numerous restaurants, hotels, and taverns, and so there were more people on the streets than had been evident near Forbes's apartment building. I followed Forbes on his southward turn, paralleling him a block to the east along Wabasha, where I encountered knots of people at almost every corner, waiting for the streetcars which regularly plied this thoroughfare.

We were now in the heart of the city, and even though the shops had closed for the night, an air of gaiety marked the streets. Merchants had illuminated their shop windows for the Winter Carnival, and many had also commissioned ice sculptures, which erupted from the fog like crystalline apparitions, gleaming and dripping in the moist night air. The thoroughfare itself was spanned at regular intervals by ornamental arches fitted out with rows of gaslights burning beneath globes of varying colors. These blazing, multicolored arches created an extraordinary effect, and I had the sensation of walking down the nave of some magnificent cathedral, beneath a roof made of nothing more substantial than fog and light.

I had little opportunity to enjoy this spectacle, however, for my mission required strict attention to business at every moment. At each cross street, I waited for Forbes to make his appearance. In every instance, Forbes arrived with clockwork precision, paused for the prescribed length of time, then moved smartly along to the next intersection. I saw him at Seventh, at Sixth (where I passed Schuneman's department store, the scene of one of Holmes's most brilliant interrogations in the affair of the Red Demon), at Fifth (where Michael Riley remained under lock and key in the bleak old jailhouse a half block away), and at Fourth. At no time could I discern anyone following him, nor did I see either of my fellow shadows.

So it was that I at last reached the blufftops of the Mississippi at the broad intersection of Third and Wabasha Streets, known as Bridge Square. Here, the Wabasha Street bridge began its long leap to the river's southern shore, though on this night the massive iron span appeared mysteriously truncated, its lights vanishing into the fog midway across the river. Here, too, along Third, was the city's historic jobbing district, now reduced to a ragged row of ill-kept stone and brick warehouses which lined the street like old maids waiting for the next dance with prosperity. And here, not far from the bridge abutment, was the beginning of what might be called St. Paul's dark zone.

All great cities, like the men who make them, have such a zone—a place removed from the clear, taming light of civilization. Here, the worst instincts of man the beast emerge, like tar oozing from the mysterious depths of the earth, and wickedness in all its infinite variety flourishes. Holmes, of course, had long sought out such places, for it was in these dismal laboratories of crime—from London's East End to Chicago's Levee—that he perfected his peculiar genius. Now, as the fog settled more densely into every crevice and corner, we were about to make our first descent into St. Paul's darkest precinct.

This netherworld, which had no particular name, formed in the early days of the city, when riverboats by the hundreds came steaming up to St. Paul, their decks crammed with brash young men in search of the main chance. Cheap taverns, brothels, gambling halls, and the like soon sprouted along the riverbank to serve this lusty population of hopeful wanderers, and by the 1860s — or so Pyle once told me — St. Paul had acquired a reputation as a "dead tough town." As the city grew and took on more civilized airs, however, the old riverfront district was left to fester, becoming a place where, as Pyle put it, "no respectable man or woman dare go after dark."

The way down into this Cimmerian corner of the city was a curious little street where, if Sherlock Holmes was right, Billy Bouquet would finally be brought to ground. Known as Bench Street, this narrow byway — no wider than an alley — was built into the face of the bluffs, angling down from Bridge Square to the ice-choked waters of the Mississippi more than fifty feet below. Short, crooked, and dark, it was lined on one side by tumbledown stone buildings, which housed several notorious "blind pig" taverns and other disreputable establishments. The other side of the street, however, offered nothing except a sheer cliff overlooking the river.[2]

From Holmes's peculiar point of view, Bench — with its isolation and its confining character — offered the ideal place to trap Bouquet. Yet as I paused at the top of the street, beneath the harsh white light of an arc lamp, I began to wonder once again whether the snare might prove as dangerous for us as for our supposed prey.

Gazing down into Bench's gloomy depths, I was not reassured by what I saw. The street seemed to drop through the swirling fog into a black hole in the earth, from which every trace of light had been banished. If Bouquet indeed followed Forbes here, as was the plan, then anything might happen, for all of us would truly be in the dark. Such were my unhappy thoughts as I took out my watch and saw that it was nearly midnight, which meant Forbes should be coming along shortly.

Then something peculiar happened. Although the night was perfectly calm and I was well dressed for the weather, a deep racking chill suddenly coursed through my body, as though I had been penetrated to the bone by a blast of Arctic wind. Shivering and shaking, I pulled up my coat collar, not realizing that this unaccountable chill was an eerie intimation of things to come. Moments later, I saw

Forbes. He was dressed in a long, high-buttoned coat and twirling his umbrella as though he had not a care in the world. Then our troubles began.

The plan was for Forbes to make himself visible at the corner of Third and St. Peter, a block west of my position, and remain there for five full minutes. This would provide us with the time needed to spring our trap. I was to go as quickly as possible to my east, toward Robert Street, where another bridge crossed the Mississippi and where a stairway led down the bluff to Bench, which at that point passed beneath Robert. I was then to station myself at the foot of Bench, just east of the staircase, and block any attempt by Bouquet to flee in my direction should he attempt it.

At about the time I arrived at my final position, Forbes was to begin his descent of Bench from Bridge Square, with Bouquet presumably behind him. Holmes would follow. Meanwhile, Pyle was to pursue a parallel course along Third, so that Bouquet could not elude us via either of the two north-south streets which intersected Bench between Wabasha and Robert. Effectively hemmed in from every direction, with his back up against the edge of a daunting precipice, Bouquet would have no possibility of escape. "It will be a perfect trap," Holmes had insisted. "Mr. Bouquet will have nowhere to go but into our grasp."

Unfortunately, Forbes now seemed to have forgotten a key detail of the plan, for instead of pausing at St. Peter, he immediately began walking toward me. This left me no choice but to turn and go as quickly as I could toward my assigned position on Bench. As I raced through the fog and darkness along Third, which was entirely deserted, I felt a rising tide of apprehension. My fear was that I would be unable to reach the bottom of Bench in time to block Bouquet's escape.

I do not know how long it took me to reach the staircase off Robert, but my heart was pounding like a piston by the time I got there. Pausing momentarily at the top of the steps to collect my thoughts (and my wind), I looked down toward Bench. It was like looking into a big black cauldron, only one filled with fog rather than steam. I took a deep breath, got my revolver from my coat pocket, and descended into the darkness.

Down I went, step by anxious step, the light growing ever more faint. I could hear the distant rumbling of a train (there were numerous tracks along the riverbank beneath the bluffs), but otherwise an unsettling quiet prevailed. The city, with its bright lights and comforting human presence, was now behind me, and I had the sense of entering an alien world. I felt my skin tingle, my pulse race, my eyes strain against the deepening darkness. Nonetheless, I continued my descent, knowing that my duty lay somewhere in the black pit below.

All the while, I fought an overwhelming urge to cry out for Holmes, whose presence nearby I could now only assume. But I held my tongue and kept my wits about me until I reached the bottom of the steps, which ended beside a small brick building. From there, it was but a few more yards to Bench Street. I sprinted toward the corner of the building, hoping to see or hear some indication that Holmes and Forbes were all right. Instead, I ran headlong into a phantom.

As I swung around the corner, the phantom appeared in the form of a large dark blur, which caught me in the crushing vise of its powerful arms. Taken completely off guard, I felt the breath rush out of my body, leaving behind nothing except a tight knot of fear in my stomach. The light was so faint that I was unable to discern the features of the men who held me with such extraordinary strength. But I knew by my captor's massive bulk that he could not be Billy Bouquet, who was much smaller than I. My mind, working at double time, now offered a better possibility: John J. O'Connor. God help me, but I had run into the Bull, and his intentions could not be honorable.

All of these thoughts flashed through my mind in the merest instant, and then instinct took over. Even though my arms were pinned, I managed to cock my revolver and thrust its barrel up into the big man's rib cage.

"Unhand me, O'Connor," I shouted, "or I will shoot you down where you stand." I meant every word of it, for I now feared that Holmes and Forbes had come to some bad end and I must do whatever was necessary to save them, even if it meant shooting St. Paul's chief of detectives.

It was then that I received a shock as great as any I have experienced in my life.

" 'Twould seem you've got the wrong Irishman, Dr. Watson," said a familiar voice, "so I wouldn't shoot just yet. Still, I can't say I'd blame you if you pulled the trigger, considerin' what a fool I've acted tonight."

"Rafferty!" I said with equal parts of relief and astonishment. "How in heaven did you—?"

"There's no time for explanations," Rafferty cut in, releasing me from his bear hug and pumping my arm with his usual gusto. "All you need know is that I'm here, that I'm wide awake—no thanks to you, I might add—and that I'm a bit more sober than I was a few hours ago. Now tell me this: Has young Forbes started down Bench yet?"

"He has. I was racing down here to get ahead of him, when I ran into you. I must say, Mr. Rafferty, that being wrapped in your arms is rather like encountering a python."

Rafferty chuckled. "My apologies for embracin' you like that, Dr. Watson. I didn't mean to give you such a fright. Problem was, I couldn't tell who was chargin' down those steps, and I didn't wish to take chances. But I'm glad you're here, because if Bouquet is somewhere out in this infernal fog, then we've got our work cut out for us, and that's a fact! Come along, then. It's time we got ourselves in position."

Still astounded by the Irishman's rapid recovery, I followed Rafferty out onto Bench Street and peered uphill toward Bridge Square. The fog was now nearly as thick as the proverbial London pea soup, and even the blazing arc lamps around the square had been extinguished as though wrapped in a dark-gray blanket.

"D--n it to hell," said Rafferty, staring into the fog. "We are runnin' blind, Doctor, and I don't like it. I don't like it at all."

"Perhaps we should call out to Holmes," I suggested. "Then we would at least know if everything is all right."

"No, 'twould give us away to that scoundrel Bouquet."

"But we don't even know if he's here," I pointed out.

"He's here, all right," said Rafferty in a tone that gave me my second chill of the night. "I can feel his venomous presence, smell the stink of him in the air, hear him sneakin' about like a beast in the night. Oh yes, Billy boy is here, and his knives are long and sharp. We must be ready for anything, Dr. Watson, anything! You see, if—"

He stopped, as though suddenly struck dumb, and I felt my startled heart skip a beat. A shout for help! I did not recognize the voice, but there could be no doubt that it came from somewhere up ahead, toward Bridge Square. Hardly had we heard this desperate scream when another sound cut through the fog like a knife. A police whistle! Once, then twice, it shrieked its warning, and my heart began to accelerate wildly. There followed a strangled cry, after which rapid footsteps could be heard in the distance.

Without another word, I began running toward the urgent sound of the whistle and whatever awaited us in the darkness.

What happened next seems to me now, as I look back on it from the comfort of our flats on Baker Street, to have been a kind of dream, a phantasmagoria played out in shadow and fog, all ending in a moment of sheer terror.

Rafferty had brought along a small lantern, and he quickly lit it before following me up Bench. The street was paved with rough cobblestones, and I could hear Rafferty coming up behind me, clip-clopping like a big draft horse as his heavy boots struck the pavement. For a man of his size, Rafferty ran surprisingly well, and he drew even with me just as I nearly tripped over a figure who lay crumpled on the cobblestones. The light from Rafferty's lantern illuminated an umbrella next to the motionless figure, and I knew at once that we had stumbled on Frederick Forbes.

"Freddie, are you all right?" Rafferty asked, bending down with his lantern to look at the young man, who now showed signs of movement. Only then did I see that Forbes's coat was open and that a dark stain had spread across his shirt near the abdomen.

Rafferty gently cradled Forbes's head in his arms and instructed him to tell us what had happened. In a weak and trembling voice, the young man said: "Stabbed . . . Must have been Bouquet . . . Here . . . never saw him until it was too late . . . I'm sorry, Shad."

"Don't worry, Freddie, you did just fine," Rafferty said as I examined Forbes's wound. It was a slashing cut to the abdomen, wide but not deep, and it was already beginning to clot. Forbes, I felt certain, would survive. I was, however, most anxious to learn where Holmes had gone. I was about to put this question to the young man, when I heard footsteps approaching from one of the intersecting streets.

Rafferty instantly sprang to his feet, a small pistol materializing out of his coat pocket. It was then that we heard yet another familiar voice sounding through the fog. "I heard the—" said Joseph Pyle, words abruptly failing him when he caught sight of Forbes's prostrate form. "My God, what has happened?"

"Mr. Forbes has been stabbed," I said. "Fortunately, it appears to be a superficial wound. But tell me, have you seen Holmes?"

"No. I heard the whistle and came running. I haven't seen Mr. Holmes since we left the vicinity of the Barteau."

Then we heard it again—a high-pitched whistle cutting through the fog. To my amazement, the sound seemed to come from far below us, at the base of the cliff. I wondered how this could be. The cliff was high and steep, and I did not see how Holmes, or anyone else, for that matter, could have gotten so quickly to the bottom of it without the aid of ropes.

Rafferty, however, soon found the answer to this puzzle. He had gone with his lantern to the edge of the cliff and gazed out over the escarpment. Immediately he turned around and said: "Let's go, Dr. Watson—there is no time to waste. They have gone over the cliff, toward the railroad tracks and the river."

"You mean Holmes and Bouquet? But how?"

"I'll explain as we go," said Rafferty. "Joseph, you stay with Freddie and get him to a doctor."

Rafferty then turned and went back down Bench at a fast trot, toward the river. I had no choice but to follow. When I caught up with him, he explained that Bouquet and, presumably, Holmes, had reached the bottom of the cliff by first jumping onto the roof of a long, tall wooden building which rose up from the base of the cliff only a few feet away from Bench. Then, he said, they had probably slid off the roof and landed in the deep snows which piled up in the narrow space between the back of the freight house and the cliff.[3]

"You and I, Dr. Watson, could not have attempted such a feat," Rafferty said as we passed beneath the Robert Street bridge, its lights almost completely obscured by the fog. "But Mr. Holmes, he's a regular athlete, he is, as is Bouquet. The question now is: Where have these two gymnasts gone to?"

We quickly reached Jackson Street, where Bench ended. We were now just a block from the Union Depot, which was served by numerous railroad tracks that ran along the river beneath the high bluffs. The fog had lifted slightly, but as I looked out across the tracks toward the Mississippi, I saw no sign of Holmes or Bouquet. Then fortune smiled on us, or as Holmes might have put it, we found ourselves in the right position to receive luck.

A passenger train was rumbling in from the east, approaching a long, low railroad bridge which curved across the river beneath the Robert Street span.[4] As the train slowed to begin its crossing, the powerful beam of the engine's lantern swept along the tracks and out over the river. In that fortuitous shaft of light I saw two moving shadows. The farthest was already across the tracks and heading out onto the river ice. The other was not far behind.

"There!" I shouted, pointing toward the shadows. "They've gone out on the river."

Rafferty let out a low growl and said: "We are in for it now. You had better pray that Mr. Holmes knows what he's about, because there's nothing more treacherous on God's earth than river ice. But I guess we'll have to follow him."

While we waited impatiently for the slow-moving train to pass by, Rafferty began to point his lantern along the tracks as though searching for something.

"Ah, here we are," he said, holding up a pair of rusted spikes which had apparently worked themselves loose from the tracks. "Take one of these, Dr. Watson, and keep it tight in your hand."

"What for?" I asked.

"It just might save your life, that's what for," Rafferty said with unusual brusqueness. "If you go through the ice—and there's a d--ned good chance that will happen—you'll want somethin' to get a grip with to pull yourself out. That spike just might be your salvation."

Once the train had finally gone by, we crossed over the tracks and scrambled down a steep embankment to the frozen river. A light layer of snow still covered the ice, and we soon found two sets of footprints leading out into the main channel. We also found blood— a small dark patch of it, still warm to the touch when I bent down to examine it. But whose was it? Given Bouquet's handiness with knives, I could only assume that the blood belonged to Holmes.

More fearful than ever for Holmes's safety, I raced out onto the ice, intent on catching up to him. Almost immediately, however, I felt Rafferty tugging at my coat.

"Go easy, go oh so easy," he warned. "River ice is like a promise from the devil himself. 'Tis never, ever to be trusted."

To demonstrate his point, he took a large stone, which he had picked up at the edge of the river, and tossed it as far as he could to one side. I heard the crack of ice and then a loud splash as the stone went into the water.

Said Rafferty: "We've got maybe four inches of ice where we're standin' right now. That's barely enough to support a man. But a stone's throw away, as you've just seen, the situation can be entirely different. There might be an inch of ice or none at all. The river's like that. The current swirls and eddies, eatin' away at the ice here and there, with no rhyme or reason to it. We're on a thin piece of Swiss cheese, Doctor, and there's no tellin' where the holes are. So I want you to move slowly and follow those footprints. Otherwise, the Mississippi just might swallow you up and spit out what's left of you next spring."

Rafferty's words had their desired effect, and I began to proceed with far more caution. We crept along, step by step, walking as gingerly as cat burglars on a creaky wooden floor. My apprehension had not abated in the least, however, for I saw more and more drops of blood the farther out into the river we went.

We followed the trail of footprints in a southwesterly direction, toward the railroad bridge. The passenger train we had seen earlier was already midway across the bridge, its lantern illuminating an island whose banks were marked by a line of tall, ghostly trees.[5] But once the train had gone past it, the island disappeared from view, and we had only the feeble light cast by Rafferty's lantern to guide us across the dark, fogbound river. Holmes, I knew, had taken along a small lantern of his own, but I supposed that in his eagerness to capture Bouquet he had not had time to light it.

I do not know how long we were out on the ice, but it was an experience I wish never to repeat. Each step we took seemed a kind of optimistic wager, a gamble that the river—winding its treacherous, indifferent way beneath us—would not at that instant decide to take us in its icy grip. Nothing I had experienced at Maiwand was as nerve-racking as this trek across thin ice, for the cold, remorseless enemy beneath our feet had no honor or purpose, and no concern for our fate.[6]

Moving carefully but steadily along, we continued to follow the footprints as they passed underneath the railroad bridge and angled off toward the island. There was no point in maintaining silence now, and I repeatedly called out Holmes's name, hoping at every instant to hear his reassuring voice. But I heard nothing except the rhythmic crunch of our footsteps atop the ice and snow. I began to wonder whether Holmes had gotten so far ahead of us that he was out of hearing range, and I was about to remark on this possibility to Rafferty when I heard a sharp crack, followed by a sudden cry and then the sickening sound of something large and heavy splashing into open water.

"My God, that is Holmes!" I said, for I knew his voice as well as my own.

Throwing all caution to the wind, I ran toward the sound of Holmes's cry. How long or far I went I cannot say, for every fiber of my being was now focused on reaching Holmes, no matter what the cost to my own safety might be. Rafferty was right at my heels with his lantern, and though I could see nothing of our position on the river, I had the sense that we were drawing near to the island. Then, suddenly, I came upon a jagged black hole in the ice. It was a pool of open water, perhaps twenty feet in circumference, and I would have gone plunging into it had not Rafferty grabbed me from behind and by brute strength pulled me back from the edge.

"Holmes!" I called out. "Answer me! Where are you?"

Rafferty shone his light out across the deadly circle of water. One set of footprints—too small, I knew at once, to be those of Holmes—led around the ice and toward the south shore of the river. Bouquet, it appeared, had made his escape. The other footprints, those of my dearest friend in the world, ended abruptly at the edge of the open water. It was then that I saw something which sent a cold dagger through my heart. At the edge of the water, standing as upright as a tombstone, was Holmes's beaver hat.

"Holmes! Holmes!" I shouted, feeling now a horrible vacancy spreading out from the pit of my stomach. But there was no sign of Holmes, no response from the cold, implacable waters of the Mississippi.

Rafferty made a sign of the cross and said in a choked voice: " 'Tis all my fault, Dr. Watson, all my fault. I should have gone with Mr. Holmes from the start, as we had planned. Now the river has got him, and I fear nothin' can bring him back."

22

I HAVE ALWAYS BEEN A HARD MAN TO KILL

"No," I said, staring down into the water. "It cannot be!"
I had once before given Holmes up for dead, in the gloomy chasm of the Reichenbach River, and the thought of doing so again was more than I could bear.[1] There are in this world only a few men who might fairly claim the right to immortality, and Sherlock Holmes was one of them. The very idea of his death was an insult to reason, for he was in life so vibrant, so teeming with ideas, so necessary to the well-being of what we are pleased to call civilization, that his demise could only be regarded as a cosmic injustice. I did not see how I could go on without him, and I felt some vital flame deep within me begin to die out, like embers fading in a hearth.

Such were my disconsolate thoughts, when Rafferty and I were startled by the appearance of a small brown creature with a long black tail. Making a curious high-pitched noise, this strange beast scurried past us and dove into the open water. Soon several of its kin came running out of the fog, ignoring us as they, too, sought sanctuary beneath the ice.

"Muskrats," said Rafferty. "I wonder why—" He stopped, as

though struck by a new thought, and said: "Doctor, do not despair yet. Quick now, follow me."

He turned and ran in the direction from which the muskrats had come. I followed, though I had no idea what had caused Rafferty to rush off with such urgency. We had gone no more than a hundred feet when I saw, in the light of Rafferty's lantern, a curious dome-like structure, several feet high, erupting from the otherwise smooth surface of the ice. It was, I later learned, a muskrat lodge, made of reeds and twigs gathered by its industrious occupants.[2]

Rafferty stopped about ten feet in front of the lodge and said: "We'll go no farther just yet. The ice is too thin."

He got down on his hands and knees, to spread out his weight on the ice, and shone his light directly at the lodge. That was when I saw the hand.

It was a large, bony hand, with extremely long fingers, and it gripped the heavy twigs which formed the base of the lodge. Holmes! It could be no one else, and I felt a surge of joy coursing through my body.

"Holmes, we are here," I shouted. "Hang on. We are coming."

There was no reply, however, and my joy drained away in an instant.

"Don't waste your time callin' to him," Rafferty said. "He's probably unconscious or close to it. We must concentrate now on gettin' to him, which will not be easy with this ice."

"I will go to him," I said.

"All right, but you'll do him or me no good if you take a swim. So listen closely. Here is what we must do."

Moments later, I found myself prone on the ice, using the spikes Rafferty had brought along to pull myself toward the muskrat lodge. Rafferty had assumed a similar position directly behind me, having looped one end of his belt around my right foot. The other end was in Rafferty's strong right hand. Yet I knew this lifeline could hardly guarantee my safety, or Rafferty's, for that matter, since there was a distinct possibility that both of us might go crashing through the ice at any instant.

The ice around the lodge had been swept free of snow, perhaps by the muskrats themselves, and it was, as Rafferty had warned me, dangerously thin. Indeed, it seemed to consist of little more than a film stretched taut across the waters below. As I inched forward, I could feel the ice flex under my weight. The sensation was that of being suspended in a swaying hammock held up by nothing more substantial than the air itself, and I felt quite certain that I would not reach Holmes without first breaking through into open water. Still, I kept going, knowing that Holmes's life now depended on my nerve and resolve.

I was within a yard of Holmes's hand when the river at last claimed me. The shock of the plunge, the way in which the waters instantly engulfed me in their deep numbing chill, is nearly beyond my powers of description. I can liken it only to the experience of paralysis, for as I struggled to keep my head above water I felt as though the rest of my body had somehow become unattached and unresponsive—a separate entity, as it were, over which I no longer held sway.

The next few minutes are to this day a blur in my mind, and I can recall only fleeting images of what happened. I know that I cried out and somehow managed to strain forward and grab Holmes's cold hand in mine. I remember seeing the lodge begin to disintegrate. I remember seeing Holmes—his white, drawn face, his matted hair, his arms and torso, his long legs, his waterlogged boots—magically emerging out of the pile of reeds and sticks. I remember holding on to Holmes's hand as the two of us were pulled backward by some powerful, mysterious force. And finally I remember the sensation of being tossed, facedown, across the saddle of a large horse—or so it seemed—and then galloping away, out of the icy darkness and into a bright, warm place.

In the light of a kerosene lamp I saw the face of a woman. She had wide, dimpled cheeks, a jolly chin, and big brown eyes, which gazed down upon me with a mixture of tenderness and curiosity.

"Where am I?" I asked, for I did not recognize either the woman or my surroundings. Swathed in thick wool blankets, I was lying on a cot in one corner of what appeared to be little more than a tar-paper shack. The woman, her eyes widening to almost bovine proportions, said something in a language unfamiliar to me. An instant later, Shadwell Rafferty appeared at her side.

"Ah, you're awake," he said. "We're at the home of Mr. and Mrs. Dvorak, residents of the West Side flats, who were kind enough to take us in after you and Mr. ah ... Baker went swimmin' in the river.[3] I don't mind sayin' I had a devil of a time luggin' the two of you here on my shoulders!"

My mind was still as befogged as the air outside, and at first I could scarcely comprehend what Rafferty had told me. "Swimming? Whatever do you mean? And where is Holmes?" I blurted out.

"You mean Mr. Baker, don't you?" Rafferty prodded, not wishing our identity to become known.

My head was clear enough now that I instantly realized my mistake. "Of course," I replied. "Mr. Baker. Tell me, is he . . ." Then it all came back to me, as though a sluice gate had suddenly been opened, pouring out a rushing torrent of memories: the fog, the chase across the river, the hole in the ice, Holmes's miraculous survival in the muskrat lodge, my own plunge into the frigid waters.

"Is my friend all right?" I asked anxiously.

"Yes, but it was a near thing," Rafferty said. "He was pale and blue and barely breathin' when we got here, but Mrs. Dvorak has filled him up with her excellent hot tea and he is doing much better. He's restin' now, for prolonged exposure to cold is like a narcotic. It puts a man asleep. Mr. Dvorak, who is a stout fellow and speaks good English, is off summonin' Mr. Hill and his private physician. In the meantime, I'd greatly appreciate it if you could take a look at Mr. Baker."

"Certainly," I said, and was about to rise from the cot when I realized that I had no clothes on beneath my blankets.

"Ah, you'll be needin' clothes, now, won't you," said Rafferty, catching my embarrassed look. "Sorry, but Mr. Dvorak and I had to undress you. Your clothes were caked with ice after I plucked you from the river. But we'll get you fixed up. Mrs. Dvorak has found some of her husband's clothes that you can wear until yours dry out."

Apologizing for their plainness, Mrs. Dvorak brought over a pair of work pants and a stout wool shirt, both of which fit me surprisingly well. I thanked her and then hurriedly dressed while Rafferty provided a screen with one of the blankets.

Once I was presentable, I went over to examine Holmes, who lay on a rough plank floor next to the big potbellied stove which heated the Dvoraks' modest domicile. Although he was wrapped in a heavy quilt, he still looked extremely pale, and his forehead felt cool to the touch. I had no medical equipment with me, but I was able to take his pulse, which was slow and weak. His breathing was quite slow as well and rather labored. I also noted with puzzlement several deep puncture wounds on his face. These wounds, however, did not appear to be life-threatening, nor could they account for the large drops of blood we had seen on the ice. This meant that the blood must have come from Bouquet, who presumably had been injured at some point during the chase.

"I must say it is quite remarkable that Mr. Baker is alive," I told Rafferty. "Not one man in a thousand could have survived what he did."

To my astonishment, Holmes now opened his eyes and said: "I have always been a hard man to kill, as you must know. Professor Moriarty could not do it, and neither could Mr. Bouquet."

I am not ashamed to say that tears rolled down my cheeks when I heard his voice. "My God, I thought we had lost you!"

Holmes smiled weakly, grasped my hand, and said: "I must confess that I was of a similar opinion when I went under the ice and began floating downriver. Had I not blundered quite by accident into the lodgings of the muskrat family, who were not in the least happy to see me, I have no doubt you would now be speaking of me in the past tense. By the way, Watson, have I ever mentioned to you what a nasty thing it is to be bitten on the face by a muskrat?"

After this remarkable account of his survival, Holmes soon fell fast asleep again and remained so while Rafferty and I transported him back to Hill's mansion in an enclosed carriage sent by our patron. Mr. Dvorak—a large, dark-haired man with a thick black mustache and merry brown eyes—had returned with the carriage, and I greeted him warmly, for he and his wife were indeed our saviors, along with the indispensable Rafferty. Before we left the Dvoraks' riverside shanty, at about two-thirty in the morning, I again offered my profound thanks to the couple, along with a twenty-dollar gold piece. The kindly Bohemians were quite delighted by this gift, which the generous Rafferty matched, and I have no doubt they were able to put their windfall to good use.

As we rode back to the mansion, Holmes lying fast asleep on the seat across from us, Rafferty recounted what had happened after I fell into the river.

"You were lucky, Doctor, as was Mr. Holmes, for bein' the fat man that I am, I was sure I'd be swimmin' soon enough myself. But I guess I'd found a solid piece of ice, for when you got your grip on Mr. Holmes, I was able to reach out and grab the belt I'd attached to your ankle. Then I just started pullin' like a draft horse, thinkin' all the while that the game would be up at any second. But I somehow got the two of you out of the water and back on good ice. You both looked as white as cod fillet fresh from the Grand Banks. I could see that Mr. Holmes was in a bad way, so I got him up on my shoulder first. You, Dr. Watson, were conscious but babblin' like a baby. I finally convinced you to climb up on my other shoulder, and then I set off across the ice toward the South Shore, which I knew wasn't far away. I followed Bouquet's footprints to shore, wonderin' every moment if the ice would hold the weight of us all. Thank God it did! 'Twas a miracle, I believe, and nothin' less. Once I got on shore, I looked for the first squatter's shack with a light in it. And that's how you ended up at the Dvoraks'.'"

I marveled at how simple Rafferty made this remarkable rescue sound. Yet I knew that only a man of his enormous strength could have pulled us out of the water and then carried more than three hundred pounds over his shoulders for a distance of a quarter of a mile or more.

"I cannot tell you how grateful I am," I told him. "Both Holmes and I would be at the bottom of the river now if it were not for you."

" 'Twas the least I could do," said Rafferty, "for I am as responsible as anyone for this awful business."

"You are too hard on yourself, Mr. Rafferty. The loss of a beloved dog, especially under such ugly circumstances, could cause any man to lose his way for a time. Neither Holmes nor I will ever hold that against you. Still, I am amazed you were able to recover so quickly from the large dose of barbiturates I administered."

"You can thank Mr. Thomas for that. I was still groggy when I came to, but he started pourin' coffee down me as fast as I could drink it, and I sobered up quick enough. Then I went runnin' over to Bench Street, hopin' I'd get there before everybody else arrived. I wasn't there more than five minutes when you came poundin' down the stairs. All things considered, I guess tonight was our lucky night."

"Indeed," I said, thinking of how Holmes regarded good fortune. "Yet I also think it is fair to say that we deserved our luck."

"Perhaps," said Rafferty as we pulled up to the gate in front of

Hill's mansion, "though Billy Bouquet also had more than his share of luck this night. Incidentally, Doctor, there's somethin' I'd like to ask you."

The question Rafferty now posed was so peculiar and so trifling, or so it seemed, that I could not help but wonder what made him ask it. But he seemed most pleased with my answer, the significance of which I would only later appreciate.

Once we had gotten Holmes inside and into a warm bed, we repaired to the library, where a blazing fire and glasses of hot brandy awaited us. Hill, Pyle, and Frederick Forbes sat in an arc of chairs arranged around the fire. The Empire Builder rose at once to greet us and inquired anxiously as to Holmes's health.

"I am confident he will make a complete recovery," I replied, "though if you had asked such a question only a few hours ago, my answer would have been far less optimistic."

"That is good news indeed," said Hill. "I should like to know everything that took place out on the river."

With an occasional assist from Rafferty, I gave Hill as complete an account as I could of our adventures on the ice and our kind treatment from the Bohemian family.

Hill listened carefully to my story and said: "As it so happens, Mr. Dvorak is a laborer for the Great Northern. I will see to it that he is rewarded for his good work this night. I can only conclude that Mr. Baker is fortunate to be alive, as—I might add—is young Mr. Forbes. Wouldn't you say so, Frederick?"

Forbes eagerly nodded his assent, a broad smile on his face, as though he were immensely pleased with himself. Such a reaction, I knew from my military experience, is quite common among men who have stared death in the eye and lived to tell about it.

"Why, he's chipper as can be," Pyle said with a grin, patting the young man on the back. "Says it was the adventure of a lifetime tonight."

"Well, I don't know if I'd go that far," Forbes demurred. He was, as usual, slouched in his chair, a tall glass of brandy resting on his lap. "But I must say the whole thing was rather thrilling, even if that devil Bouquet did almost kill me. Mr. Hill's physician said that if my wound had been an inch deeper and a few inches higher, well, let's just say it would have gone badly for me."

"Then you must count your lucky stars, Freddie, me boy," said Rafferty, "for Billy Bouquet is known up and down the Mississippi as a quick man with the blade."

Before Forbes could reply, Hill took over the conversation. Fixing me with his powerful gaze, he said: "I am curious if Mr. Baker was able to tell you anything about what happened down on Bench Street. Frederick here says that Bouquet took everyone by surprise. I am wondering how he managed such a trick."

"You are not alone in that regard," I acknowledged. "Unfortunately, Mr. Baker has not been able to talk about the matter as yet. Still, I should like to hear Mr. Forbes's account of the night's events."

"We were listening to the young man's tale just as you came in," Hill said, turning to Forbes. "Go ahead, Frederick, tell them your story."

Forbes eagerly complied, relating in great detail everything that had happened after he left his apartment and went out into the foggy night. He said the walk had gone exactly according to plan until he reached the head of Bench Street.

"I saw no sign of Bouquet, nor was there any other indication of trouble," he said. "But I must admit that the fog made me uncomfortable. I was afraid Bouquet might jump out of the shadows at any instant."

"Why didn't you wait at the head of Bench Street as you were supposed to?" I asked.

Forbes readily admitted his mistake. "The fault is mine, all mine. I simply forgot. I am, as you know, a rather nervous type, and I lost my head for a moment. I wished to get the whole business over with, if you want to know the truth."

" 'Tis understandable," said Rafferty. "Anyone would be a bit goosy in such a situation."

Forbes went on to say that he had gone about a block down Bench, toward the river, when he felt "something wrong," as he put it. "I can't really describe what it was, but I had the sense that somebody was waiting for me in the darkness. This sensation was so strong that I stopped and instinctively prepared myself for the worst. And that is when he came, without warning, from around the corner of a building. I do not mind telling you that I was very frightened. He rushed toward me, and I remember seeing something in his hand as he lunged in my direction. I jumped back, but not fast enough, I guess, for I felt the sting of the knife as it slashed through my clothes."

"Did you recognize your assailant as Bouquet?" Pyle asked.

"No. All I was looking at was that knife in his hand. After he came at me, everything happened so quickly that I can scarce give an account of it. I remember crying out and trying to grab the knife. There was a brief struggle, and then I heard a whistle and approaching footsteps. I lost my footing at some point and fell to the ground. The next thing I recall is seeing Mr. Baker. He was leaning over me and asking if I was all right."

"Did Mr. Baker say anything else to you?" I asked, for I wondered if Holmes had actually gotten a glimpse of the man we all assumed to be Bouquet.

"No. Once he saw that my wound was not serious, he went running off. Shortly afterwards, you and Mr. Rafferty arrived. The rest of the story you know better than I."

Rafferty nodded, tugged at his beard, and said: "I'm curious about one thing, Freddie. As you were strugglin' with Bouquet, do you think he might have been cut with his own knife?"

Forbes's brow furrowed in thought. He finally said: "It's possible, Shad. The way we were grappling for that knife, anything might have happened."

Hill at once grasped the implications of Forbes's answer. "Am I to take it, Shad, that you saw traces of blood as you were trailing Bouquet and Mr. Baker?"

"We did," Rafferty said, "and there was enough of it to suggest that Bouquet might have been seriously hurt."

"For all we know, then, Bouquet might already be dead," Hill noted. "But assuming that he's still with us, where do you intend to go from here, Shad?"

Rafferty smiled and said: "Home. When Mr. Baker wakes up, we'll have a talk and decide upon a course of action."

"Will you be all right at your apartment?" I asked, thinking back upon his wild outburst after finding the body of John Brown.

"I've done my mournin', if that's what you mean," Rafferty replied. "Besides, Mr. Thomas will keep me away from old John Barleycorn, at gunpoint if necessary. I'll be fine. But I do have one suggestion. I think Mr. Forbes ought to spend the night here, just to be safe. There's no tellin' what Bouquet might be up to. A wounded animal is the most dangerous kind, or so they say."

"An excellent idea," agreed Hill.

"Do you really think Bouquet would try another attack?" Forbes asked, trying his best to look brave despite an obvious quiver of fear in his voice. "I still don't understand why he came after me in the first place. Do you know, Shad?"

"I have an idea or two in that regard, Freddie, but now is not the time to discuss my theories. You just stay put here tonight, and we'll have answers soon enough."

I accompanied Rafferty to the front hall, where he retrieved his coat after rummaging for several minutes in the cloakroom. When we finally stepped out beneath the porte cochere and into the foggy night, Rafferty consulted his pocket watch and said: " 'Tis now nearly four A.M. I'll be occupied for the next couple of hours, but after that you can reach me at my apartment. Please telephone me the moment Mr. Holmes wakes up. I must talk to him as soon as possible."

"Very well," I said. "But where are you going now? I thought you had intended to go straight home."

Rafferty grinned and said: "Let's just say I have to make a little detour to gather up some evidence."

The glitter in Rafferty's eye told me that wherever he was going, it was much more than a mere detour. "You know who committed the murders, don't you," I said.

"Ah now, that would be presumptuous on your part, Doctor, most presumptuous," Rafferty replied, still grinning. "But who knows? A little presumption is sometimes a wise thing."

Then, whistling a merry tune, he walked off into the fog.

Wrapped in a thick cocoon of quilts and blankets, with hot water bottles at his feet, Holmes slept throughout much of the next day. I made it a point to check in on him regularly, but as his color was good and he appeared to be resting comfortably, I saw no need to awaken him or take additional medical measures.

Holmes's prolonged slumber—an unprecedented occurrence in the midst of a case, when Holmes might normally go days without sleep—had a curious effect on me. As the hours went by, I felt my own energy drain away, unaccustomed as I was to being deprived of the animating spark of Holmes's presence. My sense of lethargy was deepened by the emptiness which prevailed in Hill's mansion. Hill himself had gone off to his office early in the morning. A little later, young Forbes, with Rafferty's blessing, had returned to his apartment, there apparently being no fear that his life might still be in jeopardy. Pyle, meanwhile, was busily putting out his newspaper. Rafferty, too, was gone. He had stopped by briefly in the morning to check on Holmes's condition, then left just after Forbes, saying he had "important business to attend to."

After eating a late breakfast, I found a comfortable chair in the library and scanned the morning newspapers, which were preoccupied with news of the Winter Carnival. The night ahead, I learned, was to feature the carnival's climactic event, a quaint ritual known as the "storming of the ice palace." A crowd of thousands, the *Globe* informed me, was expected to converge on the palace at eight in the evening to watch as "the fiery forces of Vulcanus Rex attempt to dethrone Borealis Rex and thereby end the icy reign of winter." This event normally was held on a Saturday night, but the continued melting of the ice palace — "which has begun to droop and sag like a tired dowager," as the *Globe*'s correspondent rather cruelly put it — had forced a change of plans. There was, of course, no mention in any of the newspapers of our adventures on the river, which had in any case occurred well after all of the city's dailies had gone to press.

After exhausting the day's supply of newspapers and playing several games of patience, I determined, at about three o'clock, to take a brief nap, since I still felt quite weary from my exertions of the previous night. Hardly had I put my head on the pillow than I fell into a dreamless sleep.

"I trust you have had a good day's rest, my dear Watson," said Sherlock Holmes, peering down at me as I rubbed sleep from my eyes.

"Holmes! You are awake. What time is it?"

"Seven o'clock in the evening. A bit late to start the day, even for a gentleman of leisure such as yourself."

"Why, you should have awakened me sooner," I protested, climbing out of bed and feeling rather sheepish that I had slept so long. "I will be dressed in a moment. But how are you, Holmes? I must say that, all things considered, you look remarkably well."

This was no exaggeration. Dressed in a tweed jacket, a white shirt, and dark pants, his thin hair perfectly combed and his eyes as sharp and probing as ever, Holmes showed few ill effects from his plunge into the river other than the bites on his face. Any normal man — and Holmes, whatever else might be said of him, could never be accounted normal — would have taken days to recover from such an incident. Yet I knew from our long experience together that Holmes lived at times by the sheer strength of his will, which was so powerful that even the mortal flesh bowed to it in astonished obeisance.

As though reading my very thoughts, Holmes — who carried a large book in one hand — said: "I look well, Watson, because I refuse to look otherwise."

"If you say so. Still, those bites are rather nasty-looking. I really should like to hear more about how you managed to survive after you went under the ice."

"There is no time for that now, Watson, for we have much work to do. There has been a new and potentially sinister development in this affair."

"What sort of development?"

Slipping the book he was carrying beneath one arm, Holmes paused to adjust his shirt cuffs, which had committed the unpardonable sin of becoming folded over, and said: "It seems Michael Riley has escaped from jail."

CHAPTER

23

MR. HOLMES HAS JUST HAD
A VISION OF LIGHT

Holmes's revelation left me stunned.

"Escaped? Good God, how could that be?" I objected, for my mind went immediately back to our visit to the jail, which in its gloomy fastness had seemed to be as impenetrable as one of Torquemada's dungeons.[1]

"All that is known is that the deed was accomplished sometime within the past hour," said Holmes. "Mr. Pyle, who passed the news on to me a few moments ago, says there can be no doubt that Mr. Riley had assistance, for the lock on his cell door showed no signs of tampering. In other words, he must have had a key. It appears that none of the guards—admittedly a rather indifferent band of public servants—saw Mr. Riley slip away. Most curious of all, however, is the fact that no less a figure of authority than John J. O'Connor himself was in the jail at about the time of the escape. What do you make of that, Watson?"

In truth, I had no idea what to make of this news, and so all I could tell Holmes was that O'Connor's presence on the scene was "interesting."

"Ah, now there is a useful word," chided Holmes, "for it means nothing at all."

"Perhaps, but I have heard you use it yourself on many occasions, if memory serves me well."

Holmes smiled at my rejoinder. "You have caught me, Watson, and I must plead guilty before the bar of your infallible recollection. Still, I do not think 'interesting' is quite adequate to describe my response to the fact of O'Connor's presence."

"And just what word would you use?"

"Suggestive," said Holmes. "Extremely suggestive."

"Of what?"

Holmes gave a slight shrug. "All I can say is that the chief of detectives may have had a very good reason for wanting Mr. Riley out of jail."

I was now thoroughly at sea, rolling helplessly amid the great waves of Sherlock Holmes's mind, and I knew enough to start reefing my sails. "I will not ask you to explain your last remark," I told Holmes, "as I do not doubt you would only confuse me further. However, I am curious if you have any ideas as to Mr. Riley's whereabouts."

Holmes slowly shook his head, as though eternally disappointed by the vast perfidy of mankind. "I know little with any certainty, Watson, but I can tell you that if we do find him, there is a good chance he will be in the vicinity of Billy Bouquet. At least, such is my fervent hope!"

I grasped at once what Holmes meant, or so I thought. I said: "Then you must be of the opinion that Mr. Riley will search out Bouquet, believing him to be the real murderer."

"No, I am more inclined to think that he will be led to Bouquet, with potentially fatal consequences. You see, Watson, this dreadful case is now assuming its final form, and I do not like the look of it! The ingenious villain at the center of this affair is a person who will not hesitate to murder again and again if need be."

Something in Holmes's tone of voice and the peculiar way he snapped off these alarming words told me that he had come to some great conclusion regarding the case. Rafferty, I now recalled, had left the very same impression when we had talked in the early-morning hours beneath the porte cochere of Hill's mansion.

"By the way," I said, "have you talked to Mr. Rafferty? I believe he—"

Holmes cut in: "I know what Mr. Rafferty thinks, since we spoke at great length on the telephone only an hour ago, while you were still sleeping. He and I are in complete agreement on all the essentials of this case. We are also in agreement as to how we must proceed."

"Then you must know who killed the Uptons!" I said excitedly. "How did you finally see to the bottom of the matter?"

Holmes offered a cryptic smile and said: "I am not sure that I have seen quite as far as you imagine, Watson. But I will not deny that my eyes have been opened as a result of my experiences last night. Swimming in the waters of the Mississippi is not a winter sport which I would highly recommend, but it is not without its virtues. Indeed, I must consider it a stroke of good fortune that I went through the ice last night."

I could not readily comprehend how plunging into frigid waters and coming within an inch of death could be accounted "good fortune," and I told Holmes so.

"Then I shall have to enlighten you," said Holmes, unperturbed by my protest. "You see, there is nothing like the prospect of imminent death to sharpen a man's mind, as the good Dr. Johnson noted long ago. The river's icy waters have been my tonic, Watson. They have swept away my mental cobwebs, as it were, and thereby led me at last to the Spider who so adroitly spun them."

Holmes paused and then flourished the leather-bound volume he had been holding. "And if there were any doubt as to the identity of the 'Spider,' this book—which was delivered here while you were sleeping—provides the final piece of evidence."

He handed me the book, which was entitled *Businessmen of the Great Northwest*. It consisted, as far as I could tell after a brief inspection of its contents, of profiles of the leading capitalists of St. Paul, Minneapolis, and other cities in Minnesota.[2]

"You say the book was delivered here? By whom? And just what sort of evidence does it provide?"

Holmes took the book back, slipped it under his arm, and said: "The book was delivered to the servants' entrance by someone whom your friend from Hinckley, Miss Olson, happened to notice quite by chance. She immediately came down to tell me what she knew. As a result, I believe there can be no doubt as to who sent the book."

I was pleased to hear that Laura Olson, whom Holmes had

treated so badly in Hinckley, had now been of use to him. "Was it an acquaintance of hers who delivered the book?" I inquired.

"Better yet, Watson, it was the girl's suitor, whose name is of no importance at present. The book, however, is invaluable. A note inside of it recommended that I turn to a certain page. I did so and found the Spider, complete with a rather handsome photograph."

"I suppose you aren't prepared to tell me who sent the book," I said.

"That can wait," Holmes replied with a touch of impatience. "What is important is that even with this piece of evidence, I am still confronted with a most vexing problem. My difficulty is that while I now know who the Spider is, I am by no means convinced that I can prove he murdered either Jonathan or George Upton. And that is why we must set out as soon as possible to do what we failed to accomplish last night. We must find Billy Bouquet, for he has become the key to this whole business."

My curiosity, especially as to the Spider's identity, was now intense, and I asked Holmes to show me the book. He declined, however, saying that he did not wish to "spoil the mystery" for me.

"I suggest, my dear Watson, that you think the matter through," he said, "which is what I intend to do in my room while otherwise occupying myself with the *America*. I must also await word from Mr. Rafferty, who has promised to call me with a crucial piece of information."

Pausing to consult his pocket watch, Holmes noted that it was already nearly half past seven. He then said: "Everything now depends on Mr. Rafferty and certain men in his employ. As for you, Watson, be prepared to move on a moment's notice. We may face dangers tonight which are even greater than those which we have just endured."

Once Holmes had retired to his room, I finished dressing and went down to the library to do my own "thinking through" of the ice palace affair. Hill had gone out for dinner with several of his business friends, so I had the library to myself. Settling into a chair by the fire, I sipped a glass of sherry, smoked a fine Havana cigar, and pondered Holmes's parting comment about the dangers yet to come. It was difficult to see how anything could be more perilous than our recent adventures on the thin, shifting ice of the Mississippi. Yet I had learned long ago never to dismiss Holmes's warnings, for he had an uncanny sense of impending danger.

It also occurred to me, as I thought about the ice palace affair, how much it resembled that treacherous river ice. Indeed, the entire case seemed to drift in a swirl of crosscurrents so varied and contradictory that I did not see how Holmes had ever found his footing. Still, I took Holmes's advice to heart and did my best to untangle the affair. Over the next hour, I jotted down notes and drew elaborate diagrams. I considered the testimony of the principals, searching for inconsistencies. I mustered up all the scenarios I could think of and tested them against the known facts. In short, I tried to do exactly what Holmes, locked in his bedroom, was doing one floor above me. But in the end all of my efforts came to naught. I simply could not see the pattern beneath the chaos of events. My only consolation was that I knew Holmes himself had struggled mightily with the case, which was every bit as intricate as the rigging of his beloved model ship.

Then, as I was about to admit defeat, I had a sudden, tantalizing glimpse of the truth. It is hard to describe this fleeting apparition other than to say it was a picture in my mind's eye of something out of place. It was something I had seen, something quite obviously amiss and yet so unremarkable in and of itself that it had not registered at the time. Try as I might, however, I could not retrieve this momentary image, which had entered my consciousness like a stray bolt of lightning and had disappeared just as quickly, leaving behind only a static charge of doubt.

Sherlock Holmes, I was soon to discover, had already seen the picture which eluded me, for his agile and capacious mind, unlike my own, could indeed catch lightning.

At about a quarter to nine, not long after Hill had returned and joined me in the library, I heard the telephone ring in the main hallway. Thinking the call might be from Rafferty, I went out into the hall, where I saw a servant already on his way up the stairs, presumably going toward Holmes's room. Soon thereafter, Holmes came rushing down the steps to take the call. The conversation lasted for several minutes, with Holmes saying very little, although at one point he let out a startled exclamation.

When he hung up, Holmes turned to look at me, and I knew at

once by the determined jut of his jaw and the hard glitter in his eyes that we were about to set out on the concluding adventure of the case. This was what Holmes liked to call the "time of convergence," that moment in an investigation when the diverse lines of inquiry come together to form an iron net of guilt around the murderer. It was for just such moments that Holmes lived. They were the true sustenance of his soul, and I believe that without their stimulus he would have withered away and died, like a noble hound no longer able to participate in the hunt.

I gazed back at Holmes and felt a sense of wonder and pride that my life should be part of his, for in this moment his magnificence shone. Standing before me in the hall, his entire body charged with a kind of wild vitality, he was now most completely and joyfully himself, the one and only Sherlock Holmes, the mere mention of whose name struck fear into the hearts of criminals in every dark corner of the civilized world.

"Well, my dear Watson, are you ready to see this ugly business to its conclusion?" he inquired, knowing full well what my answer must be.

"I am. Wherever you may lead, Holmes, I will gladly follow."

"Good man! Now, here is where we stand. That was Mr. Rafferty on the telephone, and he did not have good news to report. Mrs. Riley, it seems, hurriedly left her apartment less than half an hour ago after receiving a message delivered to her door. Mr. Rafferty believes, and I concur, that there can be no doubt as to her destination."

"She has gone to find her husband," I said.

"Yes, and she is in the gravest danger imaginable," Holmes replied solemnly. "I must tell you, Watson, that this entire affair, which only an hour ago promised a quick and satisfactory ending, is now beginning to spiral out of control, with results impossible to predict. We must go at once."

"Where?" I asked as I put on my coat and prepared to follow Holmes out the door.

"To the Muskrat Club. I only pray that we are not too late!"

It was another exceptionally clement night, with the temperature still well above freezing, and as we raced along Summit Avenue in Hill's fastest sleigh, I felt a warm sense of excitement. There was, I thought, no better thing in this world than to be flying along behind a brace of high-stepping horses toward some great adventure, with the indomitable Sherlock Holmes at my side. Holmes, as always in such situations, kept to his own thoughts, and we exchanged nary a word as we clipped along through the bracing night air.

As we descended toward the business district, I noted that the streets were all but deserted. When I remarked upon this to Holmes, he reminded me that the storming of the ice palace would begin within the hour.

"I have been told that all of St. Paul turns out for this event," he said, "so I should not be surprised to find that the rest of the city is very quiet indeed."

After a series of quick turns, we reached the Muskrat Club, which was but a few blocks from the Hotel Barteau, where our adventure of the previous night had begun. We pulled to a stop in front of the club but could see no sign of activity through its darkened windows. The club members, it appeared, had gone off like everyone else to celebrate at the ice palace.

Holmes instructed me to wait in the sleigh while he "made his way" into the club, as he put it. He added: "If any officers of the law should happen to come along while I am inside, you are to make as loud a demonstration as possible to alert me to their presence. Is that clear?"

"Perfectly."

I watched as Holmes, who had brought along a lantern, stepped down from the sleigh and went up to the front door. He removed something from an inside coat pocket, after which he began fiddling with the lock. Holmes always carried a set of lock picks and other such felonious devices with him, and he was remarkably adept in their use. It took him only seconds to unlock the door and step inside. Meanwhile, I moved up next to our driver, and the two of us scanned the streets, looking for any sign of activity. I saw one distant pedestrian, who appeared to be moving away from us, but otherwise this corner of St. Paul was as quiet as an English village at three o'clock on Sunday morning.

The speed with which Holmes accomplished his expert burgling of the door had come as no surprise to me, but I was quite astonished when—mere minutes later—he emerged from the club carrying a woman in his arms.

* * *

"Help me lift her into the sleigh," Holmes said as he approached. It was only then that I saw the face of the woman.

"My God, it is Mrs. Riley!" I said as I lifted her motionless body up into the sleigh. "Is she . . . ?"

"She is alive," Holmes assured me. "I believe she has been drugged."

I checked her pulse, which was slow and weak. As I did so, I noticed the loose ends of ropes around her wrists. Some fiend had bound her, and I began to fear that the worst had happened.

Holmes caught my look of concern and said: "I do not think she has been assaulted, Watson. That was not the intent of the man who lured her here."

I was nonetheless extremely concerned about her condition, and after laying her down on the sleigh's long seat, I examined her for any obvious injuries. I could find none. Moreover, her color was good, though there were dark smudges on her face. There was one more good sign—she felt warm to the touch. I attributed this to the fact that she was well dressed for the cold, for she wore a long fox coat, gloves, and a fur hat. After covering her with a heavy blanket to ward off any possible chill, I asked Holmes what had happened.

"We will know that for certain when she recovers," he said. "Suffice it to say that she was enticed here, no doubt on the prospect of seeing her husband, and then bound and drugged. I found her in a coal bin in the basement."

"But who did this and why?"

"I will explain everything in due time," said Holmes. "For now I must ask you to accompany her back to Mr. Hill's house and make sure that she receives the care she needs. In the meantime, I must go to the ice palace. That is where this case began, and that is where I believe it will end!"

An hour later, at just after ten o'clock, I was back in Hill's sleigh, this time on my way to join Holmes at the ice palace. I had by this time assured myself that Laura Riley had no serious injuries and that the drug she had received—probably a knockout drop of the kind favored by Bouquet—would cause her no lasting harm. Hill's personal physician concurred with this assessment and also agreed to stay with the young lady until she awakened. Thus free of my medical duties, I immediately set out to find Holmes.

He had told me he planned to meet Rafferty on the western side of the palace grounds, near Giuseppe Dante's apartment building. Under normal circumstances, these directions would have been entirely sufficient, but as my driver drew near the palace, I saw at once that finding Holmes would not be as easy as I had thought.

I have witnessed many amazing sights during my years of service with Sherlock Holmes, but nothing prepared me for the fantastic spectacle which presented itself at the palace. All around the grounds, a huge and boisterous crowd—its numbers undoubtedly swollen by the mild weather—had assembled to watch the storming of the palace. This multitude, easily many thousands of people, swarmed over every inch of the grounds and spilled out onto the surrounding streets, so that all direct access to the palace was blocked. Many members of this vast throng carried torches, which flared forth in such numbers that a sulfurous odor pervaded the atmosphere. Looking across this fiery scene, I felt as though I had stumbled upon some bizarre pagan bacchanalia, a primitive rite of winter to which the good people of St. Paul had surrendered themselves with uncivilized abandon.

Yet what caught my eye even more than this wild crowd was the ice palace itself, which had been transformed by days of relentless sunshine into a grotesque semblance of its former glory. Although multicolored lights still glowed from deep within its icy ramparts, there was now about the great structure a palpable sense of decay and dissolution. Its once crystalline walls had taken on a dirty honeycombed appearance, its towers had begun to droop and sag, its domed rotunda (where we had found poor Jonathan Upton) looked to be on the verge of collapse, and water oozed from its joints like perspiration flowing from fevered flesh. The effect was eerie and unsettling, for in its decomposing state the place resembled nothing so much as some huge, misshapen beast caught in its death agony.

The storming of the palace—an extravaganza of mock warfare engaged in by teams of men dressed in rather ridiculous outfits—began only moments after I had alighted from my sleigh and begun the search for Holmes and Rafferty. Announced by a fanfare of trumpets, the battle opened with a thunderous fusillade of bombs and rockets, after which green, gold, purple, and red fireworks cascaded across the night sky. The noise from this pyrotechnic display was so great—especially from the Duseldorf cracker mines—that it brought to mind the artillery barrages of my military days. The crowd, many of whose members appeared to have amply fortified themselves with ardent spirits, shouted approval with each new blast of bombs or burst of fireworks.[3]

My sleigh driver had let me off about two blocks south of the palace, and it was about the same distance to the apartment house where I was to look for Holmes. But a walk that might on any other occasion have been accomplished in five minutes took me thirty, for the crowd was packed together so tightly that I at times had to resort to brute strength to make any headway. One reveler, a red-faced giant who held a flask in each hand, became so irate when I tried to get by him that he threatened violence upon my person, forcing me to display my pistol before he would back off.

As I fought my way through the mass of humanity, I could make out little of the actual storming, which was being staged on a high wooden platform directly in front of the palace. Normally, this mock battle would have taken place within the walls of the palace itself, but the structure was now considered too precarious for such a use. The storming seemed to go on for many minutes, and at one point I caught sight of several men in red suits "attacking" their opponents with pitchforks like those supposedly carried by Satan's minions. I also got a glimpse of the palace's chief defender, King Borealis. This rotund worthy—whose uniform included a flowing white robe, a white beard, a golden crown, and a golden scepter—looked as though he was heartily enjoying his moment of royal nonsense.

I was just nearing the front of Dante's apartment house when I heard an unmistakable voice behind me.

"Well, now, I see you've made it, Doctor," said Shadwell Rafferty, drawing up next to me and grabbing my arm. "You're just in time."

I had to shout to make my words heard above the exploding fireworks. "In time for what? Has something happened?"

"I guess you could say that," Rafferty replied. "The fact is, your friend Mr. Holmes has just had a vision of light."

I found Holmes leaning by the front door of the apartment house. Although fireworks and rockets continued to explode overhead, filling the sky with magnificent ribbons of color, Holmes appeared not the least interested in this spectacle. Instead, he stared across at the crumbling, sagging walls of the ice palace, its simple lights no match for the luminous display in the heavens above.

Such was Holmes's preoccupation with the palace that I had to call his name twice before he greeted me.

"Ah, Watson, I am glad that you have arrived," he said in an excited voice, just as the fireworks display ended with a final barrage of bombs. "Look at those lights on the palace! Just look at them! I have been in darkness and now I have seen the light. It was stupid of me, of course, to have missed such an obvious thing, but then I am afraid this case will not go down in those voluminous notes of yours as my finest hour. Yet that is the problem with the obvious, is it not? Because it stations itself so boldly and shamelessly before us, we sometimes fail to see it."

I will readily admit that I had no idea what Holmes was talking about, since there appeared to be nothing unusual about the palace's lighting. I turned to Rafferty for guidance, but his only response was to shrug his shoulders and raise the palms of his hands, as if to suggest that some things were simply beyond all human ken.

With Rafferty unable to help, I saw no choice but to admit our mutual ignorance to Holmes: "Mr. Rafferty and I would be very much obliged if you could share with us exactly what it is that has caused you to become transfixed."

Holmes reacted with a look of pained amazement. "Don't the two of you see it? It is right there," he said, pointing off in the general direction of the ice palace.

"I'm sure 'it' is," I said, "but at the moment, neither of us has the faintest idea what you're pointing at."

"I am pointing at the rotunda," Holmes said with undisguised exasperation. "Look at the lighting there and tell me what you see."

"Very well. I see light of various colors coming through the blocks of ice. The light, however, appears to be rather weak and scattered, at least compared with the light coming from other parts of the palace. But what—"

"Excellent, my dear Watson, excellent!" said Holmes, patting me on the back as though I had just made an extraordinary deduction. "The light emitted through the rotunda is, for some reason, refracted by the ice there. As a result, the rotunda is not nearly so transparent as other parts of the palace."

Holmes then paused before adding: "And that is why I now know at last the whole truth of this case."

JUSTICE WILL BE DONE

T he crowd which had gathered with such enthusiasm to watch the storming of the ice palace left slowly and reluctantly once the show was over. By about eleven o'clock, however, only a few stragglers remained on the grounds. Meanwhile, the palace itself had gone dark—its array of incandescent lights turned off for the last time. Rafferty told me that come daylight, workmen would begin cleaning up the grounds and removing various temporary structures constructed for the carnival. The palace itself would be left to die in the sun, "rottin' away like an old carcass," as Rafferty put it.[1]

We watched the ebbing crowd from the windows of a small, furnished apartment on the second floor of the building where Dante lived. Holmes, I learned, had earlier in the day made arrangements with the superintendent to rent the vacant apartment at a special daily rate.

"The gentleman thought the arrangement rather peculiar," Holmes told me as we gazed out over the palace grounds. "Fortunately, the application of an extra gold piece instantly eliminated all such concerns. Naturally, I would have asked Mr. Dante for the use of his apartment, but it seems he is gone for several days on business. In any case, the view from here will do nicely."

I said: "The view would be even better if you or Mr. Rafferty would tell me just what it is I'm supposed to be looking for."

"Why, we're lookin' for a murderer, Dr. Watson," said Rafferty with a big grin. "And the sweet thing is, Mr. Holmes believes the miscreant will do us the favor of comin' right to us."

Holmes's faith in the impending arrival of the murderer was put to the test over the next several hours. Midnight passed uneventfully, as did one and two o'clock. Nor had anything of note occurred as three o'clock approached. By this time, the palace grounds, and the streets all around, were a cold desert. As we watched and waited, Rafferty amused us by recounting tales of his days in the Nevada silver mine and later as an officer of the law in St. Paul. If even half of his stories were true—and it was always hard to tell with Rafferty how much frosting he applied to the cake—then he had indeed enjoyed a spectacularly adventurous life.

Just after three, Rafferty was regaling us with the story of the scar over his left eye, when Holmes suddenly sprang to attention.

"There!" he said, pointing to the south, where a wagon driven by a large man passed beneath one of the lamps surrounding the palace grounds. The wagon, pulled by a single horse, was small and square, with an enclosed wooden box in place of the usual open back.

" 'Tis a night-soil wagon," said Rafferty.

We watched as the driver, whose face was hidden in shadow beneath a wide-brimmed hat, stopped at the south gate. He got down from his seat, quickly opened the gate ("Note that he has a key," Holmes observed), and then climbed back up on the wagon and drove inside the grounds. Shortly thereafter, the wagon disappeared around the far side of the rotunda.

"What do you suppose he's doing?" I asked.

"Unless I am mistaken, he's dropping something off," said Holmes. "I expect he will return momentarily."

Holmes's prediction proved to be accurate, for after about five minutes, the driver and his wagon reappeared. He went back out the gate, relocked it, and then drove off the same way he had come.

"Perhaps we should go down and see what has been dropped off," I suggested.

"Not yet," said Holmes. "I think our driver will return before long."

Again, Holmes proved to be prescient, for in a few more minutes the man, minus his wagon, came striding back up the street. He paused at the gate, looked all around as though anxious not be seen, then entered the grounds by climbing over one of the low perimeter walls.

I did not know what to make of this peculiar sequence of events, but both Holmes and Rafferty seemed perfectly at ease with what had just happened. Indeed, I had the distinct feeling that I was watching scenes from a play which the two of them had already written.

Rafferty provided the next preview of the script. "I imagine our friend Mr. Bouquet will be along shortly."

"Let us hope so," said Holmes, "for there will be no show without him."

Bouquet did not disappoint. "There he is," said Holmes, directing my attention to a figure coming down the street from the north side of the palace. "I would know that quick, insolent step anywhere."

Bouquet on this occasion had discarded his feminine attire in favor of a long trench coat and a bowler hat. He walked quickly down the street, his head moving from side to side, like a sleek predator keeping an eye out for quarry. As he drew near our apartment house, he stopped, and for a moment I thought we had somehow been detected at the window. This turned out to be a false alarm, however, for Bouquet—after making one final inspection of his surroundings—turned and walked directly toward the wall around the palace grounds. As the big man had done before him, Bouquet easily scaled the low wall. He then headed directly toward the rotunda and went inside.

Holmes and Rafferty watched this scene with keen, silent interest. Finally, Rafferty said: "Well, there's only one more to go, Doctor, and then we shall have company."

"Company?"

"My associate Mr. Thomas. He's been out and about tonight, but he'll be comin' here as soon as the last guest arrives."

"And that would be?"

The answer came from Holmes: "The Spider, Watson. He does not know it yet, but tonight he will be trapped in his own web."

* * *

It was nearly half past three when the man who was the object of our long search came walking up the street. He approached the palace from the south, and as he passed under the streetlamps I tried to discern his features, but the distance was too great and the light too weak. He wore a short coat, dark pants, and a stocking cap — the sort of everyday apparel common to working men. In his hand was a small bag, which he swung with a kind of jaunty abandon as he strolled along. I noticed that he walked with a remarkably firm and confident gait, the step of a man who seemed ready for whatever the world might present to him.

There was something familiar about this purposeful walk, and I was reminded of Holmes's frequent contention that a man's style of walking reveals as much about him as anything else. Indeed, when discussing the late Professor Moriarty, Holmes once told me: "He had the light step of the Thoroughbred; there was no waste to it, and he was always moving more quickly than he appeared to be. That is why the law, which is too often in England a plodding Clydesdale, could never catch up to him."[2]

Holmes, as it turned out, was now thinking along the same lines, for he turned to me and said: "Note how the Spider walks, Watson. There is no hesitation, no deviation from the straight path, no evidence that he has any regard for, or fear of, anything."

As Holmes spoke these words, the man reached the palace's perimeter wall and vaulted over it. "Did you see that?" asked Holmes. "The two men who preceded him tonight looked carefully all around before climbing over the wall. The Spider, however, took no such precautions. That is because he is a man who believes in his own invincibility. Such men are the most dangerous of all."

After entering the palace grounds, the man went directly to the crumbling rotunda, passed beneath its arched doorway, and disappeared from sight.

"Well," said Rafferty, "it looks like everybody's arrived. You were right, Mr. Holmes. The Spider wishes to end everything tonight."

"As do I," said Holmes.

There now came a series of rapid knocks at the door to our apartment.

"That would be Mr. Thomas," said Rafferty, going over to open the door. His faithful barman stepped inside, and the two of them conferred briefly in whispered tones. Then Rafferty said: "We are ready whenever you are, Mr. Holmes."

Holmes moved away from the window and tamped out the pipe he had lit only moments earlier. He said: "Then we must go, Mr. Rafferty. But I beseech both you and Mr. Thomas to be extremely careful. There are dangerous men inside the palace, and we must not underestimate their ruthlessness or resolve."

"Oh, I'll be ready," Rafferty said, brandishing a double-barreled shotgun, which Thomas had brought him. "If it comes down to fightin', I'm your man."

Holmes nodded, and without another word we followed him out the door toward what would prove to be our last adventure in the ice palace.

Once we reached the street, we immediately split up. Rafferty and Thomas circled around toward the north side of the palace, while Holmes and I made our way cautiously toward the rotunda entrance, on the south side. Although the palace's incandescent lights had been turned off, there was a faint glow coming from inside the rotunda, as though a lantern had been lit.

"It is just as I thought," said Holmes. "The Spider has gone to the rotunda to conduct his final piece of business."

As we neared the rotunda, I noted with alarm the condition of the ice blocks which formed the great dome. The January thaw had done its work with pitiless intensity, with the result that holes and fissures could be seen in almost every block of ice. Some holes were so large that they appeared to penetrate through the blocks. All of this melting had caused the dome to slump and sag in places, and I thought it a wonder that the entire structure had not crashed in on itself. The collapse could not be long in coming, however, and I saw numerous signs warning people to stay away owing to the dangerous condition of the ice.

Nowhere was this danger more apparent than around the high, deep doorway which led into the rotunda. Crowning the arched entrance was a gigantic keystone block, easily eight feet in height. The supporting blocks around it were all but gone, and water dripped from failing joints. Still, the keystone held, as though by some miracle of the builder's art. Holmes, of course, paid no heed to this hazard, for he immediately went to the doorway and stood just inside it, beneath the perilous keystone. I followed, and when I came up next to him I heard voices.

There were two of them, coming from inside the rotunda, and I knew them both. The first was that of Bouquet, who was saying:

"You'd better have the money in that bag. I don't want no tricks from you, or you'll never see her again. I'll cut her. You know I will."

"Oh, I have no doubt as to your sincerity, Billy," said the second voice, which I heard with a shock of recognition. "Cutting is what you like to do."

"And I'll cut you, too, if I have to," came the reply. "Now let's see the money."

"It's all right here in the bag. Five thousand dollars, just as you asked. Do you want to count it?"

"Godd--n right I do. You'd cheat your mother of her last penny, you would. Now throw the bag over here, and don't try nothing funny."

"Certainly."

I heard the bag land with a soft plop. There were several seconds of silence and then a cry of outrage from Bouquet. "Why, you lying son of a b---h. You'll pay for this."

"No, Billy," came the calm reply, which was accompanied by what sounded like the hammer of a pistol being cocked. "You will pay."

The man whom I now knew to be a murderer uttered these words in a chilled, deadly tone of voice. Then he said: "You are a fool, Billy, and fools do not survive long in this world. Do you really think I care about her? You can cut her into little pieces and scatter them to the wind for all I care. You can even have your way with her first, if that is your pleasure. But I do care about money, my dear Billy, and I do not like people who try to take it from me. Did you really think I would just hand it over to you?"

Bouquet, who I now imagined to be staring down the barrel of a pistol, showed no signs of losing his courage. "If I don't get the money, you'll be found out. I've kept records, and they will hang you."

The Spider laughed, but there was nothing like amusement in what he said next: "You've been keeping records, have you. Well, now, that's an interesting tidbit, considering that you can't read or write. What've you been doing, Billy, marking down everything with little *X*s and *O*s? Or have you mastered Sanskrit in your spare time? No, Billy, I'd say you're bluffing, and if you aren't, well, I'll take my chances anyway."

"I'm not bluffing," Bouquet insisted. For the first time, I heard fear in his voice.

"Neither am I," came the response.

It was apparent that Bouquet was in great danger, and I whispered to Holmes: "Shouldn't we go in now and put a stop to this?"

"Not yet, Watson. I must first have a signal from Rafferty that he has his end of the situation under control."

"But what if—?"

I never completed my question, for a sharp report came from inside the rotunda, and there could be no doubt it was a gunshot.

Almost instantly, there was a second report, louder and deeper than the first, and Holmes said: "Now, Watson, now! Follow me!"

I drew my revolver and rushed into the rotunda behind Holmes. The scene which confronted us in that dark, eerie, and precarious space was extraordinary. Lying by the altar in the center of the room, his body bathed in a small circle of moonlight, which had squeezed through the oculus, was Billy Bouquet. A deep crimson stain spread across his trench coat, marking the spot where a bullet had torn into his chest.

The man I now knew to be the Spider stood over Bouquet, studying the fallen criminal with a look of almost scholarly detachment, as though trying to classify some exotic species of animal. His face was illuminated by a lantern (presumably Bouquet's), which had fallen to the ground so that its beam now pointed upward. In that shadowy light I saw on the man's face an expression at once cruel and bemused, and which I can best describe as a kind of joyful wickedness.

There was a pistol in the man's hand, but he calmly put it in his coat pocket when he saw us. Indeed, his coolness was quite astonishing, for he showed no hint of alarm as we approached with our revolvers drawn.

"Well, fancy meeting you here," he said, as nonchalantly as if he had run across an old acquaintance at church on Sunday morning.

"I will relieve you of that pistol," said Holmes, who came around behind him while I kept my revolver leveled at his chest.

"As you wish," the Spider replied, adding: "It was, of course, a case of self-defense."

"I do not think so," said Holmes while I went over to examine Bouquet. It took but a moment to confirm that he was dead, for the bullet appeared to have gone right through his heart.

"Think what you will," the Spider replied. "However, I am sure Mr. —"

I now heard a commotion to our rear and swung around to see two men coming through the doorway into the rotunda. One of them carried a lantern, and I saw to my relief that Rafferty had now joined us. The second man, who was being pushed forward with a short-barreled shotgun at his back, was Chief of Detectives O'Connor. He wore a wide-brimmed hat, and it dawned on me that he must have been the driver of the wagon we had seen earlier.

"You were about to mention Mr. O'Connor, I believe," said Holmes, addressing the Spider. "I fear he will not be able to provide any testimony in your favor."

"Look who I found lurkin' about like a common criminal," said Rafferty as he prodded the chief forward. "Everything was just as you suspected, Mr. Ho — Mr. Baker. You were also right about the contents of the wagon. The gentleman in question is groggy but otherwise unharmed. Mr. Thomas is taking care of him."

The Spider grinned and said: "Good evening, Shad. I see you have brought along the chief of detectives."

O'Connor, his beefy face contorted by anger, unloosed a violent stream of epithets at Rafferty, who responded by striking him on the shoulder with the barrels of the shotgun.

"Mind your manners," he said, "or I will teach you some."

O'Connor turned around and glared at his nemesis, then said: "I will kill you for this, Shad, if it is the last thing I do."

"You are welcome to try it right now," said Rafferty, bringing up the barrels of the shotgun until they pointed right between O'Connor's eyes, "though I would note you appear to be at somethin' of a disadvantage at the moment."

"It is all right, Chief," the Spider said. "These men are delusional and will pay for their actions in a court of law. I promise you that. Incidentally, Shad, there is no need for you to maintain the ridiculous fiction regarding Mr. Baker and his friend. Mr. Sherlock Holmes — the world's greatest consulting detective, or so it is alleged — needs no alias. However, he may need an attorney after I get through with him."

The man's insolence was colossal, but Holmes refused to be baited.

"No, sir, it is you who will need the attorney, and he will have to be an excellent lawyer indeed to keep you from the gallows."

"Really? That's not the way I look at it. You see, I was lured here by Mr. Bouquet on the pretense that he would, in exchange for a cash payment, offer some new information regarding the unfortunate deaths in the ice palace. I was told I must come alone. Naturally, I did not wish to do so, and that is why I asked Chief O'Connor to accompany me as a precaution. Alas, Mr. Bouquet came at me before I could call for help, and so I had to defend myself."

"That is not what we heard," said Holmes.

"Perhaps not. Perhaps you believe you heard something different as you were eavesdropping by the doorway. Such things happen. A court will decide who is telling the truth. I am sure that Mr. O'Connor will, in any event, dispute your version of events. Isn't that true, Chief?"

"You can count on that," O'Connor snarled. "There ain't a jury in St. Paul that would take the word of a bunch of foreigners nosing about in something that's none of their business. As for the killing of Bouquet, I'm sure a jury would consider that a public service."

Holmes said: "You have forgotten something, Chief. There is also the matter of the jailbreak you arranged."

O'Connor was about to reply, but the Spider broke in: "The chief had good reasons for what he did, as will be duly explained to the public. Now then, why don't you face the facts, Mr. Holmes? You've botched this affair and botched it badly. You have no proof of anything."

"Oh, there is more than enough proof," said Holmes, cool contempt in his voice, "as you will discover soon enough. You think of yourself as being invincible, but you are not. There is, for instance, the matter of the coat—an amateurish mistake if I ever saw one. As a criminal, sir, you are definitely second rate."

The coat! The mere mention of this item restored to my mind the elusive apparition I had seen earlier. Of course! It was the coat that should have given everything away. How had I overlooked such an obvious clue?

As I pondered my lack of perspicuity, I waited to see what would come of Holmes's insulting remarks to the Spider. Insult was a tactic Holmes liked to use when interrogating a suspect, and it would fre-

quently result in an angry—and revealing—reply. The Spider, however, was not so easily put off balance. A slight flushing of his face
was the only sign that Holmes's cutting words had struck a nerve.
By the time he replied to Holmes's sally, he had complete control of
himself.

"I would suggest that you are the second-rate performer in this affair," he said, addressing Holmes with his usual impudence. "The
truth is that you have nothing against me, nothing, and you know it.
You think you have figured everything out, and in a way I suppose
you have. I will deny ever uttering these words, but you are absolutely correct as to the facts of the matter. Bravo to you, sir,
bravo!"

He clapped his hands over his head and then bowed toward
Holmes, but there was in these gestures a bitter, mocking quality
that I found hard to stomach. Then he said: "Knowing facts and
proving them are two different things, as you are well aware, Mr.
Holmes. The mighty edifice of evidence you've tried to build is just
like this ice palace, which is to say it is leaking and full of holes and
will soon tumble down of its own accord. That is because the one
thing you do not have is hard proof, the kind of proof which will
stand up in a court of law."

"You will regret your hubris," I told him sharply, "and you will
not be quite so pleased with yourself when the hangman comes
for you."

The Spider stared at me, his eyes as hard and cold as bullets.
"Really, Dr. Watson, I can see no logic in your remarks. But I suppose that is a deficiency with which Mr. Holmes is all too familiar."

"Why, you—" I began, and would have cuffed the insolent cur
had not Holmes intervened by grabbing my arm.

"Do not waste your energy on him, Watson," he said. "The facts
will in the end bring this villainous murderer to justice."

The Spider laughed, the sound of his vicious gaiety echoing
through the rotunda. He said: "And what facts might those be, Mr.
Holmes? The business with the coat? That was, I admit, a minor
mistake, but I have already conjured up several plausible explanations for it. Your other 'proof,' if it can be dignified by that name, is
nothing more than a thin tissue of airy suppositions. In short, Mr.
Holmes, you are talking through that fur hat of yours, which is why
I shall now be on my way."

"And what makes you think I shall let you leave?" said Holmes.

"Because you have no choice. Otherwise, I shall have to make out a complaint against you for kidnapping, which would be most unfortunate. If you have any further business with me, you may contact my attorney, Mr. Flandreau. I think you will find him to be a most able advocate. Well, then, ta-ta, as they say."

Ignoring the revolver which Holmes still leveled at his chest, the Spider turned around, doffed his hat at Rafferty, and began walking at an unhurried pace toward the doorway.

Emboldened by this brazen display, O'Connor decided to follow suit, despite the shotgun barrels now lodged in the small of his back. "I guess I'll be going too," he said, waving one hand over his shoulder in a gesture of defiance as he began to move away from Rafferty. He added: "I'll be seeing you soon, Shad, real soon. We'll have a regular meeting, we will, just you and me and a few coppers. Meanwhile, you'd best watch your back, or somebody just might put a bullet in it."

Rafferty's response to this taunt was quick and furious. He brought up the shotgun and struck O'Connor on the back of the neck with a tremendous blow, and the big man dropped to his knees.

Rafferty then bent down and put the shotgun right up against O'Connor's forehead. "You're not goin' anywhere until I say so," he said. "Besides, we have a little score to settle, just the two of us."

Amid all this excitement, the Spider continued to saunter toward the doorway as though he had all the time in the world.

I said to Holmes: "Surely you are not going to let him just walk away, are you?"

Holmes, his face grim and ashen, said: "For the moment, Watson, I have little choice. Much as I am loath to admit it, I have insufficient evidence to bring him to trial. Be assured, however, that I shall not rest until I have such evidence and the monster we see before us goes to the gallows. Justice will be done, Watson, no matter how long it takes. Indeed, I am of a mind that Mr. O'Connor may be just the man to help us."

"I can be very persuasive," Rafferty agreed, still holding the shotgun to the chief's head.

The Spider was now at the doorway and, apparently struck by an afterthought, turned slowly around to face us. Looking languidly at Rafferty, he said: "By the way, Shad, I'm the one who broke into your office. I needed to know if you had any proof against me. That ledger book was a nice little discovery. Too bad it will never be seen again. Oh, and I wish I could tell you that I feel badly about that dog of yours, but the truth is I don't. In fact, I rather enjoyed bashing in that miserable beast's head. I thought it might throw you off your game. You see, I never did care for either you or that mangy cur."

The events of the next few seconds will be forever engraved in my memory. With a deep-throated roar, Rafferty brought up his shotgun and leveled it in the Spider's direction.

I heard Holmes say something—I think it was simply "No, no"—but whatever his words were, they had no effect. Then I heard the blast from the shotgun, so loud that my ears rang for days afterwards, as Rafferty discharged both barrels at once. I do not know, and probably never will know, whether Rafferty was aiming at the Spider or at the huge keystone of ice over his head. But it was the keystone which the spray of pellets struck, tearing it completely away from its tenuous supports.

The Spider, his features contorted by a sudden presentiment of disaster, tried to duck the double load of shot by dropping to the ground. It did him no good. The massive keystone—which I was later to learn weighed over a ton—broke loose and came crashing down with the force of an avenging god, instantly crushing to death the Spider, Frederick Forbes.

25

DECEPTION WAS HIS GREATEST PLEASURE

"Well," said Sherlock Holmes, putting down the latest edition of the St. Paul *Pioneer Press*, "it appears that Chief of Detectives O'Connor has done exactly as he was told. What a fine talent he has for lying!"

" 'Tis God's gift to the Irish," said Shadwell Rafferty, "though I must point out, Mr. Holmes, 'twas you who cooked up the fragrant stew of falsehoods which was fed to our friends in the Fourth Estate."

"I shall take that as a compliment," said Holmes with a broad smile. "Still, I should note that as a teller of outsized lies I am hardly in the league of the late Frederick Forbes, who raised prevarication to the level of an art."

"He certainly fooled me," admitted James J. Hill, who presided over the sumptuous dinner of roast duck, quail, sweet potatoes, creamed asparagus, and wild rice we were now enjoying in the dining room of his mansion. It was the evening of Saturday, February 1, barely more than thirty-six hours after Forbes and Bouquet had met their well-deserved fates, and eight of us were gathered around the table.

Besides Rafferty and Hill, our dinner companions included Joseph Pyle, Michael Riley (who had earlier in the day won his freedom in court), Laura Riley (showing no ill effects from her kidnapping and drugging), and George Thomas, the Negro barman. The latter's appearance at Hill's table had caused something of a stir among the servants, which Rafferty promptly quieted by announcing that if "Mr. Thomas is not good enough to be seated at this table, then neither am I."

As our dessert of ice cream and strawberry shortcake was served with coffee, Hill asked Holmes and Rafferty to "tell the tale," as he put it. "I should like to hear the real story, since I can only assume that the version of events which appeared in the *Globe* and other newspapers is—I will be polite about this—not entirely accurate."

Rafferty burst out in great rolling peals of laughter. "Why, Mr. Hill, the newspaper stories are not merely inaccurate. They are giant whoppers, sir, shameless mendacity on a scale not seen since Mr. Wells supposedly found that enormous skeleton skulkin' about the old mill tunnel in Minneapolis. I must say Mr. Holmes has outdone himself in the fibbin' department, and that's a fact!"[1]

Rafferty was hardly exaggerating, for the various newspaper accounts of how Billy Bouquet and Frederick Forbes met their deaths were indeed exemplary specimens of journalistic fiction. The *Globe* set the standard in this regard, rushing out a special edition under the headline: A MYSTERY SOLVED, A VILLAIN UNMASKED, A HERO DEAD. Here is how the story began:

> The final act in the most sensational murder case in St. Paul's history was played out early this morning in the ice palace, where two men—one a villain and the other a true hero—fought to the death. The dead are Billy Bouquet, a notorious criminal who has long been a stain upon the good name of the city, and Frederick Forbes, scion of one of St. Paul's most distinguished families. Forbes died in the service of justice moments after killing Bouquet in a fearsome gunfight inside the walls of the palace's crumbling rotunda. Bouquet, authorities now believe, murdered both Jonathan and George Upton. The crimes, according to Chief of Detectives O'Connor, were motivated by Bouquet's attempt to extort money from the victims.

The remainder of the *Globe*'s story was equally misleading, telling how O'Connor—convinced that Michael Riley had been framed—

staged the prisoner's jailbreak as part of an elaborate scheme to set a trap for Billy Bouquet. The story went on to state that Bouquet was lured to the ice palace after Riley threatened to "rat on him to the police." At the palace, Bouquet supposedly admitted his crimes, saying he had murdered Jonathan Upton because the young man refused to pay extortion money for some "minor indiscretion" in his past. George Upton, it was said, had then been murdered when he, too, refused to give in to Bouquet's blackmail demand.

As for Frederick Forbes, the story declared that he went to the ice palace after learning from his sister of the meeting between Bouquet and Riley. There was a confrontation, during which Forbes shot and killed Bouquet. But before Bouquet fell dead, he managed to unload both barrels of his shotgun. "By the most unfortunate of circumstances," the story went on, "this blast of shot tore into a massive block of ice spanning the rotunda's doorway, unloosed it, and caused it to fall on the heroic Forbes, killing him instantly." All of this information was attributed to O'Connor, who according to the *Globe* had "witnessed the tragic scene but was unable to prevent the fatal gunfire which erupted so suddenly and unexpectedly."

Soon after the *Globe*'s extra appeared, the other newspapers of St. Paul did their utmost to embroider this fantastic tale, much to the pleasure of Holmes, who along with Rafferty had fabricated the entire story in the span of just a few minutes after Frederick Forbes's death. It was then left to O'Connor to implant this blatant fiction with the Fourth Estate.

Now Hill was asking for the truth, and Holmes—who had the utmost respect for the Empire Builder—promised to provide it. "But first I wish to make it clear that none of what you hear tonight must go beyond this table," he told us. "I concocted the story I did—with notable assistance from Mr. Rafferty, I might add—because the real truth not only would have devastated Cadwallader Forbes but would have left a permanent blot on the family name. It would also have exposed several young women to most painful public scrutiny. And, of course, there was the problem presented by Chief O'Connor, who was prepared to invent his own version of events and perhaps even arrest Mr. Rafferty on charges of murdering young Forbes."

"Just how did you get O'Connor to come around?" Pyle inquired.

"You might say I took a page out of Frederick Forbes's book of deceit. I told the chief that if he failed to do exactly as I said, I would hand over to the proper authorities a most revealing journal kept by Forbes. This journal, I assured the chief, spelled out his involvement in an extraordinary variety of criminal acts."

"What a fortunate find!" Pyle said. "How did you get hold of it, Mr. Holmes?"

"I didn't. There was no such journal, but it is a measure of the chief's complicity in this affair that he was well disposed to believe me."

" 'Twas a clever bit of business, all right," Rafferty said, shaking his head in admiration. "You should have seen the Bull's face when Mr. Holmes described the contents of this imaginary document. The chief looked as guilty as a parson in a whorehouse."

"Are you saying, Shad, that Mr. O'Connor was directly involved in the two murders?" asked Hill.

"No. But I'd be willin' to bet he knew much more than he let on. Now, it could be that Frederick Forbes fooled the chief like he did everyone else. Or it could be the chief was just doin' what he always does, which is to sell his services to the highest bidder. No matter; the fact is, he was a party to all manner of chicanery. Springin' Mr. Riley from the pokey was just one example."

"I must confess I fail to understand the jailbreak," I said. "Why should the chief do such a thing? After all, didn't he help frame Mr. Riley in the first place?"

Holmes leaned back in his chair, his hands atop his head, and said: "He did indeed, Watson. However, I think the chief staged the jailbreak at the urging of Mr. Forbes. The plan was to bring Mr. Riley to the ice palace, where both he and Bouquet would meet their deaths at the hands of O'Connor. The postmortem story would be that the two of them had plotted the murders together and then killed each other after a falling-out. Indeed, I suspect Mr. O'Connor was prepared to tell a fine story to the world, complete with colorful testimony as to the last words of the two miscreants."

Riley, who still seemed rather stunned by his sudden turn of fortune, said: "What a fool I was to believe the chief! When he arranged for my 'escape,' he told me he had found new evidence of my innocence but needed me to confront the real villain in the affair. I was so anxious to get out from that miserable cell that I readily agreed to the scheme. Once I left the jail I was to meet the chief in the alley a few blocks away. But all I met there was a nightstick splitting open my thick skull, and the next thing I remember is waking up in that awful dung wagon and seeing Mr. Thomas's face."

Said Holmes: "I can imagine that you were none too happy about your surroundings at that moment. But do not feel foolish because of what happened. I, too, was played the fool by Frederick Forbes, who offers a remarkable case study in criminality of the most insidious kind. To the world at large, he presented himself as a rather amiable hedonist, a lover of wine, women, and song, a man without spine or ambition. But Frederick Forbes the indolent ne'er-do-well was merely a facade.

"In retrospect, I should have realized this when his father told me that as a young man, Frederick Forbes was a 'great model builder,' who had helped create the excellent version of the *Mayflower* I saw in the offices of the family business. Now, as I can state from experience, it takes dedication, tenacity, and foresight to build a ship in a bottle. Yet these are precisely the sort of qualities one would not expect to find in a young man as feckless as Frederick Forbes pretended to be. No, his true self was the Spider, an intricate weaver of webs, a planner and a thinker, and a brilliant tactician of evil. The real Frederick Forbes was a master of deception who specialized in using others to accomplish his ruthless ends and satisfy his vile passions."

After pausing to light his pipe, Holmes continued: "Let us therefore consider Frederick Forbes's catalogue of crimes. He was, to begin with, a thief, for it was he who stole ten thousand dollars from the ice palace account. The money, I imagine, went to pay off his gambling debts."

"So George Upton was right, after all," Riley noted. "He thought somebody at Forbes and Son had taken the money."

"He did," Rafferty agreed, "which is why he and old Cad had that argument in the ice palace. But I don't think Mr. Upton knew Frederick Forbes was the thief."

Holmes nodded and said: "At least, he didn't know at first, though he undoubtedly began to suspect the real truth not long before he was murdered. Still, the theft helped set in motion a chain of events which eventually led to George Upton's death, as I shall demonstrate in due time. Now, however, let us move on to Frederick Forbes's second crime, the drugging and violation of young women."

"I still find it hard to believe that Freddie could have done such a monstrous thing," said Laura Riley, "or that Jonathan would have gone along with him."

"Nonetheless, it is clear from Jonathan Upton's diary that he was lured into these horrendous crimes by your late brother," said Holmes.

Pyle now posed an interesting question: "Do you think Frederick Forbes was the sole author of these vile attacks, Mr. Holmes, or was the idea suggested to him by Bouquet?"

"We will never know for certain, but my guess is that the idea came from Forbes. Indeed, Forbes's brutish desires are probably what led him to ally with Bouquet, whom he met—as Jonathan Upton's diary tells us—at one of the 'gambling dens' on St. Peter Street. Bouquet was more than willing—for the right amount of money, of course—to serve as Frederick Forbes's procurer. And it was the ravishing of these women, crimes so heinous that they are beyond all forgiveness, which led in turn to the murders of both Jonathan and George Upton."

"I do not follow you," said Riley. "Surely you are not saying that George Upton was involved in those crimes?"

"No. What I am saying is that George Upton lost his life because of what he discovered after his son's murder."

"In other words, he read Jonathan's diary," Hill said with his usual astuteness.

"Precisely," said Holmes. "Remember that George Upton went to his son's apartment after he disappeared, no doubt in hopes of finding some clue as to his whereabouts. Instead, Mr. Upton found the diary and presumably interpreted its incendiary contents much as we did. More importantly, I am convinced he knew that Frederick Forbes was the Spider mentioned in the diary. That is why Mr. Upton later told us that he would deal with the 'traitor' responsible for his son's death. He felt that his son had been betrayed into wrongdoing by his supposed friend, Frederick Forbes."

Pyle spoke up: "But how do you conclude that Mr. Upton knew the Spider's identity?"

"If you'll excuse me, I'll show you," said Holmes, who rose from his chair and left the room. He returned momentarily with a large book, which I recognized as the same one—*Businessmen of the Great Northwest*—that had been delivered to Hill's doorstep on the night of our final adventure in the ice palace. Holmes handed the volume to me, and as I paged through it, I realized that it was one of those dull subscription books devoted to chronicling the achievements of otherwise uncelebrated merchant princes.

"I suggest you turn to page one hundred and twelve," said Holmes. I did so and found the following as part of a lengthy entry devoted to the career of Cadwallader Forbes. "Numbered among the rising young businessmen of St. Paul is Mr. Forbes's only son, Frederick. The young man, already a valued partner in his father's business, was known in his collegiate days at Yale as the Spider because of his subtle intellect, and there is every reason to believe that he will one day weave a web of prosperity for the firm of Forbes & Son."

After I had read this passage out loud, Holmes said: "Frederick Forbes and Jonathan Upton were classmates at Yale—a fact which I confirmed only this morning—and that is one reason why I think it likely that George Upton knew the Spider's identity. I was also able to verify today that a copy of *Businessmen of the Great Northwest* can be found in George Upton's personal library."

"How extraordinary," marveled Hill. "Who sent the book to you, Mr. Holmes?"

"The sender preferred to remain anonymous. However, I have no doubt that it was Jedediah Lapham, since one of his young assistants was seen delivering the volume here. As it so happens, Mr. Hill, one of your servants—Laura Olson—is romantically involved with the young man in question. She told me his name and for whom he is employed."

"Are you saying that Mr. Lapham knew all along what sort of crimes Frederick Forbes was committing?" Hill asked. "I find that hard to accept."

"Let me put it this way. I believe it very likely that Mr. Lapham knew of the embezzled money and the sexual assaults, and that he came to strongly suspect Frederick Forbes in connection with both crimes."

"Then why in God's name didn't he tell someone?" Laura Riley inquired, her tone leaving little doubt that she found Lapham's silence despicable.

"Mr. Lapham had good reasons for his silence, at least from his perspective," Holmes replied. "You see, he knew that your father would never believe criminal allegations against Frederick. It is also possible that Mr. Lapham simply had no solid evidence of your brother's wrongdoing. Still, Mr. Lapham did hint at what he knew during our conversation at the Muskrat Club, when he warned me to watch out for the 'man who wears a mask.' This was his way of telling me that the criminal was not someone obvious, such as Bouquet. My questions about the Spider must have led Mr. Lapham to recall what he had seen in his employer's copy of *Businessmen of the Great Northwest*. He then decided to pass the book on to me, albeit anonymously."

"All right, you have solved the mystery of the book," said Hill. "But what led Frederick to commit murder? Was it fear of being exposed for his crimes with the young women?"

"That is one possibility," Holmes acknowledged. "Yet I am not so sure that George Upton was prepared to make the sordid goings-on at the Muskrat Club a matter of public knowledge. After all, he knew that his own son had been involved in those crimes. Moreover, the diary also indicated that Jonathan Upton had been stealing money from his father's firm to make blackmail payments to Forbes and Bouquet. All of this amounted to more dirty laundry than George Upton wished to make public.

"Mr. Upton, however, did intend to expose Frederick Forbes's embezzlement from the ice palace account. Keep in mind that Mr. Upton had suspected for some time that money was being embezzled, and had even confronted Cadwallader Forbes on this point during their meeting in the ice palace. But it was not until Mr. Upton found his son's diary that he was able to identify Frederick Forbes as the embezzler. Young Forbes must have gotten wind of this fact, possibly from his father, and realized that he was about to be branded a thief. And so he decided that his only choice was to silence George Upton once and for all."

Riley said: "You make it sound such an easy and logical decision, Mr. Holmes. Was Frederick so cold-blooded that he could treat murder in that way?"

"He was. I believe he was a man unburdened by the weight of a conscience. The murder of George Upton in particular was a crime of pure, icy calculation. It should also be noted that Forbes himself almost certainly did not commit the actual deed. That was left to Bouquet, who I am sure demanded a hefty sum for the job. Exactly how George Upton was lured to his death we shall never know, but

my guess is that Forbes wrote him a letter to which he affixed someone else's name — perhaps even yours, Mr. Riley. The letter probably
offered a meeting where George Upton supposedly would be provided with new information about his son's death. Upton agreed to
the meeting, and that was a fatal mistake, for he was stabbed to
death by Bouquet in the dark of night. Bouquet then took the body
in a night-soil wagon to the ice palace grounds and dumped it there.
This was done in order to tie together the murders of Jonathan and
George Upton and to frame you, Mr. Riley, as the man guilty of both
crimes."

"But why me?" Riley asked plaintively.

"Ah, that is a very good question," said Holmes. "I am sure
Bouquet, having lost an ear to your combat skills, relished the
opportunity for revenge. There is, however, a far more important
reason — which I will discuss later — why you were chosen as the
scapegoat. For now, suffice it to say that you were an easy and natural target. In any event, young Forbes busily went about fabricating
evidence against you. Living as he did in the same building where
you reside, Forbes had no trouble entering your apartment and leaving various incriminating items there. He then tipped off Chief
O'Connor to make a search of your apartment. And, of course, it
was Forbes who notified the police of your whereabouts after you
eloped with his sister."

Laura Riley, her beautiful face expressing a mixture of sadness
and anger, said: "To think that my own brother could be such a monster of deceit!"

" 'Tis the sad truth, I'm afraid," said Rafferty. "There are men in
this world who live secret lives, and your brother was one of them.
Deception was his greatest pleasure."

Holmes agreed. "I believe Frederick Forbes saw himself as the
master of a secret world of his own making. In this world he was all-
powerful, a god among mere mortals. That is why he was always
looking for ways to manipulate others to serve his own dark ends.
Take, for example, one of his most inspired touches in this affair —
the threatening letters he wrote to himself to deflect any suspicion
which might be directed toward him. He was, it must be acknowledged, a brilliant actor."

"Then I suppose he also made up the business about being shad-
owed by Bouquet," said Pyle.

Holmes nodded. "He did, and in many ways it was his most dazzling deception, one which he undertook for the express purpose of eliminating Bouquet."

"I do not follow you, Holmes," I protested. "Wasn't the idea that Bouquet would try to kill you, as he had earlier?"

"That is what Bouquet, I am sure, was told. But the evidence suggests otherwise. Indeed, I believe Forbes began to see Bouquet as a distinct liability, because he was the one man who knew all his dirty secrets. It's also possible that Bouquet had begun to press Forbes for ever larger payments to ensure his continued silence. To deal with this problem, Forbes hit upon a truly ingenious solution. He convinced us that he was being followed by Bouquet, thereby setting in motion our elaborate surveillance. The truth, of course, is that we had no chance of spotting Bouquet as we trailed Forbes through the city, because Bouquet was already well ahead of us, awaiting our arrival on Bench Street. There, he had no doubt been told that he was to rush out, appear to threaten Forbes, and finally stab me as I came up to help. Imagine, then, Bouquet's surprise when, as he came out of the darkness, Forbes slashed him with a knife."

"You mean Bouquet was Forbes's intended victim all along?" Pyle asked.

"Yes, and it was probably only Bouquet's quickness that saved him, for he suffered only a minor, if rather bloody, knife wound to his thigh, as Mr. Rafferty later learned from his friend the coroner. In any event, Bouquet sensed instantly that he had been set up and fled the scene, with yours truly"—here Holmes gave a rueful smile—"in futile pursuit. Forbes's plan had been to kill Bouquet in what would seem to be a heroic act of self-defense. But when his plan went awry, he made a revealing mistake."

"The coat," said Rafferty. "Both Mr. Holmes and I noticed it at once. You see, when I bent down to look at young Forbes, to see how badly he'd been hurt, I saw that his trench coat was open and unbuttoned all the way down the front. The wound to his abdomen, which was little more than a long scratch, had bled on his shirt, but there were no stab marks of any kind on his coat. Not bein' the greatest genius in the world, it took me a while before I asked myself why Mr. Forbes had been walkin' around on a damp, chilly January night with his coat wide open. The answer, of course, is that he wasn't. Which is why, Dr. Watson, I asked you that 'peculiar' question as we were returnin' here with Mr. Holmes after our adventures on the river. You told me that Mr. Forbes's coat had indeed been buttoned when you saw him at the top of Bench Street."

"But what is the significance of all this?" I asked, for I still failed to see why the condition of Forbes's topcoat mattered in the least.

Hill, however, grasped Rafferty's point at once. "Why, what you're saying, Shad, is that Frederick must have stabbed himself!"

Rafferty laughed and said: "Ah, 'tis clear why you're the Empire Builder, Mr. Hill, for you have a way of puttin' two and two together as fast as any man I know. You are exactly right. Mr. Forbes stabbed himself, though not with much success, so that we would believe he had been attacked by Bouquet. And in order to inflict this wound without seriously hurtin' himself in the process, he had to open his coat so he could make a nice little scratch on his belly. But as you may remember, Mr. Hill, after we got back here that night, Forbes told us how he had 'felt the sting' of Bouquet's knife as it slashed through his clothes. That's when I started gettin' very suspicious. My suspicions were confirmed when I found a bloody knife in the pocket of Forbes's coat."

"So that is why you were rummaging through Mr. Hill's cloakroom before you left," I said.

"Guilty as charged, Doctor. Afterwards, I went immediately to Mr. Forbes's apartment and did a little rummagin' there as well. But the lad was d--nably clever, and there was no imcriminatin' evidence to be found. So I bided my time until Mr. Holmes awoke from his nap, and then we had a long talk. We agreed that young Forbes was our man, for Mr. Holmes had also noticed the discrepancy with the coat, among other things. It was decided we should put a 'tail' on Mr. Forbes, and I entrusted the job to Mr. Thomas here and several street urchins of his acquaintance. They were more than up to the task."

Thomas then offered an interesting explanation as to how his "lads" had managed to follow someone as clever as Forbes: "There is one person that even the wariest man in this city will pay no heed to, and that is a Negro child. Such children, it is assumed by white folks, must be entirely ignorant and shiftless. I therefore found several clever lads and had them keep a round-the-clock lookout on Mr. Forbes. I am sure he never suspected a thing."

" 'Twas a signal piece of work," Rafferty agreed, "and with Mr.

Holmes's blessin', I have since dubbed the lads the Robert Street Irregulars.[2] With the boys' expert help, Mr. Holmes and I were able to keep a close watch on Mr. Forbes, hopin' he might link up with Bouquet and we'd catch the two of them red-handed."

Holmes, who had been listening with unaccustomed patience to Rafferty's narration, said: "Unfortunately, we made one major miscalculation. We did not account for Bouquet's mounting desperation."

"Can you explain what you mean?" Pyle asked. "If I were Bouquet, I simply would have left town."

"I'm sure that was his eventual goal," Holmes acknowledged, "but first he needed money, as much as he could lay his hands on. Consider for a moment his situation. He knew that we were looking for him, that O'Connor and the police were looking for him, and that Forbes had already tried to kill him. Where could he turn? He finally decided that his only hope was to blackmail more money from Forbes. Now, Bouquet was the lowest class of criminal, but he was not without cunning. He realized that in any confrontation with Forbes, he must have an insurance policy, as it were, so that he would not be double-crossed again. You, Mrs. Riley, were that policy."

The lady shook her head, once again astonished by her own brother's perfidy. "In other words, I was kidnapped and held hostage simply as a bargaining chip."

"I fear so, madam. Still, I should have anticipated such a stratagem on Bouquet's part. I did not, for which I must beg your apology."

"There is no need for that, Mr. Holmes. You saved my life. But how did you find me?"

"It was a hopeful deduction on my part. Once I learned you had been called away from your residence on a pretext, the possibility of a kidnapping occurred to me at once. But where to find you? I tried to think as Bouquet would. Where might he hold someone for a short period of time? He needed a place which was convenient and secure, and would not have any people about. And that led me to the Muskrat Club. I knew he must have a key to the club, given his unsavory activities there, and I also knew that the club would be empty, since its members were all celebrating the grand finale of the Winter Carnival at the ice palace. Still, I was much relieved when I found you in the club's basement, Mrs. Riley."

"Not half as relieved as I," said the courageous lady, squeezing her husband's hand. "I was afraid I might never see my Michael again."

"Do you believe Bouquet would eventually have let Laura go if you had not found her?" Riley asked, kissing his wife upon the cheek.

"I think not," said Holmes. "Mr. Bouquet was not a sentimentalist. Having already killed at least once, I do not imagine he would have been put off by the prospect of killing again. Nonetheless, he did make a fatal misjudgment when he kidnapped Mrs. Riley and set up the meeting in the ice palace. Bouquet assumed that Frederick Forbes would in fact care about his own sister's life. But he did not, and so he killed Bouquet without hesitation."

Holmes now recounted the entire episode in the ice palace, ending with that extraordinary moment when the huge block of ice at last brought the life of Frederick Forbes to an end.

There was a long silence before Pyle finally spoke up: "That is quite a story, Mr. Holmes. I only wish that I could tell it to the people of St. Paul."

"Joseph, that will not be possible," said Hill curtly. "I think it best for all concerned that the truth of this matter stay inside this room. There is no use in dragging the dead through the mud. Cad Forbes, in particular, would be grievously harmed if the real story got out. Besides, it would not present a good image of St. Paul if people knew that two of its most prominent and highly regarded young men were involved in crimes of the most sordid kind."

"Well, the *Globe* is your paper, Mr. Hill, and you are free to do with it as you see fit. I predict, however, that the truth will one day come out."

"Perhaps," said Hill, "but you may be assured that it will not be in the *Globe*."

This emphatic statement brought another bout of silence, before Rafferty asked the question which was on everyone's mind: "I would be curious, Mr. Holmes, to hear your thoughts about the murder of Jonathan Upton. Why do you suppose Mr. Forbes killed his best friend?"

Holmes smiled and said: "Really, Mr. Rafferty, I thought it must be quite obvious to everyone here that he did no such thing."

26

IT IS ALL ABOUT FIRE AND ICE

Had Holmes suggested that the sun rose in the west and that the moon was made of cheddar cheese, I doubt there could have been any greater uproar at the table. Everyone began talking simultaneously, peppering Holmes with questions, comments, and expressions of astonishment. Holmes—a magician's smile creasing his face—took it all in with bemused satisfaction, immensely pleased that we had all been caught unawares by the sudden appearance of the rabbit from the hat.

"Please," he finally said above the agitated din. "I cannot answer your questions when everyone is talking at once."

It was Hill, accustomed to commanding far greater forces than our dinner party, who at last restored order. "Quiet!" he decreed in a booming voice, and the table instantly went silent. Gathering the full majesty of his presence and fixing upon Holmes the kind of gaze that could melt steel, he said: "Now then, Mr. Holmes, please explain yourself."

"Gladly," replied Holmes. "Let me begin by showing you something."

We now had our second surprise of the evening, for at Holmes's command, a servant wheeled in a small table, atop which sat an object of some kind, covered by a large white cloth. With a nod from Holmes, the cloth was removed, to reveal Holmes's model ship, which he had somehow inserted into its bottle. How he had found time to complete this intricate project was beyond me, yet I also knew that nothing was impossible when Holmes set his furious energies to a task.

"Behold the *America*," said Holmes, a distinct note of pride in his voice. "A handsome ship, is she not?"

"Very handsome," said Hill sarcastically. "Now, if you will so kind as to tell me why—"

"An excellent question, Mr. Hill," Holmes smoothly interposed. "Let me explain. I am showing you my model of a schooner yacht. As you can plainly see, the *America* is a two-master. Why two masts? Because she was built for speed. Now, a single set of sails would not have given her the speed her designers wanted, while three would have been too many for so light and agile a craft. Well, Mr. Hill, I submit to you that the ice palace affair is a two-master as well, propelled forward toward its double tragedy by two sets of sails, which were interconnected and yet operated quite independently."

Holmes now had us in the palm of his hand and knew it. Taking a deep breath, he paused to survey our eager and expectant faces, and then once again began to "tell the tale":

"Let us first turn to the question of why Frederick Forbes could not have murdered Jonathan Upton. The answer, which everyone here seems to have overlooked, is quite simple. You see, Frederick Forbes had an ironclad alibi for the night in question. He told us he was in Minneapolis with friends, and I made it a point to check his story. These 'friends'—nearly a dozen of them, some no more than chance acquaintances—all verified that Mr. Forbes did indeed attend a dinner party that evening and that he was present until after two in the morning."

"What about—" Pyle began, but Holmes had already anticipated his objection.

"What about Billy Bouquet? A good theory, Mr. Pyle, except for one problem. You see, I also looked into Bouquet's whereabouts and discovered that he spent the night in jail, on a charge of public intoxication. He was hauled in by the police at about ten o'clock in the evening after an altercation at one of the city's most notorious rum holes and was not released until the following day."

"All right," said Hill brusquely, "we stand corrected. But if Forbes or Bouquet did not murder Jonathan Upton, then who did?"

Holmes's reply was hardly what Hill might have expected: "Tell me, Mr. Hill, what is the theme of the Winter Carnival?"

Glaring at Holmes, Hill said: "Really, sir, I do not care one whit for the d--ned Winter Carnival, as it is of little use in running a railroad. Once again, I must ask you why the devil—"

"Please, bear with me," Holmes cut in, "and I think all will become clear. I asked about the carnival because its theme bears an eerie similarity to what might be called the theme of these murders. The carnival, you see, is built upon the conflict between fire and ice—the forces of Vulcanus Rex doing battle against the wintry legions of King Borealis. So it is with this case. It is all about fire and ice—the deepest passion on one hand and the chilliest calculation on the other. George Upton, as I trust we must all agree, was the victim of a hard-hearted murderer who acted solely to protect his own interests. The crime was carried out most efficiently, but there was little art or drama to it. It was, if I may say so, almost businesslike.

"Ah, but compare this unimaginative killing to the murder of Jonathan Upton. His murder, despite its icy setting, clearly was a crime motivated by some terrible passion. The murderer, as the insightful Mr. Pyle once pointed out, was not content merely to kill young Upton. He also wanted to make a statement. How else explain the almost operatic quality of the murder, especially the shocking manner in which the severed head was presented, like a bloody stage prop, to the world? It was, in other words, a deeply personal crime—brilliantly planned, to be sure, but still much different from the killing of George Upton."

Said Rafferty: "All right, Mr. Holmes, since we're playin' your game at the moment, let's talk about motive. I can think of only one feature of this case which might inspire the awful thirst for vengeance you're talkin' about, and that would be what happened to those poor young women. Are we therefore to assume that the murderer was a brother or father or even husband of one of the victims?"

"That is an excellent assumption, Mr. Rafferty."

Everyone at the table paused to consider this latest revelation from Holmes, and after a moment, I had an idea. "What about that servant girl of yours, Mrs. Riley? Does she have a brother or father who might have sought revenge on her behalf?"

"No," replied Mrs. Riley at once. "The girl is an orphan and has no brothers or sisters."

"Well, then," said Rafferty, "seein' as how we don't know who the other victims were, you're not helpin' us much, Mr. Holmes. Perhaps you'd be kind enough to give us poor mortals another clue."

Holmes said: "Very well, Mr. Rafferty, I will provide another clue. First, however, may I ask if you ever read medieval poetry?"

Rafferty was by this time so used to Holmes's manner that he registered no surprise despite the oddity of the question. He said: "Why, Mr. Holmes, I am a great lover of verse. 'Tis the soul of the Irish, and that's a fact! Would there be a particular poet you have in mind?"

"There is," said Holmes, summoning a servant and whispering a few words to him. With a nod, the servant left the dining room. His mission was a mystery to us, and we awaited his return with a sense of suppressed excitement. When the servant finally came back, he held a book, presumably retrieved from Hill's personal library.

Holmes took the volume, which had a red and black cover with stenciled lettering, and rapidly thumbed through it, obviously looking for a specific passage. "Ah, here it is. Let me read you a few lines:

'Gia era, e con paura il metto in metro
la dove l'ombre tutte eran coperte,
e transparien come festuca in vetro.
'Altre sono a giacere; altra stanno erte,
quella col capo e quella con le piante;
altra, com'arco, il volte a pie rinverte.' "

Closing the book, Holmes said: "My medieval Italian is not very good, but fortunately this edition contains a translation by Mr. Longfellow, of poetic renown. What I have just read is a passage from the thirty-fourth and last canto of the *Inferno* of Dante Alighieri. In it, Dante describes Cocytus, the ninth and final circle of hell, where the poet finds the most despicable of criminals—traitors to family, country, and God—entombed in a frozen lake. Satan himself occupies the center of this lake, beating his wings eternally in a futile attempt to escape his icy prison. He has three heads, forming a grotesque version of the Holy Trinity, and in each of his mouths he holds a sinner—Judas Iscariot in the center, Brutus on one side, and Cassius on the other."[1]

Holmes paused to let this remarkable picture of eternal damnation play upon our imaginations. Then he said: "I suggest to you that the man who killed Jonathan Upton and put his head in a block of ice did so because he believed that the young man had committed a crime so heinous that he deserved a special place in hell."

"Giuseppe Dante," said Rafferty, shaking his head as though amazed by his own obtuseness. "Of course! Of course! Then this must mean —"

Holmes completed his thought: "That Mr. Dante had a daughter. He did, and she was among the young women drugged and violated by Jonathan Upton and Frederick Forbes. But unlike the other victims, she was able to identify Upton as one of her assailants. Her father, a man of great passion and honor, then took it upon himself to wreak a terrible form of vengeance."

"But how do you know all of this?" Pyle asked.

"I know because I have spent much of the day learning the fate of Mr. Dante's daughter, whose name was Beatrice — the very name of the woman whom the poet Dante so adored. However, you may be interested to learn that it was the ice palace itself which finally pointed me toward the tragic truth of this affair. The answer, you see, was in the ice all along."

Holmes, as was his wont, did not immediately explain this tantalizing remark, which drew a babble of inquiries from the dinner party. After everyone had quieted down, he said: "Do not worry, you will all have your answer soon enough. First, however, I should like to ask a few questions of Mr. Riley, whose experience as construction superintendent of the palace qualifies him as something of an expert on the subject of ice."

"I don't know about that," said Riley, "but I'll help in any way I can."

"Good. Now then, tell me, if you would, why the blocks used for the ice palace are the size that they are. Why couldn't they be larger or, for that matter, smaller?"

Looking no less puzzled than the rest of us, Riley replied: "Well, it's largely a matter of cost and convenience. The smaller you cut the blocks, the more expensive they become, because the labor costs are higher. On the other hand, if you make them too large and thick, they're hard for the men to handle. Does that answer your question, Mr. Holmes?"

"Not quite. Tell me more about the thickness of the blocks. The standard block, I believe, is about twenty inches thick. Why not twenty-four or even thirty inches?"

Riley replied: "Well, some of it is just a matter of what looks good, I guess. Over the years, the palace builders in Montreal, who taught us much of what we know, discovered that if the ice is too thick, a palace won't show up well with electric lights."

"And why is that?"

"What happens is that the light starts to refract if the blocks get much more than two feet thick. You lose luminescence, and the palace just doesn't glow the way everybody likes."[2]

"I see. Now tell me about the rotunda. How thick are its walls? More than two feet?"

"Oh, they're much thicker, especially near the bottom. They're about four feet at ground level, and then they gradually grow thinner as you get near the top of the dome."

"So I would be safe in saying, I presume, that the rotunda, due to the unusual thickness of its walls, refracts light in a way which makes it look different from the rest of the palace."

"Yes, I suppose that must be the case, though to tell you the truth, I never really noticed it."

"I did," said Sherlock Holmes.

I now remembered Holmes's "vision of light," as Rafferty called it, while we waited for the final confrontation in the ice palace. But I did not understand the significance of this vision until Holmes reminded me of something which had happened much earlier.

Addressing the entire table, he said: "As Dr. Watson, I am sure, will recall, Mr. Dante made an intriguing observation during our first interview with him. He mentioned that he had seen a mysterious bright light shining through the walls of the rotunda on the night of Jonathan Upton's murder. Mr. Dante was very animated in his description of this light and how it moved 'like a dancing white ball.' He went on to tell us of a man he saw emerging from the rotunda, a man who wore a coat very much like one belonging to George Upton. It was a most peculiar story, and, of course, it was a complete fabrication. I realized this when I finally took a good look at the lighted rotunda and saw that it was not transparent like the rest of the palace. Therefore, Mr. Dante could not have seen the dancing beam of light he so carefully described, nor—I believe—did he see George Upton or anyone else leaving the rotunda that night."

"And Mr. Dante's big whopper, I imagine, made you very suspicious," Rafferty observed.

"It did," Holmes acknowledged. "I asked myself why he would lie about such a thing. The answer, I think, is that his hatred for the Upton family was so profound that he wished, if possible, to implicate the father in the son's wrongdoing. The description of the mysterious light was merely an arabesque designed to ornament Mr. Dante's story. Yet in the end it proved to be the major flaw in what was otherwise a perfectly planned crime."

"What happened to Beatrice after she was raped?" asked Laura Riley, in her usual blunt way. "Did she tell her father at once what had happened?"

"I do not think so," said Holmes. "I am not even certain that she was at first able to identify Jonathan Upton as one of her assailants. I do know, however, that she became pregnant as a result of the attack."

"The poor woman," I said. "It makes my blood boil to think there are men who could do such a thing."

"The world is full of such men," said Mrs. Riley in what I took to be a reprimand, "and they do such things every day. Now, if you would please, I should like to hear more of Beatrice's story."

Said Holmes: "It is not a happy story, I fear, but you shall have it nonetheless. I have learned today, through a series of telephone calls, at least the rudiments of the young woman's life. She was about twenty years of age and working at one of the dry goods stores downtown at the time of the assault last year. I do not know how Frederick Forbes 'selected' her to be one of his victims, but he may have seen her at the ice palace site with her father. She was said to be quite beautiful and possessed of a vivacious spirit. She was Mr. Dante's only child, his wife having died several years before he came to St. Paul."

"And when was that?" Hill asked.

"About five years ago," said Rafferty. "I first met him when he was carvin' some new sculptures for St. Mary's Church.[3] I never saw his daughter, though. It must have been terrible for him to learn what those men did to her."

"It was," said Holmes, "especially when her pregnancy became obvious, late last summer. I talked this morning with Mother Ursula, who is in charge of the House of the Good Shepherd here in St. Paul.[4] She told me that Miss Dante was admitted in August to the home, which provides shelter for young women who have conceived out of wedlock. She did not do well, however, and was extremely ashamed of her condition. By last November, she had grown so despondent that there were fears for her life. As a result, Mr. Dante decided to take his daughter to live with her aunt in Chicago. Mother Ursula told me that Mr. Dante hoped this change of scenery might help her. Mr. Dante himself was extremely busy with the ice palace carvings in St. Paul but intended to join his daughter in Chicago as soon as possible."

There was something unsettling about Holmes's use of the past tense, and as he continued his story, I felt a mounting sense of dread.

"It is likely that Dante visited his daughter at least once in Chicago. And though I cannot prove it, I suspect it was only then that he first learned that Jonathan Upton had assaulted his daughter."

"Why do you say that?" I asked. "Surely his daughter would have told him at once what she knew."

"To the contrary, she might have felt too ashamed to speak up," said Mrs. Riley. "Or her memory of the attack might have been vague because of the drugs."

Holmes said: "You are right, Mrs. Riley. Indeed, I suspect it may have been some months before Beatrice Dante was able to recall what had happened, so cruel and devastating was the crime of which she was a victim. Moreover, I believe that had Mr. Dante learned at once who had assaulted his daughter, he would have acted more quickly. As it was, something Beatrice Dante saw or heard came back to her, and she was able at last to identify Jonathan Upton as one of her assailants. But it was not this revelation alone which sent Giuseppe Dante on his mission of revenge."

"I fear you are about to tell us very bad news," said Pyle.

Holmes responded with a somber nod. "I am. Two days after Christmas, Beatrice Dante left her aunt's home, saying she wished to go for a walk. Several hours later, her body was found in the Chicago River. Mr. Wooldridge, with whom I also spoke today, has provided me with the tragic details. Witnesses said Miss Dante leaped into the icy waters from one of the busiest bridges in the Loop and made no attempt to keep her head above the water. The child she was carrying died with her."

The room grew silent, and I do not doubt that in all our minds there appeared the same doleful image of a young woman on a wintry day climbing over the railing of a bridge and flinging herself and her unborn child into the dark swirling waters below. It saddened me greatly to contemplate Beatrice Dante's fate, and I understood for the first time why Jonathan Upton had met so horrible a death in the ice palace. I also came to feel, as did Laura Riley, that the young man had gotten only what he deserved, although I was not certain Holmes would agree.

Holmes now continued his tale: "Naturally, Mr. Dante—who had just returned to St. Paul on the day of his daughter's suicide—was devastated by her death. He was also bent on revenge, and after he had buried his daughter, his entire life, his every thought, was devoted to nothing else. I imagine he spent every night laying his plans. The fact that young Upton was about to be married no doubt entered into Mr. Dante's calculations, and he saw the nuptials as a chance to show the world what he thought of Jonathan Upton's treachery. Before putting his plan into effect, however, Mr. Dante created a memorial to his daughter, for she was the subject of that haunting sculpture Watson and I saw on our very first day in St. Paul."

There were no questions now; we were all spellbound as Holmes narrated the wrenching saga of Giuseppe Dante's revenge.

"How Mr. Dante accomplished his vengeance can be readily inferred from the evidence already in our possession, especially Jonathan Upton's diary. Upton was probably lured to the ice palace on the pretext that Mr. Dante wanted money to take care of his pregnant daughter. What he really wanted, of course, was blood, and he got it by stabbing Upton to death. The actual murder, I believe, took place in Mr. Dante's workroom behind the rotunda. His plan, I am sure, had been to decapitate Upton at once and insert his head in a block of ice already prepared for the grisly purpose. But the night turned out to be uncommonly warm, with the temperature above freezing, and so Mr. Dante was faced with a problem."

Rafferty said: " 'Twas a nasty problem, when you think about it. There he was with a dead body, which needed to be stored somewhere until the weather froze and he could cut off the head without makin' an awful mess of the job."

"It was indeed a challenge," said Holmes, "but Mr. Dante rose to the occasion, showing the sort of bold genius evinced by the thief in Mr. Poe's ingenious story 'The Purloined Letter.'[5] There, the thief baffled the police of Paris by hiding an incriminating letter in a most obvious place. Mr. Dante did just the same with Jonathan Upton's body. A merely mediocre murderer would have gone to great lengths to hide the body, perhaps hauling it away or trying to cache it somewhere in the palace and dig it out later. Mr. Dante, however, had a much more ingenious idea.

"He simply hung the body from a hook in his workroom where he normally kept heavy coats and other winter clothes. I know this because I found a minute quantity of blood beneath the clothes hook. Of course, I cannot prove this blood came from Mr. Upton, but I am certain it was his. Covered by coats and perhaps some canvas, Upton's body was so neatly hidden that no one noticed it.

"Mr. Dante had another brilliant idea as well—he put on Upton's clothes and walked boldly past the night guard. By doing so, of course, he made it appear as though Upton had left the ice palace, thereby forestalling a search of the grounds by the police. This tactic worked beautifully, for the police looked everywhere but the palace for Mr. Upton once his disappearance was reported.

"It was probably the night after the murder, by which time the weather had turned much colder, that Mr. Dante performed the decapitation, no doubt using a saw of some kind, as Mr. Rafferty first suggested. The head was then inserted into the waiting block of ice, as was the Muskrat Club pin which Mr. Dante had removed from young Upton's coat. The pin was, in Mr. Dante's eyes, a badge of shame, and that is why he included it with the severed head."

"But how could Mr. Dante have done all of this without somebody seeing what he was up to?" asked Pyle.

"I am sure the work was done at night," Holmes replied. "Mr. Dante worked all hours in the palace, and his presence there—even well after midnight—would not have aroused suspicion. In any case, the next day Mr. Dante took the rest of young Upton's body to the city dump in a wagon of the kind normally used to carry construction debris from the palace grounds. No records were kept as to who used these wagons—at least, Mr. Rafferty could find none—but it must have been in just such a vehicle that the headless corpse was hauled away. Once the body had been disposed of, Mr. Dante had little more to do except to wait for Jonathan Upton's head to be discovered."

"That seems strange to me," said Hill. "Why did Mr. Dante hide the head beneath the altar? Why not just leave it somewhere for all the world to see, since that seems to have been his intention in the first place?"

"I can only guess the answer, Mr. Hill. But I think Mr. Dante intended that the head should be found on the day originally set for Jonathan Upton's wedding. Mr. Dante probably planned to make sure that head would somehow be 'discovered' at the appropriate time. Unfortunately for him, Mr. Rafferty and I stumbled upon the head before Mr. Dante could carry out the final part of his plan."

Thomas now raised an intriguing point. "There's one thing you haven't mentioned, Mr. Holmes, and it puzzles me. Did Frederick Forbes know the truth about who murdered Jonathan, or was he in the dark like everybody else?"

Holmes, who had lit his pipe, took a long draw of tobacco and said: "That is an excellent question, Mr. Thomas, and only Frederick Forbes, if he were alive, could answer it with complete certainty. I suspect, however, that he truly believed Mr. Riley murdered Jonathan Upton. He therefore thought it only logical to frame Mr. Riley for the murder of George Upton as well. I have found no evidence to suggest that Frederick Forbes knew what Mr. Dante had done. Nor do I believe Mr. Dante knew that Forbes had been a part of the brutal assault on his daughter. That is why this case presented so many difficulties. There were two murders, interconnected in numerous ways, yet committed by two men for entirely different reasons. I do not know that I have ever seen such a case before, and I only pray that I do not see its like again."

After another long silence, Laura Riley said: "You have painted a most sympathetic portrait of Mr. Dante, sir. And yet I must remind you that this noble gentleman appeared perfectly willing to let my Michael go to the gallows for a crime he did not commit."

"To the contrary, he had no intention of doing so," said Holmes. "He greatly admired your husband and told me so the second time we talked. Indeed, he went out of his way to inform me that Mr. Riley could not possibly be guilty of the crimes of which he was accused. But Mr. Dante did not stop there."

"What do you mean?" Mrs. Riley asked.

Holmes reached into his coat pocket, removed a folded sheet of paper, and said: "This letter was delivered to me today. It is Mr. Dante's complete confession."

There was a stunned pause before Hill finally said: "Am I to take it, then, that Mr. Dante's arrest is imminent?"

"I would not know," Holmes replied nonchalantly. "That is a question best put to the police of this city, though I doubt they are aware of Mr. Dante's role in the ice palace affair. Indeed, the only real proof of his guilt—the only evidence which I believe would stand up in a court of law—is here in my hand."

"I see," said Hill, his one good eye boring in on Holmes. "And just where might Mr. Dante be at the moment, if I may ask?"

Holmes reacted to this question as though he had just been asked for advice on the best route to Katmandu. With a quick shrug, he said: "I have no idea as to Mr. Dante's whereabouts. All I can tell you is that he left his apartment hurriedly late Thursday morning and gave no forwarding address to the building superintendent. By this time, I imagine he could be almost anywhere."

"But shouldn't we be looking for him?" Pyle asked. "After all, he has confessed to the crime of murder."

"You may do as you please, Mr. Pyle," said Holmes. "If you think it wise and just to send the law after Giuseppe Dante, I will not stop you. But I will not help you either."

"Still—" Pyle began, only to be interrupted by Hill.

"Joseph, calm down," Hill said, rising from his chair and going over toward Holmes, who sat at the opposite end of the long dining room table. Holmes rose to meet him, and the two titans—each the master of his world—exchanged long and penetrating stares.

"May I see Mr. Dante's confession?" Hill said at last.

"Of course," said Holmes. Hill took out his glasses and read the confession carefully, at one point slowly shaking his head, but otherwise making no comment.

He returned the document to Holmes and said: "What do you intend to do with this confession, Mr. Holmes?"

Holmes replied in a firm voice: "I intend to burn it, Mr. Hill, unless you or anyone else at the table objects. Indeed, I propose to poll the jury, as it were, at this very moment. Dr. Watson, where do you stand?"

"On the side of justice," I replied. "I could not in good conscience send Mr. Dante to prison or the gallows for avenging his daughter's death."

"My dear Watson, I knew I could rely upon you," said Holmes warmly. "Mr. Rafferty, what do you say?"

Rafferty tugged at his luxuriant beard and said: "I like the idea of a little fire, Mr. Holmes. 'Twill help keep us warm on this cold winter's night. Mr. Dante is already in his own hell, and there is no reason to torture him further. Burn it, I say."

"I thought you would agree with me," remarked Holmes with a smile. He then turned his attention toward Thomas, who sat next to Rafferty. "And you, sir, what do you say?"

"I am with Shad," said the loyal barman, "and always will be."

"Good. Mr. Pyle?"

Pyle, disappointment clouding his features, said: "Well, I never thought the day would come when I'd pass up a story like this one. Good God, it would be the journalistic coup of the decade! But I see your point, Mr. Holmes, and I'll not be the one to stop you from doing what you think best."

"Thank you, Mr. Pyle," said Holmes. "Mr. and Mrs. Riley?"

Laura Riley—after a quick look at her husband, during which some private and instantaneous form of communication occurred— spoke for the two of them: "Michael has what he wants, which is his freedom and his good name, and I have what I want, which is my husband. There will be no objections from us, Mr. Holmes."

Holmes nodded and turned back once again to face Hill. "Then it is up to you, sir. No man in this city has more power or influence, and if you choose to carry this matter forward because you believe the truth must be served, I will respect your decision."

Hill went over to one of the dining room windows, from which could be seen the lights of St. Paul sparkling below. He gazed out over this beautiful scene for several minutes, collecting his thoughts. Finally, he turned back toward us and said in an unusually subdued voice: "George Upton was as good a friend as a man could ever ask for, and I will miss him to my dying day. But I see no point now in calling out the dogs and bringing Mr. Dante to the dock for trial. I do not agree with what he did, nor do I think it right, but I understand the fury which drove him. This business has gone far enough, and it is time to be done with it."

He then looked directly at Holmes. "But I do have one question for you, Mr. Holmes."

"And what would that be, sir?"

The Empire Builder smiled and said: "Do you have a match?"

EPILOGUE

I SHALL CALL HIM SHERLOCK

Two days after James J. Hill had consigned Giuseppe Dante's confession to ashes, Holmes and I went with Rafferty for a last visit to the ice palace. Our train to Chicago (and from there to New York and then home via the *Campania*) was due to leave that afternoon, and I assumed this would be our last chance to see Rafferty, whom both Holmes and I had come to regard with the utmost fondness. What I could not have known then was that we would in fact see Rafferty again in connection with the strange and deadly runestone affair, of which so much as been written of late.[1]

But on this particular day, as we walked along Summit Avenue, our minds were still occupied by the ice palace case. It was a glorious morning for early February in Minnesota, as more than one passerby proclaimed to us during our walk to the palace. The temperature stood near forty degrees, the wind was but a whisper, and soft sunshine poured down from a limpid blue sky. This ideal weather, a gift from the heavens to the chilled citizens of St. Paul, had not been so kind to the ice palace, however.

As we approached Central Park, I looked in vain for the towers and parapets which had for a short time been the glory of St. Paul. But they were gone, reduced to a jumble of blocks scattered around the muddy park as though discarded by some careless giant. The rotunda where our great adventure had begun and ended was also a ruin. Its roof had collapsed, and only its thick lower walls—which had proved such a revelation to Holmes—still stood, forming a huge circle in the mud like the remains of some ancient temple whose purpose could only be guessed at. A group of ruddy-cheeked boys had taken over the remnants of the palace, constructing snow forts amid the jagged piles of ice and lobbing snowballs at one another from their makeshift redoubts.

"Well, Mr. Rafferty, it has been quite an adventure," said Holmes as we paused to gaze upon the ruins. "Both Dr. Watson and I owe you our very lives, and if there is anything we can ever do for you in return, you need only ask."

"Why, think nothin' of it," said Rafferty. " 'Twas an honor to be of some service to the two of you. I only wish you could stay a while longer, though I imagine you are anxious to get back to London."

"We are," Holmes acknowledged, "for I have no doubt that the city's criminals have been busy in our absence."

Holmes took a moment to light his pipe and then said in an utterly matter-of-fact way: "Incidentally, Mr. Rafferty, how, exactly, did you convince Mr. Dante to write his confession?"

Rafferty was not an easy man to catch off guard—like Holmes, he always seemed to be ahead of the game—but in this instance even he was taken by surprise. His blue eyes opened wide and his head jerked back slightly, as though he were trying to dodge a blow. Then a wide smile spread across his jovial face.

He said: "Well, I guess I have finally learned my lesson. I said before that you could not fool Sherlock Holmes, and I guess I'll have to say it again. You are right, of course. I did have a talk with Mr. Dante early on Thursday while you were still sleepin', Mr. Holmes."

"And at that time, I presume, you told him that you knew he had killed Jonathan Upton. I'm curious how you reached that conclusion, Mr. Rafferty."

"I got lucky. You see, when I went through Freddie Forbes's apartment, lookin' for evidence, I didn't find any evidence directly connectin' him to either of the murders. But I did come across one curious item—an old copy of the *Pioneer Press* from last year, in the bottom of a chest of drawers. I paged through it and saw that an article had been circled in red ink. The article was about Miss Beatrice Dante and her volunteer work at the Catholic Orphan Asylum. There was a picture of her too, and even though it wasn't a very good one, any fool could see she was a beauty. That's when I started wonderin' if maybe she had been one of the women assaulted at the Muskrat Club."

"And so later that morning you went to Mr. Dante's apartment and confronted him with your suspicions."

"Yes, and I suppose you can figure out the rest. Mr. Dante readily admitted what he had done—seemed almost relieved to talk to me, as a matter of fact. But I don't mind sayin' his confession left me with a bit of a problem. I wasn't interested in sendin' him off to prison, but I didn't want Mr. Riley to go the gallows either. So I told Mr. Dante to write up his confession, sign it, and then leave St. Paul as fast as he could. After that, I thought things over for a bit and decided the best thing to do was to send the confession to you, Mr. Holmes, and see what you'd do with it."

"But why didn't you simply tell us about the confession?" I asked.

Holmes provided the answer. "I think Mr. Rafferty wished to enjoy a little contest of wits. He had discovered the truth and wanted to know if I could do likewise. That is why he played dumb during our dinner gathering at Mr. Hill's mansion. Yet Mr. Rafferty also worried that I might not prove up to the task of discovering Mr. Dante's guilt, so he provided me with the confession just to be certain. This also was Mr. Rafferty's way of ensuring that Michael Riley would be released from jail. Am I right, sir?"

"You are," Rafferty admitted with a grin. "I thought that just maybe I could outsmart Sherlock Holmes—what a feather in a man's cap that would be!—but I was wrong. Still, I don't regret tryin' it."

"Ah, Mr. Rafferty, you are a most extraordinary character," said Holmes, "and always full of surprises. Well, come along now, for I have a surprise or two for you."

Less than an hour later, we were back at Hill's mansion, where Rafferty was indeed surprised to find that our dinner party of two days earlier had reassembled in the main parlor, to enjoy a glass of wine and the pleasure of his company.

"Well, now, what's this all about?" he asked nervously as he looked over the room. The Rileys, holding hands just as they were the last time I had seen them, sat on a sofa in one corner. Pyle and Thomas occupied comfortable leather chairs near the fireplace, as did Hill himself. I took a seat next to Hill, while Holmes, acting as a sort of master of ceremonies, led Rafferty to the center of the room.

"Dr. Watson and I have been thinking about how best to express our gratitude to you for rescuing us from the river and for the many other services you have rendered during our stay in St. Paul," Holmes said to Rafferty, who seemed embarrassed by so much attention. "We considered many gifts—a case of fine Irish whisky, a suit from one of Savile Row's finest tailors, or perhaps a signed first edition of one of Watson's rather sensational tales. But we rejected all of these ideas in favor of something a little more, shall we say, lively."

"Really," said Rafferty, "there's no need for this. No need at all. 'Tis been my pleasure and honor to provide what help I could to you gentlemen. Now, if—"

Holmes interrupted: "There shall be no speeches, Mr. Rafferty, and no objections. Everyone in this room is in agreement that you deserve something more than merely a polite thank-you."

"Hear! Hear!" said Pyle, whose words were followed by murmurs of assent all around the room.

"Now then, Dr. Watson, if you would, please do the honors," Holmes said.

"Gladly," I replied, and went upstairs to retrieve Rafferty's gift, which Hill had acquired for us just hours earlier.

When I returned and Rafferty caught sight of the squirming little creature in my arms, he looked more excited than I had ever seen him before. The puppy—a two-month-old bulldog, brown and white in color—reacted with equal excitement, yapping and wagging its tail with all the energy it could muster.

"We are calling him John Brown Junior," said Holmes as I presented the puppy to Rafferty. "Mr. Hill obtained him from a breeder here in St. Paul, who assures us that no better bulldog could be found between here and the Pacific."

Beaming like a child just handed a box of chocolates, Rafferty brought the puppy up to his breast and began gently petting its tiny forehead.

"Oh, he's a beauty," Rafferty said, trying to ignore the tears form-ing in his eyes, "and I think the two of us will get along just fine. There is one problem, however."

"A problem? What sort of problem?" asked Holmes with genuine alarm.

"This little fellow needs a different name. There was only one John Brown, and there can never be another. No, this young fellow needs a name of his own. I shall call him Sherlock, and I've no doubt he'll be the finest bulldog that ever lived."

Rafferty paused, then added: "And that's a fact!"

NOTES

Introduction

1. For the exact reference, see Dr. John H. Watson, *Sherlock Holmes and the Red Demon*, ed. Larry Millett (New York: Viking, 1996), 293. The manuscript itself was discovered in 1994, in a hidden wall safe in the library of James J. Hill's mansion in St. Paul. I was able to date the ice palace case because Watson himself spoke of returning to St. Paul "little more than a year" after leaving Minnesota in September 1894 (when the case of the Red Demon was concluded). There is also the fact that the only St. Paul ice palace of the 1890s was built for the 1896 Winter Carnival. In addition, it is worth noting that there are no other known cases involving Holmes between November 1895 ("The Adventure of the Bruce-Partington Plans") and October 1896 ("The Adventure of the Veiled Lodger"). Holmes and Watson thus would have had ample time to travel to St. Paul to investigate the ice palace murders in January 1896.

2. In addition to verifying that the manuscript of *The Ice Palace Murders* was in Watson's distinctive handwriting, I determined that the paper and the pencil were both of a kind typically used by the good doctor. For more details on my general authentication procedures, see *Sherlock Holmes and the Red Demon*, xi–xii.

3. A number of St. Paul newspapers devoted lengthy obituaries to Rafferty after his death on January 22, 1928. The most complete appeared in the St. Paul *Dispatch*, January 24, 1928.

Chapter One

1. Alas, no trace of the muskrat monograph has ever been found, either in Watson's records or in the scientific journals of the day.

2. "The Real Story of St. Paul's Ice Palace Murders," by the famed muckraker Lincoln Steffens, appeared in the January 1899 issue of *McClure's*. Contrary to its title, however, the article offers little beyond a rehash of earlier newspaper stories, although it does contain new information about the role of the St. Paul police in the affair. Watson's description of this article as "recent" suggests that he began writing his own account sometime in 1899.

3. Potter Palmer (1826–1902) began his career in the dry goods business but was also extensively involved in real estate. In addition, he founded Chicago's famed Palmer House hotel, which opened in 1870 and then was quickly rebuilt after burning down in the Great Fire of 1871. The case "vital to the national interest" that Watson mentions here was "The Adventure of the Bruce-Partington Plans," in which Holmes recovered top-secret English submarine plans stolen by a foreign spy. Although the case occurred in November 1895, Watson did not get around to writing about it until 1908, and that may explain why his reference here is so vague.

4. This is the earliest known reference to Chicago in one of Watson's tales and suggests that Holmes's familiarity with the city, as described in later stories, derived at least in part from his visit in 1896. For example, in "The Adventure of the Dancing Men," which concerns events occurring in 1898, Holmes remarks upon his "knowledge of the crooks of Chicago." There are other references to Chicago in *The Valley of Fear*, "The Adventure of the Three Garridebs," and "His Last Bow."

5. The *Campania* was the sister ship of the *Lucania*, on which Holmes and Watson had made their first voyage to America, in 1894. Both ships were launched by Cunard in 1893 and were considered the finest ocean liners of their time. The *America*, built for the New York Yacht Club, was a 170-ton schooner that in August 1851 won a race against fourteen British ships around the Isle of Wight. It was this race that inaugurated the America's Cup series. Under various names and owners—including a stint in the Confederate Navy—the schooner survived until 1940. The *America* has long been a favorite of model makers, so it is not entirely surprising that Holmes chose it for his first ship in a bottle.

6. Palmer's mansion—a mock-Rhenish concoction on Lake Shore Drive, complete with towers and battlements—was the closest thing to a private castle in Chicago. Perhaps the house's most unusual feature was its lack of exterior doorknobs, which meant that the only way for a visitor to enter was to be announced by a servant. Built in 1882, the house fell to the wrecker in 1950. Palmer's wife, Bertha, was one of the great figures in Chicago society and an avid art collector. The "blurry French paintings" that Watson refers to were in fact by the likes of Renoir, Degas, and Monet (the Palmers owned over thirty of his works). Many of these paintings were later bequeathed to the Art Institute of Chicago and form the basis of its magnifi-

cent French Impressionist collection. Holmes's fondness for these paintings may have been genetic, since he mentions in "The Greek Interpreter" that his grandmother "was the sister of Vernet, the French artist." As for Mrs. Palmer, she was also known for her extravagant spending, and in his highly unusual will Potter Palmer actually left a substantial sum to his successor, should his wife choose to remarry. Palmer said he did so because any future husband would "need the money." Although Watson is not forthcoming about the "urgent and delicate matter" that required Holmes's assistance, a good guess is that it involved the Palmers' son, Honore, who may have been something of a rake. For more on the Palmers and Chicago in general, see Donald L. Miller, *City of the Century: The Epic of Chicago and the Making of America* (New York: Simon & Schuster, 1996).

7. Clifton Wooldridge was an undeniably brilliant detective but also a great self-promoter who liked to call himself "the incorruptible Sherlock Holmes of America." He served on the Chicago police force from 1888 to 1910 and documented his exploits in a book entitled *Hands Up! In the World of Crime; or, 12 Years a Detective* (Chicago: C. C. Thompson Co., 1906). "Panel houses" were brothels designed with sliding wall panels, through which a man's billfold or other valuables could be removed from his pants while he was engaged with a prostitute. The "goosing slum" and the "blind pig" were both types of cheap, usually unlicensed taverns that flourished in vice districts like the Levee, which at the time of Holmes and Watson's visit occupied an area along State Street just south of the Chicago Loop.

8. Mickey Finn tended bar at several Chicago saloons before opening his own establishment—the Lone Star—in about 1895. His specialty, which earned him linguistic immortality, was a knockout potion (described as "a sort of white stuff") given to unsuspecting patrons in their drinks. Once unconscious, victims would be dragged to a back room and robbed of everything in their possession, including clothes and shoes. Finn's saloon was finally shut down in 1903, but not before he had sold his "formula" to other saloonkeepers. Eventually, a knockout drug of any kind became known in the underworld as a "mickey finn." There is a brief account of Finn's career in Herbert Asbury, *Gem of the Prairie* (New York: Alfred A. Knopf, 1940; DeKalb, Ill.: Northern Illinois University Press, 1986), 171–76.

9. Henry H. Holmes, also known as Herman W. Mudgett, was a serial killer who lived in Chicago around the time of the 1893 World's Fair. He lured perhaps a hundred or more victims, mostly women, to gruesome deaths in a fantastic house he built at the corner of Sixty-third and Wallace Streets on the city's South Side. The huge house, known as Holmes' Castle, contained trapdoors, hidden staircases, secret chambers, soundproofed rooms, a vat of corrosive acid, and even a pit filled with quicklime. Holmes was finally arrested in 1894 in connection with a murder in Philadelphia and tried in that city a year later. It was only at this trial, which ended in Holmes's conviction, that authorities learned of the earlier horrors at his "castle" in Chicago. He was finally hanged for his crimes—as Sherlock Holmes predicted—in May of 1896. See Asbury, *Gem of the Prairie*, 177–96.

10. For more on Empress Anna's pioneering ice structure, see Fred Anderes and Ann Agranoff, *Ice Palaces* (New York: Abbeville Press, 1983), 11–15.

Chapter Two

1. Leander Starr Jameson (1853–1917), with five hundred men, raided the Transvaal on December 29, 1895, as part of a plot hatched by Cecil Rhodes to overthrow the Afrikaner government there. The raid ended ignominiously with Jameson's surrender on January 2, 1896.

2. For a good account of the early St. Paul Winter Carnivals, see Paul Clifford Larson, *Icy Pleasures: Minnesota Celebrates Winter* (Afton, Minn.: Afton Historical Society Press, 1998), 41–81.

3. Cass Gilbert (1859–1934) later went on to national prominence, designing such notable works as the Woolworth Building (1913) in New York City and the U.S. Supreme Court Building (completed in 1935) in Washington, D.C. In Minnesota, his best-known building remains the State Capitol, which opened in 1905.

4. Ice, which weighs nearly 58 pounds per cubic foot, is indeed a sturdy structural material. Its tensile strength is around 300 pounds per square inch, while its compressive strength can be as high as 1,500 pounds per square inch. These figures (which assume a temperature of about 20 degrees Fahrenheit) are comparable to concrete.

5. Watson is referring here to Joseph Paxton's famed Crystal Palace, a gigantic structure of glass and iron erected in 1851 for an exhibition in London's Hyde Park. Later moved to another location, the structure was destroyed by fire in 1936.

6. Central Park and the residential neighborhood around it are gone today. The site of the park, just southeast of the State Capitol, is now occupied by a parking ramp that serves a nearby state office building.

7. Nelly Bly, who worked for the *New York World*, among other newspapers, was one of the most famous journalists of the day. She covered the aftermath of the Hinckley Fire in 1894, and Watson actually talked with her at that time; see *Sherlock Holmes and the Red Demon*, 275. Curiously, it does not appear that Bly covered the ice palace murders, even though they attracted an enormous amount of national publicity.

8. Lillie Langtry, a British actress celebrated for her beauty, made several tours of the United States, though I have been unable to find any evidence that she appeared at St. Paul's Metropolitan Opera House in January 1896.

9. The Fulton Fish Market, on the East River in lower Manhattan, was established in the 1820s and remains one of the largest wholesale fish markets in the world.

10. Lake Vadnais is located about five miles north of downtown St. Paul and is today part of a protected chain of lakes that provide much of the city's water supply.

Chapter Three

1. Nina Clifford was a legendary St. Paul madam, who operated the city's most popular bawdy house from the 1880s to the 1920s. See Paul Maccabee, *John Dillinger Slept Here: A Crooks' Tour of Crime and Corruption in St. Paul, 1920–1936* (St. Paul: Minnesota Historical Society Press, 1995), 13–17.

2. Swede Hollow, where immigrant families of many nationalities found their first home in St. Paul, remains a prominent feature of the city's East Side. The last families were evicted from the hollow in the 1950s, and it is now a park.

3. Theodore Hamm (1825–1903), one of St. Paul's most successful early businessmen, founded a brewery that eventually became one of the largest in the country. After several changes of ownership, the brewery—in operation for nearly 140 years—finally closed in 1997. Hamm's mansion overlooking the brewery was built in 1887 and destroyed by fire in 1954.

4. Although Holmes is known to have used the alias of Sigerson, a Norwegian explorer, this is the first indication that he may have spent some time in Sweden after the affair at Reichenbach Falls.

Chapter Four

1. Holmes had a long-standing interest in art, though he gives little evidence of connoisseurship in Watson's many stories. However, his readiness here to engage in a debate over two fourteenth-century Italian painters suggests that he may have known more about the history of art than he let on to Watson.

2. The "legend" of the Winter Carnival was based on Greek and Roman myth, modified to serve the cause of celebration. Boreas was the Greek god of the north wind, while Vulcanus was the Roman god of fire. These two figures remain part of the annual Winter Carnival in St. Paul.

Chapter Five

1. Jean Champollion (1790–1832) founded the study of Egyptology and was the first to decipher hieroglyphics. He did so with the aid of the Rosetta Stone, a slab inscribed in hieroglyphics and two other languages that was discovered in Egypt in 1799.

2. St. Paul's prostitution district was located near the Seven Corners area, in a section of downtown St. Paul that is today occupied by various public and institutional buildings. The old Central Police Station was on Third Street (now Kellogg Boulevard) and was within a stone's throw of Nina Clifford's brothel, among others that operated with impunity.

Chapter Six

1. Thomas Shadwell (1642–1692) was a poet and dramatist whose work is little read today. As Watson notes, he is chiefly remembered as an object of ridicule in John Dryden's famous lampoon, *MacFlecknoe*, published in 1682.

2. Pyle is correct in stating that Minnesota troops were the first offered to Lincoln. Then Minnesota Governor Alexander Ramsey happened to be in Washington when news of Fort Sumter's surrender reached the city. The next day, April 14, 1861, Ramsey offered to raise a volunteer regiment of one thousand Minnesotans to fight for the Union. See Richard Moe, *The Last Full Measure: The Life and Death of the First Minnesota Volunteers* (New York: Henry Holt, 1993), 7–8.

Chapter Seven

1. Hill began his art collection in the 1880s, eventually focusing on painters from the French Barbizon School. All told, he spent about $1.7 million to acquire his collection. The house's tracker organ, which remains in place, was built by George Hutchings of Boston and has 1,006 pipes. The thirty-six-room Hill mansion is now owned by the Minnesota Historical Society and is open to the public. See Craig Johnson, *James J. Hill House* (St. Paul: Minnesota Historical Society Press, 1993).

2. I have been unable to locate Upton's mansion, which does not appear in any of the standard architectural histories of Summit Avenue. This suggests that the house may originally have been built for another family.

3. The case of the German forger was never "written up" by Watson, and so it is not known when the episode took place or what "horrible" fate awaited Holmes had he not been able to "maintain a prolonged conversation against all odds."

4. Billy Bouquet's name turns up in several St. Paul newspaper accounts of this period, but only in passing, and very little is known of his earlier criminal career in Chicago.

Chapter Eight

1. Holmes and Watson had lunch at the Ryan Hotel during their 1894 visit to Minnesota, but Watson makes no mention of Rafferty's saloon in *Sherlock Holmes and the Red Demon*. City directories indicate that the saloon opened in 1888, just three years after the hotel itself was built, and remained in operation until 1920, when Rafferty apparently sold it. All traces of the old saloon vanished in 1962 when the Ryan was razed.

2. So-called stand-up saloons were cheap watering holes that typically had few if any tables or chairs. Instead, customers—invariably all male—stood at a long bar to have their drinks.

3. Historical accounts and photographs suggest that Watson's description of O'Connor is very accurate. Known variously as "the Big Fellow," "the Big Boy," and "the Bull," O'Connor came to St. Paul in 1857 with his father, joined the police force in about 1880, became chief of detectives in the 1890s and chief of police in 1900, all of which indicates that his entanglement in the ice palace case did no harm to his subsequent career. The police force was notably corrupt during his eighteen-year tenure as chief, when he devised the so-called O'Connor system, which permitted visiting hoodlums to hide out in St. Paul so long as they committed no crimes in the city. It was this system that led to St. Paul's becoming a haven for gangsters in the 1920s and 1930s. For more on O'Connor, see Maccabee, *John Dillinger Slept Here*, 8–12.

4. Pump-action shotguns were relatively new and expensive at this time, and the fact that Rafferty kept one behind the bar indicates he had an interest in state-of-the-art weaponry. The Winchester owned by Rafferty must have been the pump-action model introduced by that company in 1893.

Chapter Nine

1. The Hotel Barteau, built in 1889, was one of the largest apartment houses of its period in St. Paul, and one of the first to offer elegant suites of rooms as opposed to the much cruder apartments found in old-style tenement construction. The Barteau, later known by other names, was demolished in 1969.

2. St. Paul developed with two separate steamboat landings—the Upper and Lower Levees—on the Mississippi River. The river flats at the Upper Levee, located near the foot of Chestnut Street on the western edge of downtown, were home to many immigrant families in the 1890s, despite the presence of a large city dump nearby and the frequent threat of flooding.

Chapter Ten

1. The Minnesota Club, founded in 1869, was at this time St. Paul's most exclusive gentlemen's club, with a membership that included many of the city's leading businessmen. The club was at Fourth and Cedar Streets in 1896. In 1915 it moved to a new building a few blocks away, near Rice Park, where it remains today.

2. "The strange affair of Lady Carrington's codicil," as Watson describes it, appears to be another of those numerous cases that the good doctor never got around to writing about.

3. Caulfield Gardens in London was where the espionage agent Hugo Oberstein lived. Holmes and Watson broke into his house, as recounted in "The Adventure of the Bruce-Partington Plans." There are a number of other stories in which Holmes's skills as a burglar come to the fore, most notably "The Adventure of Charles Augustus Milverton."

Chapter Eleven

1. The Diebold Safe & Lock Company was founded in 1859 by a German immigrant named Charles Diebold. The company gained a measure of renown after the Great Chicago Fire of 1871, when more than eight hundred Diebold safes were found in burned-out buildings with their contents intact. The firm remains in business today.

2. There are no known copies of Holmes's monograph on the subject of safes, and it is probable that it was never published.

3. Mycroft Holmes, the great detective's older brother, worked for the British government and was undoubtedly involved in espionage to some degree. He makes his most significant appearance in "The Greek Interpreter," a story published by Watson in 1893.

Chapter Twelve

1. St. Peter Street, once lined with bars and gambling halls, long had a reputation as St. Paul's toughest street. As late as 1936, one magazine claimed in an article that "St. Peter Street is the toughest highway in the country. . . . If you want somebody killed, inquire about St. Peter Street." See *Fortune Magazine*, April 1936, pp. 112–19.

2. Kennedy Brothers was for many years the largest gun and sporting goods store in St. Paul. Gen. George Custer, legend has it, sometimes bought guns and ammunition at the store during stopovers in St. Paul.

3. House of Hope Presbyterian Church was at this time one of the largest Protestant churches in St. Paul. In 1896, the church was located downtown. Later, the congregation built a much larger church on Summit Avenue.

Chapter Thirteen

1. Hill's offices at this time were in a large brick building on Third and Broadway Streets, near St. Paul's Union Depot. He later constructed a much larger building in Lowertown for his railroad empire. The original Hill office building, constructed in 1887, still stands, but it has been vacant and awaiting redevelopment for many years.

2. This was the third St. Paul Cathedral, built in 1858 at the corner of Sixth and St. Peter Streets. It was demolished in 1914 after a much larger and grander cathedral was built by Archbishop John Ireland of St. Paul. That cathedral, one of the largest church buildings in America, stands on Summit Avenue across from Hill's mansion.

3. Holmes's fascination with cryptography is well known, and there are references to his code-breaking skills in several stories. However, this is the only mention in

Watson's work of the fact that Holmes wrote a monograph on the subject. Unfortunately, no copies of the monograph, which would be a priceless treasure, have ever turned up, and it presumably is lost, as is the case with so much of Holmes's writing.

Chapter Fourteen

1. The Globe Building at Fourth and Cedar Streets was in 1896 one of the tallest buildings in St. Paul, with a height of ten stories. Like many tall office buildings of its period, it was organized around a central atrium, or "skylit court," as Watson describes it. The building was torn down in 1959, long after the *Globe* itself had ceased to exist.

2. "Night soil" was the Victorian euphemism for human excrement, which had to be removed periodically from privy vaults in the days before widespread indoor plumbing. How best to collect and dispose of this waste was a contentious issue, and St. Paul and many other cities in the late 1800s adopted strict regulations governing the scavengers who hauled it away.

3. Pyle's account of the First Minnesota Volunteers in the Civil War is substantially correct. See Moe, *The Last Full Measure*, for good accounts of the regiment's early battles and its sacrificial charge at Gettysburg.

4. The matter of Rafferty's Medal of Honor is a curious one, since all historic accounts agree that it was a private in the First Minnesota named Marshall Sherman who captured the battle flag of the Twenty-eighth Virginia and was awarded the medal for his valor. It is possible that Pyle was simply wrong or that Rafferty won a Medal of Honor for some other act of bravery at Gettysburg. The situation is further confused by the fact that Rafferty appears to have had possession of the Virginia regiment's battle flag for many years after the war. The flag was eventually donated to the State of Minnesota and is now in the possession of the Minnesota Historical Society.

5. There is an excellent account of the Confederate disaster at Bristoe Station, which Pyle describes accurately, in Shelby Foote, *The Civil War: A Narrative: Fredericksburg to Meridian* (New York: Random House, 1963), 792–94.

Chapter Fifteen

1. What a remarkable find this is! Edward and Mollie Fitzgerald were the parents of St. Paul's most famous native son, the novelist F. Scott Fitzgerald. That the couple who discovered George Upton's body were indeed the parents of the famous novelist is clear from the *Globe*'s story, which says that the Fitzgeralds were residents of "Portland Avenue in this city." The Fitzgeralds, in fact, were living at 548 Portland Avenue in January 1896, in a row house designed, oddly enough, by Cass

Gilbert, the architect of the ice palace. Scott was born on September 24, 1896, which means he was in utero at the time his parents made their shocking discovery. Later, of course, Scott was to write a wonderful short story entitled "The Ice Palace," published in 1920 and set in St. Paul during the Winter Carnival. See Dave Page and John Koblas, *F. Scott Fitzgerald in Minnesota: Toward the Summit* (St. Cloud, Minn.: North Star Press, 1996).

2. The city of Red Wing is about fifty miles southeast of St. Paul on the Mississippi River. The St. James Hotel, where the newlyweds Michael and Laura Riley were taken into custody, is still in business.

Chapter Sixteen

1. Charles Dana Gibson (1867–1944) was a talented illustrator who in 1890 introduced the so-called Gibson girl in a drawing for *Life* magazine. The Gibson girl — tall, slim, and often dressed in a flowing off-the-shoulder gown — soon became a national sensation, her image conveying a new ideal of American womanhood.

2. Holmes himself often lamented his inability to understand women. In "The Adventure of the Illustrious Client," for example, he stated that a woman's "heart and mind are insoluble puzzles to the male."

Chapter Seventeen

1. Magee's Café was one of St. Paul's most popular dining spots in the 1880s and 1890s. Described by one magazine of the period as St. Paul's leading "epicurean resort," the restaurant — located on Jackson Street not far from the Union Depot — was said to attract the "best class of business and professional men."

2. Cavendish Square, located just east of Baker Street in London, is cited in two other of Watson's tales — "The Resident Patient" and the "Adventure of the Empty House." However, neither story mentions any murders in which the victims were disemboweled, and so this intriguing reference must be to one of Holmes's unknown cases.

3. The "new federal building" Watson refers to here is the large federal courthouse built in St. Paul between 1892 and 1902. Renovated and restored in the 1970s, the building is now known as Landmark Center and houses a variety of cultural organizations.

Chapter Eighteen

1. The jack pine twins were young prostitutes who gave Watson a very difficult time when he tried to interview them during the adventure of *Sherlock Holmes and the Red Demon*. One of the twins, Dora Olson, was subsequently killed in the forest

fire that swept through the town of Hinckley, but her sister, Laura, survived. Watson later helped secure a job for Laura Olson as a maid at the Hill mansion.

2. This was the original Ramsey County Jail, built in 1857–58 and every bit as grim a place as Watson describes it here. The old jail was torn down in about 1900 and replaced by a new one—also since demolished—a few blocks away.

3. Dartmoor was a name often used for Princetown Prison, located in Devon in the southwest of England. Some of England's most violent criminals were sent to the prison, built in 1809. Much of the action in *The Hound of the Baskervilles* takes place in the Dartmoor area, now a national park.

4. The "Masterman stock fraud case" must be yet another of those tantalizing adventures Watson never saw fit to write about.

Chapter Nineteen

1. Riley's comment here is a measure of how famous the boxer John L. Sullivan (1858–1918) was in Victorian America, even though by 1896 he had already lost his heavyweight championship to James J. Corbett. Sullivan was in St. Paul on a number of occasions and was reputed to have become so angry one night while drinking at the Ryan Hotel that he cracked a bar made of solid mahogany with one smash of his fist.

2. Holmes is correct in noting that the collection of "night soil," as the term suggests, was a nocturnal activity. In fact, St. Paul—like many other cities—permitted the collection and transportation of night soil only after dark, presumably so as protect the citizenry from too much exposure to such an earthy, if essential, public service.

Chapter Twenty

1. The so-called bloody angle was a point near a clump of trees in the center of the Union lines along Cemetery Ridge at Gettysburg. The 15,000 Confederates who formed Pickett's charge used the trees as a marker as they made their hopeless advance. The First Minnesota was stationed near this critical point and took part in the desperate hand-to-hand fighting by which the Confederates were ultimately repulsed.

2. Drury Lane was the heart of London's theater district. Surprisingly for a man as theatrical as Holmes, he does not appear to have frequented London's playhouses, since there are few references to theatergoing in Watson's stories.

Chapter Twenty-one

1. The twin-towered church mentioned by Watson here is Assumption Catholic Church, sometimes called St. Paul's "German cathedral." Constructed in 1874, Assumption still stands and is the oldest church left in downtown St. Paul.

2. Bench Street, now known as Second, today bears little resemblance to the historic street described by Watson. All of the old buildings along the street were removed in the early 1930s when the city built Kellogg Mall Park atop the river bluffs. Second now runs beneath the park and carries little traffic.

3. The "long, tall wooden building" Watson refers to here must have been the freight house of the St. Paul & Omaha Railroad. Old photographs show that it was indeed built right up against the bluffs and that its roof could have been reached by someone jumping from Bench Street, as Bouquet and Holmes did. The freight house, like numerous other railroad buildings once found along the river, is long gone.

4. The railroad bridge mentioned by Watson was the Chicago Great Western swing bridge, built in the 1880s. It was replaced in 1913 by a lift bridge, which is still in use.

5. The island with the "tall, ghostly trees" was Raspberry Island, which later became known as Navy Island when the U.S. Navy built facilities there. In recent years, however, the island's original name has been restored.

6. Maiwand was the battle in Afghanistan on July 27, 1880, in which Watson was wounded while serving with a British regiment. Oddly enough, Watson's own accounts of the battle do not agree as to whether he was struck by a bullet in the leg or the shoulder.

Chapter Twenty-two

1. The Reichenbach River in Switzerland was, of course, the scene of the famous battle to the death in 1891 between Holmes and Dr. Moriarty, as described in "The Final Problem." Watson thought Holmes had perished with Moriarty when the two men went over the precipice, but he learned three years later, in "The Adventure of the Empty House," that Holmes had in fact survived.

2. Holmes's famous luck seem to have been very much in evidence in this remarkable episode. Muskrats normally build their lodges in the calm, shallow water of marshes and ponds rather than in river channels. However, as the Mississippi flows past downtown St. Paul, it forms a slow-moving backwater area on one side of Raspberry Island, and it was there Holmes must have found the muskrat lodge that undoubtedly saved his life after he plunged beneath the ice.

3. The Dvoraks lived in an area of St. Paul known as the West Side flats. Like the Upper Levee flats across the river, the flood-prone West Side flats were home to many poor immigrants. Today the flats are protected by high levees and have been turned into an industrial park.

Chapter Twenty-three

1. Tomás de Torquemada (1420–98) was a Dominican monk who organized the infamous Inquisition in Spain. Since there is no evidence that Watson ever visited Spain, it is doubtful he ever actually saw one of the dungeons used during the Inquisition.

2. I have been unable to locate a copy of *Businessmen of the Great Northwest* to learn when and where it was published. However, books extolling the virtues of local business leaders—whether in St. Paul or elsewhere—were common in the late nineteenth century. Almost all of these books were of the subscription variety, which means they were sold in advance to the wealthy men who would be featured, always in a most flattering fashion, in their pages.

3. Exactly what Watson meant by "Duseldorf [sic] cracker mines" is unclear, but they must have been an especially loud sort of fireworks, presumably with some connection to the city of Düsseldorf in Germany. There is a detailed account of the pyrotechnic display at the storming of the ice palace in the St. Paul *Pioneer Press*, January 23, 1896, p. 1.

Chapter Twenty-four

1. In the early days of the Winter Carnival, ice palaces were indeed left to simply melt away, as Rafferty says here. However, in the modern era, St. Paul's ice palaces (the most recent built in 1992) have been torn down at the end of the carnival because of concerns over safety and liability.

2. Although Watson says it was Holmes's "frequent contention" that how a man walks reveals much about him, this particular observation is not found in any of the doctor's other stories. However, there is a celebrated scene at the beginning of *The Hound of the Baskervilles* in which Holmes makes a series of startling deductions simply by analyzing a man's walking stick.

Chapter Twenty-five

1. Rafferty is referring here to a hoax concocted in the 1860s by a Minneapolis accountant named Edward Wells, who claimed to have discovered the remains of an eight-foot-tall prehistoric man in a mile-long cave beneath the city. In fact, the "cave" was an abandoned mill tunnel that harbored nothing except the usual colony of bats. There is an account of Wells's prank in "The Nesmith Cave Hoax: A Communication," *Minnesota History* 11 (March 1930): 74–75.

2. The name given to the group of young boys hired by Thomas is, of course, a reference to the celebrated Baker Street Irregulars. These were, in Watson's words, "six dirty little scoundrels" whom Holmes employed on various surveillance missions. The Irregulars appear in *A Study in Scarlet*, *The Sign of Four*, and "The Crooked Man."

Chapter Twenty-six

1. Judas Iscariot and Brutus are well known for their acts of betrayal, but Cassius' name may be less familiar. He was Gaius Cassius Parmensis, a Roman politician and writer, who participated with Brutus in the assassination of Julius Caesar in 44 B.C. Cassius was eventually executed by the emperor Octavian in about 31 B.C.

2. Riley's remarks about ice are correct. In 1992, for example, the builders of the Winter Carnival Ice Palace in St. Paul were very careful about using blocks no thicker than twenty-two inches so as to avoid any possibility of light refraction.

3. St. Mary's, built in 1867, was one of the oldest Catholic churches in St. Paul at this time. Unfortunately, the old church was demolished in the 1960s, and none of Dante's sculptures are known to have survived.

4. The House of the Good Shepherd was a large Catholic institution in St. Paul that offered assistance to what were in Victorian times called "delinquent girls"—i.e., unwed mothers.

5. Holmes, despite occasional claims to the contrary, appears to have been quite an admirer of Edgar Allan Poe. It is known, for example, that Holmes once had a cat named after Poe's fictional detective C. Auguste Dupin; see *Sherlock Holmes and the Red Demon*, 204. Dupin is the detective who solves the mystery of "The Purloined Letter," a story published in 1845. Despite Holmes's reference here to "Mr. Poe's ingenious story," he once told Watson, in *A Study in Scarlet*, that Dupin "had some analytical genius, no doubt; but he was by no means such a phenomenon as Poe appeared to imagine."

Epilogue

1. Here is another revelation from Watson, one which indicates that he and Holmes must have returned to America—and presumably to Minnesota—for a third time. Unfortunately, no manuscript by Watson is known to exist for the "strange and deadly rune stone affair," and what the case might have involved can only be surmised. It would seem likely, however, that Holmes and Watson somehow became involved in investigating one of several mysterious runestones found in western Minnesota in the late 1890s. The most famous of these, the Kensington runestone, contains a runic inscription purportedly carved by a group of Norsemen who traveled to the area in 1362. Discovered in November 1898, the Kensington stone has long been the subject of controversy, although the vast majority of scholars regard it as a hoax.

AUTHOR'S NOTE

Like its predecessor, *Sherlock Holmes and the Red Demon*, this book is a work of fiction inserted into a background that contains a good deal of historical fact. There was, for example, an ice palace built in St. Paul in 1896—the city's last such structure of the nineteenth century. However, the 1896 palace was not in Central Park, did not include a large dome of ice, was not designed by the famed architect Cass Gilbert, and in fact melted well before the Winter Carnival was completed, because of unseasonably mild weather.

The palace I created for this book is much closer in size and splendor to the magnificent St. Paul ice palaces of 1886, 1887, and 1888 than to the one built in 1896, which was called "Fort Karnival" because of its fort-like appearance. And while a glittering dome of ice makes for a fine setting for murder and mayhem, such a structure would in truth be extraordinarily difficult to erect, because of ice's tendency to move (or "creep," as engineers call it) in response to changing atmospheric conditions. No such gigantic ice dome has ever, to my knowledge, been attempted, in St. Paul or anywhere else.

This book also mixes real and fictional characters. James J. Hill, of course, was a real person, as was his assistant and newspaper editor, Joseph G. Pyle. John J. O'Connor was also a genuine chief of detectives (and later chief of police) in St. Paul, and I suspect he was every bit as tough a customer as I've portrayed him here. Another historic figure is William Best, the railroad engineer mentioned briefly at the outset of the story. Best, as some readers will recall, plays a much more significant role in my earlier Sherlockian adventure. And yes, Edward and Mollie Fitzgerald were indeed the parents of F. Scott Fitzgerald, who was born in St. Paul and spent much of his early life at the fringes of Summit Avenue's high society. There is, however, no evidence to suggest that the famed novelist's parents ever stumbled upon a dead body in an ice palace. The other major characters are all fictional, even though I'd like to believe that somewhere in St. Paul's long and colorful history there was once a bartender at least a little like Shadwell Rafferty.

With a few exceptions, such as the entirely fictional Muskrat Club, the streets, places, and buildings mentioned in this book are also genuine, even if in many cases they have long since succumbed to the irresistible tide of progress. Central and Rice parks, the Ryan Hotel, the old Ramsey County Jail, the Barteau and Costanza apartments, Hill's own mansion, and even Raspberry Island (near which Holmes took his plunge into the frozen Mississippi) are among the authentic settings used for this book, and I have tried in every instance to depict these buildings and places as accurately as possible.

Finally, I should add that I have done my best in this book to adhere to the official Holmes canon as established by his creator, Sir Arthur Conan Doyle, in the fifty-six short stories and four novels in which he featured the great detective. My task was simplified by the fact that the year 1896 was not a very active one for Holmes and Watson in the canonical stories. Indeed, according to Conan Doyle, the duo took on only three cases that year, all between October and December. I therefore thought it not too presumptuous to bring Holmes and Watson back to Minnesota in January 1896, since it seems they were not otherwise occupied.

Larry Millett is the author of six Sherlock Holmes adventures. He is also an architectural historian whose well-known books include *Lost Twin Cities* and the *AIA Guide to the Twin Cities*. As a reporter for the *St. Paul Pioneer Press,* he covered many beats and also had the honor of writing clues for the newspaper's legendary Winter Carnival Medallion Hunt, which annually attracts thousands of treasure seekers. He lives in St. Paul.